"Welcome, daughter of Samular," intoned a faint, rusty voice.

Bronwyn whirled, startled by the unearthly sound, and found herself looking straight into glowing red eyes, set into a skeletal face.

She swallowed a scream and fell back. At second glance, she understood what manner of being she faced. Ancient, rusty robes hung in tatters about the lank form. Where flesh once had been, there was only bone wrapped in papery gray. Lank strings of white hair straggled out from beneath the cowl of a once-white cape. Yet there was life, of a sort, in those glowing red eyes. This was a lich, an undead wizard, and one of the most feared and powerful beings known.

The creature advanced. "Daughter of Samular," it repeated. "You have little need to fear me. I have waited long for this day, and for one such as you. The Fenrisbane—its time has come? You have come for it, and for the third ring?"

Because it seemed the thing to do, and because she was not certain her voice would serve her, Bronwyn nodded. . . .

THE HARPERS

A semi-secret organization for Good, the Harpers fight for freedom and justice in a world populated by tyrants, evil mages, and dread concerns beyond imagination.

Each novel in the Harpers Series is a complete story in itself, detailing some of the most unusual and compelling tales in the magical world known as the Forgotten Realms.

THE HARPERS

Thornhold

Elaine Cunningham

THORNHOLD

Distributed to the book trade in the United States by Random House, Inc. and in Canada by Random House of Canada Ltd.

Distributed to the toy and hobby trade by regional distributors.

Distributed worldwide by Wizards of the Coast, Inc. and regional distributors.

Cover art by Brom. Map by Sam Wood.

FORGOTTEN REALMS and the TSR logo are registered trademarks owned by TSR, Inc.

TSR, Inc. is a subsidiary of Wizards of the Coast, Inc.

First Printing: August 1998
Printed in the United States of America.
Library of Congress Catalog Card Number: 97-062374

9 8 7 6 5 4 3 2 1

8584XXX1501

ISBN: 0-7869-1177-8

U.S., CANADA, ASIA,	EUROPEAN HEADQUARTERS
PACIFIC, & LATIN AMERICA	Wizards of the Coast, Belgium
Wizards of the Coast, Inc.	P.B. 34
P.O. Box 707	2300 Turnhout
Renton, WA 98057-0707	Belgium
+1-206-624-0933	+32-14-44-30-44

Visit our website at **www.tsr.com**

To my father, who, unlike Hronulf, Dag, and Khelben, was always there.

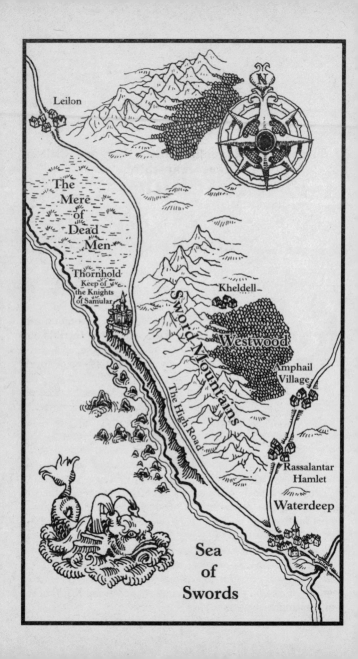

Prelude

27 Tarsakh, 927 DR

Two young wizards stood on a mountain-top, staring with awe at the terrible outcome of their combined magic.

Before them lay a vast sweep of spring grasses and mountain wildflowers. Moments before, they had beheld an ancient and besieged keep. The keep was gone, as were the powerful creatures who had taken refuge within. Gone, too, were any survivors—sacrificed to the war against the demons that spilled up from the depths of nearby Ascalhorn. Gone, leaving no marks but those etched in the memories of the two men who had brought about this destruction.

They were both young men, but there the similarities ended. Renwick "Snowcloak" Caradoon was small and slight, with fine features and a pale, narrow face. He was clad entirely in white, and his flowing cloak was richly embroidered with white silk threads and lined with the snowy fur of winter ermine. His hair was prematurely white, and it dipped in the center of his forehead into a sharp widow's peak. His bearing bespoke pride and ambition, and he regarded the result of the joint casting with satisfaction.

1

His companion was taller by a head, and broad through the shoulders and chest. His hair and eyes were black, and his countenance browned by the sun even so early in the year. An observer might be forgiven for thinking him a ranger or a forester, but for the unmistakable aura of magic that still lingered about him. There was a deep horror in his eyes as he contemplated what he had done.

A gaping scar on the mountain, a charred skeleton of a fortress—that would have been easier for the mage to accept than this serene oblivion. He had never heard a silence so deep, so profound, and so accusing. It seemed to him that the mountains around him, and everything that lived upon them, bore stunned and silent witness to the incredible force of magic that had swept away an ancient dwelling place and all those who lived within.

From somewhere in the budding trees below them, a single bird sent forth a tentative call. The song shattered the preternatural silence, and the awe that held the two wizards in its grip. By unspoken agreement, they turned and walked downhill. The memory of what they had done hung heavy between them.

But the mage was not content to leave the matter. He turned to his fellow wizard. The expression on Renwick's face stopped him in mid stride. Renwick looked content, almost exhilarated. Dreams of power, immortality—Renwick had often spoken of these—were bright in his eyes.

Suddenly feeling in need of support, Renwick's companion rested one hand on a stout oak. "The rings you used in the casting," he demanded. "What else can they do?"

The younger wizard gave him a supercilious smile. "Why do you ask? Was this day's work not enough for you?"

The other mage's temper flared. He fisted both hands in the folds of Renwick's white cloak, lifted him bodily from the ground, and slammed him against the oak tree.

"Tell me where you found those three rings, and the nature of their power!"

Renwick only smiled. "What they were meant to be, I do not know. What use I have made of them . . . you will not know."

Renwick's calm demeanor shamed his companion. There were better ways to control the situation. He released Renwick and took a step back. "You know you cannot stand against me in spell battle," he pointed out.

"I do not intend to," Renwick retorted smugly. "The rings, and a partial knowledge of the power they wield, are in the hands of an adversary you cannot defeat."

This set the mage back on his heels. Even among the elves who had raised him, there were few who could match his command of magic.

"You do not ask me of whom I speak. Pride forbids it, I suppose," Renwick observed. "I will tell you nonetheless. Samular holds the rings, as will his descendants after him."

"The paladin?"

"Samular is not just any paladin. He is destined for legend. With my help, of course."

The mage began to understand, could even admire the sophistry of this ploy. Paladins were noble warriors, knights dedicated to the service of their gods. They served kings, protected the weak, and upheld law and justice. Evil in any form was anathema to them; they simply could not abide it. No other single group of men were as widely admired. If the three rings were in the hands of the paladin Samular, and if he used their power for good, then the mage could hardly wrest the artifacts away without appearing to be an enemy of all things noble.

"A paladin's way is righteous and good," Renwick taunted softly, in echo of the other's thoughts. "If you do not stand with him, you are against him."

He could not deny the truth in this, but felt compelled to add another truth. "So much power cannot be easily contained," continued the elder mage, a man who, nearly two centuries later would come to be known as Khelben Arunsun. "You will not be able to keep the rings secret forever. Some day they will fall into other hands, and be used for other purposes."

Again the pale wizard Renwick smiled. "Then it is in your best interest to make certain that this does not occur. Once the tale begins to be told, who knows where it will end?"

One

5 Mirtul, 1368 DR

The young woman, by all appearances a pirate down on her luck, paused at the base of the hill. There was little cover so close to the sea, and the wind that sent her cape whipping about her shoulders brought memories of a winter not long past. The woman cast a quick look over her shoulder to make sure the path behind her was still clear. Assured, she swept aside the dead branches concealing the small opening to a sea cave.

A lone bat darted out of the darkness. She instinctively ducked—a quick, agile motion that sent her long braid of brown hair swinging up to drape over her shoulder. She flipped it back, then took a torch from her pack. A few deft taps of knife against flint produced sparks, then flame. Instantly the stone floor of the cave exploded into life. Rats fled squeaking in alarm, and crabs scuttled away from the sudden burst of light.

"Waterdeep, the City of Splendors," murmured Bronwyn, her lips curved with affectionate irony. Since taking up residence in the city four years ago, she had spent more time doing business in places like this than she did in her posh shop on the Street of Silver.

There was little splendor in the hills south of the great port city. The tang of the sea hung heavy in the still air, along with the smell of dead fish and the even less pleasant odor of the nearby Rat Hills, a length of shore that served as repository for the city's garbage. She ducked into the small opening and stood, taking stock of her surroundings. The cave was cold and water was everywhere, dotting the cave floor in dank puddles, drizzling down through the moss and lichen that festooned the walls, and dripping like drool from the fang-shaped rocks hanging down from the ceiling. There would be even more water when the tide came in.

That thought quickened Bronwyn's step down a steep, uneven path. As she went, she trailed one hand along the damp wall for balance and kept a wary eye on the shadows beyond the circle of her torch's light. Bats, rats and crabs represented the cream of cave society. She fully expected to encounter worse.

She carefully skirted a broad pool that nearly spanned the stone ledge. Bronwyn hated water, which lent a touch of irony to her seafaring guise.

She lifted her hand to her head to ensure that her rakish scarlet kerchief was still in place and that the cheap bronze hoops evocative of Nelanther pirates were still secured to her ears. This was the Smugglers' Caves, and as the old saying went, "When in the Coldwood, shiver." Her years of slavery had taught her that survival meant adapting.

At that moment the path curved sharply. After a few more steps, it opened into a cavern. A crack far overhead let in a bit of light. Bronwyn eyed the ravine that suddenly appeared beside the path, looking like a deep, broad gash in the mountain's stone heart. At the bottom of the ravine, running swift and deep and eerily silent, was an underground river. Bronwyn suppressed a shudder and went to work.

She shrugged the pack off her shoulder and took from it a large rag, then a small axe finely crafted from mithral and mahogany. A lifelong appreciation for fine things prompted her to wrap the axe carefully before placing it behind a boulder and obscuring it from view with a pile of pebbles.

That done, she dropped to her belly at the ravine's edge and reached down the steep rock cliff, feeling around until she found the rope she had tied there several days ago, when she had scouted and prepared the meeting place. The rope was virtually invisible, for it was long enough to drape down the ravine walls on either side. The slack middle was held underwater by the swift flow of the river. Hauling up the wet rope was hard work, and by the time she'd finished, Bronwyn's old leather gloves were soaking, her palms raw.

Bronwyn took a few moments to catch her breath and shed her ruined gloves, then she again shouldered her pack and tucked one end of the rope in her belt. She scrambled up a steeply winding incline to a point that overhung the path below—a spot she'd chosen because of the concave hollow beneath, between her and the path. This way, if her luck went bad and she was forced to use the rope to swing back across the ravine, she wouldn't splat like an overripe apple against a sheer stone wall.

When the rope was secured and hanging in a loose, unevenly draping curve, Bronwyn removed from her bag an oddly shaped bit of iron, which resembled the outline of a potbellied caldron with a narrow neck and a wide rim curving on either side. This she turned upside down and placed over the rope. Taking a firm grip on the curved handles, she squeezed her eyes shut briefly and leaped out over the ravine.

Bronwyn slid down the rope toward the far side, rapidly at first, and then slowing as she reached the lowest point. When she came to a stop, a few feet from the far cliff, she swung her feet up and wrapped her booted ankles around the rope—just in case. She released one side of the handle and lunged for the rope. Her fingers closed around it. With a sigh of relief, she shimmied the rest of the way across the rope and crawled gratefully onto the solid ledge.

She left the rope where it was and hurried along the edge of the ravine. After about a hundred paces, she found what she sought: a small opening at the base of the rock wall that looked ridiculously like an oversized mouse hole.

Bronwyn dropped to the ground and crawled into the tunnel, a short passage through the stone wall into another network of tunnels. It was not the quickest route to the agreed-upon meeting place—far from it—and it was a very tight fit. This was, of course, the point. Bronwyn could wriggle through the small tunnel, but those with whom she was about to deal could not.

She emerged from the tunnel and lit another torch. A few hundred paces took her to the entrance to the meeting place, a small, damp antechamber carved into the stone by eons of dripping water.

The scene within was less than inviting. A relatively flat slab of rock had been propped up on several boulders to serve as a table. On this table lay scattered the remains of a rather unpalatable meal: dried bread, odoriferous blue-green cheese, and mugs of sludge-colored beer brewed from mushrooms and moss. This repast had just been consumed by three of the ugliest dwarves Bronwyn had ever seen.

They were duergar, a race of deep-dwelling dwarves who were gray of beard and skin and soul. The enmity between mountain dwarves and duergar was nearly as bitter as that which existed between elves and their subterranean counterparts, the drow. Bronwyn did business with all of these people—but cautiously.

Each member of the filthy trio raised a hand to his brow to shield his eyes from the bright torchlight. "Came you alone?" one of them demanded.

"That was the agreement," she said, nodding to the third and smallest duergar. "Speaking of agreements, there were supposed to be only two of you. Who's that?"

"Oh, him," the duergar who'd first spoken replied, flapping one hand in a dismissive gesture. "A son, could be mine. He comes to watch, learn."

Bronwyn considered the third member of the party, the only one she hadn't dealt with before. Duergar were usually thin and knobby, but this little one was the scrawniest of his kind Bronwyn had ever seen. She raised her torch and squinted. He was no more than a boy. The other two duergar sported stringy gray beards, but this one's receding chin was as bald as a buzzard. And he still had all his teeth, which he was busily picking with a black-rimmed fingernail.

The duergar boy removed his finger from his mouth and ran his tongue over his teeth to collect the dislodged bits. He caught Bronwyn's inquisitive gaze. She nodded in greeting. As he regarded her, a slow, knowing leer stretched his lips. Evil wafted from the young duergar, as tangible as the foul steam that rises off a chamber pot on a cold morning. Bronwyn shuddered, chilled by such malevolence in one so young.

The leader noted her response. He snarled and back-handed the youngster, who yelped like a kicked cur. The boy sent a baleful glare at the human, as if the blow were somehow her fault.

Bronwyn pretended to notice nothing of this. She picked up a small stone knife from the table and helped herself to a hunk of the smelly cheese. Among duergar, this was regarded as taking liberties, perhaps even a small challenge. The second adult glowered at her but did not speak. He had never spoken in Bronwyn's presence, though the three-foot iron tipped cudgel he carried lent a certain eloquence to his silence.

She held his gaze and popped the cheese into her mouth. She kept her expression bland, almost smug, silently stating that she had the upper hand in this situation and saw no reason for concern. A necessary bit of bravado when dealing with such as these duergar, but it was a bad moment for Bronwyn. As she awaited a response, her stomach roiled in a mixture of apprehension and revulsion. But her luck held twice over. The duergar's cudgel stayed down, and so did the pilfered cheese.

For form's sake, Bronwyn sneered at the silent duergar and turned her attention back to the leader. "Where are the gems?"

He grunted in approval at her handling of the matter, then took a filthy leather bag from his belt and spilled the contents onto her outstretched palm.

As the golden stones spilled through her fingers, Bronwyn kept her face carefully neutral even though she knew at once that this necklace was extraordinary. The gems were amber, reputed to be the lifeblood of trees that once had grown in the lost Myconid Forest. The delicate silver filigree, though old and much tarnished, was of exquisite workmanship. Elf-crafted, certainly. It was among the most magnificent pieces of gemcraft Bronwyn had ever beheld. Even so, her fingers prickled when they touched the amber. Perhaps because her senses had been honed to a fine edge by a lifetime of dealing with magic-rich antiquities, perhaps it was merely her imagination, but she could have sworn that she sensed the faint, distant echo of fell magic.

She forced herself to pick up the necklace again and study it as if she were merely appraising weight and color. "Nice," she admitted casually, "but your price is too high."

The duergar leader knew the game of barter as well as anyone. "Five hundred gold, not a copper less," he said stoutly. "And weapons. Two of them."

Bronwyn smirked. "Where I come from, merchants know the value of their wares. But since amber isn't your usual stock in trade, perhaps I can cut you some extra rope."

"Yeah? How much?"

She tugged thoughtfully at one of her oversized earrings. "I could stretch the price to fifty gold, and a battle-axe. I found a good one; two-headed, well balanced for either throwing or hand fighting. It's dwarf-crafted, of course—a very good journeyman piece by a gold dwarf smith. The axe head is mithral, the handle is polished mahogany set with chips of garnet and tourmaline. Interested?"

"*Hmmph!*" The duergar leaned over to one side and spat. "Got no use for pretties. Less for gold dwarves."

But Bronwyn did not miss the gleam of avarice in his eyes. Duergar were far more likely to be scavengers than smiths, and she had yet to meet one that didn't crave fine dwarven weapons. She gave the priceless necklace a casual shake. "This quality amber in a new, fashionable setting would sell for about two hundred gold in the bazaars. I'll give you half that."

The duergar started to work up another wad of spittle, then apparently decided a more dramatic gesture was in order. He pantomimed drawing a knife and plunging it into his heart. "Sooner that, than take a hundred gold!" he swore. "Four hundred, and the axe."

"The axe alone is worth five hundred, easily."

"Not likely! But since you and me go back a ways, even trade—the stones for the axe."

Bronwyn sniffed. "I'll give you two hundred gold, but you can forget the axe."

The duergar slammed the table with a slate-colored fist, incensed at the thought of losing this prize. "Gimme the axe, *and* the two hundred gold, and call it a deal. Call it a *theft,* is more like it!"

Bronwyn took the complaints in stride. She had expected protests; in fact, it seemed to her that the duergar had given in far too easily. There was more trouble to come—of that, she was certain. That puzzled her, given the presence of the duergar lad.

"Done." She placed a bag on the table. "Two hundred gold, paid out in five-weight platinum coins. Go ahead and count it."

A hint of red suffused the duergar's gray face. Most likely, Bronwyn surmised, he couldn't count that high, much less cipher out the coin exchange. "No need," he muttered. "You're good for it."

Bronwyn noted, not without satisfaction, that the duergar spoke whole and simple truth for what might have been the first time in his life. She prized the reputation she'd worked hard to earn. Promise made, promise kept.

In a few words, she told them where they would find the second part of their payment. "The axe is yours, you have my word on that. It'll take time to get to it, that's all—time that I'll use to put some hard road between us. I haven't forgotten what happened after our last deal."

"Me, neither. I was sorry to lose Brimgrumph. He was a good hand at fighting, but he got too much in the habit of it. Didn't know when to quit," the duergar said piously.

It was the longest speech Bronwyn had heard from him, and the most self-serving. If the ambush that had capped their last transaction had succeeded, this duergar would no doubt have been quick to claim his share of the take. But it had failed, and his henchman had died. Bronwyn's steely gaze announced that she rejected his attempt to slough off the responsibility.

"Cross me once, expect me to watch you. But cross me twice, *you* best watch out for *me*," she warned.

The duergar shrugged. "Fair enough," he agreed.

Too easy again, Bronwyn thought. As the silent duergar pocketed the gold, Bronwyn gathered up the necklace and loosened the strings on her bag. Not a common bag, but one that she'd bought from a Halruaan wizard at a cost that represented nearly a year's worth of sales. The thing was worth every copper. It was a magical tunnel that whisked whatever she tucked inside to a well-guarded safe in Curious Past, her shop in an elegant section of Waterdeep. Bronwyn had learned long ago one basic truth about the business of acquiring rare antiquities. Finding them was one thing; *keeping* them was another matter entirely.

A small movement caught her eye and stayed her hand. The stone knife she had borrowed moved of its own accord—not much, but a little, just enough so that the tip pointed to the amber in her hand.

Lodestone, Bronwyn realized. The knife had been carved from a stone that felt and followed the energies in metal—or in this case, in amber. The duergar meant to track her and reclaim the necklace once they thought themselves beyond the traps that she always lay to cover her retreat.

Cross me twice, she thought grimly.

She kept her expression carefully neutral as she rose from her stone seat. She even turned her back as she walked away, allowing the duergar spokesperson time to pick up the tattling stone knife. When she reached the mouth of the cave, she turned and stared coldly into the cunning eyes of the treacherous creatures, then dropped the amber necklace into the sack. It disappeared into a magical vortex. The stone

knife spun in sympathetic flight, slicing deeply across the
duergar's palm.

His shout of pain and outrage tore the smirk from his face.
Bronwyn turned and fled, running like a deer for her escape
tunnel.

She dashed around a sharp turn and stooped, dropping her
torch to snatch up a stout staff she'd hidden among the rubble
beside the path. The three duergar followed in a thundering
crescendo of iron-shod boots. When she judged the moment
right, she leaped out in front of the first two onrushing duergar, staff held level with the ground, held waist-high and
firmly braced.

The duergar had no time to halt. They ran right into the
staff, one on either side of Bronwyn, catching the wood just
below the throat. Their heads snapped back, and their feet
flew out from under them. A dull, deep boom rumbled
through the cavern as the two hardy creatures slammed down
flat on their backs, arms flung out wide. Bronwyn danced
back.

The young duergar came on, trampling his fallen kin in his
eagerness to get at Bronwyn. The gleam in his eye and the
small, pitted axe he held high overhead announced his deadly
intent.

Quickly Bronwyn pivoted to her right. Seizing one end of
the staff with both hands, she hauled it back. Feeling like a
child preparing for an extremely high-stakes round of stick
ball, she swung out high and hard. The staff whistled through
the air and connected with the duergar's weapon arm. Something—either arm or axe handle, Bronwyn wasn't sure
which—shattered with a sickening crack. The youth dropped
the axe on one of his dazed elders and kept coming.

Bronwyn stooped and reached for the cudgel that had
rolled free of the adult duergar's hand. Too late she realized
that she should have made a different choice; the iron-bound
club was too heavy for her to lift.

There was no time to go for another weapon. Bronwyn
came up in a springing lunge, her chin tucked. Her head connected hard with the young duergar's belly, stopping his

charge. His breath wheezed out in a sharp, pained grunt, and they fell together in a tangle of arms and legs.

Bronwyn thrashed and kicked, but she was in too close to do much damage. The duergar youth did little better. Winded and favoring a garishly broken arm, he landed a few blows but couldn't put much force behind them. Suddenly he devised a better strategy. He seized one the bronze hoops in Bronwyn's ear and yanked it hard. The sudden, tearing pain surprised a scream out of her, and brought a wide grin to the creature's beardless face.

Angry now, Bronwyn felt about for her fallen torch. Her finger closed on the handle, close enough to the pitch-covered wood to feel the lingering heat. She thrust the still-hot end into the duergar's face.

He shrieked and released her, clutching at his eye with his one good hand. Bronwyn rolled aside and leaped to her feet, nimbly evading the grasping hands of the duergar leader. The two adults had shaken off the surprise attack, and were starting to gather their wits and reclaim their weapons. Bronwyn turned and fled for her escape tunnel.

Arms pumping, she ran full out down the path, the three duergar huffing along behind. The small tunnel came into view. She dropped to her knees and slid the last few paces, then flopped down onto her stomach and scrambled into the low tunnel. Frantically she dragged herself forward before one of them could grab her ankle and drag her back.

Almost through. Almost safe.

Something bumped her foot, startling her. Her head jerked up and connected painfully with the stone ceiling. Suddenly she realized why the duergar had brought the scrawny youngster with them. She was not the only one who had scouted the cavern. They must have anticipated this evasion—and brought along a duergar small enough to pursue her through the tunnel.

For some reason, that realization inspired more anger than fear. The young duergar was already hurt, and this was far from over. She would kill him if she had to. Surely his elders knew that.

Bronwyn scrambled out of the tunnel and ran for the ravine, steeling herself for the swinging jump ahead. She reached the rope and crawled out to the marked spot. Gripping the rope tightly with one hand, she sawed at the rope behind her with her knife. The rope was almost shredded through when she heard the young duergar's terror-filled scream. His wail rose in pitch as it faded away, and then ended altogether in a resounding splash. Bronwyn cursed under her breath. The young duergar, half blinded and no doubt off balance with pain, had stumbled and fallen into the river.

The shouts of the older duergar and their thundering footsteps brought Bronwyn an odd sense of relief. They had found another way into the cavern. They would save the youngster before he was swept too far downstream.

Suddenly her rope rose in a sharp, hard jerk. She dropped her knife and hung on with both hands as she gazed back in disbelief at the path. The duergar were focusing their attention on her, rather than on the boy in the river below.

Anger swept through Bronwyn, chasing away the nearly paralyzing fear of the water below. She shouted a dwarven insult—one that was almost guaranteed to inspire a tavern brawl, retributive murder, or small-scale war.

Again they tugged on the rope, harder this time. The fraying rope gave way, and Bronwyn swung out over the ravine. She forced herself to keep her eyes open, her attention fixed on the rapidly approaching stone. As soon as she cleared the ledge, she released the rope and threw herself into a side roll.

The maneuver absorbed some of the impact, but still she hit the stone floor with bruising, numbing force. She rolled several times and slammed into the wall hard enough to leave her dazed and aching.

Another angry shout ripped across the divide. "You made a deal!" the leader howled. "The gold *and* the axe!"

Bronwyn rose painfully to her feet and glared across the divide at the dancing, hooting duergar. After all this, he had the gall to accuse *her* of reneging on their deal.

Still, he had a point. She had the necklace, and she'd

promised the axe in exchange. She went to where she'd left the fine weapon, then fisted her hand and drove it into the pile of pebbles that hid it. Raising the gleaming axe high, she hauled it back for the throw.

The axe spun across the divide, directly toward the angry duergar. They squawked and dived for cover behind a pile of boulders. When they heard the heavy *thunk!* of metal against rock—several feet below their position—they darted out and skidded to a stop at the edge of the ravine. There, on a small ledge perhaps ten feet below the path, lay the axe.

"Oops," Bronwyn said casually.

Leaving the duergar to solve the dual problem of retrieving their axe and their young henchman, she turned and started up the steep path to the surface. There was little doubt in her mind which they would consider the more important.

* * * * *

Dag Zoreth had forgotten what the river sounded like when it ran wild in the spring. Faint and sweet, both impatient and laughing, the River Dessarin sang in the distance, its voice as familiar as a childhood lullaby. A wave of sharp, poignant memory assailed him, a memory almost powerful enough to drown out the remembered screams, and the terrible thunder of hooves.

He took a long, steadying breath to ground himself firmly in the present. "Wait here," he curtly told the men with him.

They had not anticipated this. They tried to hide their surprise, but Dag saw it all the same. He didn't miss much, and he gave away less—which was, in no small measure, the reason why he was the one giving the orders.

Dag understood the men's reaction all too well. He knew what they saw when they looked at him. A slight man who stood a full head shorter than most of his guards, a man who had little expertise with the short, jeweled sword on his hip, a man exceedingly pale of skin from many years spent within walls; in short, hardly the sort of man who might venture off alone into the wild foothills. Usually, Dag Zoreth didn't waste

much thought on such matters. But here, in this place, childhood memories were strong—strong enough to strip him of
his hard-won power and leave him feeling small and weak,
once again the child despairing of ever reaching the mark set
for him.

He felt the old despair now, a shadow in the memory of his
father's deep, ringing voice intoning, "When you hear the
Dessarin sing just so, it is time to turn off the road."

Dag Zoreth pulled his horse's reins toward the south, tug-
ging so sharply that the beast whinnied in pain and protest.
But the horse followed his command, just as the heavily
armed men behind him waited obediently on the eastbound
road to Tribor.

He rode for several minutes before he got his bearings. The
old path was still there, marked not by the passage of feet and
horses, but by the slender trees that grew in the once-open
space. It was remarkable, Dag Zoreth mused, how fast a tree
could grow once it was out from beneath the heavy shadow of
the older forest.

A song slipped into his mind, unbidden and unwelcome. It
was a marching song, an old hymn of praise to Tyr, the god of
justice. His father had often sung it to mark the passage to
the village. The path and the song were of like length, his
father used to say. Dag Zoreth knew that before he finished
humming the final chorus, the forest would give way to a
clearing, and the village would be spread out before him.

A small, cynical smile tightened his lips at the thought of
actually giving voice to the song. He doubted that his own
god, Cyric the Mad, had much of an ear for music.

But habit proved to be stronger than caution. As he rode,
Dag recalled the verse and marked out the measure in the
silence of his mind. When the remembered song was over,
Dag Zoreth did indeed find himself in the clearing he sought.
Along the edges young trees had made great strides toward
reclaiming the forest.

Dag Zoreth slid down from his horse. He was unaccus-
tomed to riding, and the trip had introduced him to a legion of
unfamiliar muscles. Though the journey from his home in

Darkhold had been long and hard, his body had adamantly refused to take on strength and muscle. There was nothing wrong with his will, however, and he thrust aside the throbbing pain as a lesser man might flick aside a fly. He left his horse to graze and began to circle the clearing.

The site was familiar and strange all at once. The buildings were gone, of course, burned to the ground in that terrible raid more than twenty years ago. Here and there he caught a glimpse of charred wood or scattered foundation stone under a tangle of spring-flowering blackberry brambles, but the village of his birth was irrevocably gone. And lost with the village was the heritage Dag Zoreth had come to reclaim.

Frustrated now, he looked around for something, anything, that would provide a marker. The years had changed him even more than they had altered the forest, and he no longer saw things with the eyes of a boy who had yet to weather his seventh winter. Then, his whole world had been comprised of this tiny village in the foothills south of Jundar's Hill. His world was wider now and vastly different from anything he could have imagined during his years in this sheltered enclave—different from everything, of course, but the raid that had ended his childhood.

Dag Zoreth took another long breath, massaging his temples with both hands as he dredged his memory. A sudden, sharp image came to him: a red leaf framed with jagged points, drifting lazily down, and then disappearing against the brighter crimson of his brother's shattered chest.

He spun on his heel, quickly, as one might retreat from some chance-glimpsed horror. Tilting back his head, he scanned the treetops. There had been an oak tree over the place where his brother died. There were oaks in plenty, but none of them looked familiar. Perhaps he should have come in autumn, when the leaves turned color. He smiled slightly at the foolish thought and shook it aside as quickly as it came. He had the power to claim what was his, and the will to use it. Why should he wait?

But the years had changed and filtered his memories, just as the forest had closed in around his childhood home. There was no mortal way that Dag Zoreth could retrieve what was lost. Fortunately, the gods were less encumbered by issues of time and mortality, and they were occasionally willing to share their insight, one glimpse at a time, with their mortal followers.

Though he dreaded the task before him, the young priest's hands were steady as he pulled the medallion bearing the holy symbol of Cyric from beneath his purple and black tabard. Dag Zoreth wore the colors of his god at all times, even though he knew better than to go abroad flaunting the priestly vestments and symbols of Cyric. It was Dag Zoreth's opinion, based on his own experience and his own ambitions, that people who claimed no reason to fear and hate Cyric's priesthood, simply hadn't lived long enough to find one.

The young priest closed his eyes and clenched his fist around the medallion. His lips moved as he murmured a prayer for divine guidance.

His answer came suddenly, with a cruel force that slammed Dag Zoreth onto his knees, and into the past. "The hymn," he muttered though a rictus-grin of pain. "Cyric must have heard the hymn." Then the thought was gone, swept away by more than twenty fleeing years.

Dag Zoreth was a child again, kneeling not in a new-growth forest, but in the darkest corner of a smoke-filled cottage. His small, skinny arms clutched a butter churn, and his black eyes were wide with terror as the bar on the door splintered and gave way. Three men strode in, their eyes burning with something that both repelled and fascinated the shrinking child.

One of them backhanded Dag's mother, who had leaped forward to defend her children with the only weapon that came to hand—a long-handled iron skillet. The ridiculous weapon fell from her hand and clattered to the hearth. Again the man struck out, and his mother's head snapped back. She went down hard, striking the hearthstone with an audible crack. Blood bloomed like an obscene crimson flower against her too-pale face. But somehow she found the strength to haul herself up, to dart past the man who strode purposefully

toward the wide cradle at the far side of the room. There lay
Dag's twin sisters, shrieking with fear and rage and flailing
the smoky air with their tiny pink fists. His mother threw
herself across the cradle, scooping both little girls into her
arms and shielding them with her own body as she cried out
in prayer to Tyr.

The man drew a sword and swung it up high. Mercifully,
the churn obscured Dag's view and he never actually saw the
blow fall, but he knew what the sudden silence meant. In the
rough, angry exchange that followed the sword's fall, Dag
read his own fate.

He shrank back, flattening himself into the indentation his
impish little sister had carved into the thick wattle-and-daub
wall. It was a hiding place for her "treasures"—smooth or
shiny rocks, a bluebird feather, and whatever other small
wonders she discovered around the village. Dag fervently
wished that his sister had dug deeper, turning her trove into
an escape door. He held his breath and willed himself to dis-
appear into the crevice, the smoke, and the shadows.

The men searched the cottage, tossing over the chests and
beds in their haste to find the boy before they were overcome
by smoke from the smoldering thatch roof. They did not move
the churn, probably because there was no apparent place
behind it for a child to hide. Finally they gave up the search,
concluding that Dag had bolted as his sister had done.

She had left the cottage well before the fire had started.
Ever curious, she had gone to investigate the noise caused by
the approaching raiders, evading their mother's frantically
grasping hands and wriggling through the one small window
left unshuttered. Her old night tunic had caught and torn on
the shutter hook. Instinctively she'd clapped her hand to the
little crimson birthmark on her bare hip—no doubt a defensive gesture honed by Dag's frequent teasing. Then she was
gone, the soles of her small feet flashing as she spilled headfirst out of the window. Dag wondered, briefly, what had
become of her.

Dag waited until the men had left his home, then he
slipped out of his cubby and crept over to the side window. He

left his mother and his baby sisters behind without a glance, all the while hating himself for his cowardice. Though he was but a child, he was the son of a great paladin. He should have fought. He should have found a way to save his family.

His thin fingers shook as he tugged at the latch holding the shutters closed. For a few terrible moments he feared that he would not be able to open the window, that he would be forced to choose between dying in the smoldering building, or walking out into the arms of the men who had come to steal him away. Terror lent him strength, and he tore at the latch until his fingers bled.

The metal bar gave way suddenly. The shutters swung outward, and Dag all but tumbled over the low sill and into the herb garden that framed the side of the house. He lay where he fell, crouching low amid the fragrant plants until he was certain that his precipitous move hadn't drawn attention. After a few moments, he cautiously lifted his head and darted a wide-eyed look over the clearing.

What he saw was like something from the lowest layers of the Abyss, horrors that no son of Tyr's holy warrior should ever have had to endure.

Mounted raiders circled the village, swords raised to cut down any who might try to escape. The thunder of their horses' hooves echoed through a hellish chorus of voices: the shouts of the raiders, the screams of the dying, the terrible keening grief of those who were yet alive. Above it all was the roar and hiss of the hungry fires. Most of the village houses burned freely, and bright flames leaped and danced against the blackness of the night sky.

Nearby a roof timber crashed to the ground, sending an explosion of sparks into the smoke-filled clearing. The sudden light illuminated still more horrors. Crumpled, blood-sodden bodies lay about the ground, looking more like slaughtered geese than the people Dag had known from his first breath. Surely that couldn't be Jerenith the trapper over there, gutted like a deer, his own bloody knife lying at his feet. The young woman draped limply over the stone circle of the village well, inexplicably naked and nearly black and purple with soot and terrible bruises, could not be pretty Peg Yarls-dotter. Wasn't it just this morning that she'd given Dag a honey cake, and kindly assured him that his father would return to the village before first snow?

A familiar voice, raised in a familiar cry, seized the boy's attention. A wave of relief and joy swept through him. His father, the bravest and most fearsome Knight of Tyr in all the land, had returned at last! The child's terror melted, and with it disappeared the pain of long days spent watching for his father's horse, envying the boys whose fathers stayed in the village to tend less exalted tasks.

Suddenly brave, Dag leaped up from the herb garden and prepared to race to his father's side. There could be no better or safer place in all of Faerûn than on the broad back of a paladin's war-horse, shielded by his father's strong sword arm and implacable faith.

He ran three steps before he realized his mistake. The voice was not his father's after all, but that of Byorn, his older brother. His brother was fighting, as his father would have fought. As he, Dag, should have fought.

Not yet fourteen, not quite accounted a man, Byorn had the courage to pick up a sword and face down the men who rode into his village with cold steel and burning torches. And his voice, when he called out to Tyr for strength and justice, held the promise of matching his father's deep, ringing tones.

Hero worship battled with terror in Dag's dark eyes as he watched his brother flail about with a blood-streaked weapon. It was plain even to Dag that Byorn lacked skill and strength, but the youth fought with a fervor that kept two grown swordsmen at bay, and left neither unscathed. A third man sprawled on his back nearby, his head lolling to one side on a throat torn open, and his eyes still wide with the surprising knowledge that Death could wear a beardless face.

No wonder it was Byorn who wore the family ring, thought Dag with more admiration than envy. Their father had given Byorn the ring not only because he was the oldest of the five children, but because he was the most worthy.

The ring.

Once again, Dag's fear retreated, this time before the grim fire of purpose. He was not quite seven, but he sensed in his bones and his blood the importance of that ring. He believed he would have done so even if he had never heard the fireside stories of the great Samular, a noble Knight of Tyr and his own distant ancestor. The ring must be kept safe, even if the children of Samular could not. By now, Dag understood with cold certainty that there would be no safety, no rescue, for any of them.

He crept around the back of the house and into the cover provided by the remnants of a neighbor's summer garden. On his hands and knees, he scuttled between long rows of withering vines toward the place where his brother stood and fought like a true son of Samular's blood. He was almost in the clear when Byorn slipped and fell. He heard the raider's shout of triumph and saw the killing stroke descend.

With a sharp, painful gasp, Dag dragged in a lungful of smoky air to fuel a scream of rage and horror and protest. All that emerged from his lips was a strangled whimper. Nevertheless, he kept moving steadily forward until he reached Byorn's side.

His brother lay still, horribly still, in a silent patch of blood-soaked ground. None of the raiders paid Byorn any heed now that he was no longer putting up a fight. They'd left the boy at once and turned their attention to ransacking the few remaining buildings. Dag understood: they were searching for the descendants of Samular. That was the only treasure this tiny, hidden village had to offer. He had heard the men in his own house, berating the soldier who had killed two valuable infant girls with a stroke meant only for their mother. Byorn's death must also have been a mistake. The men had come for children, and to Dag's adoring eyes, Byorn was already a man grown. With a sword in his hand and a battle-prayer to Tyr on his lips, Byorn must have fooled the raiders, as well.

Dag took his brother's limp hand in his. He tugged at the family ring, all the while fearing that Byorn's fist would clench to protect and keep, even in death, what was rightfully his. But valiant Byorn was truly gone, leaving the battle in the hands of his younger brother—a boy of nimble mind, to be sure, but cursed with a body too thin and frail to ever bear the burden and glory of Tyr's service.

But if a quick mind was all he had, he would use it as well as any warrior his weapon. A simple resolve, perhaps, but it struck Dag with the weight and force of prophecy. For just an instant, the forgotten years rose up before him. Dag understood what he had only sensed the first time he'd lived through the raid: this moment's insight would shape and define his life. Then, suddenly, the years receded, the adult was gone. But resolve calmed the child, focused him.

Again Dag tugged at the ring. Finally it came free from Byorn's finger. Dag's first thought was to bolt into the woods with it, but he knew instinctively that such sudden and obvious movement would draw attention to him. He could not outrun the men and their horses. He dared not keep the ring with him, for he would surely be captured sooner or later. What, then, was he to do with it?

The answer came to him in the form of a single, crimson leaf. It floated down, drifting as gently as a newly freed soul, and came to rest on Byorn's torn jerkin. Dag swallowed hard at the sight of the terrible wound, and he jerked his gaze upward, in the direction from which the leaf had come.

There was a knot in the tree. A small one, but sufficient to his purpose. Dag slowly rose to his feet, hardly daring to breathe.

"There's another one! And he's got the look of the paladin about him, too!"

It took Dag a moment to realize that the man was talking about *him*. Once, long ago—just yesterday, just this morning, less than an hour ago!—he would have been thrilled to his soul by any comparison to his famous father. Now all the raider's words inspired was a terrible, burning rage.

His mother and two of his little sisters were dead. Byorn was dead, and Dag had been left alone to finish a task that should never have fallen to any of them. His father should have been here. But he wasn't. He wasn't. What good could there be in any man if he was never there, not even when his own children were in grave danger?

Dag heard the crescendo of running feet behind him. Inspiration came like a jagged lightning flash, and he acted on it at once. He flung himself at the tree and thrust the ring into the knot hole. He did not move away, but clung to the tree as if it were his mother. Terrified sobs shook through him, though his eyes were dry and his fear now completely overshadowed by cunning.

Let the men think him a foolish child, mindless with grief and terror. Their opinion would not alter his fate. They would take him away, but at least the ring would be safe.

The ring.

Dag Zoreth slammed back into the present, as suddenly as if he had been jolted awake from a nightmare involving a long, terrifying fall.

Every muscle in his body screamed with pain, but he hardly noticed the physical agony over the fresh torture of remembered grief. Several dazed moments passed before he realized that his hands were bleeding, his fine clothes muddy and torn. He must have moved through the village in concert with the Cyric-given dream, tearing at the gods-only-knew-what in his remembered attempt to dislodge the window shutter, crawling through the wild tangle that had once been a garden in a desperate struggle to reach his long-dead brother.

"I moved through the dream," Dag murmured, suddenly understanding the practical implication of this. He raised his eyes, fully expecting to see a spring canopy of gold-green oak leaves overhead.

There was no oak tree, but the silvery leaves of a pair of aspens fluttered nervously in the quickening breeze.

A quickening breeze. Dag took a long breath and considered the subtle, acrid scent borne on the wind. Yes, it would rain soon, one of the quick, violent thunderstorms that he had so loved as a child. Even then, Dag had reveled in the power and drama of those storms, shrugging off any thought of the destruction that they all too often left behind.

A thunderstorm! Inspiration struck again, and Dag began to tear at the vines and brambles before him. In moments, he had uncovered a blasted, blackened stump. Shards of an ancient tree lay nearby, and weirdly shaped mushrooms grew from the black powder of rotted limbs. It was the very oak tree Dag sought, struck by lighting many years ago and burned nearly to the ground.

The ring was not easy to find amid the ruins of the tree. As Dag searched, the gathering storm swallowed the sun and deepened the shadows that shrouded the clearing. Dag's horse whinnied nervously. The priest ignored these warnings. Rain began to pelt down as his searching hands raked through the debris, and soon the forest around him shuddered with the force and fury of the storm. Another man might not have found the ring at all, but it seemed to call out to Dag, urging him on.

He reached for a clump of mud and crushed it with his fingers. He felt something hard, and caught a glimpse of gold. Eagerly he reached for the small wineskin attached to his belt and poured the contents over the encrusted band—barely noticing the sting when the wine met his battered skin. He scrubbed the band clean on his ruined tunic and rose to his feet, his family treasure tightly clutched in one triumphant, bleeding fist.

Dag examined the ring by the light of another livid flash. Arcane marks scored the inside of the band. He had seen the marks once as a child and had assumed they were only a design. Now he could read the cryptic runes: *When three unite in power and purpose, evil trembles.*

Three, Dag mused. He knew of only two rings. As the pattern took shape in his mind, he began to understand why Malchior, his mentor, was suddenly so interested in Dag's family history. It seemed likely to Dag that his childhood memories of the rings' importance were based on more than legend. If Malchior was nosing about, there was real power to be had. Luckily the old priest knew nothing about the ring. Or perhaps he did; few high-ranking members of the Zhentarim were known for altruism. Surely Malchior did not go through the trouble of seeking out Dag's lost past, and the location of his birth village, just to put his former acolyte's mind at ease. Well, be that as it may, Malchior would not find him a docile tool, nor would power of any sort leave Dag's hands without a bloody struggle.

Dag started to slip his family ring onto his index finger, as Byorn had once worn it.

Pain, quick and bright and fierce, lanced through him. Astonished, Dag jerked off the ring. He dashed his rain-soaked hair from his eyes and held the ring out at arm's length, gazing at it with a mixture of puzzlement and reproach. He was a descendant of Samular—how could the ring turn on *him*?

The answer came swiftly, borne on a wave of fierce self-anger. He should have seen this coming. He should have known this would happen. The ring had probably been blessed, consecrated to some holy purpose in which he, Dag Zoreth, could have no part. Samular had been a paladin of Tyr; Dag Zoreth was a strifeleader, a priest of Cyric.

On impulse, Dag took the medallion from around his neck, a silver starburst surrounding a tiny, carefully sculpted skull. He undid the clasp with fingers made slippery by mud and rain and his own blood, and then he slipped the ring onto the chain. He did up the clasp and put the medallion back in its proper place over his heart. The ring was hidden securely behind the symbol of Cyric.

Let Tyr—if indeed the god of justice condescended to observe someone such as Dag Zoreth—make of this what he willed.

Dag whistled for his horse and stiffly hauled himself up into the saddle. The return trip would have to be swift, for he could not wear the ring for much longer. It burned him now, even separated from his body by layers of purple and black garments and a light vest of fine elven mail. But there was another who would wear the ring for him, someone as innocent as he himself had been on that long-ago day, when an oak tree had wept crimson leaves over Byorn, the last worthy son of Tyr's paladin.

Worthy or not, Dag fully intended to use the ring. After all, he was of Samular's bloodline. He would reclaim his heritage—in his own way, and for his own purposes.

Two

There were other fortresses in the city of Waterdeep that were larger and more impressive, but Blackstaff Tower was without doubt the most secure and unusual fastness in the city.

Danilo Thann was a frequent visitor to the tower, and had been since Khelben Arunsun took him under his stern tutelage some twenty years earlier. Of late, it seemed to Danilo that the archmage's summons were increasing in frequency, and that the demands he made upon his "nephew" and former student were growing by the day.

Today he walked openly through the invisible doors that allowed passage through the black stone of the courtyard wall, and again into the tower. This much was expected; he then sauntered in *through* the wooden door of the archmage's study, not bothering to open the portal and in casual defiance of any wards that might have been placed upon it.

This was a typically arrogant gesture, one that no one else in the city would dare to attempt. Danilo hoped that Khelben perceived these acts as statements of his intention to remain independent of the archmage's plans for him, but he suspected that this very insouciance was in no small measure the reason for his frequent presence in Blackstaff Tower.

He was late, of course, and he found the archmage in an unusually foul state of mind. Khelben "Blackstaff" Arunsun, the archmage of Waterdeep, did not often pace. Such was his power and his influence that matters usually went as he willed them to go. But at the moment, he roamed the floor of his study like one caged and extremely frustrated panther. Under different circumstances this might have afforded Danilo a bit of wry amusement, but the report he had sent to his mentor was disturbing enough to ruffle his own composure.

Khelben stopped pacing to glower at the man who was his nephew in name only. There was little similarity between them, other than the fact that they were both tall men, and that either of them would kill without hesitation to protect the other. The archmage was solid, dark, and of serious mien. He was clad in somber black garments, whereas Dan was dressed in rich shades of green and gold, bejeweled as if for a midwinter revel, and carrying a small elven harp. He was, much to the archmage's dismay, committed to a bard's life. It was a constant source of conflict between them—a conflict that supported Danilo's suspicion that the archmage still hoped his nephew might be his successor as keeper of Blackstaff Tower. Danilo supposed that Khelben's reasoning was sound enough. If he were forced to tell the whole truth—an event that, fortunately, did not often occur—Danilo would have to admit that he was more skilled with a spell than with harp or lute.

He set the harp on a small table and made a quick, complex gesture with his hands. Immediately the harp began to play of its own accord, a lilting elven air of which Danilo was particularly fond.

This brought a scowl to the archmage's face. "How many musical toys does one man need?" he grumbled. "You've been spending too much time at that thrice-bedamned bard school, neglecting your duties!"

The young bard shrugged, unconcerned by the familiar reprimand. Never mind, he thought wryly, that evidence of

the archmage's particular artistic outlet stood in every corner
of the room. Khelben painted; frequently, passionately, and
with no discernible talent. Oddly skewed landscapes, por-
traits, and seascapes hung on the walls or stood on easels.
Half-finished canvases leaned in rows against the far wall.
The scent of paint and linseed oil mingled with the more pungent odor of spell components, which wafted in from the
adjoining storage chamber.

Danilo walked over to the sideboard that held his favorite
painting—an almost-skilled rendition of a beautiful, raven-
haired half-elf—and poured himself a glass of wine from the
decanter of elven wine he'd given Khelben as a gift.

"New Olamn *is* my duty," he reminded the archmage. "We
have had this conversation before. The training and support
of Harper bards is an important task. Especially in these
days, when the Harpers so badly lack focus and direction.
And by the way, you have some paint on your left hand."

"*Hmmph.*" The archmage glanced down at his hand and
glowered at the green smear, which promptly disappeared.
He snatched up the small scroll that lay near the magical
harp and tossed it to his nephew.

Danilo deftly caught it, then draped himself over Khelben's favorite chair. The archmage also sat, in a chair with
carved legs that ended in griffin's claws gripping balls of
amber. In direct reflection of Khelben's mood, the wooden
claws drummed like impatient fingers.

"How many magical toys does one man need?" Danilo
echoed wryly, and then turned his attention to the information on the scroll.

A few moments passed as he read and translated the coded
message. His visage hardened. "Malchior is a strifeleader,
commander of the war-priests in the Zhentish keep known as
Darkhold," he paraphrased grimly. "Damn! Bronwyn has
done business with suspect characters before, but this is
beyond the pale."

"Malchior cannot have that necklace," Khelben said firmly.
"You must stop the sale and bring the stones to me."

The bard's eyebrows rose, and his gaze slid over the

severely-clad archmage. Khelben's only ornaments were the silver threads in his black hair, and the distinctive streak of white in the middle of his neatly trimmed beard. "Since when did you develop a passion for fine antique jewelry?" Danilo asked in a dry tone.

"Think, boy! Even in its humblest form, amber is more than a pretty stone—it is a natural conduit for the Weave. This amber came from Anauroch, from trees that died suddenly and violently. Imagine the power required to transform the ancient Myconid Forest into desert wasteland. If even a trace of that magic lingers in the amber, in any form that can be tapped and focused, that necklace has enormous magical potential. It can also gather and transfer magical energy—" Khelben broke off, looking faintly startled, as if, Dan noted, he was suddenly considering that thought in a new light. The archmage rose and resumed his pacing. "Apparently we shall have to keep a closer watch on Malchior and his ambitions."

"In our copious spare time," Danilo murmured. He lifted one brow. "Here's a happy thought. When you say 'we,' perhaps you are employing the *royal* 'we,' and excluding your humble nephew and henchman?"

Khelben almost smiled. "Keep thinking in that manner," he said. "They say that dreams are healthy."

"Uncle, may I be frank?"

This time, the archmage looked genuinely amused. "Why stop on my account?"

"I am concerned about Bronwyn. Stop frowning so—nothing is out of the ordinary. All has been done as you requested. I have arranged to have her watched and protected. I have quietly fostered her shop as the right place to acquire gems and oddities, ensured that her acquisitions are seen on those who mold the whims of fashion, made certain that she receives social invitations likely to build her reputation and her client list. In short, I have kept her busy, happy, and here in Waterdeep.

"But may I be damned as a lich if I know why, and damned thrice over if I am proud of my part in the manipulation of a friend and a fellow Harper!"

"Consider it 'management,' then," Khelben answered, "if the other word displeases you."

Danilo shrugged. "A goblin by any other name is just as green."

"What a charming bromide. Is that the sort of thing you're teaching in the bard school?"

"Uncle, I will not be distracted."

The archmage threw up his hands. "Fine. Then I, too, will be blunt. Your words display far more naïveté than I would have expected from you. Of course the Harpers must be managed. The decisions an agent must make are often too important, too far-reaching, to leave entirely in one person's hands."

"Unless, of course, that person is yourself."

Khelben stopped his pacing and turned slowly, exuding in condensed form the wrath and power of a dragon rampant. "Have a care how you speak." he said in a low, thrumming voice. "There are limits to what I will endure, even from you."

Danilo held his ground, though he better understood the true scope of Khelben's power than did most who stood in awe of the great archmage. "If I offended, I beg pardon, but I only speak the truth as I see it."

"A dangerous habit," Khelben grumbled, but he subsided and turned away. He clasped his hands behind his back and gazed out a window—a window that shifted position randomly, and that was never visible from the outside of the tower. The current vista, Dan noted, was especially impressive: the luxury of Castle Ward, crowned by the majestic sweep of Mount Waterdeep. A trio of griffons from the aerie at the mountain's summit rose into the sky, their tiny forms silhouetted against sunset clouds of brilliant rose and amethyst. Danilo watched them circle and take off on their appointed patrol as he waited for the archmage to speak.

"You have no doubt wondered why we keep such close watch on Bronwyn, a young Harper whose missions mostly entail carrying messages."

"No doubt," Danilo said dryly. He folded his arms and stretched his long legs out before him. "What was your first portent of this? The many times I demanded to know why I was made a mastiff to herd this particular sheep?"

"Sarcasm ill becomes you," Khelben pointed out. "You would not be so flippant if you understood Malchior's possible interest in Bronwyn."

"Then tell me." Dan traced a rune over his heart, in the manner of one schoolboy making a pledge to another. "I shall be the very soul of discretion."

The archmage's smile was bleak and fleeting. "I have never found you to be anything less, but you must accept that this is a tale best untold. I would like to keep it so. Go now, and get that necklace before it falls into Malchior's hands."

"Bronwyn values her reputation for making and keeping deals. She will not thank me for interfering."

"She need not know of your involvement. It would be better so. But if that is not possible, use whatever means needed to separate her from the necklace."

"Easily said," Dan remarked as he headed for the door.

Khelben lifted a skeptical brow. "Timid words, from a man whose first contribution to the Harper cause was his ability to separate women from their secrets."

The young Harper stiffened, then turned. "I will do as you say, Uncle, but not in the manner you imply. I resent this assignment, and I deeply resent your assault on my character."

"Can you deny the truth in my words?"

Dan's smile was tight and rueful. "Of course not. Why do you think I resent them?"

* * * * *

Steam filled the room and Bronwyn, who had had time after returning to the city to clean up, dress up, and take certain precautions, squinted into the mist. As her eyes adjusted, she noted the gray-bearded man lounging in the vast bath, his fleshy pink arms spread along the rim. His black eyes swept appreciatively over her. "You are prompt, as well as beautiful," he said in courteous tones. "I trust you have the necklace?"

Bronwyn closed the door behind her and settled down in a cushioned chair. "I would not risk carrying it with me, for fear of being waylaid. My assistant expects to send it by courier."

"Just as he anticipates your imminent return, no doubt," the man said dryly.

She responded with a demure smile. "Such precautions are needed, my lord Malchior, as my experience has proved many times over." Especially when dealing with the Zhentarim in general, and priests of Cyric in particular, she noted silently. Noting his scrutiny, she spread her hands in a self-deprecating gesture. "But I will not bore you with my little stories."

"On the contrary, I am sure I would find them most entertaining."

There was a soft tap on the door. "Another time, perhaps," Bronwyn murmured as she rose to answer it. She accepted a pile of fresh linen towels from the maid, closed and locked the door firmly behind her. From the center of the pile she took a small box roughly fashioned from unpolished wood.

Bronwyn set the box down on a small table and lifted the lid carefully, so as not to get splinters in her fingers. The priest eyed the homely box with distaste. His eyes rounded, however, when she spilled out the contents—several exotic smoking pipes already filled and tamped with a fragrant and highly illegal form of pipeweed. She did not miss the sudden light in his eyes as he regarded them. She did not come blind into this encounter and knew more about this man and his habits than she liked to contemplate.

"Forgive me if this offends you, my lord," she said, careful to keep any hint of irony from her face and voice. "This was a feint, just in case the lad who smuggled this box into the festhall was set upon by thieves, who would expect to find either valuables or some type of contraband. A thief would likely take the pipes and discard so rude a box, not suspecting that the box has a false bottom."

She deftly pried it loose and lifted the necklace from its hiding place. She stooped and held it out to the priest, who took it with eager hands. He closed his eyes and smoothed the amber beads over his forehead. An expression of near-ecstasy suffused his plump face. As his eyes opened and settled on her, Bronwyn suppressed a shiver. Despite the man's high rank and considerable personal wealth, his eyes held a degree of greed and cunning that marked him as kin to the worst duergar scum. Bronwyn suspected that his reasons for purchasing the amber had little to do with furthering the good of humankind.

"You have done well," he murmured at length. "These are . . . more than I had expected. It is said that amber holds the memory of magic. Perhaps your touch, your beauty, has added to their value."

His words sent a crawling sensation skittering over her skin, but Bronwyn forced herself to smile graciously. "You are too kind."

"Not at all. Now, let us proceed to the matter of payment. You wished information in addition to gold. Why don't you join me? It would be more congenial to talk together in comfort."

Bronwyn deftly unclasped her belt, then stepped out of her shoes. With a quick, fluid motion, she pulled the dress over her head, and turned to drape it over the chair.

She turned back to the bath, catching the priest in an unguarded moment. His eyes were fixed on the curves of her hip, and narrowed in lewd speculation. Bronwyn set her jaw and stepped into the water. Public bathing was a part of life in Waterdeep, as in most civilized cities. She did not see it as a prelude to further intimacy, but there were those who did.

"This is much more pleasant," Malchior said. "Perhaps when our business is concluded, we might enjoy the other amenities this fine festhall has to offer."

Such as the adjoining bedchamber, Bronwyn supposed. "Perhaps," she said pleasantly, though now that she had met the man, she would rather kiss a water snake—at fifty fathoms.

"What can you tell me of the *Sea Ghost?*" she asked, naming the ship that had forever changed her life.

Malchior's plump shoulders rose in a shrug. "Little. The ship was indeed a Zhentish vessel, but it disappeared some twenty years ago. Given the pirate activity in the area, it was assumed that the ship was attacked, looted, and scuttled."

Bronwyn knew that already, and all too well. "Was there any attempt to trace the cargo?"

"Of course. A few weapons were recovered, and a few bits of jewelry, but most of the cargo disappeared into the markets of Amn."

He continued to talk, but his words melted into the remembered haze of sound and smells and sensations: terror, captivity, humiliation, pain. Oh yes, Bronwyn remembered the markets of Amn. The cacophony of voices that she could not yet understand, the prodding hands, the sudden knell of the falling gavel that announced a slave sold, a fate sealed.

"I'm afraid I can tell you little more. Perhaps if you told me more about the precise piece you are seeking?"

Malchior's words seeped into her nightmare, drawing her back into the present. Her eyes focused on his greedy face, the cunning knowledge that whatever she sought was worth more to her than the priceless amber necklace. She managed a wry smile. "Surely you don't expect me to answer that. Can you tell me about the origin of the cargo? The ship's owner, her captain? Even the name of a crewman? Anything you know, even details that may seem insignificant, might prove helpful."

The priest leaned forward. "My voice begins to fail, with all this shouting back and forth across this lake. Come closer, and we will talk more."

The bath was big, but not that big. Bronwyn rose and moved closer to the priest, taking care to stay beyond reach of those pudgy hands.

But he made no attempt to reach for her. "I must admit, your interest in this old matter intrigues me," Malchior said. "Tell me what you know about *Sea Ghost* and her cargo, and perhaps I can be of more help."

"I don't know much more than I told you," Bronwyn said honestly. "It was a long time ago, and the trail has long since gone cold."

"And I would doubt that your own memory extends back so

far," he commented. "The ship was sunk more than twenty years ago. You were perhaps four years old?"

"About that," she answered. In truth, she wasn't sure of her exact age. She remembered very little: most of her early memories were swallowed up in terror. Before she could capture it, a bleak sigh escaped her.

Malchior nodded, his eyes shrewd in his round face. "Forgive me if this seems over-bold, but I could not help but notice your interesting tattoo. It looks a bit like a crimson oak leaf. Perhaps you are a follower of Silvanus?"

Her first impulse was to laugh at this notion. Silvanus, the Oak Father, was a god revered by many druids, and she was most assuredly not of that faith. But it occurred to her that Cyric, Malchior's god, was exceedingly jealous of any sign of fealty to another power.

"I was once rather . . . fond of a certain young woodsman," she said lightly. "And he, in turn, was fond of oak leaves. So. . . ." She let the word trail off and shrugged. Let him assume from that what he would. The birthmark on her backside was no one's business but her own.

"Is that so?" Malchior leaned forward. "I have great sympathy for a man's desire to leave his mark on you. In time, perhaps you could be persuaded to wear mine. Take her!" he called out.

Bronwyn's eyes widened, then darted to the door. The first hard kick resounded through the room, straining the bolt she'd carefully put in place.

She was out of the tub with a single leap and then dashed for the window. The splashing behind her—barely audible over the continued pounding at the door—announced Malchior's pursuit.

He moved fast, especially for a fat man. The priest seized her from behind, one fleshy arm around her waist and another flung around her throat. He was strong, too. Bronwyn wriggled like a hooked trout, but could not break free.

"Hurry, you fools!" he shouted out. "I can't hold her forever!"

Bronwyn thrust a hand into her hair and yanked out the

stiletto she had hidden in the thick coils. The weapon was designed for precise, careful attack, but there was no time. She stabbed back over her shoulder and met yielding flesh.

But the narrow knife did not strike hard or deep. Malchior yelped and tightened his grip. Again she struck, this time punching into the bones of his hands. She tore at the blade, then lashed out a third time.

Finally he released her—just as the door burst open in an explosion of wood. Bronwyn darted a quick look over her shoulder. Three men charged into the steamy room. There was little time for escape, but fury prompted her to turn back to the priest, and slash the point of the tiny blade across his sagging jowls.

Then she was gone, racing for the window. She flung aside the drapes and kicked open the wooden shutters. The latch gave, and she plunged out the window to the street below.

Time stood still as Bronwyn fell. An instant, no more, before she struck the quilted awning that her assistant had stretched between this building and the next, two floors down from the room that housed the private bath. She bounced slightly, then felt about for the tunic that was supposed to have been left there. She found it, quickly pulled it over her head, then rolled to the edge of the awning. She lowered herself down and dropped to the street, then took off at a run for the safety of her shop.

To her immense relief—and her surprise—she was not pursued. Perhaps Malchior decided not to take the risk. After all, Zhentish priests could hardly afford to advertise their presence, even in a city as tolerant as Waterdeep. He had the necklace, and at a ridiculously low price. No doubt he considered the bargain well made.

But why then had he called his men? The attack made no sense. She had already received payment, so it was no attempt to defraud her. Perhaps he had learned that she was a Harper. That would be reason enough for him to kill her. But his words indicated that he planned to keep her, not kill her. Did he have ambitions of turning her, making her into a hidden agent of the Zhentarim?

Bronwyn pondered this as she wove back through the city, following a complex path that took her through alleys and into the back room of a pipeweed shop whose owner was friendly to Harpers and their small intrigues. She emerged from the shop shod in the slippers she'd left there, her tunic decently covered by a linen kirtle and her wet hair hanging in a single braid. Thus attired, she could walk without notice through the elegant market area, just another tradeswoman on some errand for her household, or a servant indulging the whim of a mistress.

Finally she turned onto the Street of Silks, marveling again at her good fortune to have secured a lease on a shop in this posh district. Convenient to the Market and the wealthy Sea Ward, the street was a long, broad avenue of shops and taverns that catered to Waterdeep's wealthy. Only the finest merchandise and the most skilled craftsmen found a place on this street. The shops reflected this status. Tall buildings, constructed of good timber and wattle-and-daub, or even fine stone masonry, were decked with carved and painted wooden signs, bright banners, and even small beds of flowers. The street lamps glowed brightly, casting a golden light upon the elegantly dressed people who strolled the cobbled paths. Minstrels were plentiful, and as Bronwyn walked down the street, the music shifted around her in a pleasant kaleidoscope of sound. The dinner hour was long past, and most of the shops had closed, but in Waterdeep there were diversions to be had at all hours. Taverns and festhalls stayed open until breakfast. Lavish private parties and smaller, clandestine celebrations kept many of the more privileged citizens happily occupied until daylight. Those who earned their living with hard labor and skilled crafts were more likely to sleep and rise with the sun. Bronwyn heartily wished that she were one of them.

She was not surprised to see that the lights in her shop were still burning. She unlocked the door and stepped into the warm, appealing jumble of curiosities and treasures. Her assistant, a white-haired, rosy-cheeked gnome woman who went by the name Alice Tinker was studying an emerald ring through a jeweler's glass. She looked up when Bronwyn entered, not bothering to lower the glass. The result—one normal gnomish eye, one magnified to a size more fitting to a blue-eyed beholder—set Bronwyn back on her heels.

Alice laughed merrily and set down the glass. "Busy day we had, eh?"

"Aye," Bronwyn agreed on a sigh. "Did you have time to sketch the piece I sent through?" So tired was she that the words sounded muzzy even to her own ears.

"That I did. I've matched the color with some bits of amber we had hereabouts, and I'll use that as a guide to add the proper tints on the morrow."

Bronwyn nodded. She kept a portfolio of such sketches, a record of the rare pieces that passed through her hands, under lock and spell-guard in her safe. Some of the drawings she did herself, but most of the work fell to Alice's small, capable hands. The gnome was a positive treasure. She kept the shop and wrote up sales while Bronwyn was out adventuring and making deals. The two of them were a true team, and the success of Curious Past belonged to them both. To be sure, Alice tended to treat her employer like her own oversized child, but Bronwyn was willing to overlook that single lapse.

"Tomorrow will be soon enough," she agreed and turned to the stairs that led to the chamber she kept over the shop.

"Oh! One thing more," Alice called after her. "That young bard was in earlier, looking for you. Says it's important he talks to you at your earliest convenience. Something about a necklace."

That would be Danilo, of course. Again, tomorrow would be soon enough. "Fine. Good." Bronwyn said, and staggered up the stairs.

Alice followed her to the base of the stairs, her fists planted on her hips and her brown, apple-cheeked face filled with motherly reproach. "Look at you, child! Dead on your feet! I keep telling you to take some time off, laze around the shop a bit."

Ignoring the gnome's continuing harangue, Bronwyn climbed up to her chamber, intending to fall face first onto the bed and hoping she could stay awake that long.

But when she reached the chamber, all thoughts of sleep fled. In the center of the room, leaning on his staff and regarding her with a somber, measuring gaze, stood the most feared and powerful wizard in Waterdeep.

Bronwyn gaped at Khelben Arunsun, the Master Harper who ultimately directed her activities, but whom she had never met. She considered herself well versed in the custom and protocol of a dozen races and threescore lands, but for the life of her she could not decide which of three equally compelling responses she should chose:

Should she bow, flee, or faint?

* * * * *

Two men, both clad in the purple and black of Cyric's clergy, strolled through the villa's garden. A bright moon lit the white-pebbled path. Though it was still early spring, the air was scented with the fragrance of a few timid flowers. Three fountains played merrily into tiled pools.

"I have been hearing interesting things about you," Malchior said, slanting a glance at the man who had been his most talented and promising acolyte.

Dag Zoreth inclined his head in acknowledgment—and evasion. His mentor knew too much about him, had made a study of the family from which Dag had been torn. Some of this information he had recently shared: the location of the village from which Dag had been stolen, the rumors of power inherent in the family bloodline, the current post held by his illustrious father. He often wondered what else Malchior knew. He also wondered how the priest got that livid cut down his left cheek—and he envied the man who had put it there.

"It would appear that you have a more intriguing tale to tell," Dag commented, raising a finger and tracing a line down his own cheek.

The older priest merely shrugged. "You recently traveled to Jundar's Hill and rode alone into the foothills along the

Dessarin. I am curious, my son, what prompted you to take such chances just to visit the site of your home village?"

So that was it. Word had reached Malchior faster than Dag had expected. "I, too, am curious," he said. "What you told me of my past intrigued me, but there are still many holes in my story. I sought to fill some of them."

"And did you?"

"One or two." Dag turned a stony gaze upon the older priest. "You told me that the raid was the work of an ambitious rival paladin. But the men who attacked were Zhentarim soldiers. Looking back from where I stand, I can see that plainly."

This clearly took Malchior aback. "How is this possible? You were a child."

"I know," Dag said simply. "The matter is between me and my god."

There was little Malchior would say to counter this pronouncement. For several moments they walked together in silence. "This villa, your new responsibilities," he began, "these things you have earned. I have something more for you. A gift." He paused to add weight to the coming words. "You are not the last of Samular's bloodline. Your sister also survived that raid and is alive and well."

Dag froze, stunned by this revelation. It did not occur to him to challenge Malchior's words; indeed, as the realization sank home, he wondered why he should be so surprised. He remembered the Cyric-given vision, the bold and curious little girl diving headlong from the small window to investigate the coming raid. His sister Bronwyn, dimly remembered as the bane of his young existence. Of course. *He* had been spared—why not the girl?

A sister. He had a sister. Dag was not certain how he felt about this. Vaguely he remembered his father's deep, disapproving voice lamenting the little girl's bold ways—and wondering why her older brother was not half so intrepid.

"How is she? Where is she?"

"In Waterdeep," Malchior answered. He grimaced and touched the livid cut on his face. "And trust me, she does well enough. I met and spoke with her earlier this very night."

So that was Bronwyn's work. The years had passed, but still she had the courage to act when Dag held back. This did not please him, but the discomfited expression on Malchior's wounded face most assuredly did.

"For a paladin's daughter, she is quick with a knife," Dag commented with dark amusement. "You are not usually so incautious as to overlook a hidden weapon."

"A naked woman," Malchior grumbled, "with a stiletto hidden in her hair. Men must be cautious in these treacherous times."

This time Dag laughed aloud. "Oh, that is priceless! Wouldn't the great Hronulf be proud?"

The older priest shrugged. "She is an interesting woman, a finder of lost antiquities who has made it her life's work to collect pieces of the past. Ironically, she has not been able to recover her own history. Yet she is clearly desperate to do so. She was willing to trade a gemstone artifact for information. You could exploit this. And you should." Again he grimaced. "I ran into some . . . interference. Had I not prepared for that possibility and importuned Cyric aforetime for spells to take me to this place, the night would have ended more disastrously than it did. Clearly, we are not the only ones in possession of this knowledge. Your sister is watched, protected. If you do not stake claim to this woman and whatever power she wields, someone else will."

"Yes," Dag murmured. "What do you suggest?"

Malchior's eyebrows rose. It had been some years since his former student had asked for advice. "I have given into your hands the man who betrayed your father, and you. Use him. Let him lure your sister to a place where you can, shall we say, exert a degree of brotherly influence."

The young priest nodded. "Well said. And what, if I may be so bold, do you hope to gain from any of this?"

"Gain? We have known each other for many years. You have been like a son," Malchior began. When Dag began to chuckle, the priest gave up the attempt and shrugged. "There is power in your family. I don't understand its precise nature.

That is for you to discover. But I trust that you will do so and
share your discovery with me."

"Really?" Dag imbued the single word with a great deal of
skepticism. Malchior was not a man to be trusted, and he
assumed that all other men dealt as he did.

"Let us say that there is power enough for both. I desire your
success with all my heart, for it is a stepping-stone to my own."

That, Dag could believe and understand. "Very well. When
Bronwyn is under my influence, when I understand the scope
of my heritage, then you and I will speak again."

"I am satisfied to wait." Suddenly the priest's jovial expression disappeared, and his eyes were as flat and hungry as a
troll's. "You understand, of course, the price of failure."

"Of course," Dag said smoothly. "Have I not inflicted it
often enough? Ask any failed man under my command the
price of his failure—but first, prepare to summon his spirit."

Malchior blinked, then began to laugh. "Well enough. A
drink then, to seal our agreement." He linked his arm with
Dag's, and together they strolled back toward the darkness of
the villa.

*   *   *   *   *

"Forgive the intrusion," Khelben Arunsun said in a deep,
faintly accented voice, "but circumstances demanded that we
meet and speak. Please, sit down."

Still too dazed for thought, Bronwyn sank down on the
nearest available seat—the old sea chest that held her
linens. The archmage took the chamber's only chair. Staff in
hand, he looked uncomfortably like a magistrate about to
pass judgment on some unknown crime.

"It has come to my attention that you have accepted a
commission from a priest of Cyric, a man known as Malchior."

How had he learned of this so soon? Bronwyn shook off
this second surprise and marshaled her wits. "That is so,
Lord Arunsun."

"What precisely was your thinking in this matter? Need I

remind you that conspiring with the Zhentarim is hardly an approved Harper activity?"

"True enough, my lord. But it *is* part of my job. I was recruited by the Harpers for my contacts. A wide range of customers seek my services."

"And simple prudence dictates that you set limits. Correct me if I err, but was it not your intention to deliver gemstones containing significant magical power to Malchior of Cyric?"

"Yes, but—"

"What do you know of the man? What is the nature of your dealings with him?"

Before Bronwyn could form a defense, a tap at her open lintel distracted both her and her visitor. A familiar, fair-haired man lounged against the door post. He held up one hand to display a length of golden beads and silver filigree.

Bronwyn's eyes widened at the sight of the amber necklace. For a moment, she forgot the daunting presence of the archmage. "Damn it, Dan, what are you doing with that?"

"I should like to know that, myself," Khelben intoned in a grim voice. He rose and faced down the younger man. "Why did you bring the necklace here?"

"Why wouldn't I? It belongs to Bronwyn," Danilo said.

"No, it doesn't," she gritted out. "I received payment. The bargain was made."

"Was it?" Her friend's usually merry face showed deep concern. He walked into the room and sat beside her on the sea chest. "From what I hear, there was a slight downturn in the course of bartering. Something about an attempted kidnapping and a leap from a fourth floor window? Why are you so angry about a little assistance, Bronwyn? They might have killed you."

This argument did nothing to lessen Bronwyn's ire. "Obviously, they did not succeed. I was away before your . . . friends . . . made an appearance." She gave him an impatient little shove. "Don't you realize what you have done?"

His eyebrows rose. "I thought I did. Obviously you are of a different opinion, and the archmage quite clearly holds a distinct third. Since I am sure he will share his thoughts with me at a later time, no doubt in four-part harmony, why don't we discuss *your* views?"

Bronwyn leaped to her feet and strode to the little window that overlooked the city. "Promise made, promise kept. That's my reputation and the most valuable thing I possess. This is the first time I have not delivered. You have undermined more than a single deal. Now do you understand?"

The silence stretched out for a long, tense moment. "The necklace has great magical value and must be properly safeguarded," Khelben said.

Bronwyn struggled to hold her temper. Hadn't the archmage heard a word? Or did such minor things matter nothing? After all, what regard does a dragon have for a mouse?

"I'll keep it in my safe," she said in a stiff tone. "Danilo can tell you what magical wards have been placed upon it."

Her friend rose and placed one hand on her shoulder. "What price did the necklace command? I will see that Malchior is amply compensated. Although that will not fully satisfy him, it may serve to restore your honor in his eyes and your own. We owe you that."

"And more." She tipped back her head to glare at her friend. It was a relief, not having to hide her irritation. "You'll have to forgive me if I prefer to collect at some later time."

A faint smirk lifted one corner of the bard's lips. "Lord Arunsun, I do believe we are being thrown out."

Bronwyn glanced at the archmage. "I didn't mean—"

"Of course you did," Dan broke in smoothly. "And not without justification. Get some rest. The day's . . . bargaining has taken a toll." Before she could respond, the two men turned and left her chamber by the back stairs. Bronwyn sat staring after them, all thoughts of sleep vanished.

* * * * *

As the Harpers walked down the stairs, Khelben began to transform. His broad form compacted and lengthened into that of a lithe young man, and his clothing changed from somber black to shades of forest brown and green. The silver streaks disappeared from his hair and beard, and his face took on a faintly elven appearance.

Danilo had seen this so many times that he did not remark on it. The archmage seldom went about the city wearing his own face. In fact, neither man spoke at all until they had reached the alley behind Curious Past.

"What were you thinking, bringing the necklace to Bronwyn's shop? Now she is aware that Harpers are watching her."

"We took on that risk when we sent men to the festhall," Danilo said bluntly. An alley cat streaked out from behind a crate, yowling as if in protest. No doubt their appearance had spoiled a long and patient stalking of some prey, likely a rat. Danilo was not fond of such, and he quickened his pace. "Bronwyn is no fool. Surely she realizes that she got away too easily and suspects that someone detained Malchior's thugs."

Khelben lengthened his stride and fell into pace. "And now, thanks to your misguided gesture, she knows without question. Given Malchior's involvement, this has become a delicate situation."

"Enlighten me."

They emerged onto Selduth Street, which at this hour was bustling with tavern traffic, as well as the paid escorts and would-be suitors who gathered on nearby Jester's Court. The lighting was dimmer here, in deference to ale-sodden heads and a desire for discrete dalliance. Khelben shot a quick look around to see if anyone was paying too close heed to their conversation, then started walking back west toward the Street of Silks. Even an archmage, Dan noted, instinctively sought the safety of a well-lit street.

"You have known Bronwyn for perhaps seven years. I have been searching for her for more than twenty. She is the daughter of a famed paladin—Hronulf of Tyr, who is of the bloodline of Samular Caradoon, the paladin who founded the order known as the knights of Samular. From your expression, I surmise that you recognize those names."

"I have been schooled in history," Danilo said, nimbly avoiding a drunken and weaving passerby. "Pray continue."

"Then you also know that Hronulf's family was thought to have been destroyed in a raid on his village more than twenty years ago. Hronulf believes that all his children were killed, but I had doubt on the matter and kept searching until my suspicions were confirmed. One child, now a man grown, is beyond my reach. But Bronwyn I can and must influence. She has no knowledge of her heritage, and there is ample reason to hope that she is never enlightened."

Danilo stopped abruptly and caught the archmage's arm. "Am I to understand," he said in a low and angry voice, "that for nearly seven years, you have known that two of Hronulf's children live, and *he* does *not*?"

"Do not pass judgment on that which you do not understand," Khelben cautioned. "You would do better to attend to the task at hand. We must learn who, if anyone, knows of Bronwyn's secret—including Bronwyn herself. And that is where you come in."

Khelben started walking, leaving Danilo standing with his jaw dropped and his mind churning with suspicion. Determined to find the truth of the matter, he trotted up to Khelben's side and fell into step.

"Seven years ago, you sent me to Amn to recruit a likely agent, a woman not yet twenty years old. Bronwyn and I became friends."

"So you said."

"The report and recommendation of a potential Harper includes many things, including, I might add, whether or not a person has any identifying marks." Danilo's tone was tight, kindling with growing wrath. "And I reported Bronwyn's birthmark. That was the identifying mark, was it not? The mark that confirmed that she was Hronulf's daughter?"

"Yes. What of it?"

Danilo inhaled, his breath whistling through clenched teeth. "You sent me to Amn, intending for me to see and report this."

"You were both young and unattached. It was reasonable to assume that nature would take its predicted course," Khelben said. "And you are, I might add, predictable in this matter."

The bard let out a low, furious oath. "I cannot believe this, not even from you. Is there no part of my life beyond the Harpers' reach? And you! To thus manipulate those who put trust in you . . . this is beyond belief."

"Calm yourself. That was long ago. No harm came of it. You even remained friends."

"Friends, indeed!" he sputtered. "What kind of friend will Bronwyn think me when she learns that I used and betrayed her thus? Will she believe it was without intent or knowledge? Will she believe that I had no part in keeping her past, her *family,* secret from her?"

"Lower your voice." Khelben glanced at a pair of interested passersby, and drew Danilo into a side street. "It is long past and a small matter. Let it go. This was not the first time you used charm and persuasion to learn a woman's secrets. I doubt it will be the last."

"Not the last?" Dan folded his arms and glared into Khelben's borrowed face. "I have made certain personal commitments. Does that mean nothing?"

"You have a prior commitment to the Harpers," Khelben pointed out, just as angry now as his nephew. But his anger was cold—to Danilo's eyes, almost inhuman. "If your Arilyn cannot accept this, then she proves herself unworthy of her Harper pin, as well as your continued regard."

Danilo considered himself an easygoing man, but this was treading where he allowed no man to walk. "I may have to hop back to my house as a frog," he gritted out, "but by Mystra, it will be worth it."

He fisted his hand and swung hard, connecting squarely with Khelben's jaw.

The archmage stumbled back a few steps, startled by the first physical attack he had received in what was no doubt centuries. For just a moment, his magical disguise slipped. Danilo confronted not a strong young man with elven blood, but an aging wizard. So old did Khelben look, in fact, that Danilo's heart thudded with mingled guilt and grief. It was one thing to deck a man wearing a magical disguise of his own apparent age, another entirely to look upon the dumbfounded face of the man who was in fact his own grandfather.

Then the moment passed and the powerful archmage of Waterdeep stood with his hand on his jaw, looking exactly as he always did: stern, powerful, and determined to have his way in this matter and all others.

Danilo turned and strode off, too full of fury and turmoil to care if retributive lightning was forthcoming.

*   *   *   *   *

All thoughts of sleep forgotten, Bronwyn quickly dressed herself in dark breeches and shirt, then slipped down her back stairs. She hailed a three-copper carriage on the street and gave the driver an address in the Dock Ward, the rough and dangerous part of town where sea met city. There was a warehouse just off Keel Alley that boasted a cavernous cellar. This was a favorite gathering place for denizens of the underground realms. When her duergar "friends" were in town, they invariably stayed there.

Bronwyn got to the warehouse without incident and crept into the building. The warehouse was vast, resembling a miniature city with narrow, wood-planked streets between structures formed by stacks of wooden crates and piles of sacks. It was fully as dangerous as the larger city beyond its walls. When Bronwyn saw a pair of luminous eyes, narrowed in challenge and hunkered low to the floor, she instinctively reached for her knife. A low, angry growl curled through the dusty air toward her. Bronwyn recognized the sound and relaxed. It was only a scrawny cat, such as many warehouse owners kept to limit the number of rats. The unearthly glow of the cat's eyes was merely reflected light from a crack high on the wall and the street lamp beyond.

She made her way through the maze of barrels and crates to the back corner of the warehouse. There stood a large, squat keg. She flipped open the knothole and squinted inside.

There was no floor beneath the barrel, just a ladder that led down into the cellar. A small, smoky fire burned in a stone hearth, and the haunch of rothé spitted over it sizzled and spat. The light of the fire fell upon several gray faces. Bronwyn counted five duergar, including the two she had dealt with earlier that day. The young duergar was not with them, but his elders did not seem to mourn his loss overmuch. The silent duergar sat contentedly munching a hunk of half-cooked rothé, while the leader played dice with the others and argued in a low, angry voice. The huge, empty ale mug at his elbow suggested Bronwyn's next course of action.

She tied a bit of thin, sturdy cord to the handle of a crate stacked overhead, then wriggled the crate forward a bit so that its position was less than secure. Then she took a place behind a nearby stack of crates and waited for the duergar to emerge. The way she figured it, the rental on his ale would expire shortly, and not even the filthy deep dwarves would permit him to end his lease in the cellar dining hall.

Sure enough, before long she heard the creak of heavy iron boots on the rickety ladder. When the duergar passed her, intent upon reaching the alley door, Bronwyn sprang. She reached over his shoulder, seized his beard, and jerked it up and back, then laid her knife to his bared throat. With her free hand, she began to loop the end of the cord onto his belt.

"That necklace you sold me," she whispered. "Where did you get it?"

The duergar started to wriggle, then thought the better of it. "Not telling," he mumbled. "Not part of the deal."

"I'm adding it on, as payment for damages. Who sold it to you? " She gave the knife an encouraging little twitch to speed his answer.

"A human," the duergar said grudgingly. "Short beard, big grin. Runs to fat. Wears purple."

The picture was forming clearly enough in Bronwyn's mind, but she wanted to be sure. "Does this human have a name?"

"Calls himself Malchior. Now turn me loose, and go bother him. I got things to do," the duergar complained.

Bronwyn lowered her knife. She gave the duergar a kick that sent him sprawling—and that brought the crate and several below it tumbling down on him. She turned and fled.

Before the other duergar could so much as investigate, she had put two alleys and a shop between them.

As she made her way back to Curious Past, two conclusions tumbled through Bronwyn's mind. First was the irrefutable fact that Malchior had set her up for no reason that she could fathom. And second was her growing conviction that the duergar had given her this information far too easily.

*   *   *   *   *

Early morning sunshine poured in through windows of fine leaded glass. An impeccably dressed servant unobtrusively placed a breakfast tray on a nearby table. Dag inhaled, enjoying the complex scent of sausage pasties, fresh-baked bread, and even a pot of the Maztican coffee that was becoming so popular in the decadent southern lands.

"Will that be all, my lord?"

Dag Zoreth paused in the act of surveying his new domain and glanced at the elegant, dark-clad man who'd addressed him. Emerson was a gentleman's gentleman: a polished, accomplished, and supremely capable servant who could probably run a small kingdom with great success and aplomb. The manservant was precisely the sort of amenity to which Dag intended to become accustomed.

"One thing more, Emerson. Sir Gareth Cormaeril will be calling this morning. He expects to meet with Malchior. Do not disabuse him of this notion. In fact, should he pose any questions at all, evade them."

The manservant did not so much as blink at this odd litany. "Shall I announce him, sir, or send him in directly?"

Dag's lips thinned in a semblance of a smile. "By all means, send him in at once. This meeting is more than twenty years overdue."

Emerson responded with an admirable lack of curiosity and a quick, perfect bow. After the manservant had shut the elaborately carved door behind him, Dag settled down in a deeply cushioned chair and took a moment to let the sheer luxury of the room flow over him.

Intricately patterned carpets from Calimport, many-paned windows accented with colored glass and framed with draperies of Shou silk, furniture carved from rare woods and softened with tapestry-covered pillows, shelf after shelf of beautifully bound books. The fireplace was tiled with lapis, and the chandelier that lit the room with scores of extravagant beeswax candles had the sheen of elven silver. Not a single item in the room was less than superlative, and nearly all were in shades of rich blue and deep crimson—the most difficult colors to achieve, and the most expensive.

This was the library of the Osterim guest villa, a small but lavish manor that was part of the Rassalanter Hamlet in the countryside east of Waterdeep. A complex of manors, cottages, and stables, it was maintained by a wealthy merchant for his use and that of his guests. This was widely known. It was less known that Yamid Osterim was a captain of the Zhentarim. His impeccable credentials as a merchant gave him access to secrets and trade routes; his cunning allowed him to pass along much of this information in such manner that never once had a hint of suspicion touched him.

Malchior, Dag's mentor and immediate superior, had enjoyed access to Osterim's hospitality for many years. That privilege he had passed on to Dag, along with the services of the inestimable Emerson—and the control of Malchior's paladin.

In preparation for Sir Gareth's visit, Dag had added his own unique touch to the room's décor. The hearth blazed with magical fire—strange, unholy black and purple flames that cast an eerie purple light and sent macabre shadows dancing across the carpeted floor. It amused Dag to flaunt the colors and the power of Cyric, in unspoken mockery of Sir Gareth's ability to bear such proximity to evil.

The door opened and a tall, well-made man in vigorous late life stepped into the room, helmet tucked respectfully under his left arm and snowy hair smoothed into precise waves. His bright blue eyes widened in surprise when they fell upon a slight, dark young man instead of the substantial and falsely jovial priest he clearly anticipated.

"Welcome, Sir Gareth. It was good of you to come," Dag Zoreth said, inflecting the words with irony.

The knight's look of puzzlement deepened. "I had little choice in the matter, young sir. I was summoned."

Dag sighed and shook his head. "Paladins," he said with mild derision. "Always this need to state the obvious. Sit, please."

"I have no wish to intrude upon your leisure. My duty is with another. Only accept my apologies for this intrusion and I will leave you and seek him—"

"Malchior will not be attending," Dag broke in smoothly. "He sends his regards and his desire that you see in me his replacement."

Sir Gareth hesitated. "I do not know you, young sir."

"Do you not? I have chosen the name Dag Zoreth, though you may well have heard me called by another. You knew my father extremely well, if the stories tell truth." Dag nodded at the older man's right arm, which hung withered and useless at his side. "You took that wound saving his life. Or so they say."

The color drained from the paladin's face, but still he stood as straight as a sentry.

"Oh, sit down before you fall," the priest said irritably.

Sir Gareth moved stiffly to the nearest chair and sank into it, his eyes riveted on Dag's face. "How is it possible?" he whispered. "Hronulf's son. This cannot be true."

"If you are looking for my father's likeness in me, do not bother," Dag said with a touch of asperity. "As I recall, we were never much alike. But perhaps this little trinket will convince you of my claim."

He lifted a silver chain from around his neck and handed it to Sir Gareth. The old knight hesitated when he glimpsed the medallion bearing the symbol of Cyric. He forgot his scruples, however, when he caught sight of the ring behind it. He took the chain and studied the ring carefully.

After a few moments Sir Gareth lifted his gaze to Dag's face. "You do not wear this ring," the paladin said. "I suspect that you cannot."

That was true enough, but Dag shrugged it aside. "Someone can wield it for me. If the ring is in my control, it matters little whose hand it bedecks."

An expression of shrewd speculation flashed into the knight's eyes, coming and going so quickly that Dag wondered if he had only imagined it. But he remembered it, as he remembered all things Malchior had told him about this man Dag now owned.

"There are two other rings," Dag continued. "My father wears one. Where is the third?"

Sir Gareth reluctantly handed back the ring. "Alas, we do not know. The ring was lost to the Holy Order long years ago, during the time of the great Samular."

The priest studied the older man's face for signs of hesitation. Malchior had advised him that Sir Gareth never lied, yet often managed to speak truth in highly misleading fashion. It was difficult, Malchior had warned, to tell whole truth from artfully contrived prevarication. Dag suspected that Sir Gareth himself would be hard-pressed to tell the difference. According to Malchior, the knight was a master at the art of rationalization. Sir Gareth worked hard, desperately hard, to conceal from his brothers in the Order—and from himself, most likely—the fact that he was a fallen paladin. The grace of Tyr was no longer with him and hadn't been for a very long time. In light of this, Dag concluded with grim, private amusement, Sir Gareth could hardly object to carrying a bit of Cyric-granted magic.

The priest reached into the folds of his purple tabard and removed a small black globe. This he handed to Sir Gareth. "You will carry this with you, keeping it on your person at all times. When I wish to contact you, you will feel a sensation of cold fire. I will not try to explain this—you will know what it is when you feel it. When this occurs, hasten to a private spot and draw the globe out of its hiding place. The touch of your hand will open the portal—and dim the pain." Dag smiled thinly. "But I'm sure that warning is twice unnecessary, since alacrity and fortitude are both knightly virtues."

Sir Gareth took the globe with an unwilling hand. He drew

back in horror at the image within: Dag's pale, narrow face, back lit by purple flames.

"Speak into it in a normal voice. I will hear you," Dag continued. His eyes mocked the knight, who hastily put aside the globe and wiped his fingers as if the touch not only burned, but sullied him. "With this device, you can continue to serve the Zhentarim, as you have for nearly thirty years."

Dag's words were a deliberate insult, and were received as such. Sir Gareth's jaw firmed and his chin lifted. "Think what you will, Lord Zoreth, but I serve the Order still. The Knights of Samular venerate the memory of Samular, our founder. In serving you, a child of the bloodline of Samular, I am fulfilling my vows."

"Twisted," Dag Zoreth said with mild admiration. "Perhaps you can enlighten me on another matter. I am curious . . . have you any idea what kind of diversions a priest of Cyric finds amusing?"

The priest smiled at his visitor's reaction. "You blanched just now. I will take that as a yes. How, then, do you justify the use of your Order's funds to finance Malchior's leisure activities?"

Sir Gareth's face was ashen, but his gaze remained steady. "Whatever else he may be, Malchior is a scholar and most knowledgeable in the lore and history of my Order. It is right and fitting that some of the Order's monies support this work. I have no firsthand knowledge that these funds were used in any other manner."

"A fine distinction, and one that I'm sure you find soothing," the priest commented. His face hardened and the dark amusement in his eyes vanished. "Permit me one more question. By what possible light could you justify condemning children to death?"

The former paladin dropped his head into his hands, as if the weight of his unacknowledged guilt was too heavy to bear. "I had no hand in what happened to Hronulf's children."

"Did you not? Did you not sell some of your Order's most precious and closely guarded secrets? If that led raiders to my father's village and to me, I suppose none of the taint clings to your garments."

Sir Gareth sat up abruptly, his shoulders squared. The awareness of imminent death was in his eyes, but he was still paladin enough to meet his anticipated fate squarely.

"It is rather late for you to die a martyr," Dag said coldly. "Killing you slowly and painfully would be vastly amusing, but all things considered, it would be administering simple justice. That is the purview of *your* god, not mine."

"Then what do you want from me, priest of Cyric?"

"No more than Malchior wanted," Dag said. "Information is worth far more to me than the brief satisfaction I would derive from your demise."

The knight studied him, then nodded. "If the knowledge is mine, it shall be freely given."

Dag doubted this, but information received from Sir Gareth would be a fine starting place. He would check and confirm and expand upon what he learned from this wily knight, and only then would he act.

The priest leaned back in his chair. "Speak to me of my father," he said. "Tell me all about him—and tell me everything you know about the fortress he commands."

This Sir Gareth did, at great length and in admirable detail. He described the old fortress known as Thornhold, its defenses, the terrain around and beneath it. He yielded up information to which few men, even among the Knights of Samular, were privy. Hronulf, it seemed, had trusted his old friend with many secrets. As Gareth spoke, a plan began to take shape in Dag Zoreth's mind.

When the meeting was over and the paladin had gratefully left, Dag Zoreth rose and walked over to the hearth, deep in thought. The magical flames caught his eye and diverted him. The Fires of Cyric was a spell of his own devising, and one of his favorites. The fire itself was deep purple, and the heart of each leaping spire was utterly black. The colors of amethyst and obsidian, the colors of his god, glowed with intense and unnerving power. The fire was a symbol of Dag Zoreth's ambition, and the path to power that had suddenly opened before him.

Who would have thought, he mused as he gazed at a dancing flume, that something so very black could also be so beckoning and bright?

Three

 Algorind reigned his horse around a pile of boulders that had fallen onto the path from the cliff above. They were too large for one man to move; he would have to note this in his report so Master Laharin could send more men on the next patrol. Keeping the paths between the river and the Dessarin Road clear and safe was one of the duties of the young paladins who trained in Summit Hall—a duty that Algorind was glad and proud to shoulder.

This was his first solitary patrol, and his first time riding Icewind, the tall white horse that he had spent long days breaking to saddle and bridle. Icewind was not a true paladin's mount—that Algorind had yet to earn—but he was a fine beast. Algorind settled happily into the rhythm of the horse's long-legged stride and allowed his thoughts to stray to the evening ahead.

Tonight, three young paladins would be inducted into the Order. They would become Knights of Samular through an ordeal of faith and arms, and by the grace of Tyr, god of justice and might. The prospect of witnessing this ritual filled Algorind with sublime joy.

All his life, he had longed to be a knight. By the happiest of

circumstances, his father, a nobleman of proud lineage but
light purse, had delivered his third-born son to Summit Hall
before his tenth birthday to be raised and trained by the
Order. Algorind had not seen his family since, but he did not
feel loss. He was surrounded by young men of like ambition,
future priests and paladins devoted to Tyr's service. Were not
all the young acolytes his brothers? And the masters of the
hall more than father to him?

These thoughts contented him as he fulfilled the last hour
of his watch. Other than the dislodged boulders, the patrol
had been without incident. Algorind was almost disap-
pointed; he had hoped to contribute to the Order's latest venture. The knights, during their training forays into the
surrounding countryside, had discovered and routed clans of
orcs. The surviving beasts roamed the hills, terrorizing travelers and farmers. May Tyr grant that the last of them be
found soon, Algorind thought piously, and the evil they represent vanquished.

A muffled cry caught his ear, followed by a chilling riff of
guttural laughter that could not possibly have come from a
human throat. Algorind drew his sword and held it aloft as he
spurred his horse on to battle.

The white horse thundered around a bend in the path,
down a rock-strewn hill and toward a scene that kindled Algorind's wrath. Four orcs—great, monstrous creatures with
stringy muscles covered by filthy greenish hide—were tor-
menting a lone messenger. The man was on the ground and
curled up tight, his arms clutching his many garish wounds
as if he could hold in life by sheer will. The orcs were circling
him and prodding at him with their rude spears, looking for
all the world like a small pack of sadistic tomcats worrying a
single mouse.

The orcs looked up at Algorind's swift reproach, their
sneers frozen by sudden terror into skeleton-grins. As he
closed in, Algorind lifted his sword high and to his left, and
dealt a terrible sweeping blow. The keen sword caught one of
the monsters in the throat and cleaved head from body with a
single stroke.

Algorind reined his horse around to face his remaining foes. The three of them had abandoned their blood sport and stood to face him, their spears braced and leveled at the white steed's breast. The young paladin sheathed his sword and took his lance from its holder. He raised it high, a chivalrous salute too deeply ingrained to withhold from this unworthy foe, and then couched it under his right arm. He leveled the lance at the foremost orc and urged his horse into a full, galloping charge.

The horse ran straight at the braced weapons, its wild whinny ringing free as if to acknowledge the danger and defy it. But Algorind had no thought to endanger his steed. This was a tactic they had practiced together many times in the training arena of Summit Hall. His eye measured his lance at twice the length of the orcs' spears, and he silently began the rhythmic prayer to Tyr that would count off the measure of his attack.

At just the right moment, he raised himself in the stirrups and pulled up on the reins. On command, the mighty horse leaped. Algorind's lance caught one of the surprised orcs just below the ribs and bore him up and over his shrinking comrades.

Mustering all his strength, Algorind hurled the lance forward as if it were a giant javelin. The effort did not launch the weapon, but countered the force of the impaled orc and kept the paladin's arm from wrenching painfully back. Before the horse's hooves touched down, Algorind pushed out to the side with all his might, casting aside the lance and the dying orc.

The horse landed, cantered a few paces, then wheeled. Two orcs remained. Algorind could not surprise them again. He swung himself down from the saddle and drew his sword.

The orcs rushed at him, spears level. Algorind stood his ground. When the first orc was nearly upon him, he swept the sword up hard, catching the spear and turning it toward the sky. He spun, sliding his blade off the upturned spear and bringing it down and around as he turned. The edge sliced across the orc's belly, spilling the contents. The creature stumbled several paces more before he tripped on his own entrails and fell on his face, never to rise again.

Algorind turned to face his final foe. The orc circled him
cautiously, using the longer spear to keep the paladin and his
blade at a safe distance. "Challenge," the beast grunted.
"Same weapons, one to one."

The young paladin recoiled in surprise. How had a base
creature such as this orc learned anything of the paladin's
creed? By the rules of his Order, he could not refuse a challenge given, unless the challenger was clearly outmatched.
On the other hand, the messenger was badly wounded, perhaps dying. Algorind glanced toward the fallen man. His
tunic was sodden with blood, his breathing shallow. To
make matters worse, the sun was near to setting, and the
wind whistled sharply over the bleak hills. The man needed
aid and warmth, and soon. A paladin was pledged to aid the
weak. How, Algorind puzzled, was he to chose between
these duties?

Algorind eyed his opponent. The orc was the largest of his
kind that Algorind had ever seen. He easily topped seven
feet, and though his slack greenish hide showed signs of lean
times, he was still nearly as broad and thick and fierce as an
owlbear. A carved medallion bearing the bloody claw symbol
of the evil god Malar hung on a thong around the orc's neck.
The wooden disk was nearly the size of a small dinner plate,
but it did not seem out of proportion to the creature who
wore it.

Yes, this was a foe worth fighting. Algorind could not see
his way clear to deny the challenge.

The paladin hooked his boot under one of the spears the
fallen orcs had dropped. A quick kick sent the weapon spinning up. He sheathed his sword with one hand and snatched
the spear out of the air with the other. The orc grinned horribly and spun his spear in challenge, holding it out level before
him like a quarterstaff. Algorind mirrored this stance, and
the challenge was on.

Orc and paladin circled each other, their eyes alert and
their hands tightly gripping the long, stout wooden staves
they held out level before them. From time to time one of the

staves flashed forward, to be met by an equally deft parry. The irregular rhythm of wood against wood rang out, slowly at first, then increasing in tempo into a percussive flurry.

As the battle went on, the orc's confident sneer hardened into a grimace. Fangs bared, the beast bore down on the young paladin, thundering blow after blow upon his skilled opponent. But Algorind answered each strike, meeting the frenzied rhythm and adding his own thrusts and feints to the clatter of the duel.

The young paladin was breathing hard now and admitted himself sorely tested by the orc's unexpected skill. But he kept his focus and his courage and concentrated on working the monster's staff up high. A risky strategy, given the differences in the opponents' strength and stature, but Algorind saw no other choice. Rather than allow himself to be intimidated by his opponent's great size, he would use it to his advantage.

Suddenly Algorind spun the blunt end of the spear down. He accepted the blow that slashed through his relaxed guard, allowing the wooden haft to thump painfully into his chest as he hooked the lower end of the spear behind the orc's boot. A quick twist jerked the orc's feet out from beneath him. The creature fell heavily, flat on his back.

Algorind spun the spear quickly and planted the crude stone point at the orc's throat. "Yield," he said, before he remembered to whom he spoke. Such mercy would have been appropriate in a fight between honorable opponents, but this was a creature of evil, not a man of honor. How could Algorind suffer him to live? And how could he *not*, now that the offer of quarter had been extended?

Fortunately the orc resolved this dilemma. He spat and tipped back his head defiantly, baring his throat as he chose death over surrender.

The paladin struck, leaning hard on the spear and finishing the evil creature in a single quick, merciful stroke. That accomplished, he turned to the messenger.

Algorind gently turned him onto his back and immediately realized two things: first, the man could not possibly survive his hurts, and second, he wore the white and blue tabard that proclaimed him a member of the Knights of Samular. A second, closer look revealed the courier's pouch still strapped to the wounded man's shoulder.

"Brother, take ease," the young paladin said gently. "Your duty is done. Here is another to take it from you. The creatures are vanquished, and the hall is but an hour's ride. I will carry your message for you."

The man nodded painfully and swallowed hard. "Another," he croaked out. "There is an heir."

Algorind's brow furrowed in puzzlement. With his last strength, the messenger wrenched open the latch on the pouch and drew from it a single sheet of parchment. The words written upon it filled Algorind with awe, and his lips moved in grateful prayer to Tyr.

There was another. The great Hronulf, commander of Thornhold, would not be the last, after all. An heir to the bloodline of Samular had been found.

* * * * *

"Almost home," panted Ebenezer Stoneshaft as he thundered through the deeply buried tunnel.

"Home" was a warren of dwarven tunnels under the Sword Mountains, not far from the sea and too damn close to the trade route just to the east and the human fortress above.

He'd been gone quite a while this time, but it was all so familiar: the damp scent of the tunnels, the faint glow from the luminous moss and lichen that decked the stone walls, and the old paths marked with subtle runes that only a dwarf could read. There had been some changes, though, some new additions. Ledges carved into the walls, and steps and such. At the moment, Ebenezer didn't really have the leisure to examine these innovations closely.

Running full out, the dwarf rounded the tight curve in the tunnel, his short legs pumping. The clatter of his iron-shod boots against the stone floor was all but lost in the rattle and clamor behind him.

Right behind him.

In his ears rang a cacophony of hisses that sounded like a fire-newt left out in the rain, and screeches that would make an eagle cock its head and listen for pointers. Who'd-a thought, he grimly noted, that a mob of over-sized pack rats could raise such a ruckus?

Granted, it was a big pack, as osquips went. Dozens of clawed feet scrabbled against the stone as a score of giant rodents chased after Ebenezer in hot and angry pursuit. And for what? He'd taken a mithral chisel from their pile of shiny trinkets—only one, and only because it was his to take. Belonged to his cousin Hoshal, it did, a dour and reclusive dwarf smith who would string Ebenezer up by his curly red beard should he get wind of any kin of his being slacker enough to leave a good tool just lying about.

Ebenezer almost stopped. Come to think on it, how *did* that chisel end up in an osquip trove? It was a family jest that Hoshal could put his hands on any one of his many tools or weapons sooner than he could grab his own—

"Yeow!"

A sharp nip stole the remembered quip from Ebenezer's mind, and sheared a chuck of thick boot leather—and a good bit of the skin beneath—from the dwarf's ankle. Fortunately for Ebenezer, the osquip only grazed him. If the critter had gotten a good grip, Ebenezer would have ended up hopping the rest of the way back to his clanhold. An osquip's teeth were large, protruding squares that could gnaw through stone—pretty damn good practice for biting off a dwarf's foot.

Ebenezer whirled, hammer in hand, and whacked down hard on the head of the offending rodent. The huge, wedge-shaped skull shattered with a satisfying crunch. The sudden attack set the others back on their heels for a moment, which was all Ebenezer needed. He was off and running again, and even had a few paces lead to spare, before any of the osquips got their six or eight or even ten legs back into the habit of forward motion. But once they did get going, they could roll along right smart. At this rate, noted Ebenezer, they would

all come thundering into Stoneshaft Hold before the priest
was done with the wedding blessing.

Grim humor lit the dwarf's slate-blue eyes as he envisioned
the reception his kin would muster to receive their unexpected
visitors. It had been many years since the Stoneshaft clan had
been troubled by osquips—giant, hairless, many-legged
rodents who were nearly as ugly as a tea-totaling duergar—
but they killed the critters on sight, just on principle, and also
to keep the numbers down. If they didn't, the rodents could
raise a horde in the side tunnels even quicker than humans
could fill one of their surface cities. Their ugly, naked yellow
hides—osquip hide, not human—made good leather, too, and
wherever there was mining to be done and people too lazy to do
it without the aid of magic, there were wizards who were only
too happy to buy osquip teeth as a spell component. For all
these reasons, osquip-bashing was a favorite dwarven sport.
So here he was, bringing a pack of the damn things right into
the clanhold. The dwarves would have a merry time of it.

If the gods were kind, thought Ebenezer with a grin, the
fun he was bringing would get him off the spit for being late to
his sister's wedding. At the very least, maybe Tarlamera
would vent most of her temper on the osquips before turning
it on him.

Ebenezer burst from the tunnel to emerge in a small cavern. He shot a look over his shoulder and groaned. There were
perhaps fifty of the critters behind him now—they must have
picked up recruits along the way. That was a bit much, even
as wedding presents went. Maybe he should whittle the pack
down a mite before making his entrance.

The dwarf considered his options. He could stand and
fight, but this many osquips were a bit much even for him.
Ahead of him flowed a deep underground river. For the
briefest of moments he considered plunging into it. Osquips
weren't much for swimming, even with so many legs to do the
paddling. He could count on at least half of them drowning.
On the other hand, his own chances were even less optimistic.
The clan kept hunting cats that liked water better than
Ebenezer did, and they feared it less. It might be that he

could swim, but he'd never actually taken to the water to test it out.

"Stones," he muttered darkly. Still running, he spun on his heel and veered sharply to the right, sprinting down a small, dark side tunnel that led toward the clanhold.

A sudden, sharp hiss on the path before him brought him up short. There, her orange ears flattened back against her head and her fangs bared in her customary welcome, crouched Fluffy, his sister's ginger cat.

Instinctively, Ebenezer danced back. He was leery of cats, even the sawed-off critters that humans kept as pets and mousers. Four-legged elves, they were, right down to their haughty airs and deft, dangerous paws. Fluffy was easily ten times the size of a surface cat, and she had a disposition to match Tarlamera at her surliest. For once, and for all those reasons, Ebenezer was almost glad to see the beast.

"Rats," he panted out, stretching the truth a bit as he pointed to the roiling pack of swiftly approaching osquips. "Get 'em!"

Fluffy cast him a supercilious glare, but her tail lashed as she eyed the rodents. With a fearsome yowl, she launched herself into flight and came down in the center of the pack. The creatures fell back, yipping and squealing in surprise. Had they possessed more intelligence, the osquips would have realized that the lot of them were more than a match for a tunnel mouser. But the ancient instincts of their kind stuck with them, and most of the creatures scuttled away like cockroaches at the sight of this rodents-bane.

Some of the osquips recovered quickly enough from the shock, and a score of them abandoned the cat to follow their original quarry. Ebenezer did not stay to help the cat chase down stragglers; she would not have thanked him if he had. Keeping the tunnel free of vermin was her job, and she was every bit as territorial as a dwarf when it came to matters of land held and defended.

As he ran, the dwarf tugged a kerchief from his pocket and mopped his face. He suspected he looked a sight, what with all the running. His reddish brown hair was exceedingly curly at the best of times. At the moment, he was as lathered as a racehorse, and at such times his hair sprung up into wild clusters of small, tight ringlets. Ebenezer's beard was another matter. Long and full and defiantly red, it had the decency to just hang there. A beard any dwarf would be proud of, it was. For all his odd ways—and according to his clan, his ways were plenty odd—he was a dwarf who appreciated tradition. So what if he hated mining, preferring the sway of a horse to the measured rhythm of the pickax? Whose affair was it if he kept his upper lip clean-shaven, rather than sporting the usual thick mustache? What stone was it engraved on, anyway, that a dwarf had to wear a mustache? All the damn thing did was guarantee that he would keep smelling his dinner, hours after the fact. Thank you, but no.

Ebenezer grimaced with amusement when he realized that he was rehearsing for the arguments to come. Well, no matter. He'd been gone a long time, and with each moon phase that had passed, the measure of his clan's more annoying tendencies shrank just a bit more. Fact was, he was looking forward to the brand of contentious peace that meant hearth and home.

He wove his way through a henge of statues, a circle of ten-foot stone dwarves that honored heroes of the past, and bolted down the final tunnel toward the clanhold's cavern. He burst out into the open, to be confronted with the slack-jawed astonishment of his kin.

His Da, a burly, gray-bearded dwarf with a belly the size of a boulder and a heart to match, was the first to recover. "Osquips!" he howled, his eyes gleaming wildly as he took his hammer from his belt. "Didn't I tell you, Palmara, the boy'd be back in time, and bringing gifts?"

Ebenezer's mother sniffed and reached for her pick. She buried it deep in the skull of an onrushing rodent and kicked the twitching thing aside. Long years together had blurred the differences between the dwarf pair; except for the feminine cut of her dress tunic, Palmara Stoneshaft was nearly indistinguishable from her mate. She gestured with her bloody pike. "There's two more over there. You, Gelanna!

Back off them critters. I saw 'em first!"

For several moments the ceremony was forgotten as the
dwarves busily chased down the invading osquips. Ebenezer
edged his way toward the center of the cavern. The stone
lectern that served as podium for their contentious clan meet-
ings had been turned into an altar, now abandoned as the
priestess of Clangeddin joined gleefully into the sport. Tarlamera and her soon-to-be-husband, a likely little sprout of a
dwarf who was not more than fifty and not much more than
two hundred pounds, stood with arms folded and eyes filled
with mingled amusement and frustration. Osquip-bashing
was fun to watch, but no dwarf willingly stood still when
there was mayhem to be had. But Tarlamera wore the ceremonial apron, and she would get stomped by every other
maiden in the clanhold if she messed it up with rodent guts.
Regrettable, but that was tradition for you.

"You're a lucky dwarf, Frodwinner. You got yourself the
prettiest dwarf maid in a hundred caverns," Ebenezer said
and meant it. His sister was a picture, with her normally wild
red beard neatly plaited and her hair tamed into bright
ringlets. On her, those damned ringlets looked good.

The dwarf maid snorted, but her eyes were fond. "About
time you showed. Staying long?"

It was a familiar question, and edged with a sarcasm that
predicted Ebenezer's answer. "Long as I can stand to," he
admitted. He softened the remark with a shrug. "I'm not one
to stay put. You know that."

Tarlamera shook her head in puzzlement and swept her
hand toward the clanhold's vast courtyard. "In all the wandering you've done, have you ever seen a place to equal this
one?"

Ebenezer shook his head, honestly enough. The Stoneshaft
Clanhold was impressive, yet cozy. Ceremonies, celebrations,
and mock battles took place in the great hall, a fine cavern
with a smooth, level floor and richly carved walls. Over the
centuries, Stoneshaft artisans had carved many a frieze
depicting dwarf victories and frolics. Several small tunnels
led out of the hall, and stairs carved into the walls wound up

to higher levels. Some of these openings led to private family homes, others to the forges and gem-working shops that kept the clan happily employed. Miners they were, of course, and smiths, but clan Stoneshaft was also renowned for the fine, bold wearable art they made of gems and metals. A few dwarves served as merchants, trading the finished goods for materials not easily found. Ebenezer worried about this. His kin were too isolated, too clannish and race-proud to understand that some humans posed more of a risk than others.

"Dying down, it looks like," offered Frodwinner, nodding toward the other dwarves. The osquip-bashing frenzy was over, but for a few final thumps. Already most of the creatures had been dragged away. Most likely, Ebenezer mused, to be thrown into the river. The swift-moving current would bear them away, and whatever the river denizens didn't eat would wash ashore in the hydra cove. A lot of mouths to feed there, Ebenezer concluded.

A few minutes more and the cavern was clear. Some of the dwarves cranked up buckets of water from the wells and sluiced the stone floor, sending the last traces of the battle down several small openings in the floor that were covered with finely crafted iron grates.

"Can we get on with this?" demanded Palmara Stoneshaft, fists planted on her ample hips. "Got me a daughter to wed, a son to welcome back. And lookit!" she added, pointing toward the festive board that stood waiting over to one side of the cavern. "The stew's getting cold, and the ale warm!"

These practical considerations marshaled the wedding guests and sent the priestess scurrying back to the altar. Ebenezer fell back and swept his gray-bearded mother into a fierce hug that had her bellowing in happy protest.

The ceremony was brief, solemn. The celebration that followed was anything but. All of Clan Stoneshaft gathered at tables, telling tall tales and exchanging extravagant insults until the last stew pot was wiped clean and more than half the kegs of wedding ale drained dry. At a sign from Palmara—who as mother of the bride was master of the festivities—a score of musicians leaped onto the tables and set up a merry din with their horns and pipes and drums. The dwarves fell to dancing with a zest and vigor that rivaled their battlefield exploits.

A rare sense of contentment swept Ebenezer as he watched his kin leap and whirl and thunder their way through the intricate patterns of a circle dance. He was glad to be home. The knowledge that he'd be nearly as glad to leave in a tenday or so did nothing to diminish the moment's pleasure.

But even now his feet got to twitching. He reached for his bag and removed from it pipe and weed before he remembered that Palmara Stoneshaft would have nothing of that in *her* cavern. Ebenezer had picked up the habit in his travels, and he liked a good pipe now and again. But the Stoneshaft dwarves frowned upon such vices and had made loud complaints about the smoke last time he'd visited. Ebenezer had pointed out—reasonably enough, it seemed to him—that in a clanhold warmed and scented with the smoke of forges and hearth fires, a wisp or two more made no never mind at all. But they couldn't see it. With a resigned sigh, Ebenezer pocketed his pipe and headed for the nearest river tunnel.

He walked along the river for maybe an hour, puffing contentedly and enjoying the wild rush and gurgle of the water. The river got right riled up, come spring, what with all the melting snow from the Sword Mountains high overhead, but that was the only intrusion of the upper world. The tunnels were pleasantly chilly and dark. Not safe, exactly—the Stoneshaft clan had to deal with vermin ranging from osquips to kobolds to drow—but there was a nice secure feeling to having a rock ceiling overhead, and walls on every side. It was a world apart from the light and bustle that held sway under the sun.

Ebenezer finished his pipe and got out flint and stone to light another. The spark and flicker was echoed by another light, far ahead and filtering out of a side tunnel. Ebenezer pursed his lips and squinted. Light so far underground was odd, and generally a bad sign. Anybody who belonged in the tunnels could see well enough without it.

As the thought formed, a trio of tall, scrawny figures emerged from the side tunnel, their gaunt frames clearly silhouetted against the light of their own torch. Ebenezer spat, then swore. Humans. Bad enough they squatted on the mountain above, but they had no call to be in the dwarven tunnels. How'd they find out about these warrens, anyhow? Only a handful of humans knew anything at all about the Stoneshaft clan, and they were a closed-mouthed bunch.

Suddenly Ebenezer remembered the chisel he'd taken from the osquip hoard. He pulled it from his belt and studied the mark carved into the mithral handle. Yes, it belonged to his Uncle Hoshal. No doubt there—there was Hoshal's mark, big as a gnome's nose. But how had the rodents got hold of it? Ebenezer dredged his memory, trying to conjure the image of Hoshal's grim, pockmarked face at the edge of the wedding celebration. He could not. Hoshal was not one for festivals, but come to think on it, he was powerful fond of wedding ale. His absence, combined with the fact of humans in the tunnels, looked suspiciously like problems brewing.

"Stones!" Ebenezer swore again. He tucked the chisel back into his belt and followed after the three intruders.

*   *   *   *   *

Algorind hastened back to Summit Hall, the body of his brother paladin decently covered and lashed to a makeshift litter Algorind had fashioned from branches. Dragging this burden added extra time to his journey, and the ceremony of induction was already underway when Algorind came to the monastery gates.

Darkness enveloped the hills, and the sand-colored stone of the outer walls seemed to melt into the terrain. If not for the bright lights rising from the chapel and his own detailed knowledge of the area, Algorind might not have seen the monastery at all. Many travelers passed by in full sight of the tower watchmen, never once seeing the monastery. That seemed to Algorind a remarkable thing, considering the vast size of the complex.

The gatekeeper, a strapping young paladin who was often Algorind's training partner, looked his friend up and down. "You saw battle," he said, a note of unseemly envy in his voice.

"Orcs." Algorind dismissed the creatures with a shrug and gestured to the slanted litter. "They fell upon this messenger. They have received Tyr's justice, but I was not in time to save this brave man."

"I'll see to this brother. You'll be wanted in the chapel." The paladin stripped off his spotless blue and white tabard and handed it to Algorind. Gratefully, the young man accepted the loan and quickly donned the fresh garment. The two men were of a size—both being an inch or two over six feet, their flesh hard-chiseled by nearly constant drilling with sword and lance and staff. Algorind smoothed down his curly, close-cropped fair hair, and hastened to the chapel that, along with the training field, dominated life at Summit Hall.

He halted at the arched entrance. His brothers were singing, a hauntingly beautiful chant extolling the justice of Tyr and the courage of the young men who had chosen this path. That meant the ceremony was nearly over.

Algorind felt a stab of disappointment. He had seen men invested before, but nothing moved or inspired him as much as this sacred ceremony. It was his dream, and all his life had been lived in expectation of a moment such as this. Witnessing an investiture made him feel that much closer to his goal. Much had led up to this moment: the years of training at arms and devotions, the paladin's quest, the trial by ordeal, the night of wakeful prayer in the chapel, the ritual bath and the donning of the white robes and new tabard. Algorind was still in training and expected a year or more before he would be granted a paladin's quest.

He lingered near the open door, head reverently bowed as Mantasso, the High Lord Abbot—a massive warrior who despite his rank still trained the clerical acolytes at arms—prayed for Tyr's blessing. The ceremony of investiture, the giving of the sword and the ceremonial drawing of blood as a symbol that life was forfeit to service, was the task of Master

Laharin Goldbeard. It was an ancient ceremony, conveying
honor with the touch of a sword but conducted with more
solemnity by the Knights of Samular than romantic tales of
chivalry suggested. Algorind watched with awe and deep
longing as the regally tall paladin conducted the final dub-
bing ceremony, accepting the sword of each young paladin in
turn, and imposing upon them a reminder that their lives
were forfeit to the service of Tyr. Finally the young paladins
sheathed their new weapons, still stained with their own
blood, and rose as full Knights of the Order.

The hymn resumed, this time swelling on a note of exulta-
tion. Algorind joined in with all his heart, and swept out of
the chapel with his brothers.

Almost immediately, news of the slain messenger spread
throughout the hall. Algorind was summoned to Laharin's
study to deliver his report.

Algorind hurried to the keep, the large building that dominated the north end of the complex, and climbed the stairs to
the tower that held the Master's inner sanctum. The tower
room was circular, its furnishings simple, even austere. The
only flash of color in it was the vivid yellow hue of Laharin
Goldbeard's bright whiskers and thinning hair. The Master
sat in a high-backed wooden bench behind a table of polished
wood. The chairs that flanked and faced the table were hardly
designed for comfort, and no tapestries softened the stone
walls. A shelf held tokens of great deeds accomplished, as well
as a single row of dusty books. Two tall, narrow windows and
a trio of squat candles provided light enough to see, if not to
read. Scholarship was not scorned, exactly, but neither was it
numbered among the Order's knightly virtues.

Algorind came in when he was bid and took one of the
chairs facing Master Laharin. He nodded respectfully to the
other men who flanked the paladin—Mantasso and two of the
highest-ranked priests, and three elder paladins, including
Sir Gareth Cormaeril, a nobleman and paladin of great fame,
retired from active service to the Knights of Samular by a
grievous wound more than thirty years ago. Despite his
injuries and his life of enforced inactivity, the old man was

tall and strong still. He had arrived at the fortress just that morning—shortly before Algorind had left on his patrol—after a two-day ride that would exhaust many a younger man. At the moment, he looked the part of an elder statesman, clad in dignified garments of somber blue hue, his white beard neatly trimmed and his bright blue eyes keen and watchful.

The men listened carefully as Algorind gave his report. "You have done well," Laharin admitted when the tale was told—extravagant praise, coming from the master paladin. "The task that now falls to us, however, is more difficult than your feats at arms."

"This is no easy matter," Sir Gareth agreed. "Our brother Hronulf has long believed his family dead. Now we learn that there is a son. Unless this lost son—no less than a priest of Cyric—accepts Tyr's grace, there is little we can do for him. His child, however, is another matter."

Mantasso folded massive arms and stared the knight down. "The message says that the little girl is kept in safe fosterage, happy with the family who has raised her from birth, and innocent of the evil her father has chosen. Have we any right to disturb this?"

"Not only right, but duty," Laharin said sternly. "Of course she must be brought under the care and instruction of the order. And the possibility, however slight, that she may have in her possession one of the Rings of Samular adds urgency to the matter. But how to proceed?"

"With your indulgence, Master Laharin, I propose that the answer is right before us," Sir Gareth said in his courtly manner. "What of this lad? I hear tell that he is the best and brightest of the crop, and more than ready for his paladin's quest. Charge him with finding the girl and the ring."

A heartbeat passed, and then another, before Algorind realized they were speaking of him. They were thinking of granting him a paladin's quest! He had not expected such honor for another year at least!

"I take it you are willing," Laharin said dryly, studying Algorind's shining face.

"More than willing! Grateful, my lords, to serve Tyr and

his holy Order, in this manner or any other."

"He is eager, that is without question," grumbled Mantasso. The big priest stirred impatiently, drawing an ominous creak from his wooden chair. "Before you continue, I must speak my mind on this matter!"

"Of course," Laharin said in a tightly controlled voice. "Why should this matter be different from any other?"

Algorind blinked, astonished by this sign of disharmony among the Masters. Mantasso, who was watching him keenly, noted this and shook his head in exasperation.

"I mean no disrespect to any present," the big priest said, "but this youth belongs in the clergy, not the military order. Is it not our mandate as servants of Tyr to use all our gifts in his service? All? Algorind possesses learning and languages, a quick mind, and a potential for both scholarship and leadership. His knowledge of map lore is remarkable, and he is well spoken and comely. In the priesthood, he could go far and accomplish much, influencing many to the cause of Tyr. But how many paladins live to see their thirtieth winter? Even their twenty-fifth? Perhaps two or three in a hundred! You venerable gentlemen in this chamber are not the rule, but the rare exception!"

"And Algorind is not exceptional?" retorted Laharin. "We are well aware of the young *paladin's* gifts and potential. The Order needs men of his talent and dedication. The matter is settled." He turned to Algorind. "You have your duty, brother. See that you fulfill it well."

Algorind rose, too full of joy for words, and bowed deeply to the Master. He left the study to attend to his quest, certain that nothing could exceed the glory of this moment.

Sir Gareth followed him and hailed him to a stop. The famed paladin offered Algorind his hand, clasped wrists with him as if Algorind was already a fellow knight. Nor did he leave the matter there. They walked together, and Sir Gareth offered him guidance and advice, instructing him on what steps must be taken once the child was rescued.

Such fellowship was more honor than Algorind had ever dreamed of. He listened carefully, storing each detail in his carefully trained memory. By the time Algorind's gear was packed and his white horse readied, Sir Gareth pronounced him ready.

"You will bring honor to the order, my son," the great man assured him with a kind smile. "Remember the knightly virtues: courage, honor, justice. To these, I add another: discretion. This is a subtle matter. It is important that you tell no man what you do. Will you so swear?"

Nearly giddy with excitement and hero worship and holy fervor, Algorind dropped to one knee before the paladin. "In this matter and all others, Sir Gareth, I will do as you command."

* * * * *

It took Bronwyn nearly two days to track down Malchior.

First, she had to find and question the Harper agents who had carried out Danilo's bidding and kept Malchior's men from following her. That was no small task, for secrecy was a habit deeply ingrained among the Harpers, and many were reticent to share secrets even among their own. Fortunately, one of Danilo's henchmen, Nimble, was a halfling with bardic pretensions. The ditty he composed of the event—his own role dramatically enhanced, naturally—made the rounds of the taverns and meeting places frequented by the short folk. Alice Tinker had heard the song on her evening out, and had brought the tale—along with the loudly protesting halfling—back to Bronwyn.

Nimble's tale, when shorn of ornamentation, was of little real help. The priest had disappeared, leaving only a puff of acrid purple smoke. Bronwyn searched the city, calling in every marker she had for information, as well as indebting herself so deeply that the favors she owed, if placed end to end, would keep her busily employed until snowfall. But finally, her efforts bore fruit and led her to an elf who possessed deep resources and an exceedingly dark reputation.

"You owe me," the elf said unnecessarily as he handed her a roll of parchment.

Bronwyn grimaced as she took the parchment, imagining
the sort of payment that this particular contact was likely to
call in. She unrolled the scroll and whistled in appreciation. It
was plans for a medium-sized villa. In tiny script, the elf had
noted magical safeguards, hidden doors, concealed alcoves for
guards, and other closely guarded secrets. She raised suspicious eyes to her benefactor.

"How do you know all this?"

He gave her a supercilious smile. "My dear, I *own* that
building. Since the man you seek has paid his rent in
advance, you can do as you like with him—but mind the furniture and do try not to get blood on the carpets."

"I'll do my best," she said dryly. After exchanging a few
more dark pleasantries with the elf, she took her leave and
headed for the North Ward.

At night, this district was quiet, with most of the wealthy
residents either behind the walls that surrounded the villas
or off pursuing pleasures in a more boisterous part of town.
As she walked along the broad, cobbled streets, she wondered
how the residents of Waterdeep's most traditional neighbor-
hood would react if they knew that a priest of Cyric was in
their midst. Probably, their response would be much like the
elf's. As long as the priest paid his bills and kept to himself,
he was no real threat.

Bronwyn had ample reason to think otherwise. Malchior
had gone through a great deal of trouble to meet her. Tonight,
she was determined to discovery why.

She circled around the Gentle Mermaid festhall, a massive
and excessively tasteless stone structure that sprouted more
turrets than a hydra had heads, as well as numerous balconies
decked with elaborate wrought iron. The building took up the
interior of an entire block; she quickly skirted it and cut down
Manycats Alley. She glanced up at the lifelike stone heads that
lined the eaves of several buildings up ahead, remembering
the tavern tales claiming that they sometimes spoke to
passersby. But the only voices she heard were those of the
stray cats that scrapped over the leavings of butcher shops
that plied their trade by day. The scent of these shops hung

heavy in the still, mist-laden air. Bronwyn lifted a fold of her cloak over her nose and picked up her pace, careful to avoid the pair of tabbies battling over a length of seafood sausage.

Not far from the shops, she found the back wall of the villa's enclosed garden. She ran her fingers over the stone. The latch was exactly where the elf had claimed it would be. Vowing to be generous in her repayment of this particular debt, Bronwyn pressed the latch and waited until the stone door swung open. She slipped through the opening and into the shadows of the grape arbor that cut down the middle of the garden.

At the end of the arbor, hidden from casual view by lush vines, stood the first guard. Bronwyn remembered him as one of the Zhentish soldiers who had stormed the bathhouse in response to Malchior's summons. For a moment she hesitated. It was no small thing to kill a man, but he had been very willing to kill her—or to take her captive on Malchior's behalf, which would surely have proved to be worse.

She slipped up behind the guard, a length of thin, strong rope held between her hands. With a quick, sudden movement, she plunged her hands through the vines and wrapped the garrote tightly about his throat. A small, strangled noise gurgled from him, growing in volume as he worked his fingers under the rope. He was far stronger than she. With a flash of panic, Bronwyn realized he would soon be able to sing out an alarm.

She leaped up, planting both feet against the arbor trellis, and leaned back, hauling at the rope. After a moment, the man went silent. Bronwyn tied the garrotte firmly to the trellis, then edged around to the other side. The man's bulging eyes bore witness to the effectiveness of her attack. She took a long, steadying breath and slipped into the icehouse.

The villa was well appointed, even to the small, thick-walled building that stored blocks of ice cut from the nearby river, a luxury in the coming months of summer. The house was nearly full now, and as cold as midwinter. Bronwyn drew her cloak closer about her as she edged through the narrow aisle between the blocks.

At the end of the aisle she found another hidden door. Bronwyn slid it aside and stepped into a dark, small tunnel. She felt about for the promised shelf and the candles kept there. She lit one and proceeded down a narrow passage to a flight of steep stairs.

According to the elf landlord, this passage led through the back wall, up into the most lavish bedchamber. Surely she would find Malchior there. She only hoped that she would find him alone.

Bronwyn crept along the passage, then up a flight of steep wooden stairs. She moved slowly, easing her way along so that no creak would betray her presence. With each step, she felt increasingly uneasy. There were no cobwebs in the tunnel, no sign of mice. How could a passage so well-used be secret?

Just as she considered turning around, the passage ended at another door, this one a sliding door of thin wood, hidden by a tapestry. Malchior was apparently alone, and at prayer. Bronwyn clamped her eyes shut and tried not to listen as the dreadful cadence of the chant rose and fell. Knowing that Malchior worshiped Cyric was one thing; it was quite another to stand by while the dark and evil god was invoked.

Finally Malchior finished his devotions. Bronwyn could hear his grunt of exertion as he hauled his bulky frame up off his knees, and then the creaking protest of the wooden floor as he walked past.

The next part was the riskiest. Bronwyn eased the door aside, edged past the tapestry, and peeked into the room. Malchior was not alone, after all, but the young woman with whom he'd shared the evening was already thoroughly, messily dead. So much for the elf's carpets, Bronwyn noted grimly. The tawdry, much-patched feminine garments cast over a chair suggested that the woman had been from the Dock Ward, perhaps a tavern wench who'd been lured to the villa by one of Malchior's men with the promise of easy coin, earned by enduring an old man's brief embrace. How could she know that the jovial, rotund priest took his pleasure in death and the power that came with the dealing of death?

Bronwyn's heart thundered as she drew her knife and waited. She watched as the priest poured himself a glass of deep red wine from a silver decanter and raised it to the dead woman in salute. He sipped, closing his eyes as if savoring a pleasant memory. Then, humming lightly, he sauntered toward the bath—and past the tapestry.

She leaped out of her hiding place and kicked out hard. Her booted foot all but disappeared into the vast, fleshy belly, but the shot had the desired effect. Malchior wheezed like a bellows and went down.

Bronwyn seized a handful of his hair and dragged his head back. Stepping behind him, she placed her knife hard against his throat. "Shout out and you're dead," she informed him in a low, furious tone.

It took Malchior a few minutes to marshal his facility for speech, but when he did reply it was with admirable aplomb. "I am quite capable of discerning the obvious," he wheezed out. "Speak your mind. My bath is cooling. Or better yet, you may disrobe and join me."

She almost had to admire the man's gall. "The *obvious* question, then, is this: why did you try to take me the other night? Was it another of your games?"

"A pleasant thought, but no," the priest replied. His voice was stronger now, but there was fear in his eyes as he noted the fury on Bronwyn's face. "Not a game. I wouldn't dishonor you with trivial matters. You are not some tavern wench, to be lightly used and easily discarded."

"I'm flattered. What, then?"

He lifted his hands, palms up. "It was nothing personal. I am of the Zhentarim. You are the daughter of a sworn enemy of the Zhentarim. A man who wishes to live long does not leave dangerous whelps to grow fangs and to scent the trail of vendetta."

Bronwyn froze. Nothing, nothing that she had ever seen or experienced, nothing that could have come out of this terrible man's warped and evil imagination, could have stunned her as did those few simple words: You are the daughter of . . . *someone.*

"Who?" she demanded urgently. "Who is your enemy?"

The priest laughed, sending ripples undulating through his rolls of flesh. "My dear, I am a priest of Cyric. I have more enemies than this whore had *fathers*."

The sly emphasis he gave to the last word was nearly Bronwyn's undoing. Malchior had toyed with her. He was doing it still. She looked at the knife she held at his throat and longed to pull it back hard and deep. Yet if she struck, she would never find the answer she had spent twenty long years seeking. She took a steadying breath and tamped down her anger.

"Tell me my father's name. Tell me, and I'll let you live."

"Promise made, promise kept?" he mocked her. "Where is my necklace?"

"That was none of my doing," she hissed. "As you yourself say, a priest of Cyric has many enemies." A new threat occurred to her. "You handled the amber. I wonder what interesting secrets a skilled mage could discern from the echoes your magic left behind."

That thought stole the smugness from Malchior's eyes, if just for a moment. "And this necklace. Is it now in the possession of such a mage?"

"It could be. It was given back to me, but I'd be happy to part with it for a good cause."

Malchior considered this. "I will give you your father's name, if you keep the amber in your possession for, say, three moon cycles."

"Done."

"You may find this information amusing, given your, shall we say, *resourceful* methods of doing business," the priest began slyly.

"Out with it!"

"Oh, very well," he said, pouting. "I'm getting a crick in my neck anyway, the way you're holding my head back. Not that you are unpleasant to look at, but perhaps you might release your grip on my hair? And this knife is most uncomfortable—"

"Speak!"

The priest tsked at her impatience. "You are the oldest and only surviving daughter of Hronulf Caradoon, a paladin of

Tyr. A knight of some sort or other, I believe."

Through the daze that enveloped her, Bronwyn felt herself nod slowly. That name stirred long-forgotten memories, and images that she could not quite conjure—like dreams, forgotten past retrieval. The enormity of it dazzled her. Her father had a name. *She* had a name!

She eased her knife away from the priest's throat. Then she flipped her hand, palm up, and drove the hilt of the knife hard into Malchior's temple.

His eyes rolled back, showing the whites, and his body sagged forward. Bronwyn released her grip on his hair, and he fell facedown onto the carpet he'd ruined with the tavern wench's blood.

Bronwyn cautiously stooped and placed her fingers just below the man's ear. Life still beat in him. He would awaken far too soon, to do more evil, but that was the deal she had made. His life, and the promise that whatever secrets he had inadvertently confided to the amber necklace would be kept from prying eyes.

Promise made, promise kept.

She rose and slipped back behind the tapestry. She would leave by a different path from the one she had taken in, but this first step was the same. As she made her way through the escape route her elf associate had carefully marked out, Bronwyn tried not to regret what she had done. She kept her promises, whether made to man or monster. It made good sense. Even if a person was totally lacking in honor, that did not render him incapable of recognizing and appreciating honor in others. She did well—for herself, her clients, and the Harpers—because people knew her reputation and were willing to deal with her. But there was another reason for this stern policy, one even more important and deeply personal. If once, just once, she allowed herself to break the primary rule that guided her path, would she be any different from the people with whom she dealt?

A new voice in her mind—new, yet disturbingly familiar— added a quiet addendum. And if she broke the rules, could she truly be a paladin's daughter?

Four

Ebenezer stalked down the river path, as stealthy as one of Tarlamera's cats. Most humans he knew thought dwarves were about as subtle as an avalanche, but the truth was, any dwarf worth navel lint could travel his tunnels as silently as an elf walked the forest.

For that reason and a host of others, what happened next was downright embarrassing. One moment Ebenezer was walking along behind the three humans, well out of range of their torchlight and their limited vision. The next, he was netted like a fish.

The heavy ropes thumped down on him, hard enough to knock him on his backside. With a craftsman's instinctive appreciation for made things, Ebenezer noted that the net was strong and heavily weighted along the edge, then threaded through with another rope like a drawstring on a leather coin bag. Ebenezer was hard pressed, though, to imagine humans strong enough to draw it shut. He looked up through the web of rope and saw the pair of grinning half-orcs on the ledge above. One of them raised his hand to his nose in a tauntingly obscene gesture, and then the two of them began to haul him up.

The first jerk swept the rope drawstring underneath him and toppled him over. Angry now, the dwarf reached for his hunting knife and began to saw at the net. One strand pinged open, then another. He was almost within reach of the half-orcs when the net gave way. Ebenezer wriggled through the opening and fell heavily to the stone path below.

The impact of dwarf meeting stone rumbled through the cavern. The humans turned and lifted inquisitive eyes to the ledge above. The half-orcs shouted out a warning and began to scramble down the sheer stone wall toward their prey.

Ebenezer whirled, axe in hand, to face the approaching humans and their half-orc henchmen. The eager grin on his face faded as his eyes fell on the one holding the torch. He was a tall man, wearing a short purple and black robe. His shaved head was as bald as the skull emblazoned on his oversized medallion. Ebenezer knew that symbol and didn't much like it. A priest. Men, he could fight, but add a lying coward of a human god into the mix, and suddenly Ebenezer didn't much like his odds. But there was no time to consider the matter. The half-orcs finished their climb and came at him, weapons in hand.

For many moments the ring of steel against mithral rang loud over the spring song of the river. Then another sound edged into Ebenezer's consciousness, a low, ominous chanting. Dread seized him, and he flailed frantically in an effort to cut down the fight and get to the priest before it was too late.

But his axe began to grow heavy, and his limbs slowed. Even the sweat-soaked ringlets of his hair began to relax, hanging straight and limp before his increasingly bleary eyes. The song of the river, too, began to slow, until the rush and babble seemed to become words that he could almost, but not quite, make out. Soon, even that faded away, and there was only darkness, and silence.

He awoke later, stiff in every limb and with a headache that no amount of ale could produce. Cautiously, he sat up. He lifted his hand to his head and bumped against wood. Blinking rapidly, he managed to clear his vision and began to sort out what was what.

First off, he was in a cratelike cage. A good, sturdy one, made of thick slats of wood. Instinctively his hand dropped to his axe loop. The weapon was gone, of course. His cage was in a small alcove, a little cave just off the river. It appeared to be a treasure trove of sorts. His captors were avid collectors—Ebenezer recognized some of the items he'd seen in the osquips' hoard. His captors had gone through the trouble of keeping him, rather than killing him outright. Which—and this pained him to admit—would have been the sensible thing to do.

"Seems like I'm some sort of treasure," Ebenezer muttered, more to raise his spirits than from any belief in his own words. "About time someone recognized what I'm worth."

But even as the words formed, the dwarf began to realize the truth behind them. There was only one reason for them to keep a dwarf alive, something that any dwarf worth lizard spit would happily die to avoid.

He'd been captured by slavers.

* * * * *

The gate to the western wall of Darkhold creaked open. Dag Zoreth's horse, recognizing the Zhentarim fortress as home, suddenly shook off fatigue, nickering and prancing in its eagerness for the stable. Dag absently reined in the horse and fell into ranks behind his scouts. He, unlike his steed, was not particularly keen on entering the fortress that had been his home for several years. The time he'd spent away, and the knowledge that he was on the verge of acquiring his own stronghold, enabled him to view the Zhentish fortress with new eyes.

Darkhold was as grim and forbidding as any place Dag had ever seen or imagined. The castle itself was enormous, constructed on an exaggerated scale from huge blocks of red-streaked gray stone. Legend had it that blood was mingled with the stone and mortar. Dag did not doubt it. An aura of evil and death emanated from the castle as surely as the smoke rose from the spike-encircled chimneys of its many towers. Set in a deep valley, surrounded on three sides by steep, sheer stone cliffs, and on the other side by the high, thick wall through which his caravan had just passed, the fortress was virtually impregnable. The valley floor that lay between the gate and castle was flat and rough and littered with stone, barren but for a winding brook that sang sadly on its path over jagged rocks and a small, besieged copse of trees.

The massive outer gate clanked shut behind them, and Dag rode through the bleak valley to the inner wall surrounding the castle. Thirty feet tall it was, and nearly as wide. The four-man patrols that walked the wall met and passed each other with room to spare.

The caravan paused at the end of a deep moat and waited while the iron portcullis rose. The bridge swept down to meet it, gears grinding in a chilling metallic shriek that sounded to Dag like a playful dragon raking its claws over a sheer slate cliff.

Dag and his men crossed the bridge into a massive court-yard. He swung down from his horse and handed the reins to an instantly attentive soldier. After a few terse words to his men—reminding them of the penalty they would suffer for divulging any aspect of the trip—he strode through the great open door, and through a banner-draped hall with impossibly high ceilings, sized to accommodate the long-dead giants who had built the fortress.

He stopped before one of the giant-sized doors that led out of the hall. A smaller door had been cut into the center of the massive portal, one more manageable for the current, human inhabitants. Dag felt every saddle-sore muscle as he walked stiffly up two spiraling staircases and down another hall toward the richly appointed suite of rooms that served as his private quarters.

Dag had earned such luxury. He had served Darkhold as part of the new cadre of war-priests since its inception nearly four years ago. During that time he had risen to a position of considerable power among the clergy, second only to Malchior. Even Kurth Dracomore, the castle's chaplain and the not-so-secret informant of Fzoul Chembryl, ruler of far-off

Zhentil Keep, observed Dag with a wary and respectful eye.

The young priest nodded to the pair of guards who paced through the hall on some errand. He could afford to be gracious—his preparations for the conquest of Thornhold were going extremely well. He had sent word to Sememmon, the mage who ruled Darkhold. Sememmon had applauded his plan and bid him return to the fortress for his pick of men to take to his new command. The mage approved of initiative and ambition, as long as those who possessed it did not threaten his own position. And Dag Zoreth had no ambition to rule in Darkhold. He preferred to claim his own territory. This conquest did not represent the zenith of Dag Zoreth's ambitions—far from it—but it was a reasonable next step. It would add to the rapidly growing power of the Zhentarim, and also bring him great personal satisfaction.

A faint purple haze lingered on the door latch—a warning to those who might be tempted to enter uninvited. Dag quickly disabled the spells that guarded his door and stepped into his chamber. Immediately the lamp beside the door turned on of its own accord, even as he was reaching for flint and stone. The room was suddenly warmed by golden light, the rich, spicy aroma of scented oil—and the soft, heady, and menacing sound of seductive female laughter.

Before the startled priest could unleash a defensive spell, the shadows at the far side of the room stirred. A slim figure, an elf woman of supassing beauty, rose from the bed and stepped into the circle of light. She was clad only in a sleeping gown of fine, deep red silk. Her long flaxen hair had been left unbound to ripple over the pale gold skin of her shoulders.

Dag's heart missed a beat, then thudded painfully. It had been many years since she had come to his chamber, and never had they met so in Darkhold.

A small, knowing smile lifted the elf's exquisite lips as she regarded the dumbfounded priest. Surely she knew that apprehension, not desire, glazed his eyes and stole the scant color from his face. But as if to taunt him, she gathered up a handful of her clinging skirts. "You recognize this gown, perhaps? I wore it the night our child was conceived."

"Ashemmi." He spoke her name in an admirably controlled, well-modulated tone. "Forgive me if I seemed somewhat surprised. I had thought you wished to forget the brief time we shared."

"I forget nothing. Nothing." She floated closer, skimmed the tips of her fingers down the line of Dag's jaw, then touched the point on his forehead where his dark hair dipped into a pronounced widow's peak. She tipped her head to one side, regarding him. "You have grown more handsome. Power does that to most men."

"By that measure, our lord Sememmon is second only to Corellon Larethian himself," he said dryly, naming the elven god who epitomized male beauty.

Ashemmi laughed—a beautiful, uniquely elven sound that reminded Dag of fairy bells and delighted babies. But she eased away from him, which was exactly the response that Dag had intended to evoke with a mention of the wizard who was her lord and lover.

Her face clouded slightly as she recognized his ploy. "Sememmon is secure in his position," she said firmly. "All the more so now that you plan to establish your own hold. He was growing wary of you, you know." Her voice rose in a coquettish lilt, and one eyebrow lifted in subtle challenge.

Dag understood, and fell at once into the almost-forgotten rhythm of subtle predation. At this art, Ashemmi was a master. With a few words, the minx intertwined the deadly competition of Darkhold's hierarchy with a tantalizing reminder of her considerable personal charms. A volatile balance indeed. Anything he said, whatever note he struck, could be dangerously wrong. This knowledge quickened his pulse, and rekindled the dark pleasure he had last tasted nine years before. Dag was not a man for simple carnality, but this was a game he appreciated, and this was a woman who played it well.

His equilibrium restored, the priest strode over to a small table and pulled the stopper from a bottle of fine elven spirits. He poured two goblets and handed one to the elven sorceress. She raised it to her lips, savoring the scent and the taste with tauntingly slow and disturbingly thorough enjoyment—all the while eyeing him over the edge of the goblet. Dag merely sipped his drink and waited for her to have her say.

Finally she tired of this ploy and set the goblet aside. "You are patient, my poppet. You were always so. Once, I found it rather . . . charming."

"Times have changed," he observed in a bland tone that nonetheless managed to convey a dozen shades of meaning.

A brief, appreciative smile flitted across the elf's face. Next to power and beauty, Ashemmi appreciated subtlety above all else. She came closer, close enough to envelope him in the scent of her perfume—an enticing and incongruous mixture of night-blooming flowers, musk, and brimstone. "Times have changed," she agreed. "I have lately come from another visit to Zhentil Keep. The signs of its destruction are almost vanished."

"Gratifying," Dag commented, then took a casual sip of his wine.

"Very." She reached out and took the goblet from him, turned it and slid the tip of her tongue over the place on the rim his lips had touched. "It is a time to rebuild what once we had, and to seek new . . . heights."

"You were always ambitious," he said, deliberately taking her words only at face value.

This amused her. She set the goblet down and began to walk in a slow circle around him. "Opportunities are great for those who have the strength and wit to take them. You could do very well. Your devotion to the Zhentarim is beyond question, and your spells are stronger than those of any other cleric in the fortress. Indeed, you rival the spell power of all Darkhold's wizards but two!" She paused when she came around to face him, closer than she had been before. So close that he could feel the heat of her, and the ice. He sternly banished the awareness of her from his eyes, even when she reached up to unleash the clasp of his cloak. The dark garment fell unnoticed to the floor.

He cleared his throat before he could think better of it. "You flatter me."

"Not at all. I say nothing more than truth." Ashemmi toyed with his medallion, tracing her finger over the engraved sunburst pattern.

Instinctively Dag clutched the medallion, and the secret hidden behind it. He could not risk her or anyone else discovering the ring. On the morrow, he would have it sent to his daughter for safekeeping. To distract a suddenly interested Ashemmi from the source of his concern, he lifted the medallion over his head and dropped it in a silver vase that stood on the table.

A flicker of triumph lit the sorceress's eyes. Her hands dropped to his belt, to which were affixed his weapons and his bag of potions and prayer scrolls. From another woman, this would be nothing more than a logical next step. Not Ashemmi. Dag had set aside one sign of power: she sought to strip him of another. Trust Ashemmi, with her passion for irony, to seek to geld him thus.

Dag captured one of her roving hands. He reached for her wine goblet and closed her fingers around it. "Why these questions, this sudden passion for 'truth?' I never noticed that it held much interest for you before."

Suddenly the elf's golden eyes turned hard. She took a step back and impatiently flung the goblet aside. "Let us speak plainly. You have intelligence, talent, ambition, and the good will of those who rule in Zhentil Keep. Why do you insist upon besieging a fortress? What have you to prove?"

So that was it. Somehow, she had heard of his plans, and was puzzled by them. "You ascribe too many complications to my thinking. My motives are simple," he informed her. "I merely wish to command my own stronghold. The fortress I desire is, regrettably, not currently under Zhentish control. Correcting this problem is a small matter." He paused and slid one hand through the silken curtain of her hair to cup the nape of her neck, then tightened his grip just to the point of pain. "But truly, your concern for my well-being is most touching."

She arched back to lean into his grasp, and her lips curved in a feline smile. "Why would I *not* be concerned? After all, you are the father of my only child."

Dag's heart quickened at this second reference to the child that, to his way of thinking, was his alone. Ashemmi had been happy enough to turn over the babe eight years earlier, fearing that her climb to power might be hampered by a half-breed brat clinging to her silken skirts. All she had asked from Dag—no, demanded of him—was a vow of absolute secrecy. This was the first they had spoken of the child, or of much else, in eight years.

He smoothed his hand down her back and made an effort to steer the conversation onto a safer path. "Your concern is noted, but the reward is worth the risk. The fortress will be a good acquisition for the Zhentarim. It is strategically located on a major trade route."

"And it is far from Darkhold. Let us not forget that. You could have your precious child at your side and not concern yourself with any need to share her—or the power she carries."

The priest felt the blood drain from his face. This seemed to amuse Ashemmi. Again she cocked her head and studied him. "Now I understand the whispers of the common soldiers," she purred. "Do you know what they say of you, when they feel certain that they will not be heard? You are so pale and austere, so light of step and delicate of frame that you seldom make a sound, barely cast a shadow. You unnerve them. They say that you resemble a vampire in all things but the fangs!"

Beneath the obvious insult in her words lay several layers more, reminders that Dag Zoreth was a small man, a physical weakling in a fortress of warriors. But he smiled nonetheless. His hand dipped lower, his fingers dug into firm and yielding flesh. "If you desired to do so, you could inform them that my teeth are sharp."

Her laughter bubbled over again. "It is so much more amusing to let them learn at their own peril." She sobered quickly, and moved beyond reach of his punishing caress. "We were speaking of your plan for an assault on a mountain fortress. Surely you know of the difficulties inherent in a siege! It is a long and costly process. The fortress you desire is but a few days' march from cities unfriendly to our cause, which greatly lowers your chances of success. Do you think Waterdeep would allow a Zhentish army to lay a lengthy siege, when in five days they could muster enough fighters to engage you in open warfare?"

Dag had considered all of this and prepared for it. He captured a lock of her pale gold hair, let it slide between his fingers, and skimmed his hand down the slender length of her. "Set your mind at ease. I do not intend to lay siege to the fortress."

"No? What, then? You cannot believe you can conquer it outright. There are not enough warriors in the whole of Darkhold to accomplish such a feat. Nor could you move a force of the needed size without drawing attention. The alarm would be sounded before you left the Greycloak Hills! What then?" she demanded again.

His eyes grazed the feminine form that Ashemmi's crimson gown did little to hide. "It is dangerous to reveal too much to an enemy. Or have you not heard?"

She smiled again, darkly, and her arms lifted to twine around his neck. "If enemies are well matched, battle can be a pleasant diversion. Tell me, and then we need talk no more."

Dag reminded himself of his vow to have nothing more to do with this viper in elf form. "I have been preparing this attack for a long time. Arrangements have been made to ensure a successful, if unorthodox, escalade."

"You can do better. I remember well," she breathed in his ear.

He stepped back while he still could. "Content yourself with this: the capture of this fortress will not deplete Darkhold's military strength. I do not plan to shatter the Pereghost and his commanders against the fortress walls," he said, naming Ashemmi's chief rival for the position of second-in-command. He inclined his head in a brief, ironic bow. "I apologize for any inconvenience this might cause you."

They studied each other in silence. Dag Zoreth had no intention of telling Ashemmi that he would gain much more from the assault than the possession of a fortress. She already knew too much, as her presence here demonstrated.

"You have been forthright. Now it is my turn," she said, as if she followed the path his thoughts were taking. "You are planning to bring the child to your new command."

Dag's heated blood suddenly cooled. "Why should you care? You gave her into my hands willingly enough. I have kept my pledge. Few know I have a daughter, and no one knows who gave birth to her. No one need ever know, least of all Sememmon."

Ashemmi's smile was that of a cream-sated cat. "Ah, but perhaps I *want* him to know. Why should he care whom I bedded some ten years ago? It is of no consequence—unless, of course, the child that resulted is of the bloodline of Samular. . . ."

Dag had been dreading this revelation since Ashemmi's first mention of their child, but even so the implications staggered him. Why should Ashemmi want his daughter, unless she knew of the power the little girl could command? He fervently hoped that if Ashemmi had received this information from Malchior, it was by theft or magical spying. The thought of these two conspiring together was more chilling than a ghost's embrace. If Malchior learned of the child's existence, there would be no safety for her. But surely Ashemmi would not give up such valuable information, not when she could hoard the girl's power for herself! Unfortunately, with a subtle, treacherous creature such as Ashemmi, there was no knowing for certain.

He decided to bluff. He closed the distance between them and his hands skimmed down her back, cupping her intimately and drawing her close. "Samular, indeed," he murmured into her hair. His voice revealed nothing more than mild, derisive amusement. "What is some long-dead paladin to you and Sememmon? Perhaps you two are thinking of changing your occupation and allegiance?"

Ashemmi sniffed, but apparently did not deign that comment worthy of rejoinder. "There is power in the bloodline of Samular, even more than you realize."

His hands stilled. Her bald claim stunned him, intrigued

him. Given what he already knew—and his suspicion that
Malchior had not told him all—he did not doubt the possibility that Ashemmi's words held truth. He drew back a little
and met her probing gaze. "What precisely do you want from
me?" he asked bluntly.

An expression of distaste darkened Ashemmi's golden
eyes. "Must we spell out our terms? Haggle our way to agreement like vulgar merchants?"

"Indulge me."

The elf smoldered, then shrugged. "Very well, then. I want
the child brought here. I wish to explore her potential. Then
we will see between us what use might be made of it, and
her."

This was more than Dag could bear. For years he had
bided his time, not risking a possible revelation of his heritage until he was in a position to protect the innocent child
who carried, unknowing, the bloodline of Samular. All this,
Ashemmi could carelessly undo, and she would just as easily
toss the girl aside if there was no benefit to keeping her.

He thrust the sorceress away from him. "It is a poor excuse
for a mother who would so exploit her own child," he said
coldly.

"And a poor excuse for an ambitious warlord who would
not," Ashemmi snapped back. "Remember yourself, and while
you are about it, bear *me* ever in mind. This situation presents opportunity to us both, provided we are clever and discrete in how we proceed."

"And speaking of discretion, how will Sememmon respond,
when he learns that you have been keeping this matter from
him?" he retorted.

The blatant threat set Ashemmi's eyes aflame. "*If* he or
any other person in Darkhold learns of the child from you, it
will be from conversing with your spirit. I will tell Sememm-
mon, in my own way and at a time that suits my purposes. *I!*
Agree, and you and your misbegotten brat might be permitted
to live out your meager, allotted span. Am I understood?"

Dag Zoreth regarded the elf with a degree of loathing
normally reserved for the creatures that occasionally oozed

up through the fortress midden. "Of course, Ashemmi. I understand you very, very well."

"Good," she purred, drawing out the word. She languidly swept her arms high, and her gown dissolved into a swirl of crimson mist. The haze floated out to envelope Dag, as intoxicating as smoldering poppies.

Ashemmi's smile was hard and enticing. "As long as we understand each other, let us have one more secret to keep from our lord Sememmon."

For one long moment, Dag wavered on the precipice of indecision. He could step back, he could turn away and quit this room, leaving Ashemmi naked and furious. He could.

Instead, he breathed in deeply of the mist. He held the enchanted fragrance until the power of it nearly burst him asunder, and then he moved through the crimson cloud toward her.

* * * * *

On the second day after he had received his quest, Algorind reined his horse to a stop on a hill overlooking a cozy valley. Smoke from the evening fire rose from a snug stone cottage. Geese strutted contentedly near a small pond, and a small herd of rothé cropped at the grass in an enclosed pen. Soil had been turned for a kitchen garden, and already a few neat rows of seedlings rose from the rich soil. He caught the sound of a woman's teasing voice and the bubbling response of happy, childish laughter.

As he gazed at the homey scene, Algorind marveled that an evil man should have provided such ease and comfort for his child. By all appearances, this was a goodly household, unknowing of the alliance they had made. Perhaps they knew nothing of their fosterling's heritage. But surely, if they were goodly folk, they would see the wisdom in turning the child over to him for her good and that of the order.

At that moment the cottage door opened, and a tall, brown-haired woman strode out. She held her apron bundled up before her with one hand, and with the other began to strew grain for the chickens and geese. They came running in eager response to her clucking calls.

Algorind's eyes widened. At first glance, the woman was seemly enough, modestly clad in a simple linen shift draped with a long kirtle. But the color of her kirtle alerted and alarmed him. It was a deep, vivid purple, a color that was expensive and difficult to achieve, and a hue that no simple, decent goodwife would wear.

Her husband came out of the lean-to that served as a horse barn, and Algorind's hand went to his sword. Not a human at all, but an elf. Algorind's practiced eye measured the elf's gait, his way of holding himself, the watchful readiness of his posture and his face. This was no mere farmer, but a well-trained warrior.

The truth came to him then. The priest of Cyric had arranged his daughter's fosterage with evil subtlety. Who would suspect a simple farm family of harboring a Zhent's child? Who did not assume that the elves were goodly folk, best left to go about their business? These were no simple folk, happy in the gift of a child that the gods had not seen fit to send them, but hirelings of an evil priest. The deception kindled Algorind's wrath. He drew his sword and urged Icewind into a charge.

As he thundered down the hill, the woman shrieked and fled into the cottage. The forgotten grain cascaded among the squawking, scattering chickens. Algorind came at the elf with a mighty swing. The elf deftly dropped and rolled aside. He came up with a long knife in each hand and deadly intent in his catlike green eyes.

Algorind dismounted and strode forward. He met the elf's first darting blow, swept it easily aside, riposted. The elf met his thrusting attack just as easily. For several moments they stood nearly toe to toe, in a ringing exchange of blows delivered with nearly equal skill and passionate conviction.

In his training, Algorind had learned of many styles of sword play. This elf fought like a Sembian, a two-handed style of quick attack, a street-fighter's technique best suited for a short, decisive battle and a fast retreat.

"You fight well," Algorind panted out between parries. "But you are far from home."

The elf hesitated, startled by this pronouncement. The sudden sharp pain in his inhuman eyes brought something rather like pity to Algorind's heart.

"It is a sad and evil world," the paladin continued, "when goodly men or even elves are drawn into the plans of evil men."

Algorind barely dodged a vicious slash. "It is the *good* men who sent me here!" the elf snarled, speaking for the first time. He advanced in a flurry of slashing, darting attacks. For many moments it took all the paladin's skill merely to hold him back.

"The tanar'ri Vladjick," the elf said, his voice raw with exhaustion and bitter rage. "Do you remember that story?"

The paladin did, and acknowledged it with a brief nod. A terrible demon, a tanar'ri, had been summoned by an evil man's ambition. Years before Algorind was born, knights of the Order of Samular had marched against the creature. The battle had been long and fierce, and the tanar'ri had fled into the forest north of Sembia. An elven community lay between the paladins and their evil foe. The elves had resisted the passage of the knights through their forest, thus allying themselves with the evil tanar'ri. Many good and noble knights had fallen in the fierce fighting. Ever since, some of the order had remained wary of elves and their unknowable, inhuman ways.

"I remember it," the elf gritted out. "I will always remember it! The knights slaughtered my family for no better reason than that we were elves, and we were in the way."

Again he advanced, but this time emotion outbalanced control. Algorind caught one of the elf's flailing wrists in his left hand and stuck the elf's other hand aside with the hilt of his sword. The elf was slight, almost frail. It was a small matter to hurl him back, to advance with sword leading. A single, decisive thrust finished the battle and silenced the lying elf forever.

Breathing hard, Algorind went to the cottage. He hoped

the woman would be more inclined to see reason.

The cottage was empty, the back window open. Algorind circled around, easily picked up and followed the tracks of the woman's feet into the small orchards beyond.

He followed her through the spring-flowering trees and cornered her against the high stone wall of a pig pen. She whirled, the child in her arms, and entreated him wordlessly, her face streaked with desperate tears.

For a moment Algorind hesitated, wondering if he had been tragically misinformed. Woman and child were both slender, and both had brown hair decently plaited. But there the resemblance ended. The woman was human: the child, half-elf. Surely *this* was not the daughter of Samular's blood-line!

"Don't hurt her," the child said in a remarkably clear, bell-like voice. There was more anger than fear in her tip-tilted elven eyes.

"I have no wish to harm you or your mother, child," he said gently.

"Foster mother," corrected the child, showing a regard for truth worthy of a child of Samular.

"Woman, is this the child of Dag Zoreth, priest of Cyric?" Algorind demanded.

"She is *mine!* She has been mine since her birth! Go away, and leave us alone," the woman pleaded. She set the child on the ground and pushed her behind her purple skirts, shielding the girl with her own body.

This put Algorind in a quandary. Surely this brave and selfless response was not the behavior of an evil hireling. He fell back a few paces, sword still ready in case of sudden treachery. His eyes remained on the purple-clad woman, but his focus drifted past her and his lips moved in prayer. The power that Tyr granted all paladins enveloped him. In the name of the God of Justice, Algorind weighed and measured the woman before him.

Pain struck him like tiny knives to the temples. An image came to him, that of a purple sunburst and a glowing black skull. Algorind drew in breath in a quick, pained gasp. Tyr

had spoken: the woman was allied with evil—great evil. She
followed the mad god Cyric.

But Tyr was also merciful, so Algorind drew himself back,
away from the god-given insight. "Woman, will you renounce
Cyric and the evil bargain you have made? Give the child into
my hands and live."

Her eyes flamed, and she defiantly spat at the ground by
Algorind's feet.

Algorind's way was clear, yet still he hesitated. Never had
he killed a woman, much less one who was unarmed and
untrained. And certainly never in the presence of a child.

"Run, child," he advised kindly. "This is not for your eyes."

But the girl was as stubborn as her foster mother, and she
stayed where she was. All that was visible were her tiny
hands, clutching at the woman's bold purple skirts. Algorind
summoned a silent prayer to steady his resolve and to drown
out his own protests against this terrible duty. He struck a
single, merciful blow. The woman slumped to the ground. The
child regarded him over the body of her foster mother, the
purple skirts still fisted in her hands and her eyes wide with
terror. Then, suddenly, she turned on her heals and ran like a
rabbit.

Algorind sighed and put away his sword. His paladin's
quest was growing more perplexing by the moment.

*   *   *   *   *

Bronwyn did not sleep well that night. In the room above
the Curious Past, she tossed and twisted in her bed. Her
dreams were filled with long-forgotten images, childhood memories awakened by Malchior's revelation. Her father's name
was Hronulf. He had been a paladin of Tyr. He had expected
something of her, something important. As a child, she had not
understood what that was, and she could not piece together
enough images to gain an understanding.

She awoke before dawn, determined to find answers. From
what she'd heard of Tyr's followers, the early hour would be no
deterrent. Quickly she dressed and slipped down to the shop.

Alice, her small brown face tight with motherly wrath, was already awake and waiting for her. She brandished her feather duster at Bronwyn with a gusto that would not have been out of place had she been wielding a flaming sword. "And where do you think you're going at this hour?"

Bronwyn sighed and leaned against a green marble statue she'd retrieved from Chult. "I have business, Alice. A business, I might add, that *employs* you."

The gnome snorted, not at all cowed by this reminder of her status. She shook a stubby brown finger at Bronwyn. "Don't think I don't know what time you came in last night. You're up to something, and I want to know what. Let me help you where I can, child," she said in a gentler voice.

"All right," Bronwyn relented. "I'm going to the Halls of Justice to talk to some of the paladins there. I might have found word of my father."

The gnome sank down to sit on a carved chest. "After all these years," she said faintly. "Who gave you this word?"

"A Zhentish priest. The one who commissioned the amber necklace," Bronwyn answered. Anger at Malchior's treachery crept into her voice. "He's up to something, and I intend to know what."

"Yes, I suppose that's for the best," Alice murmured absently. "You'll be back this morning?"

"Not before highsun. I've got to stop by the Ilzimmer gem shop on Diamond Street. They're repairing and cleaning the gold setting on that emerald piece."

"Fine. I'll pick up something from the market for a midday meal," the gnome said.

Bronwyn nodded her thanks and walked out into the dark streets. The sky overhead was beginning to fade to silver, and many of the street lamps were guttering as the night's supply of oil ran low. Despite the early hour, the city was not sleeping. Though the Street of Silks was considered by the wealthy to be a place to shop, dine, or seek entertainment, many hard-working merchants lived above their shops and taverns. Smoke rose from chimneys as servants and goodwives started the breakfast fires. A cart rumbled past, drawn by a pair of

stolid oxen and guided by a sleepy-eyed driver. Wheels of
cheese and casks of new milk filled the cart, and the somno-
lent cat lying atop a cask opened one eye to regard Bronwyn.

She quickly reclaimed her horse from the nearby public
stable and set off toward the temple of Tyr. The Halls of Justice was a complex of three large buildings, somber, square
edifices of gray stone that formed a triangle around a grassy
field. It was not a grim scene, however. Banners hung in a
bright row from the balcony of the main building, standards,
no doubt, from the various paladins' orders. Though the sun-
rise colors still streaked the sky, a dozen or more men and
three women were already busy with weapons training.

Bronwyn stated her business to the young knight at the
door. His courteous manner warmed and brightened at the
mention of Hronulf.

"You are in good fortune, lady," he said in animated tones.
"Sir Gareth Cormaeril is in residence today. He was a great
friend of Hronulf's and a partner in arms in their youth. You
will surely find him in the exchequer's study, attending to the
business of his order. Shall I escort you there?"

"Please." Bronwyn listened carefully as the young man
continued to extol Sir Gareth, Hronulf, and the former great
deeds of the mighty warriors. He told the story of the Zhentarim attack and the terrible wound that Gareth received
defending his friend's life.

"Sir Gareth serves the Order of the Knights of Samular
still as exchequer in charge of funds. Hronulf, of course, is
still on active duty."

Bronwyn's heart thudded at this news. *Her father was still
alive?* For some reason, that possibility had never occurred to
her. She had hoped only to hear stories of him. Never had she
dreamed that she might see him again with her own eyes.

The chatty young knight kept talking, but Bronwyn did
not hear another word until she stood at the door of Sir
Gareth's study. The knight made the introductions and left
her there.

Sir Gareth was a handsome man in late middle life, robust
still despite the wound that rendered his right arm virtually

useless. He graciously received her and sent a servant for tea.

"You wish to know of Hronulf Caradoon," he said. "May I inquire what the source of your interest might be?"

Bronwyn saw no reason to prevaricate, yet instinct and habit prompted her to tell less than the whole truth. "I have been looking for my family for many years. It is possible that Hronulf might have information that will help me in my search."

Sir Gareth leaned back in his chair and regarded her thoughtfully. "That is most interesting. Hronulf, too, has suffered a loss of family. I am certain he will be most sympathetic to your plight and will do all that is in his power to aid you. Of course," he said with a faint, proud smile, "he would do so regardless."

The warm regard in the knight's blue eyes touched her. "I am told that he is your friend."

"The best I ever had, and a better man that this world deserves," Sir Gareth responded. "But meet him, and judge for yourself."

The knight reached for ink and parchment and wrote a few words. He sprinkled the ink with drying powder, then shook the excess away. He rolled the letter into a scroll and handed it to an attentive scribe. "My seal," he instructed absently, and then turned back to Bronwyn.

"Bear this letter to Hronulf, as my introduction. He is captain of the fortress known as Thornhold. Do you know it?"

"I have heard of it. Off the High Road, perhaps two days' ride north of Waterdeep?"

"That is correct. Ah, thank you," he said, taking the sealed missive from his assistant. He handed the scroll to Bronwyn. "Do you desire an escort? I am not at leisure to accompany you myself, but I would gladly send trusted men to guide and protect you."

Bronwyn smiled her thanks and shoved aside the hint of resentment that his paternalistic tone inspired. It was a gracious offer, and should be graciously received. "You are very kind, Sir Gareth, but I will be fine on my own."

"Then may Tyr speed your path. You leave soon?"

"Today," she agreed.

He rose. "Then I will not keep you. If you would be so kind, bear my regards to my old friend."

She agreed and took his offered hand, then swiftly left the Halls of Justice. She passed the Ilzimmer shop without stopping to inquire about the progress of the commissioned repairs. After all, her client's family had been missing the emerald brooch for over a century. A few days more wouldn't alter matters much.

The Street of Silks was lively with mid-morning commerce by the time Bronwyn arrived at her shop. But to her surprise, the door to the Curious Past was closed, and a sign proclaimed that the shop would open after highsun.

Bronwyn frowned as she fumbled in her pocket for her extra key. This was unlike Alice. The gnome was the most faithful shopkeeper in all of Waterdeep, which was saying a great deal. What could have happened to inspire her to close the shop during the busy morning hours?

Memory edged into Bronwyn's mind, bringing with it questions she had not had time to consider, and a suspicion that made her heart hang like lead in her chest. The Harpers had known where to find her the night she'd met with Malchior. Either they had followed her footsteps during the entire tumultuous day—which was unlikely—or they had been informed of her intended meeting place. Malchior and his henchmen had received word of the meeting place shortly before the appointed time. Only one other person knew her plans.

Alice.

Bronwyn thrust the key back into her pocket and turned her steps south, toward the tall, smooth black tower where all Harper business seemed to converge. As she worked her way through the crowded street, Bronwyn reminded herself that she was accustomed to treachery and betrayal, that she faced it every day and made deft provisions to survive it. It was nothing new, and usually it was nothing personal.

Why, then, did her eyes burn so painfully with unshed tears?

*   *   *   *   *

Ebenezer stared glumly at his cage. The wooden slats were hard and thick enough to keep a whole den of beavers busy until sundown. Without knife or axe, he had little hope of getting free.

Yet that was precisely what he had to do. Humans and half-orcs in the tunnels, catching dwarves and sticking them in cages. That was trouble. Spellcasting priests were even worse, and who knew how many more of them were roaming around? He had to get free and bring warning to his clan.

The dwarf rose up on his knees and took another look around. The men had returned a while back and had crated up the osquips' trove. Zhents, they were, and intent on plunder. The cave was full of stout boxes, locked and wrapped with chains. There was nothing lying about handy that he could use as tool or weapon, even if he could find a way to reach it. Nothing at all but a few paces of stone ledge and a long drop to the river.

Inspiration struck. Ebenezer scuttled to the far side of his cage, crouched, and launched himself at the opposite wall. The cage tilted, then crashed onto its side. He shook his head to clear it, then repeated the maneuver. He moved the cage over to the ledge, one painful crash at a time, and prayed to every dwarven god who'd ever wielded a hammer that he could finish the job before the racket brought back the dwarf-stealing Zhents.

Ebenezer paused at the very brink of the ledge. One more time, and he'd crash to the stone path below. The cage simply could not survive the impact, and he would be free.

"This is gonna hurt some," he admitted, then hurled himself against the cage one last time.

* * * * *

To Algorind's dismay, the child did not take kindly to her rescue. She fought him until they reached Rassalanter Hamlet, where he gratefully turned her over to the nurse Sir Gareth had employed. After downing a a cup of strong tea, the child fell asleep, and stayed asleep in the privacy of a covered carriage, until they reached Waterdeep.

With great relief he entered the grounds of Tyr's temple, and sent word ahead to Sir Gareth as he had been instructed to do. In moments, the old knight met him at the gate, on horseback and ready to travel. To Algorind's surprise, Sir Gareth led him not into the complex, but down the street toward the sea.

"This matter required great secrecy," Gareth reminded him. "If the child is to find safe, appropriate fosterage, few can know of her arrival in Waterdeep."

"But surely she would be safe in the Halls of Justice," Algorind ventured.

The knight looked at him kindly. "Many visitors come to the Halls of Justice, seeking aid or information. We cannot risk that the child's presence be discovered. Some might come to us with questions. Why place the brothers in a position where they must either betray us or lie? What they do not know, they can deny in good faith."

"I'm sure that is wise," Algorind agreed, though for some reason he still felt somewhat troubled.

"It is necessary," Sir Gareth said firmly. "You may leave the child in my hands now, your duty complete."

Algorind hesitated. "What would you have me do now? Return to Summit Hall with word that the child is safely in your hands?"

"No, better that you ride first to Thornhold with a message to Hronulf. He should have word of his granddaughter."

The knight reached out and placed a hand on the young paladin's shoulder. His face was grave. "I have a new charge for you. Stay with Hronulf for as long as needs be. I fear that perilous times are coming, and I would feel more content for my old friend's safety if I knew that a young knight of your skill and valor guarded his back."

"I will happily do as you ask, but I am not yet a knight," Algorind felt compelled to add.

Sir Gareth smiled, but his eyes had the faraway expression of a man who regarded distant glories. "Do this, and I swear to you that you will die as a paladin should, fighting alongside fellow knights."

* * * * *

As he entered Khelben's study, Danilo recoiled in suprise. There was a slight swelling to one side of the archmage's jaw, where Dan had struck. His lingering ire vanished, replaced by guilt and puzzlement. Khelben could easily heal himself— why would he choose not to?

"Our last discussion seems to have made more of an impression upon you than I intended," Danilo ventured.

The sharp, sidelong look Khelben sent him showed a hint of self-deprecating humor that most men would think entirely foreign to the archmage's character.

"Apology accepted," Khelben said brusquely. "Now, to the matter at hand."

He nodded toward the other occupant of the chamber, a gnome woman who sat clenching the arms of a too large chair, her feet stuck straight up before her like a child's.

"Alice," Danilo said warmly. "It's good to see you again."

"Save the pleasantries," the archmage cut in, "and listen well. A situation has arisen that requires me to divulge information that until now was best left unspoken."

Khelben strode over to his writing desk, absently picked up a quill, and crumbled it in his hand. "Alice tells me that Malchior has given Bronwyn information on her past. She is even now talking to Tyr's followers. This creates a grave situation and puts her in considerable danger."

He dropped the ruined pen into a wastebasket. A small, claw-tipped orange hand reached up and caught it from the air. The smacking, chewing sounds that followed spoke of the discrete disposal that awaited any discarded written drafts that might otherwise reveal the archmage's business.

"It is certain that members of the Zhentarim know of Bronwyn's identity. Soon the paladins of Tyr will know this, as well. They may tell her of the power that her heritage brings. Paladins and Zhents will wish to exploit it, and her."

Danilo nodded slowly. He hadn't resolved his anger at Khelben's machinations, or his own sense of confusion over his part in uncovering Bronwyn's identity, but at least he was beginning to see Khelben's reasoning. He didn't like it any better, but understanding helped. A little.

"And what is this power?" he inquired.

The archmage grimaced. "I do not know the whole of it," he admitted, "but this much I can tell you: the Knights of Samular have in their possession three rings, artifacts of considerable power. They can be worn and wielded only by blood descendants of Samular."

"Which Bronwyn is," Danilo put in.

"Yes. What these rings can do, and where they are held, I do not know. Hronulf wears one of them, another was lost in the raid on his village. The third has been missing for centuries."

The archmage turned to Alice. "And this is where you come in. Find out what Bronwyn knows, and report back at once."

"I'm to tell her of the rings, aren't I?" Alice asked anxiously. "It won't be easy admitting to her that I've been keeping watch over her these four years and more, but the time has come."

"Not yet," Khelben cautioned. "You are to act as you always have. Watch, listen, and report."

"But—"

He cut her off with a single stern glare. "Find out what she knows," he repeated. "And that is all."

The dismissal was unmistakable. Alice slid off the too-tall chair and nodded her head in a curt, barely respectful bow.

Danilo watched her go, fully understanding how she must feel. The little gnome considered Bronwyn a friend, and yet she kept secrets from her because it was her duty as a Harper to do so. Clearly, it didn't sit well with the proud former warrior. It didn't sit well with Dan either, if truth must be told. He wondered how much longer either he or Alice would be able to give duty greater weight than friendship.

Five

Bronwyn stopped when she was perhaps a hundred paces from Blackstaff Tower. It was one of the oddest buildings in a very unusual city. A tall, flat-topped cone of seemingly unbroken black stone, it was surrounded by a curtain wall of the same dark substance, a wall without any apparent doors.

She circled around, not quite sure what she was looking for. Then, she noted a basket at the foot of the wall, a tall wicker basket such as a merchant might use to haul goods to the market stalls. There were a few baskets of that sort in the back room of the Curious Past. Bronwyn edged between two nearby buildings and settled down to wait.

After a short time, the basket began to move, dragged by the handle by a small, white-haired gnome. Bronwyn caught her breath in a half sob as she recognized Alice.

Even through her pain, Bronwyn had to admire the gnome's ploy. Emerging through an invisible wall was one thing, and would surely seize the attention of any who witnessed it. But who would notice a gnome tradeswoman, who appeared only to be stooping to adjust her load before proceeding on her way? Alice had obviously planned to slip through the wall behind the basket, wait for an opportune moment, and then go on her way. It was well done.

Bronwyn followed, keeping at least thirty paces between herself and the treacherous gnome. At least she now knew how the Harpers had been keeping an eye on her business. That Alice reported directly to Khelben Arunsun, the Master Harper, was a matter of some concern. Bronwyn could see no reason why she warranted such lofty attention. No doubt the archmage was concerned about her contact with Malchior. Members of the Zhentarim seldom ventured into Waterdeep, and their activities were carefully monitored. And as she herself had noted, a skilled mage could probably get a good deal of information from the amber necklace that Malchior had handled. Khelben had not been happy to lose it.

Anger welled up anew, momentarily stopping Bronwyn in her tracks. Khelben must have ordered Alice to bring him the necklace. And this, after Bronwyn had pledged to Malchior that she would keep it safe from those who could read magic's secrets. Once again, it seemed that the Harpers were forcing her to renege on her word. That, she simply could not allow.

When she reached Curious Past Bronwyn threw open the door with a force and fury that brought a shower of plaster shimmering down off the wattle-and-daub walls and rattled the rare things displayed on the shelves. Two startled halfling customers and one equally surprised gnome shopkeeper stared up at her in astonishment.

"Where is the amber necklace?" she demanded of Alice.

The gnome's brown face furrowed in puzzlement. "In the safe, child, where you left it. Please browse—I'll be back directly," she said to the customers. The gnome shot a glance toward her personal version of a shop's cat—a sleek, keen-eyed raven named, appropriately enough, Shopscat. The raven hopped down from his perch, positioning himself so that the halfling matron's fingers were within easy reach of his wicked, yellow beak.

Alice and Bronwyn hurried into the dusty jumble of baskets, boxes and barrels that was the shop's back room. Behind them they heard a sharp squawk, followed by a halfling's

startled squeal. "Think about it," the raven advised, one of
several phrases it used to good effect.

The gnome sighed and shut the door behind her. "I'll have
to hurry before Fillfuphia cleans out the place. Bronwyn,
there are things you must know. Sit, child."

Bronwyn sat, settling down on a suspiciously familiar basket. She swallowed the lump that rose in her throat. "I have a
few questions for you, too."

"They'll have to wait. Please listen well. This is not easy to
say, and I'd hate to have to repeat any of it."

"Go on," Bronwyn said cautiously. She gripped the edges of
the basket so tightly that the wicker edges bit into her still-
sore palms. This response was the last thing she'd expected
from Alice. The gnome was always calm, competent. *Never
show them what you're thinking*, Alice had often cautioned
Bronwyn; this was a rule that governed all their business
dealings and, it would seem, their dealings with each other.
But for the moment at least, Alice had cast aside her own
rules. The gnome's slightly prominent eyes glistened with
tears, her face was drawn and pained, and her form shook
with emotion too strong to repress. In short, Alice was a precise mirror for what Bronwyn herself was feeling.

"Child, you're not the only Harper in this shop. I was
assigned to watch and protect you, without telling you why. I
didn't know why, until recently, other than a general knowledge of who and what I was to look out for. But the pot is
heating up. . . ." In a few terse words, the gnome told her what
Khelben had said about the Zhentarim, the paladins, and the
family artifacts.

As Bronwyn listened some of the pain of betrayal seeped
away, but her determination was stronger than ever. "I need
to go to Thornhold," she said. "I have to see my father."

"Of course you do, child." The gnome looked at her
shrewdly. "But that's what they expect you to do. There might
be problems. Unless, of course, we can distract them."

Bronwyn nodded as a plan started to fall into place. But
one question remained. She met and held Alice's gaze. "We?"
she asked pointedly.

"We," the gnome said firmly. "You do what you must, and I'll help you however I can." Alice hesitated, then held out her hand, offering both an apology and a pact.

A clasp of the wrist, Harper to Harper. Bronwyn understood the gesture and found it inadequate to what Alice offered and what they shared. She struck the tiny hand aside. Before the shock in Alice's eyes could turn to hurt, she gathered the little gnome into her arms. The two women clung together in a brief, fierce embrace.

After a moment Alice cleared her throat and drew back. "Well, I'd better go see what Shopscat is squawking about," she said hurriedly, dashing the back of her hand against her eyes.

"Good idea," Bronwyn replied, though she had not heard the raven's raucous voice since they'd left the shop. A fond smile curved her lips as she watched the gnome scurry out to the shop. Then she wiped her eyes and climbed the back stair to her room, to collect her thoughts and to prepare for the trip ahead.

*   *   *   *   *

The small sea cave, located to the south of the Stoneshaft tunnels by a half day's brisk walk, measured six paces from side to side. Ebenezer marked off the width again, then again, pacing distractedly as he considered his predicament.

It wasn't much of a cave. Exceedingly small, it was littered with dried seaweed, crab claws, and broken shells. Various mussel-like critters clung to the stone walls and ceiling, and the floor was a combination of cliff rock and ocean sand. Not exactly homey by the dwarf's standards, but it served him now as a combination haven and prison. The large boulder he'd shoved into the opening nearly covered the mouth of the cave, keeping it secure—for now. Ebenezer wasn't sure what he'd do when the tide came in. Drown, most likely. He could hear the sea and even smell its salty tang, though that was hard to do over the much closer and far more foul aroma outside.

"Off the chopping board and into the stew pot," Ebenezer muttered. It was a dwarven cliché, but since it fit the situation so perfectly he thought he could maybe get by with using it, just this once.

Glumly he reviewed the steps that had led him to this predicament. He'd survived the drop from the ledge onto solid stone below just fine and had kicked his way out of the splintered crate—only to lose his balance and splash into the river. Ebenezer had never learned to swim, and now he knew why. Being in cold, moving water was damned unpleasant. He'd been tossed and buffeted about for what seemed like hours, going under more times than he could count. The only thing that had kept him from drowning was sheer cussedness— that, and the large rock that he'd slammed smack into. Fortunately, the rock was not the only one of its kind, and once his eyes had uncrossed he'd been able to make his way to shore. Problem was by then he was well past the warren of Stoneshaft tunnels and the only way back was up the river he came down on. Thank you, no. So he'd taken to the surface by the quickest tunnel and headed south along the sea's shoreline— noisy, nasty thing, that sea—to a point where he could scale the nearly sheer cliff and get up to the Trade Way. Ebenezer's thinking was that the road was the fastest way back to the tunnels' entrance. Unfortunately, he had a long walk ahead— at least a half day, the way he figured it. He suspected that he would be too late.

That was what the "chopping board" looked like. The "stew pot" was no improvement. Ebenezer sighed and edged closer to the mouth of the tiny cave.

A skeletal hand lashed out toward him. The dwarf leaned back, and the grasping claw swiped past, so close that the smell of rotting flesh nearly knocked him on his backside.

"That was close," Ebenezer admitted as he backed away. "Good thing I shaved off the mustache, or he might 'a got a grip."

The dwarf adjusted the boulder that blocked most of the cave's mouth and settled down to think. Men, he could fight. Orcs, goblins, even elves if it came to that. But he had no idea

what the creatures outside his cave were—or, more accu-
rately, *had been*. Wasn't enough left of the things to tell. And
even if he knew what style of fighting was called for, he had
no weapons to fight with. Yep. This was a stew pot, all right.

Ebenezer ventured another peek over the rock. On the
rocky shore beyond his hiding place, three misshapen creatures, their flesh so bloated and rotten as to render them
unrecognizable, paced hungrily. The dwarf knew that
undead creatures abounded in the Mere of Dead Men, but
this was the farthest away from the swamp he'd heard of
them coming.

"Lost, are you?" he bellowed out at them. "Head north,
then. Follow the sea. When the going gets mushy underfoot,
you're almost home."

There was more than bravado prompting his words.
Ebenezer knew a zombie when he smelled one. Someone had
raised up these poor creatures, turned dead men or whatever
else they'd been into rotting, unthinking warriors. It was a
long shot, but he figured the zombies might just listen to him,
lacking another master to tell them what to do.

As it happened, his words had an effect—though not the
one he'd anticipated.

"Hello the cave!" shouted a clear, young baritone voice.
"Are you unhurt, friend?"

The shout came from the direction of the road. Ebenezer
scrambled to his feet. "Got no complaints," he hollered back,
"other than being pinned down by three very dead people who
forgot to lie down and quit."

There was a pause, silence broken only by the sound of
approaching hoofbeats. "I see them."

The young man's voice held repugnance, but no fear. That
worried Ebenezer. "You got company, I hope?"

"I am alone," the voice answered calmly, "but the grace of
Tyr is with me."

One man, confident in the favor of some human god. The
dwarf groaned and slumped against the cave wall. He slid
down and sat and tried his best not to listen to what was sure
to come. Zombies were not tidy fighters and generally liked to

tear their prey messily apart.

To his surprise, the young man's voice lifted in a song, a hymn by the sounds of it. Wouldn't be well received in a tavern, leastwise, being slow and solemn and not real catchy. But Ebenezer felt its power and was drawn by it. He scrambled to his feet and peered out over the boulder.

A young man, curly-headed as a lamb and nearly as fair, approached on a tall white horse. The three zombies staggered toward him, a fact that disturbed the man's composure not at all. He merely lifted one hand to the sky and pointed the other at the undead creatures. His song lifted, swelled to a shout of power. "In the name of Tyr, I command you to yield to your fate!"

Instantly, the creatures sagged and fell. Rotten flesh dissolved, bones made brittle by long contact with unnatural, prolonged decay gave way and crumbled into powder.

Ebenezer shouldered the rock out of the way and emerged from the cave. "That's a good trick," he admitted.

The young man nodded. "You are most welcome, friend dwarf. It was a good thing that I heard your shouts. Now you must excuse me."

"Hold on," the dwarf said, catching the horse's reins. "I gotta get word to my clan. Can you take me where I need to go?"

"Icewind could not long carry the two of us," the young man said, nodding at his splendid white horse, "and my duty takes me elsewhere."

"But this is important!"

"Then may Tyr speed your steps and provide a means for your swift journey."

"Might could be that he already has," Ebenezer muttered. He reached up and seized a handful of the man's white and blue tabard, and yanked him down off the horse.

They tumbled together, and the young man reached for his sword. Ebenezer grabbed the first weapon that came to hand—a rock about twice the size of his fist—and slammed it between the human's eyes. The young man groaned and fell limp.

Ebenezer hopped to his feet. "Sorry about that," he muttered, relieved to see that the human still breathed. Borrowing a horse in dire straits was one thing, outright killing a man who'd done him a good turn was quite another. But, as the man had said, Tyr would provide. It'd be downright ungrateful for Ebenezer to ignore such a thoughtful and timely gift.

The dwarf seized the horse's reins and led the beast over to the boulder. He climbed onto the rock and just barely managed to hoist his foot into the stirrup. He hauled himself up and settled down in the saddle. Unlike most dwarves, he liked horses and rode when he could. This was the finest horse he'd ever had. It wouldn't be easy to give the beast back, but Ebenezer determined that he would find a way to do so.

"I'm off, then," he advised the man, who was beginning to shake off the effects of the blow. "If you've got problems with that, you might want to take it up with Tyr."

Ebenezer shook the reins over the white horse's neck, and headed northward toward his clan and home.

*   *   *   *   *

Danilo was a frequent visitor to Curious Past. Until now, he not given much thought to his role in fostering Bronwyn's business. He liked rare and beautiful things, and so did many of his wealthy peers. It was a small matter to send them Bronwyn's way, a favor no larger than he would do for any friend. The difference was that he was doing this at Khelben's direction and for the express purpose of keeping Bronwyn in Waterdeep and under the eye of the archmage.

As he stood before the tall, trim building that housed the shop, Danilo wondered what Bronwyn would think of this involvement or how she would react if she knew that her shop—like many others on this street and others—was in fact owned by the Harpers. Perhaps he should tell her outright, Danilo mused as he pushed open the large oak-plank door. Perhaps he should tell her everything he had learned about her heritage. But Khelben insisted that doing so would endanger her. In Danilo's opinion, the archmage was overly cautious and often downright miserly with information, but how could he be certain that Khelben's warnings were not valid?

"Think about it," advised a raucous, inhuman voice, speaking almost in his ear.

Danilo jumped, then turned to find himself face to beak with a large raven. A wry smile curved his lips. Odd that the raven's standard rejoinder meshed so perfectly with his ambivalent state of mind.

"I assure you, my dear Shopscat, I have been doing precisely that. Is your mistress in attendance?"

The raven merely cocked his head and eyed the shiny gold hoop in Danilo's ear. Danilo clapped one hand to his ear and took several judicious steps back. Shopscat was a shoplifter's bane, but the raven occasionally showed himself unable to discern which valuables belonged in the shop and which the shoppers were entitled to take with them by right of prior ownership.

"He doesn't understand you, and he doesn't answer back," Alice Tinker said, coming out from behind the counter.

"I stopped by to see Bronwyn," he said bluntly. "Is she about?"

"You missed her," Alice said, her blue eyes wide and ingenuous. "Just. She left for Daggersford this morning. Took the South Gate out," she added helpfully.

"Really."

"She's on commission. Some paladin sent her off looking for an old sword. A paladin's sword. Not exactly magical, but blessed—though exactly what the difference might be, I couldn't tell you. It seems it was lost, some two hundred years back in an important battle with lizard men. Bronwyn heard tell of a sword that might fit the bill. The marsh has been receding, you know, and there's a boy in Daggersford who found an old sword when he was out digging mussels. She's off to see if these swords are one and the same."

"My, that's quite a bit of information," Danilo observed lightly.

Alice shrugged again. "That's what I do. Anything else you need to know?"

"When do you expect her back? Daggersford is—what? About two days' ride? I imagine she'll need a day or two to conduct her business, and then about the same time back."

"Yes, that sounds about right," the gnome agreed.

As well it should, Dan noted. Daggersford and Thornhold were almost equal distances from Waterdeep, albeit in opposite directions. He suspected that Bronwyn probably did leave by the South Gate, only to blend in with a northbound caravan, return through the city, and slip out the North Gate with yet another caravan. She had used such ploys before, to good effect. And he had to admire the bit Alice had added about the paladin's commission. That was simply inspired. Clearly, the Harpers would not want to alert the paladins to their interest in Bronwyn, and they could hardly knock at the doors of the Halls of Justice and demand to know what errand they'd sent Bronwyn to attend. The reasonable thing for the Harpers to do would be to pursue her to Daggersford and ensure her safety.

Well, that is what the "Harpers" would do. Danilo, personally, had other plans. He stooped and kissed the gnome's brown cheek. "Thank you, Alice."

"What for?" She sniffed and scrubbed at her cheek with one hand. "I gave you my report, same as always. You'll pass along the report, same as always. Business as usual."

"I'll pass along *the report you gave me*," he said, giving the words deliberate emphasis.

Awareness dawned in the gnome's eyes, and a small, grateful smile curved her lips. She cleared her throat and turned aside. She opened a glass-topped table and snatched up a pair of teardrop earrings; silver, set with moonstones and sapphires. They were beautiful, and perfect for Danilo's half-elf partner.

"These are elven, and if I remember aright, the elf festival of Springrite is just around the corner."

He counted out the price and put the gold coins into the gnome's hand. "Arilyn will love them. She may even *wear* them. You are an excellent saleswoman, Alice," he said, punctuating his remark with another kiss to her cheek, "and an even better friend."

Danilo turned and left, shooing off the suddenly suspicious raven and noting, with great satisfaction, that this time the gnome permitted his heartfelt kiss to remain where he'd left it. And as he went, he sent up a silent prayer to Selûne, the goddess of moonlight and the patron of all seekers, that Bronwyn would find her way safely to Thornhold, and that there she would find what she had been seeking so long.

*　*　*　*　*

Dag Zoreth had heard stories about the vastness and complexity of the underground world, but all of them paled before the reality. The tunnels and caverns beneath the Sword Mountains went on forever, delving far deeper than he had imagined a man could go. Dag Zoreth had never been so far underground. It was oppressive in a way that no fortress dungeon, no matter how dank and fearful, could ever duplicate. Perhaps it was the knowledge that tons of rock and soil loomed overhead, or the constant danger posed by the river that careened through the heart of the mountain.

The river path was wet and treacherous. More than one man had fallen down the steep embankment, to be swept away to his death. They had been forced to slaughter one of the pack mules who'd fallen and broken a leg amid the uneven stones. The noise of the rushing water was nearly deafening, and the only light was the luminous moss that grew in uneven patterns on the tunnel walls.

But Dag had chosen the path for its very hazards. The river's roar would drown out the sounds of the approaching army, and the glowing moss made torchlight unnecessary. It was never easy to surprise dwarves. Taking out their outposts—a reclusive smith and some far-ranging mining parties—would help. One of the miners had yielded up some interesting news. Not willingly, of course. He had died without speaking, despite the Zhentish soldiers' most creative

efforts to wrest information from him by torture. The dwarf's
spirit had been more accommodating. Grudging even in
death, the dwarf had given up, bit by bit, the fact that most of
the Stoneshaft clan had gathered to celebrate the wedding of
the patriarch's youngest daughter. There would be days of
festivity and merriment. Wedding ale, a particularly potent
brew, would be abundant.

None of the soldiers believed that this guaranteed an easy
time of it. Dwarves were fearsome fighters whose prowess
and ferocity only seemed to rise with the level of ale in their
bellies. But what the Zhentarim had in their favor was surprise, in the form of access to tunnels that, until recently, no
one but the paladins of Thornhold knew existed.

Sir Gareth's information proved accurate, though Dag had
taken care to verify it wherever he could. Finally they reached
the last tunnel, the one that led to the Stoneshaft clanhold's
great hall.

A call for silence and readiness passed down the line, moving swiftly by blow and gesture. Dag watched as the soldiers
loosened their weapons and removed extras from the nearly
empty packs on the mules. The animals would stay back with
the drovers, for they would be useful in the new trade routes
that would follow this conquest. When all was ready, Dag
nodded to his captain, and the soldiers crept forward.

Excitement, dark and compelling, welled up in Dag's
heart. He had seen battle before, but only from a distance. His
superiors at Darkhold deemed him too valuable to risk in
close combat. He had earned his position in the war-clerics
through his command of strategy and the clerical spells he
had developed with Cyric's blessing. This was the first time
he would smell the blood and the fear, taste the potent wine of
destruction.

He fell into place behind the fighters and began murmur-
ing a low prayer. Into it he poured all his long-repressed
anger, his hatred, his desire for blood and power and death.

The evil spell gathered force and power, growing until it
felt to Dag like a living thing, a third being born of Cyric's
dark power and his own unfathomable yearning. The power

reached out and seized the soldiers with unseen hands, swept them along into the vortex of what Dag felt, saw, and summoned. Soon the men were running, thundering down the tunnel with weapons aloft and eyes glittering with bloodthirst.

The dwarves heard and came running out to meet them, as Dag had intended for them to do. They came barreling down their tunnel and into an antechamber, a vast work of art so grimly beautiful it nearly distracted Dag from his terrible devotions.

Almost, but not quite. Dag's voice lifted into a sound like shrieking wind. The spell tore free of his throat and whirled into the chamber.

Power, visible only to his eyes, swept with maelstrom force to engulf and encircle the massive stone statues that ringed the chamber. Instantly the statues began to tremble.

The dwarves paused, startled into temporary inaction by this harbinger of the one thing their kind feared above all others: earthquake.

But the reality of Cyric's wrath was something both less and more terrible. The wondrous statues of long-dead dwarf heroes turned on their descendants. They tilted inward, breaking free of their pedestals with thundering booms, and then crashed into the dwarven throng.

Some of the dwarves were fleet enough of foot and wit to escape back down the tunnel, but dozens were crushed beneath falling stone. The Zhentish soldiers rushed into the swirling cloud of dust.

The sounds of furious battle echoed through the tunnel that led to the great hall. Though the Zhentarim had the strength of numbers and arms and magic, Dag did not count the dwarves out yet, not by any means.

He had reason to know how fiercely people could fight to defend their homes and family. He had seen his brother Byorn die doing just that, living longer than he should have against odds far greater than any sane man would face. Young Byorn's face rose up before him now, bringing with it a stab of poignant loss. Dag ruthlessly thrust the memory aside.

He began the chant of another dark spell, one that he himself had developed as a Darkhold war-cleric, one that he had taught to the men and women under him. Dream-pursuit, he called it. It slowed the limbs of their opponents, made each motion as languid and heavy as if they were moving through water. The spell duplicated, with precise and deadly effect, the feeling one had in a nightmare of being pursued and unable to run. Only this spell was not a dream, but grim reality.

The spell took effect, turning the dwarves' battle effort into a slow, macabre dance. Dag studied the surviving dwarves for signs of value. When he saw one he thought might do, he limned the prospective slave in faint purple light, which served both to freeze the dwarf in place, and to mark him as beyond limits. His men knew better, even in the grip of the spell-enhanced battle-lust, to thwart Dag's demonstrated will.

Dag found himself enjoying the process of selection. Each dwarf that died by his command was an offering to Cyric, god of strife. But this offering held something more, something so exhilarating that it bordered on blasphemy. Cyric received, but only the offerings Dag Zoreth chose to give. He pointed, and a dwarf lived. A red-bearded female, probably a gem smith judging from her rich ornaments. A beardless child. Another. That one with the hammer uplifted to crush a soldier's skull. A stout female with festive garb and a long gray beard. No, that one was too old to be of lasting value. The purple light surrounding her vanished, and a Zhent's sword slashed in.

It was over too soon. In the relative silence that followed the slaughter, Dag's heart pounded so hard that he was certain all could hear it. That mattered not. His men would not think less of him for it. His dark pleasure was mirrored on the face of every surviving Zhent.

Dag took a long breath, gathering himself and turning to the next task. "Chain the captives, no more than three together," he instructed. "Drive them to the surface. The wagons are ready?"

"They are, my lord," his captain answered.

Dag nodded. Slavery was outlawed in much of the north-lands, and he had deemed it imprudent to march the dwarves overland. Enclosed wagons offered a degree of security. The dwarves would be shipped to the south and sold in the markets where dwarven lives and skills had a price. The money would go to Zhentil Keep, ensuring that there would be little discussion over whether Dag would be permitted to hold what he had conquered.

The task, however pleasurable it might have been, was not yet done. There were tunnels to explore and tunnels to seal. And then, the best of all . . .

The destruction of Thornhold and the reclamation of Dag Zoreth's birthright.

Six

When she neared the top of the winding path, Bronwyn slid from her horse and stood, looking up at the fortress her father commanded.

Her father. She had said the words often in the silence of her mind and had even practiced them aloud a time or two on the way to Thornhold.

The trip had been indecently short. Two days' ride was all that had separated her from the truth of her past. Worse, she had long known of this stronghold of the order of paladins, had known exactly where it lay; not far north of Waterdeep, on the sea cliffs, north of Redcliffs and the Red Rocks, straight west of Kheldell and south of the Mere of Dead Men. She could have come here any time had she but known what she would find.

Bronwyn took a long, steadying breath and took stock of her surroundings. The fortress was impressive, forbidding. It was built of gray stone, set against and near the top of a hill that swept up high, and then fell in a nearly sheer drop to the sea. She could smell the sea and hear it, too—a distant, restless crashing against an extremely inhospitable and rocky shore. A few sea birds circled overhead, and their poignant cries gave voice to the inexplicable loneliness that swept over her in waves.

It was a strange feeling, no doubt inspired by her bleak surroundings, but still utterly at odds with the coming reunion. Bronwyn shook off the dark mood and studied the fortress itself. A thick wall surrounded the keep in a tall, curving sweep—no corners to obscure the watchmen's vision, no dead areas where arrows could not reach potential invaders. Two tall towers rose high over the wall, each crowned with the blue and white banner of the Knights of Samular. There was no other ornamentation; unlike the small city castles of Waterdeep and the exotic keeps Bronwyn had seen in the southern lands, this one was somber and stolid, build for strength and nothing more. There were no glass-covered windows, no balconies, no ornamental stone-work—nothing that would provide a handhold or an entrance for an enemy intent upon escalade. The arrow slits were exceedingly narrow. Crenellations were spaced evenly along the top of the wall and fitted with wooden shutters for extra security.

After several moments of this scrutiny, Bronwyn began to wonder where an observant eye ended and a coward's hesitation began. She gathered up the lead reins of her horse and walked toward the massive wooden gate. There was a smaller door in the gate; this opened to her knock, and an elderly man came out to greet her. It seemed to Bronwyn that he was surprised, probably because she was a young woman traveling alone. She had read that some of the holy orders had little to do with women and thought of them, when they thought of them at all, as weaker beings requiring protection. But she could not fault the old man's manners. In courtly tones, he asked her name and what aid she required.

"I have business with Hronulf of Tyr," she responded politely. "My name I will tell to him alone."

The paladin studied her for a moment, his rheumy eyes intense. Then he nodded. "There is no real evil in you," he said. "You may enter."

Bronwyn bit her lip to keep it from turning up in a wry

smile. *No real evil*. That was a resounding endorsement if ever she'd heard one. Oddly enough, that carefully qualified praise had a familiar ring to it, one that was shadowed by a vaguely remembered emotion. Bronwyn tried to find words to describe that emotion. Quiet despair? No, that was not quite right. It was, however, uncomfortably close to the mark.

She pondered this as she followed the old paladin. He turned her over to another man, also well advanced in years, who led her through the bailey courtyard. Here, at least, was bustling life, and Bronwyn gratefully gave her natural curiosity free rein.

Perhaps a score or more servants, common folks tending the tasks needed by any community, busied themselves in and around the small wood and plaster buildings that were set against the interior wall. Clustered about the bailey—the castle courtyard—were animal pens, a brewery, and a chandler's workshop pungent with the scent of melting tallow and cooling candles. The scent of lye soap was heavy in the air, and a pair of servants, arms bared to the elbows, leaned over large wooden tubs and scrubbed garments up and down rippled washboards. A wheelwright was melding the broken spoke on a cart's wheel, while the anxious merchant stood by offering suggestions. Through another open door, Bronwyn caught sight of a loom bright with the blue and white design of the order.

Oddly enough, there appeared to be no women among the servants. That puzzled Bronwyn. After all, her very existence proved that the Knights of Samular was not a celibate order.

She was tempted to ask her guide about this but upon second consideration decided that he was not the confiding sort. When told to take Bronwyn to the fortress commander, he had responded with folded lips and a curt bow. He had bid her to follow him and then turned away. Not a word had he spoken since, and Bronwyn had seen frowning faces less eloquent than the stiff lines of his back and shoulders. Not the confiding sort at all. She hoped that her father would be more approachable. At this point, though, and for no reason that she could express or explain, Bronwyn felt unwilling to place many coins on that bet.

Her guide led her through the bailey and to one of the towers. They climbed a broad stone staircase. Near the top, her escort stopped before a door fashioned of stout oak planks banded with iron.

"This is Hronulf's chamber. He should be finished with his devotions by now." With that, the paladin turned and left Bronwyn alone in the hall.

This was it. She had waited for this moment for over twenty years—longed for it, worked for it. Suddenly she felt strangely reluctant to proceed. Muttering an imprecation, she lifted a hand and knocked.

Almost at once, the door swung open. A tall man, taller than Bronwyn by at least a head, stood in the portal. Although he was of an age when most men would be accounted elderly, he was still in fine trim, and he stood with the balanced poise of a warrior. Broad shoulders and powerful arms declared his prowess with the sword that hung at his hip, and he wore a tabard of white linen emblazoned in blue with the symbol of Tyr—a balanced scale, set upon the head of an upright warhammer. His hair was thick and iron gray, as were his mustache and neatly trimmed beard. Keen silver-gray eyes peered kindly at her from a ruddy, comely visage that wore its years exceedingly well.

Before Bronwyn could speak, the color drained from the paladin's face. He sagged and grasped the door lintel. Instinctively, Bronwyn reached out to steady him, but he quickly recovered himself, shaking off the moment of shock.

"Forgive me, child. For a moment you reminded me of someone I once knew."

"Who?" she asked. The word spilled out before she had time to consider.

"My wife," he said simply.

My mother, she thought.

The silence stretched between them as the paladin waited courteously for her to state her business. But Bronwyn's facile speech utterly deserted her. Finally the paladin spoke. "Surely, you did not come to listen to an old man's tales of the past. How may I help you, child?"

Bronwyn took a long breath. "Sir, I came from Waterdeep to speak with you. I have gone over what I wished to say many times in my mind, but that didn't seem to help. I don't know quite how to tell you. . . ."

"Simple words are best," he said. "A straight arrow flies truest."

The words stirred a memory in some distant corner of her mind. She had heard them before, and others like them. "I was raised in Amn as a slave, taken there when I was very young. I do not remember my age, or my village, or even my family's names. All that I carried with me was my given name and a small birthmark on my lower back that looks a bit like a red oak leaf. My name is Bronwyn."

The paladin turned so pale that for a moment Bronwyn thought he might collapse. She gently, but firmly pushed him back into the room and into a chair.

He gazed up at her for a long moment, his expression utterly incomprehensible. It occurred to Bronwyn that he might be testing her, as the guard at the fortress gate had done—the man who had found "no real evil" in her. Bronwyn decided that she could not bear and would not abide another such grudging acceptance.

Her chin came up and her shoulders squared. "I am told that you lost a child of my age, a child who bore a similar name and birthmark. I am told that I am she. If this is so, I will be content to leave this place with the truth. If I have been misinformed, I will seek my family elsewhere. Either way, I ask nothing from you. If you have any doubts about my intent, test me in whatever manner you see fit. Take the truth from my heart in fair exchange, for the truth I ask."

As she spoke, she studied the old knight's face. She might not have a paladin's god-given insight into the minds and hearts of others, but she possessed finely honed powers of observation and instincts that had been right more often than not. So she noted the slow return of color to Hronulf's face, and the return of light to his eyes. She dared to hope that simple shock, not suspicion, colored his silence.

Hronulf slowly rose to his feet. Bronwyn noticed that though his face was composed and his bearing tall and proud, one white-knuckled hand gripped the back of the chair as if for support—or, perhaps, as a tangible sign that he was not yet ready to let go of the "truth" he had believed for twenty years.

"Of your own will, you would step into the scales of Tyr's justice?" he murmured.

"I will."

He nodded thoughtfully and his grip on the chair eased a little. "None but the righteous would make such bold claims. I do not require such tests."

"But I do," Bronwyn said urgently. Until this moment, she had not fully realized how desperately she needed to know. "I have long heard that a paladin can discern truth. Will your god tell you if there is truth in the story that brought me here?"

"I can but ask." The paladin's eyes grew distant once more, as he sought in prayer a level of insight and enlightenment that only his god could give him.

Moments passed, long moments that were heavy with the weight of Bronwyn's twenty years of exile. She waited, scarcely breathing, until the unseen vision faded from Hronulf's eyes, and his gaze once again focused upon her. Bronwyn knew, before a word was spoken, what Tyr's answer had been.

"Little Bronwyn," Hronulf murmured, studying her with desperately hungry eyes. "Now that I see the truth of it, I understand that my heart knew you at once. You are the very image of . . . of your mother."

This both pleased and saddened Bronwyn. She lifted one hand to her cheek, as if seeking in her own face what she had lost. "I do not remember her."

Hronulf took a step forward, both hands outstretched. "My poor child. Can you ever forgive me for what you have endured?" he asked, his voice quavering, pleading. "The fault is mine, though I did not lightly let you go. When you were not found among the slain, I . . . I sought you for many months. I would never have given up . . . until the day I wept over the remains of a girl child that I believed to be my own."

His terrible guilt smote her heart, and she took both his hands in hers. "I don't blame you," she said hastily. "For many years I've been trying to find the truth of my past. There weren't many paths to follow, and every one ended against an alley wall. I make a living finding lost things, things that most people despair of finding. If I could not find my way back to my own past, how could you, who had every reason to believe your quest had ended, be expected to do better?"

Hronulf smiled faintly. "You have a good heart, child, your mother's heart."

"Tell me of her," she urged.

They sat down together, and the paladin began to speak of the past, slowly and with strange awkwardness. At first Bronwyn thought the source of the difficulty was the barrier formed by lost years, but soon she realized that the reason ran deeper still. Hronulf had been seldom at home, and thus he had few memories of her in the scant time they had been a family. He did not know her. She wondered if he could ever have known her better, even if the raid had never occurred.

Not much time passed before he ran out of remembrances. He rose, looking relieved to have some plan of action in mind. "Come," he said. "I will show you the castle."

*   *   *   *   *

Ebenezer's luck, which had been notably bad of late, took a happy turn. At just the right time, he had met up with a southbound caravan and arranged with its master to have the paladin's horse returned to the Halls of Justice at Waterdeep. It took some talking and some coin, but the dwarf parted company with the merchant satisfied that all would be done as he had asked. Ebenezer headed north with a clear conscience, his debt discharged. It seemed likely that sooner or later, the young man who was so all-fired fond of Tyr would end up at that god's temple and would there reunite with his lost steed. No harm done him, other than a bit of wear to his boot soles.

Ebenezer veered off the trade road into the foothills. The entrance to the Stoneshaft tunnels was not far off the road and so cleverly hidden that only a dwarf could see it. He found the place—a steep hillock surrounded by a dense stand of young pines—and ran his hands over the rocky wall until he found the subtle pattern in the stone. He put his shoulder to the rock door, heaving and grunting until it eased inward. He ducked quickly through the opening, which slid shut behind him with a solid thud.

He stood for a moment or two, giving his eyes a chance to adjust to the darkness and rubbing at his numb backside with both hands. He hadn't been on a horse for some time, and his legs and rump burned with fatigue. But he shrugged off the stiffness and took off down the tunnels at a steady, rolling run. Most humans Ebenezer knew thought of dwarves as slow and quick to tire, but any dwarf worth a pile of fingernail pairings could roll along at a smart pace for as long as he had to.

Ebenezer figured it was getting near to sunset by the time he reached the river. He strained his ears, trying to hear something, anything, over the infernal din of the rushing water. The closer he got to the clanhold, the more anxious he felt about his kin. Quickening his pace and ignoring the treachery of the wet, uneven path, he sprinted full out past several caverns and passageways toward the tunnel that led to the heart of the dwarven clanhold.

The smell hit him suddenly, twisting his stomach and sending his heart plummeting into his boots. There was no mistaking that smell; any dwarf who had ever raised an axe in battle knew it well. Coppery, heavy, strangely sweet, and utterly sickening—the smell of spilled blood turned black and dry, bodies gone cold.

Terrible, numbing dread swept through Ebenezer like a winter storm, robbing him of strength and will and forward motion. He skidded to a stop. A single keening cry burst from his throat—the first and last mourning he would allow himself before he knew the whole of it. He forced himself into a run while he could still trust his legs to carry him where he needed to go.

He stopped again at the entrance to the Hall of Ancestors, stunned by the destruction of a monument that had stood for untold centuries. The ancient stone dwarves had toppled and lay in broken pieces among the dwarves their fall had slain.

Ebenezer stooped by the nearest dwarf and clamped his jaw shut to bite off a cry. The Stoneshaft patriarch, his Da, had led the charge. The old dwarf had not been killed by the falling statues; that was horrifyingly clear. Stone dwarves did not wield swords and spears with such slow, cruel expertise.

Ebenezer lifted his gaze, blinking hard to clear his suddenly blurred vision. Several humans lay sprawled nearby, bearing the unmistakable marks of a dwarven axe. Ebenezer took some comfort in this. His father had not died easily, but he had died well.

He rose and wandered through the chamber, his rage building with every dwarf he identified—and growing hotter still with each dwarf that he could not. Ebenezer was no stranger to battle, but the carnage here was of a sort seldom seen. The stamp of unmistakable pleasure, of long and lingering evil, was upon each cold and tormented dwarf.

Ebenezer found more of the same inside the great hall. Not a single dwarf lived. Stoneshaft Hold had been decimated, and the bodies of his brutally slain kin left to molder in the empty halls.

Grief numbed him, mercifully slowing his wits and numbing his heart. He moved in a daze through the devastation, tending the dead, marking their names in his memory. Time slowed down, became utterly without meaning. His face was as set as granite, his eyes dry and hard as he gathered the bodies of kith and clan into a single grave.

Hours passed. In some dim corner of his mind, Ebenezer marked the time, and knew that far above him, a plump waxing moon rose over the Sword Mountains. But in this place, the dwarf knew only darkness and the terrible task before him. He did not stop for rest until all of Clan Stoneshaft had been decently laid to rest beneath a pile of mountain stone.

When the task was done, he slumped to the ground and

tried to put words to the nagging fear in the back of his mind.

The ruined face of young Frodwinner rose up in memory. Of all the Stoneshaft dwarves, he had died the hardest and best. He'd taken enough wounds to kill a trio of dwarves and kept on fighting. Seven humans and four half-orcs had fallen to his axe. Of course, Frodwinner had more to lose than nearly anyone else in the clan. He was just two days into a wedding feast, wed to the prettiest, feistiest dwarf maid in a hundred warrens. Frodwinner and Tarlamera should have had centuries of life before them. Frodwinner had been barely fifty. He was just a kid. Just a kid.

And with that lament, Ebenezer found words for his concern:

There had been no children among the slain.

This realization slammed into Ebenezer like a hobgoblin's fist. His first response was relief—like most dwarf clans, his had not been blessed by many children. He loved kids, loved every one of the rowdy little scamps. But if they were not here, where were they?

As the dwarf thought about this, he also realized that he had not accounted for several adult members of the clan, including some of his own near kin. His Da rested in the cairn, beside the cantankerous, beloved dwarf woman who had borne him nine stout children. Most of these offspring, Ebenezer's brothers and sisters, also slept beneath the stone. Tarlamera was not among them.

He sat upright. Why hadn't he realized that earlier? Tarlamera was the sibling closest to him in age and temperament. They'd fought their way through a happy childhood, and hers was the face he always sought first in a crowd of his kin. Why hadn't he looked for her and noted that she was not to be found?

Ebenezer had heard tell of people who got through rough spots by blocking out important things, not thinking about them until they were armed and ready, so to speak. Maybe that was what he was doing. Funny, but until now he would have called that sort of thing soft-headed.

But the time for protective denial was over. Ebenezer

began to sort through the grim facts, and a pattern became clear. Most of the clan's best fighters had been slain, as well as those who spent their days tending to the practical needs of the clan: hearth mothers, brewers, coopers, cobblers. All of the elderly dwarves were dead, and the few that had had the odd infirmity. The missing members were those who had special skills—skills that no one could master quite as well as could a dwarf. Their best miners were gone, including Tarlamera, whose instincts for the stone were so keen Ebenezer suspected she could smell deposits of ore and gemstones from fifty paces. The best gem workers were missing, and the finest smiths. A few of the females of breeding age. The children.

In short, everyone who had value in some distant slave market.

Rage, cold and fierce and all-consuming, rose like bile in the dwarf's throat. There was yet another thing he'd conveniently blotted out: his own capture by a passel of Zhents. Suddenly he realized the true and devastating nature of his fear.

Slavery.

Ebenezer hauled himself to his feet, grabbed some weapons, and left behind the graveyard that had been his home. He struck out for a secret tunnel—a steep, curving passage that led up to the stronghold some humans had built on the mountain above a few decades past.

Knights, they called themselves. They were a bunch of smug-faced meddlers who kept themselves busy tidying up the area of trolls and bugbears and so forth, reminding Ebenezer of dwarf grannies fussing about the clanhold, forever straightening up the furniture and dusting off the whatnots.

If there were answers to be found, Ebenezer was certain that the nest of those troll-hunting, minding-the-world's-business, pain-in-the-back-of-the-lap humans was a reasonable place to start looking.

* * * * *

Bronwyn followed her father down the tower stairs back into the bailey. The first signs of real animation crept into Hronulf's voice as he described the fortress to her, its history, its defenses, and the good work that the paladins did for travelers who passed by. He stopped here and there to chat with the servants and exchanged bluff greetings with the other knights. To each knight, he introduced her pointedly and proudly as his lost daughter. Oddly enough, that did little to warm Bronwyn's heart or make her feel wanted. It was almost as if he felt a need to justify her presence here. But Bronwyn noticed the deep affection and respect that all the fortress inhabitants showed their commander. Those who knew Hronulf, clearly held him in highest regard. This reminded her of the knight who had sent her here.

"I met Sir Gareth Cormaeril in Waterdeep," she said. "He sends his regards."

Hronulf's face lit up. "You have seen him? And he knows who you are? This news must have brought him great joy!"

"I told him my name, but he did not seem to connect me with you in any way, not even when I told him I was seeking you out in hope that you might have information about my lost family" Bronwyn said. "He commented that you had lost family, too, and would most likely be willing to give me whatever aid you could, but he did not put the pieces together."

"Sir Gareth was a great knight and a good friend," Hronulf stated. His eyes suddenly went bleak. "It was he who found you, or so he thought—a child slain when goblins overran a southbound caravan. Perhaps his affection blinded him, then and now. He was afraid for me, so great was my grief. Although beholding your dead child is a terrible thing, not knowing what has become of her is much worse. Having settled my mind and his that you were dead, he was not looking for Bronwyn Caradoon when he beheld your face."

"That's possible," she admitted, though she was disturbed at the possibility that she might have been found, had not Sir Gareth been so quick to pronounce her dead. Something else occurred to her. "Did Gareth know my mother?"

"Oh, yes. Gwenidale was a woman of good family, and her

brother was a paladin, Gareth's comrade and mine. He fell before his twenty-third year, but he was a great knight. But it has been many years since any living man has gazed upon fair Gwenidale's face. Do not fault Gareth in this matter." Hronulf smiled faintly. "He and I are aged men. The eyes fail, and even the fondest memories do not always come to our command."

As they talked, they continued their tour of the fortress. Hronulf led her through the chapel, and pointed to the stairs that led up on either side of the back wall. They climbed the stairs on the right and emerged on the walkway that encircled the wall. Her father's pride in his domain, his obvious concern for all those under his care, made one thing perfectly clear to Bronwyn. Thornhold was truly his home, not the village she could barely remember. This place, these men, had always been first with him.

That made her curious and angrier than she liked to admit. She decided to prod a bit. "There are no women here," she observed.

"A traveler, from time to time," Hronulf said. "I believe that there is a female hire-sword with the caravan currently under hospitality."

"So the knights don't bring their families here." That bothered her deeply, especially in light of her own history.

"Few knights have families," the paladin said, then hesitated. "It is a hard life, and full of danger. There are often matters of fealty—sworn service to god or king—that must be discharged. Some men who live to their thirtieth year and beyond marry. Most do not."

"You did," she pressed. "You had a family and left us in a small forest village." The words came out like a challenge. Bronwyn wished she could have been more diplomatic, but her need was too great. She needed to hear some word of explanation, some reason for the horror that had destroyed her family and shaped her life.

Hronulf did not answer right away. He paused before the door of a long stone building that spanned the distance between the two towers, the roof rising up steeply to meet in the center in a soaring arch. Through the open door, Bronwyn could see the raised altar with the scales of justice above. Light filtered in through windows set high on the stone walls, falling in thin, golden slants on the knights who knelt or prostrated themselves in prayer.

"It was my duty to marry," Hronulf said simply. "The bloodline of Samular must be carried on. Which reminds me, there are family matters of which we must speak. Come."

That was no answer at all. Hoping that he would offer better, Bronwyn followed him back up to the tower. He closed the door and bolted it. This struck Bronwyn as a strange precaution, given their secure surroundings. She was even more puzzled when he took an ancient sheet of parchment from a small, locked wooden chest. "Can you read?" he asked.

"In several languages, both modern and ancient."

The response seemed natural enough to her, but it seemed to displease her father. "Such pride is not seemly."

"Not pride," she said with complete honesty. "Necessity. I'm a merchant. And, I suppose, a scholar of sorts. I find lost artifacts, which means I have to study a wide variety of materials and speak to many sorts of people to find what I'm looking for."

"A merchant."

He spoke the words in a tone that could have served just as well if he'd said, "a hobgoblin." Bronwyn suddenly knew how a cat felt when its back went up. She swallowed the tart response that came quickly to her tongue and reached for the parchment.

The style of the script was old, the ink faded and blurred, but Bronwyn got the gist of it well enough. The fortress of Thornhold, and most of the mountain upon which it stood, did not belong to the Holy Order of the Knights of Samular. It was the property of the Caradoon family.

"There is a copy of this writ of succession in the Herald's Holdfast," Hronulf said. "Upon my death, you must make provision for the fortress and see that it is used as it has been for these many centuries." He looked keenly at her. "Are you wed?"

"Not even close," she said dryly.

"Chaste?"

Under any other circumstances, she would have answered that question with derisive laughter. Now she merely felt puzzlement, edged with the beginnings of anger. "I don't see what that has to do with this discussion," she said stiffly.

Hronulf apparently heard in this his answer, and not the one he'd been hoping for. An expression of grave disappointment crossed his face. He sighed, then his jaw firmed with apparent resolve. He rose and went to his writing table. Seating himself, he took up a quill. "I will write you a letter of introduction," he said, dipping the quill into an inkwell. "Take it to Summit Hall and give it to Laharin Goldbeard of Tyr. He commands this place and will find a suitable match for you."

Bronwyn's jaw dropped. She dug one hand into her hair and shook her head as if to clear it. "I don't believe this."

"The line of Samular must continue," Hronulf said earnestly. He blew on the writing to dry it, then set the parchment aside. "You are the last of my five children, so the responsibility falls to you. You seem well suited to it. You are young, comely, and in apparent health."

This was more than Bronwyn could take. "Next I suppose you'll be telling me that children are my duty and destiny."

"And so they are."

Bronwyn had a sudden, sharp feeling of empathy for a brood mare. She rose abruptly. "I am tired, father. Are there guest quarters in this fortress that will not be too sullied by a woman's presence?"

He rose with her, and his visage softened somewhat as he studied her. "You are overwrought. Forgive me. I gave you too much to think about too soon."

"I'm adaptable," she assured him, wondering even as she spoke if perhaps she had finally come up against the edges of her flexibility.

"We will talk more in the morning. There are secrets known only to the descendants of Samular that you must hear. You must understand your family responsibilities."

This time, Bronwyn could not hold back a small, grim

smile. Until this moment, she had always been fond of irony. To Hronulf of Tyr, family responsibility apparently meant the continuation of the bloodline of Samular. Yet in doing his duty, he had left his family vulnerable.

She was not even the slightest bit tempted to point this out to her father. So vast was the gulf between them that Hronulf was unlikely to ever see this matter as she did. If she married well and produced sons to follow Tyr, he would be content. Nothing else she could do, nothing else she *was,* could possibly matter. In any way that truly counted, she was as alone now as she had been before she'd entered Thornhold.

Bronwyn reminded herself that she had never really expected to have a family. She had merely sought to learn about her past. If she could think of this meeting with her father as a means to that end, then maybe the ache in her chest would subside.

So she took the scroll Hronulf handed her and the small leather book that he bid her read in order to learn more of the family's creed and purpose. Bronwyn still had a thousand questions, but the answers seemed finally within her grasp. The answers, that is, to all questions but one:

Why was the knowledge of her past, this fulfillment of her dreams, not nearly enough?

* * * * *

Elsewhere in Thornhold the dinner hour was ending and the Knights of Samular scattered, each to his preferred rest and ease. One aging paladin, once known throughout eastern Faerûn as Randolar the Bear, made his way up a narrow stair to his chamber. He retrieved a book from his modest bed-chamber, a fine tome brimming with exciting tales told with admirable brevity, and betook himself to an even smaller room—a tidy latrine set into the thick wall of the keep. There he ascended the throne of the common man and happily settled down to read.

So engrossed did he become in the tale that, at first, the muted curses seemed nothing but echoes of the vanquished villain's ire. It came to him, slowly, that the voices were real, and that they were coming from the midden shoot below him. After a puzzled moment, Randolar realized that someone was climbing up the interior of the keep wall, an invader determined enough to risk the sort of unpleasant reception he had just received. It also occurred to him that since this was not the only privy in the keep, there might be other, similarly determined invaders.

The old paladin leaped to his feet and dragged in air to fuel a shout of alarm. Before he could utter a sound, the privy's wooden seat flew up and slammed against the wall with furious force. Randolar spun just as the head and shoulders of a black-bearded man, grim-faced and covered with the leavings that coated the midden, emerged from the shoot.

Propping himself on one elbow, the invader lifted a small, loaded crossbow. His grimy finger jerked at the trigger. The bolt tore into Randolar's chest, and he slid slowly down the wall onto the cold, stone floor. His last thought was deep mortification that a knight of Tyr should die so, his last alarm unsounded and his breeches tangled about his ankles.

*   *   *   *   *

On a hilltop not far away, Dag Zoreth stood on the watchtower of a conquered outpost, his eyes fixed on the fortress. All was in readiness. His minions had done well. Even Sir Gareth had delivered above expectations. According to Dag's scouts, a young woman had entered the fortress several hours ago. His reunion with his lost family promised to be more complex and fulfilling than he'd dared to hope.

And it would happen soon. By now, his advance soldiers should have made their way up the unprotected midden chutes. They were handpicked men, among them some of the most skilled and silent assassins known to the Zhentarim, and the best archers. It was their task to quietly slip into the fortress. Three assassins would work their way up to the winch room, a small upper-floor chamber where the machinery that lifted the portcullis was housed. The others would take out the men who walked the walls and watched from the high turrets, and work their way to the gate.

Dag was suddenly distracted by the sensation of cold fire that stabbed at his left side—painful, yet not entirely unpleasant. He slipped his hand into the leather bag that hung at his belt and removed from it the source of his discomfort, a small globe like the one he had given Sir Gareth.

The face in it was dusky gray, vaguely elven in appearance, and seamed with scars earned over long decades of service to evil. The half-drow assassin gave a single, curt nod.

Dag smiled and slipped the globe back into his bag.

"They have secured the winch room and are ready to raise the portcullis," he said to his captain, a bald, black-bearded man who was more than a head taller than Dag and nearly twice his breadth. What Captain Yemid lacked in strategic innovation, he made up in sheer brute force and the corresponding ability to pass along orders and make them stick. "Sound the charge," Dag commanded.

Yemid thrust a ham-sized fist into the air. Instantly one of the men lifted a curved horn to his lips and winded the signal for attack. A score of heavy cavalry thundered toward the fortress, huge war-horses, barded with plate armor and bearing fully armored warriors. Behind them came the next wave, another twenty mounted soldiers who would chase down and slay any who managed to escape. Finally came the infantry, fifty men, well armed and well trained, fortified with the battle frenzy that came in the wake of Dag Zoreth's Cyric-granted spells.

It was not a large force, but it would more than suffice. Thirteen men were already in the fortress, killers as silent and deadly as ferrets hunting aging roosters and nesting doves. Dag only hoped there would be enough killing for his men to sate their bloodlust; if not, some of them were likely to turn on each other, seizing the opportunities of battle confusion to settle some old insult or petty rivalry. It was not an uncommon occurrence among the Zhentarim.

A senseless waste, Dag mused as he kicked his horse into a run. It was better to hoard anger like treasure, building and nurturing it until it became a weapon, one that could be unleashed to good effect.

Nearby, one of the soldiers fell from his horse, an arrow protruding from his chest. Good. There was still some fight in the paladins. To minimize his own risk, Dag leaned low over his horse's neck as the steed galloped past the infantry. He kept his eyes fixed on the great wooden door in the fortress wall.

The portcullis rose in a series of quick, sharps jerks as the assassins winched it up. The knights of Darkhold swept toward the wooden door, long spears leveled before them.

Four of them struck the gate at nearly the same instant. The two halves of the wooden door burst inward, a gratifying testament to the invaders' success in throwing the bars. Zhentarim fighters poured into the breached wall. Dag spurred his horse on viciously, determined to enter the fortress before the fighting was done.

* * * * *

In Hronulf's tower chamber, Bronwyn was the first to hear the alarm. She poised, her hand on the door, and then spun back to face her father. "That horn. I know that signal," she said grimly.

Hronulf nodded and strode for the door. "Zhentarim. You stay here—I must go to the walls."

Bronwyn seized his arm, all thoughts of anger forgotten. "It's too late for that. Listen."

The faint sound of battle seeped through the thick stone and stout oak. Hronulf's eyes widened. "They are inside the fortress!"

She nodded. Her mind raced as she tried and discarded possible plans. "Is there a back way out of here?"

The paladin smiled grimly and drew his sword. "Not for me. Thornhold is my command. I will defend it or die."

Before Bronwyn could respond, the first crashing assault struck the chamber door. The oak panels buckled, and even the iron bands that bound them bulged inward.

Hronulf thrust his sword back into its sheath and took a richly carved band of gold from his hand. He seized Bronwyn's left hand and slipped the ring onto her index finger. Though it had fit the paladin's large hand just a moment before, it slid into place on her slim finger and stayed there, comfortably snug.

"Listen well," he said, "for the door will not hold much longer. This ring is a family heirloom of great power. It cannot fall into the hands of the Zhentarim. You must protect it at all cost."

"But—"

"There is no time to explain," he said, taking her shoulders and pushing her firmly toward the wall. He reached around her and pressed hard on one of the tightly fitted stones. A passage opened in the seemingly solid wall, a rounded, dark hole just above the floor. He gestured to the opening. "You must go," he insisted.

Bronwyn wrenched herself away from him and dived for the pair of crossed swords displayed on the wall. She tugged one free and brandished it at the buckling, cracking door.

"I just found you," she said from between clenched teeth. "I'm not leaving."

The paladin's smile was both sad and proud. "You are truly my daughter," he said. For a moment their eyes met, and it seemed to Bronwyn that he was actually seeing her—*her,* not a reflection of her long-dead mother or a conduit for the bloodline of Samular—for the first time. "Bronwyn, my daughter," he repeated with a touch of wonderment. "Because of who you are, you will do as you must. As will I."

With that, he knocked the sword from her hand and seized her by the back of her jacket. Spinning her around, he grabbed her belt with his other hand and lifted her from the ground. As if he were a half-orc bouncer and she a rowdy patron at a tavern, he hauled her back for the traditional Dock Ward Drunk Toss. She hit the smooth stone floor, skidded on her stomach, and disappeared head first into the tunnel.

Beyond the hole was a steep, smooth incline. Down she

slid, the wind whistling in her ears as she picked up speed.
But even so, she heard the solid thump of the stone wall's clo-
sure, the terrible splintering of the wooden door, and a deep,
ringing voice singing out to Tyr as the paladin began his final
battle.

* * * * *

Dag Zoreth swept through the door into the bailey and
leaped from his horse. Darting a look around, he saw that
most of the fighting was over. Many of the fortress servants
had been slain. Their bodies were lying limp and sodden in
heaps, like so many beheaded chickens ready for plucking.
Soldiers were rounding up the survivors and forcing them to
their knees in a single precise row. A pair of priests worked
their way down the line, casting the spells needed to discern
character and allegiance.

This was an unusual precaution—usually castle servants
were considered plunder, regarded as simple fools eager to
save their skins and their livelihoods by serving whatever
lord controlled the fortress. Dag knew that his priests considered the testing process a nuisance and a waste, but he
thought otherwise. The influence of a paladin was insidious.
On his orders, any man who displayed too strong or steadfast
an alliance with the forces of righteousness was to be slain.

In Dag's opinion, it was a highly sensible precaution.

His eyes fell on Yemid, on foot now and in rapid pursuit of
a retreating servant. Dag caught the captain's arm. "Where is
the woman?"

Yemid blew out a sharp, frustrated breath. "Gone, my lord.
The men have searched the fortress from dungeon to turret."

Dag's brows drew down into a deep, angry frown. He had
not considered the possibility that his sister might possess
magic. She was said to be a merchant, not a mage. But he
knew as well as any that magical trinkets were available, provided one had the gold to trade for them. Even so, most
devices he knew of had limited range and power. If she had
escaped in this manner, she had not gone far. "Send out

patrols, range out as far as needs be. Find her!"

Yemid spun and bellowed out the orders. A dozen men took to their horses and galloped from the gates.

"And the keep commander?" Dag persisted, determined not to be cheated entirely. "Where is he?"

The captain hesitated, then nodded toward the line of Zhentish bodies neatly laid out, prepared for cremation, resurrection, or undead animation, as suited Dag's whim. "There's some of his handiwork," he said. "They pinned the old man down in a tower chamber. Even so, it took some doing to drop him."

"Drop? Him?"

The deadly chill in those words stole the color from the huge soldier's face. "I swear to you, Lord Zoreth, the man was alive when I saw him. He took a wound, though. Looked serious." He tossed aside the spiked cudgel he liked to use for in-close fighting, and turned his back to the furious priest. "I'll take you to him."

Dag followed the soldier to the back of the fortress, up winding stairs to a tower room in the keep. A pair of guards bookended the shattered door, barring the entrance with crossed spears. Dag took note of their small wounds, their slashed tunics, and the bright marks on the chain mail beneath where a keen sword had slashed or stabbed. These men were numbered among the elite of Darkhold, fighters hand chosen by the Pereghost himself, yet even they had not remained unscathed by Hronulf's blade.

A small, tight smile stretched Dag Zoreth's lips. It was rare that childhood memories lived up to their luster. His perception of his father's battle prowess clearly proved to be an exception.

"The paladin commander lives?" he demanded.

"Aye," one of the guards said grudgingly. "On your orders."

Dag nodded in satisfaction. "Step aside."

The guards hesitated, exchanging a glance that mingled foreboding and indecision. "I would be doing less than my duty if I didn't warn you," ventured the man who had already spoken. "Several good soldiers died underestimating that old man."

"So noted." Dag's eyes narrowed in menace. "Fortunately for me, I am not a *good* soldier, but a priest of Cyric. Do you understand me, soldier?"

The threat was a potent one. Both men saluted smartly and moved aside. Dag stalked past them and into the room, dark head held high, his black and purple cape flowing behind him like a storm cloud. He was exhilarated rather than daunted by the prospect of facing the tall, powerful paladin who even in his late years could dispatch a half score of Darkhold's best. Perhaps he might still have to look up at Hronulf of Tyr, physically, but he would do so, for the first time in his life, from a position of power. There was an irony in this that pleased him.

But Dag was robbed of this small triumph. The father he had come so far to vanquish was no longer a warrior to be hated and feared, but an old, dying man.

Hronulf of Tyr sat stiffly upright on a chair. He held his sword out before him, the point resting on the floor, one hand on the hilt, in a manner that recalled a monarch and his staff. His other hand was fisted, and driven into a gaping wound just below his ribs.

Dag Zoreth turned slowly to his guide. "It is as you said. He was gravely wounded, against my express orders."

The captain nodded and swallowed hard. The knowledge of his coming death was written clearly in his eyes.

But Dag shook his head. "I do not kill bearers of bad news, either for entertainment or to demonstrate that I am a man to be feared. Good messengers are hard to find, and good captains even harder. You've served me well, Yemid, and I will award you accordingly. But if you fail in the assignment I am about to give you, you *will* taste my wrath."

"Of course, Lord Zoreth!"

"Go find the man who dealt this wound and do likewise to him. But first, stake him to the ground. Gut him so that he dies slowly, so that his screams will call hungry ravens to help finish the task."

Again Yemid swallowed hard—bile, if the sudden greenish tinge to his skin was any indication. "All will be done as you say." He saluted and left the room with a haste that spoke more of grateful self-preservation than of any real zest for his duty.

Dag dismissed the guards and shut what was left of the door. When he was alone with his captive, he folded his arms and stared down at him coolly.

"I am a priest," he said in a coldly controlled tone that revealed none of his wrath, or his elation. "I could heal you. I could stop that pain instantly. I could even offer you protection from the soldiers who stormed your fortress, or a quick death fighting, if you so prefer."

Hronulf lifted his eyes to Dag's pale, narrow face. "You have nothing that I could desire."

"That is not strictly true." Dag made a quick, complex gesture with both hands, unleashing a spell he had prepared. An illusion rose in the air between them, the glittering image of an ornate golden ring. "Unless I have been misinformed, you want this very much. And it is mine."

The paladin's eyes blazed. "You have no right to it!"

"Again, not true. I have every right to the ring." Dag lifted his chin. "I am your second-born son, whom you named Brandon in honor of my mother's father. I took the ring from the hand of my brother Byorn, after he fell in a battle he should never have had to fight."

"Lies!"

"Cannot a paladin discern truth? Test me, and see if there is any deceit in my words."

Hronulf fixed a searching gaze on the priest. His eyes went bleak as the truth came to him, but his face hardened. His gaze pointedly swept Dag's black and purple vestments, then fixed upon the symbol engraved on his medallion. "I have no son, Cyricist. My son Byorn died a hero, fighting against the Zhentarim."

Even though he had expected them, these words struck Dag's heart with painful force. "Did he really? Have you never wondered how the closely held secret of your family's village reached Zhentarim ears? Or for that matter, how a Zhentilar band managed to unravel the secrets of this fortress? Look, and wonder no more!"

Dag snatched the black globe from its hiding place and
held it before his father's eyes. The purple fire burned high,
casting unholy light upon the face of Hronulf's oldest and
most trusted friend.

"How may I serve you, Lord Zoreth?" inquired the image of
Sir Gareth Cormaeril.

Shock, disbelief, and sudden bleak acceptance flashed
through Hronulf's silver-gray eyes. He lifted his gaze to Dag's
coldly vindictive face. "Gareth was a good man. To corrupt a
paladin is a most grievous evil and a black stain on the souls
of all who had a hand in his downfall. You will not find
another here who will have aught to do with you, Cyricist."

With great effort, Dag kept his face neutral. "I've come to
claim my heritage and meet my sister," he said. "Where is
she?"

"This is a fortress of the Knights of Samular. No women
reside here."

"Finally, you speak something resembling truth," Dag said
coldly. "But let us not play foolish games. We saw a young
woman enter this fortress. We did not see her leave."

"Nor will you. She is beyond your reach, Cyricist."

Dag merely shrugged. "For now, perhaps, but the day will
come, and soon, when the three rings of Samular are reunited
in the hands of three of his bloodline. Tell me what that
means. What power will that unleash?"

"It matters not. You do not wear the ring. You cannot."

"Perhaps not, but my daughter *can,* and she will do as I tell
her. Soon my sister will do the same. As long as I command
the power, it matters not whose hands wield it." The priest
unfolded his arms. He held out one hand and took a step forward. "It is time for you to bequeath me my inheritance. The
second ring, if you please!"

Pain flared in the paladin's eyes as his fallen son
approached, for the evil of Cyric burned men such as Hronulf
as surely and painfully as dragonfire. Dag Zoreth saw this,
expected it. Nevertheless, he kicked the regal sword out of
Hronulf's grasp and snatched up the paladin's hand between
both of his own.

"No ring. The other hand, then," he demanded. In defiant response, Hronulf raised his bloodied fist and spread the fingers so that the priest could see that there was no ring upon them.

Dag's face darkened as anger rose in him. "Once, when I was no more than seven winters of age, I hid such a ring for safekeeping in a hole gashed into an oak, rather than have it taken by the raiders. Could it be possible that you have done much the same?"

"I do not have the ring," Hronulf stated.

"We shall see."

Dag did not doubt that the paladin spoke the truth. He knew that by all that was reasonable, he should find a way to heal the man and question him, but Dag was beyond reason. Rage, grief, the madness of his life of terrible isolation—a torrent of emotions too many and complex to catalogue or understand—tore him over the edge. In one swift motion, he plunged his own hand deep into the paladin's wound.

A roar of agony and outrage tore from Hronulf's throat. Dag suspected that the touch of a priest of Cyric caused pain greater than the paladin would know if a dwarven smith quenched a red-hot iron in his belly. This pleased Dag, but it was not quite enough to sate him.

Dag held his father's anguished eyes as he began to chant the words of a spell. The god Cyric heard his priest and granted the fell magic. Dag's frail fingers suddenly became as sharp and powerful as mithral knives. Up they tore, through walls of muscle and flesh, and closed surely around the paladin's beating heart.

With one quick jerk, Dag Zoreth pulled the heart out through the wound and showed it to the dying paladin. Then, just as quickly, he threw the heart into the hearth fire.

Dag Zoreth spun on his heel and stalked from the room, still chanting softly. The last sounds Hronulf of Tyr heard were the hissing, sputtering death of his own heart and the voice of his lost son, cursing him in Cyric's name.

Seven

The sounds of battle faded swiftly as Bronwyn plummeted down the steeply sloping shaft. Down she slid, picking up speed as she went.

Dimly she realized that the tunnel was carved into the thick wall of the keep and that she had fallen down what was a nearly vertical drop. She wrapped her arms over her head and steeled herself for whatever would come at the bottom of the shaft.

But the tunnel curved suddenly, sliding her into what seemed to be a spiraling arc. She suspected that the tunnel was sweeping down through the curved wall, but she could not be certain. Balance and sense of direction had abandoned her, swept aside by the speed of her headlong slide. There was no time to consider her situation, to plan or even to react. She had no choices, no options, but to surrender to the force that held her in its grip. This she understood without words or even conscious thought, and the understanding raised her frustration into simmering rage. Was there nothing in her life, nothing at all, over which she had any control?

Suddenly Bronwyn realized that the tunnel had widened. She no longer felt the walls rushing past her, brushing her

along one side and then the other. And she no longer felt the
ripple of the closely fitted stones beneath her. The floor over
which she careened was still smooth but seemingly of solid
stone.

She was inside the mountain now, Bronwyn realized, and
still falling.

Her speed hadn't lessened much, but at least she had some
room to maneuver. She wrenched herself to one side, tucking
her knees up against her chest and then kicking out as hard
as she could. Neither her outstretched hands nor her kicking
feet managed to graze a wall, but stretching herself out full
length had some effect. Her wild slide began to slow. Bronwyn
dared to hope that the ride was almost over.

Just then she hit another curve. Her weight shifted, sending her into a spin. Completely out of control now, Bronwyn
tumbled and rolled. She flailed about wildly, seeking something, anything, to hold onto that might halt her wild ride.
There was nothing; the stone floor and walls were smooth and
sheer. She was grateful for that. If the tunnel had been rough,
she would have been torn and battered past recognition, but
at the moment, she would almost welcome a boulder in her
path if it would stop her precipitous slide.

Then, suddenly, one was there—or at least, something
that closely resembled a boulder. She caught a glimpse of it,
silhouetted against some faint, distant light far beyond. She
threw her arms over her head to ward her face, and then
plunged headfirst into a hard, rounded wall.

Fortunately for Bronwyn, the "wall" had some give to it. A
startled *oof!* wheezed out, and strong, stubby arms and legs
thrashed about in a brief, desperate attempt to hold position
on the steep incline. For just a moment, Bronwyn grappled
with her unseen "rescuer" as they both teetered on the edge of
a fall. They lost the battle, and the slide resumed in a tangle
of arms and legs and a flurry of gruff-voiced and exceedingly
earthy curses.

The tunnel began to level out, and Bronwyn slowly skidded
and spun to a stop. She had no idea where she was, but at
least there was a bit of light—a soft, greenish glow, probably

due to the phosphoric lichens that grew in some underground caverns. Bronwyn lay flat on her back, willing the whirling shapes and colors to sort themselves out into images she could use. With one hand she groped for her knife, in case she needed to defend herself against what she could not yet see.

A few paces away, Ebenezer groaned and rolled up onto his knees. He hurt from beard to boots, but his belly had definitely taken the worst of it. Physical pain was something he knew, something he could handle. Compared to the agonizing grief of his clan's destruction, a few aches and pains was almost a relief. A distraction. So was the anger that welled up when his eyes settled on the small, disheveled woman sprawled out on the stone floor of the cavern.

Ebenezer rose to his feet and staggered over to the dazed human. "Well, are you gonna lie there all day?" he demanded in a querulous voice.

She opened her eyes and squinted in the direction of his voice. Her head bobbed around a bit, as if she were trying to peer through a swirling haze.

"A dwarf," she muttered, and her eyes drifted closed again. "No wonder I thought I'd run into a boulder."

"You weren't far wrong," Ebenezer said in a tight, rumbling growl, "only boulders generally don't go taking revenge when they're attacked."

That got her attention. Her eyes popped open, and she pulled a long knife out of a sheath attached to one side of her belt. She hauled herself onto her feet, looking so wildly unsteady that Ebenezer confidently waited for her to fall. She wobbled a mite, but stayed up. Dropping to a respectable crouch, she held her knife in a practiced, blade-down grip.

A fight, then. That was fine with Ebenezer. He pulled from his belt the hammer he'd taken from Frodwinner's cold, clenched fist.

"You're wrong. I didn't attack you," the woman stated as she began to circle around him.

He turned with her, rubbing his aching belly. "Yeah? What would *you* call it?"

"Falling."

Despite his anger, Ebenezer had to admit that there was something to that. When humans wanted to bombard someone, they didn't generally use their own bodies as missiles. Ebenezer granted that this human might not have deliberately halted his process up to the fortress, but he still had ample justification for wrath. His clanmates had been slain or captured. Ebenezer would kill any Zhent he saw in Stoneshaft tunnels, starting with this one.

"Falling, eh?" Ebenezer echoed bitterly. "Get ready to fall a mite further. I'm-a gonna send you and all your kind straight to the Abyss."

He circled her, measuring her height and balance and stance. Humans, in his experience, were fairly predictable. When they saw a hammer or axe coming at them, most of them instinctively ducked. But it seemed that their instincts didn't take into reckoning the measure of a dwarf's height and reach. Ebenezer noticed that oftentimes all they managed to do was lean into the coming blow. Aim at the shoulder, and he'd get the head. A good deal, by his measure.

He lashed out, swinging the hammer in a high, side-sweeping blow.

But this human didn't respond as Ebenezer had anticipated. She dropped flat to the cave floor, rolled in the opposite direction of his hammer swing, and came up behind him. Her knife slashed across the seat of his leather breeches.

He whirled at her, one hand clutching at the sudden, stinging breeze. "You've fought dwarves before," he observed coldly. That confirmed his suspicions. Not many humans took on a dwarf, not unless they had a powerful personal grudge or a bunch of friends close at hand. Judging by the devastation of the clanhold, she had a big bunch of friends.

The woman danced back a few paces. Her big-eyed gaze darted around the cavern as if searching for a means of escape. "I've known some dwarves, that's all." She lifted one eyebrow and gave him a small, knowing smile. "One of them, I knew very well."

Her meaning was unmistakable, but Ebenezer wasn't buying that. Humans and dwarves did very little cavorting, and no serious courting to speak of. "Bah!" he scoffed. "What would a dwarf want with the likes of you?"

She proceeded to tell him, in detail so vivid that he was certain his cheeks were as red as his beard. Ebenezer liked a good tall tale as much as the next dwarf, but he was in no mood to swap boasts with a murderous Zhent wench. He cut her off with a quick advance, followed by a series of hammer-swings that kept her dodging and retreating for several long moments.

"You're quick," he gave her, when they both paused for breath. "But trying to distract me just ain't going to work!"

"No?" The woman smirked and lunged forward with a knife feint.

Ebenezer leaned back away from the blade. She sprang at him before he could right himself. He did his best to bring the hammer up and around, but she was already in too close.

Her weight slammed into him—a pretty good hit for such a scrawny thing, but Ebenezer was used to harder hits, and he didn't expect to go down. He wouldn't have, except for the large stone right behind him. Seems that he had been a mite distracted, after all. Never saw the rock. It hit the back of his knees, which buckled and folded on him. Ebenezer toppled back, much to his mortification.

The woman went down with him, writhing and scratching and spitting mad, impossible to hit in so close and just generally as hard to hold as a trout. Little and puny she might be, but she fought with a fury that would have had Tarlamera's cats sitting up and taking notice.

Embarrassed now as well as angry, Ebenezer wanted nothing more than to be finished with this. He palmed the stone floor in search of his hammer. Nothing. He cast a look to one side—and hollered when the damn female sank her teeth into his exposed ear. The weapon lay well out of reach. Ebenezer swore and shoved the two-legged she-cat away. He scrambled to his feet and then dived for the hammer.

The woman spat blood and leaped after him. Her arms wrapped around his ankles. Down he went, flopping onto his already abused belly. His chin hit the stone with a mind-numbing crack. Worse, his outstretched fingers fell short of the weapon's handle.

She scrambled over his back and grabbed the hammer, then flung it away as far as she could. Ebenezer heard the crack of mithral on stone, then the slithering, metallic slide down the steep bank into the river.

That was one blow too many for him. Ebenezer bucked once, easily throwing her off. He staggered to his feet and stabbed one stubby finger at her in furious accusation.

"Now you're starting to get me riled," he bellowed, with typical dwarven understatement.

The human was already on her feet, circling again, those big eyes all wild looking and wisps of her brown hair sticking up every which way. It occurred to Ebenezer, briefly, that she looked almost as angry and crazed and grief-ravaged as he felt.

"Getting *riled*, are you?" she gritted out. "Then I suppose it won't make much difference if I do *this*—"

She leaped at him, cat-quick, and fisted both her hands in his long red beard. Ebenezer yowled in pain and fury and outraged dwarven dignity.

But the wench wasn't done with him yet. She leaped up, yanking back hard on his beard as she tucked up her knees and then kicked out, planting her booted feet squarely into his belly. She went down onto her back, dragging Ebenezer down after her. His hands braced out to catch himself when he fell, partly by instinct and partly because he didn't much like the idea of wiping squashed human off his tunic.

Things didn't quite work out that way. The woman hit the floor first and kicked her feet up and out. Ebenezer felt the cavern shift weirdly, and his boots described a fast arc over his head. Over he went, flipping like an oat cake on a griddle. He soared over the woman and landed hard on his backside.

Quick hands swept his beard up past his face, crossed, then pulled back down. Before his head crashed to the stone, Ebenezer felt a quick, strangling tug. Disbelief coursed through him, along with a fresh wave of anger. The woman had the stones to try to strangle him with his own beard!

Ebenezer struggled to his feet, dragging the stubborn woman up with him. He twisted this way and that, but she clung to him like a burr on a mule and only tightened her grip. His lungs began to burn, and his vision turned dark around the edges. The pounding of his own heart grew until the roaring in his ears thundered and rolled like the ding-blasted sea.

This was *not* the sort of death that would earn him a place in the hall of heroes. Determined not be brought down in this ignominious fashion, Ebenezer staggered over to the cavern wall. If he could get there before he fell, if he could slam her up against the stone a few times, maybe he could break her grip.

He was almost there when her stranglehold suddenly loosened and her weight slid down his back. Ebenezer dragged in a ragged breath and dug his fingers beneath the suddenly slack strands of his beard. He started to pull, but stopped suddenly when he saw what she had seen.

"Stones," he muttered in a voice raw from near strangulation.

*   *   *   *   *

The conquest of Thornhold was complete. Dag Zoreth walked through the fortress reviewing the work his men had made of the job.

They had certainly been thorough. Only a few of the servants remained alive. The man who kept and butchered the pigs and chickens, for instance, the brewer, a few of the kitchen staff. Most of the fortress's inhabitants had been too infected by the paladins whom they had served and were even now turning to ash on the massive bier.

Smoke rose in dark, fetid clouds from beyond the fortress walls. The slain paladins and their followers had been tossed onto a burning pile of driftwood and old straw. Such fuel did not produce the hottest fire, but Dag's new castellan—a thin, dark man who would have been handsome but for the livid brand on one cheek—was a practical steward and manager,

and he decreed that Thornhold's supply of firewood and timber was too dear to waste on such matters. Dag had been content to yield the decision to the castellan; after all, the man
had ably managed the estates of an Amnian nobleman, until
the discovery of his dalliance with the man's wife had led to
his discharge and disfigurement. Dag cared nothing about a
man's habits, and the castellan's advice seemed sound
enough. And if the paladins did not burn completely, what of
it? Did not the ravens and wild beasts of the Sword Coast
need to eat?

The celebration inside the fortress that night was raucous
and long. The soldiers raided the cellars and brought casks of
ale and wine up to the keep's dining hall. Several of the
slaughtered animals, along with leeks and root vegetables
from the cellar, went into a huge pot for stew. The men
feasted and drank and sang and boasted until the moon had
set, and stayed doggedly at it until most of them were snoring
at the table with their faces pillowed in their gravy-soaked
trenchers.

Dag held himself apart from this, watching and waiting
quietly until he was certain he would have the privacy he
needed. There was one more thing he must do, the one final
thing that would make the victory truly his.

When the night sky had faded from obsidian to sapphire,
when dawn was not long in coming and the fortress silent but
for a few drunken snores, Dag walked into the chapel and
closed the heavy doors behind him.

A few squat candles still burned on the alter, and more in
the plain iron sconces set into the walls. Most of the flames
had winked out or diminished into fading wisps of blue sink-
ing into tallow puddles. Unusually fine candles, they were.
Dag had noticed earlier that the chandler's shop produced a
good supply of tall, thick candles, big enough to burn through
a day or a night. A pity, Dag mused, that the talented chandler had held so steadfastly to the path of righteousness. Had
the man shown a bit more flexibility, he might have lived to
bedeck Cyric's altar. Dag could envision the chapel lit by
scores of enormous, deep purple tapers.

But perhaps he could do even better. Dag walked up the
wide stairs that led to the altar and stood for a moment gazing up at the wooden scales of justice, the symbol of stern Tyr,
then he closed his eyes and began to chant.

Power filled the chapel, and with it a ghastly purple light
as tall flames rose from the spent candles. The priest opened
his eyes and studied the long, writhing shadows that danced
against the wall. No, not danced—fought. Shadowy paladins,
milling about in an endless battle they could never win. The
spectacle pleased Dag, as he suspected it would please Cyric.

Proof of his god's pleasure was not long in coming. A low,
thrumming boom sounded through the chapel, and the symbol of Tyr tilted slowly and crashed to the altar. Flames from
the candles leaped up to engulf the wooden scales, consumed
them utterly, then rose higher still. The unnatural fire converged, rose into the air, and took the shape of a livid purple
sunburst. As Dag watched, awestruck, a darkness appeared
in the heart of the manifestation, growing larger until it took
the form of an enormous black skull.

Dag slowly dropped to his knees, his ambitions both
humbled and confirmed by this great sign of Cyric's favor. He
raised his hands, which were still stained with dried blood,
and began to chant anew. This time, his words formed a
prayer of supplication, importuning Cyric to accept the gifts
of conquest and intrigue and strife and to guide him as he
sought the next step in his path to power.

The priest was confident that his god would be with him.
The gift he offered was far more than a chapel of Tyr, its sanc-
tity polluted by foul magic and its grim majesty rededicated
to Cyric. In Dag's mind, he could bring no greater offering to
his dark god than the death of a great paladin of Tyr, a
descendant of the mighty Samular himself, the man who had
been his father.

*   *   *   *   *

Bronwyn saw the torchlight before she heard the soldiers'
approach. The sudden appearance of four armed Zhentilar

shocked and sobered her, and the blinding red haze of her anger slipped away. With sudden clarity, she realized that this dwarf was not her enemy. The poor fellow probably made his home in these tunnels. It seemed unlikely he was allied with the Zhentarim; in fact, he looked no happier to see the soldiers than she was. She released her grip on his beard and pushed him away.

"Stones!" he spat, and though his voice was rough from her ill-treatment, the venom and vitriol in that one word marked it as a dwarven curse.

Bronwyn felt the need to let loose a few soft curses of her own. This drew a quick, curious stare from her red-bearded opponent.

"Aren't you with them?"

"I thought *you* were," she shot back. The enemy of my enemy, she thought grimly. "We fight or run?"

"You lost my hammer," he groused, "which narrows down the choices a mite."

At that moment, one of the soldiers caught sight of them. He pointed and shouted, and the four men kicked into a running charge.

"Run," Bronwyn decided.

The dwarf jerked his head toward the river and was off at a fast, rolling trot. Bronwyn followed, but she ached in every joint and sinew, and her movements felt stiff and awkward. Her eyes widened as they fell upon the slick, uneven path that wound along the very brink of the riverbank's incline. If she kept up with the dwarf's breakneck pace she ran the risk of slipping and tumbling down into the fast-moving water. If she did not, if she lost sight of the dwarf, she could well spend the rest of her life wandering around these tunnels. Which might not be such a long time, if the Zhent patrol found her.

Bronwyn suddenly had grave doubts about the wisdom of tossing her lot in with this dwarf. As if he sensed her hesitation, he skidded to a stop and shot a look over his shoulder. He extended one stubby hand to her.

"Grab hold," he hollered, his deep voice rising over the roar and crash of the river. "No dwarf worth snail slime has ever slipped on this path. I won't be letting you fall."

For some reason, Bronwyn believed him. She ran to him
and seized the offered wrist. Immediately he was off, and at a
pace faster than she would have believed possible.

Behind them, they heard a startled shout, followed by a
splash. She and the dwarf exchanged a quick, fierce grin.

"One down," she panted out.

"Good start," he admitted.

At that moment, Bronwyn's feet flew out from under her.
She fell hard on her backside and her right elbow and began
to slide. Instantly she twisted to the left, as the dwarf dragged
her back from the steep bank. Another pull jerked her back
onto her feet. Without missing more than a beat, she and the
dwarf were running again.

"Told you I'd keep a grip," he bellowed. "Got my word on
it."

As she nodded her thanks, some of the desolation lifted
from her heart. Suddenly Bronwyn found it wasn't hard at all
to keep pace with the dwarf.

*   *   *   *   *

Algorind tried to count his blessings. The sun was bright,
and the cold breeze that blew off the Sea of Swords seemed
almost balmy in comparison to the chill winds that had buffeted the hills around the monastery throughout the long winter. He had been given a paladin's quest, and the first part of
his journey was complete. Now he was en route to Thornhold
to bear great and glad news to Hronulf of Tyr, the paladin
whose fame and virtue had been an inspiration to Algorind
for as long as he could remember. He had life, health, faith,
and a fine sword at his side.

What was a lost horse, in comparison to that?

Even so, the memory of the ungrateful, treacherous dwarf
rankled. Algorind had to admit that he knew little of the
world, but surely this could not be common behavior. He had
always heard dwarves spoken of as gruff, but honorable. Why
did the little red-bearded fellow accost him and steal his

horse? It was poor payment, after Tyr had been gracious enough to save his life.

Algorind was also concerned about the delay. On foot, it would take him nearly a day longer to reach the fortress. Losing his horse was a serious matter, for he would not be given another by the order. He would have to earn his next steed, which would add another task to his quest and greatly delay his investiture as a Knight of Samular. Ah, well, he conceded with a sigh, patience was among the knightly virtues.

But there was still more. Sir Gareth's cryptic parting words continued to trouble him. The old knight had importuned Algorind to stay with Hronulf and watch his back. What prompted this sudden concern? A paladin's life was fraught with danger, that was true enough, but was there some specific, expected threat to the famous knight?

Another thought hit Algorind. Hronulf was getting along in years. Perhaps his health was failing. Perhaps Sir Gareth feared that the news Algorind brought would throw Hronulf into decline. As joyful as word of a new-found granddaughter might be, there was no discounting the terrible shock of learning that his lost son was alive, but an enemy. Better a dead son than a living priest of Cyric.

Many and troubling were the puzzles before him, but as Algorind walked, the beauty of the spring day beguiled him and lightened his heart. The High Road was broad and even underfoot and often shaded by tall oak trees and majestic pines. Berries, small as his thumbnail and red and sweet and bursting with juice, grew in profusion along the roadside. The birds sang with the sweet urgency of springtime as they sought mates and built nests to cradle their coming young.

It was all new and delightful to him. Algorind had not been so far from Summit Hall since the day he had been entrusted to the order, but for all that, he knew precisely where he must go.

This he knew because he had committed to memory all the maps in the monastery library—most of which he had brought with him as part of his apprentice fee. Algorind's father and older brothers had had little use for such things,

preferring the glittering life of Cormyr's capital city to anything so dusty and unpleasant as travel. But Algorind had
loved maps for as long as he could remember. Even as a small
child, he had coaxed the use of them from every traveler and
merchant who passed through his father's doors, committing
each line and dot and squiggle to memory. He knew where the
mountain passes lay, where the rivers sang swift and treacherous songs, what hills were likely to contain lairs of orcs or
goblins or worse. In Algorind's opinion, all knowledge was
useful, but this was information he would most assuredly
need if he was to travel the world in Tyr's service.

This was the first time he had had the opportunity to com-
pare the reality of the wide world with the careful image he
had crafted in his mind. For the most part, the two matched
with admirable consistency. There ahead was the low stone
building built by followers of Tyr as a travelers' rest. Here the
path ahead veered away from the sea to run through some
low, rock-strewn hills. The terrain was rougher there, and the
trees gave way to small, determined shrubs. Some might find
the stretch of land bleak and forbidding, but Algorind was as
delighted as a child to see his maps come alive.

Suddenly he caught sight of something that no map could
prepare him to face. To the north of him a cloud of thick, oily
black smoke rose into the sky.

The sound of rough voices seized his attention and drew
his gaze to the hills east of the Trade Way. Next he heard the
sound of horses' hooves against the stony path and a foul
curse from one of the riders. Clearly, this was no patrol from
Thornhold.

Or was it? The rising smoke and the portent of Sir Gareth's
words of concern gave birth to a terrible suspicion. If trouble
had come to Thornhold, Algorind must know of it.

He thought quickly. The horsemen undoubtedly followed a
path through those hills. Algorind had once seen it marked,
on an extremely detailed map shown him by an elven sage.
The path was treacherous and narrow, and at one point it
followed the wall of a steep cliff, with nothing but a deep
ravine on the other side.

Algorind took off at a run, circling around and bending low as he hurried through the low-growing scrub pine. He listened carefully to the sound of the coarse men's speech, judging their progress and quickening his pace to match it.

He found the pass and scrambled up a rocky incline that overlooked the path and the ravine beyond. He crouched down behind some rocks to watch and wait, and then sank lower as the men came into view.

There were four of them, and they wore on their black over-tunics the twisted rune that was the emblem of Darkhold. Zhentish soldiers, certainly. That made Algorind feel a bit better about what he was about to do. Laying ambush was hardly a noble task for a paladin, but these men were clearly evil, and great odds required greater valor. This took some of the sting from the needed act.

When the men were almost past his position, Algorind leaped at the one who rode rearguard. He seized the man on his way down and carried him from the horse. They fell together. Algorind delivered two quick, jabbing punches to the Zhent's throat and temple. The Zhent instantly went limp. Algorind swung himself up onto the startled horse and drew his sword.

The remaining soldiers had noted their comrade's fate. They wheeled their horses around and drew their weapons. Urging their mounts on with vicious kicks, they came at the paladin in full fury.

Fortunately for Algorind, the path was too narrow for two to ride abreast. The first attacker thundered toward him, sword held high. Algorind caught the blade with his, tugged the reins of his borrowed mount to the left, and gave the joined swords a deft twist. Jousting was an art much practiced at Summit Hall, and Algorind unhorsed his opponent with ease. The Zhent hit the ground hard, landing just off the path. He rolled down the punishing, stone-studded ravine. His curses swiftly rose into howls of pain, then faded away.

While their comrade was still rolling down the ravine, the two remaining men came on. The foremost had a wicked spear, which he held couched like a lance under one arm.

Algorind waited until the man was nearly upon him, then leaped from the saddle toward the onrushing blade, slashing down with his sword as he went.

His blade caught the spear shaft, and his weight forced the point of the spear down. It struck the ground and dug in hard. Algorind rolled aside beyond the reach of the horse's thundering hooves. He heard the man's rising wail as the bent spear lifted him from his mount and hurled him into the air.

Before the heavy thud announced the man's impact onto solid rock, Algorind was already back on his feet, sword ready. He leaped directly into the path of the last rider. The startled horse reared up, dumping its rider onto the path. Before the fallen soldier could collect himself, Algorind was there, one foot pinning the man's sword arm down, and the tip of his blade at the man's throat.

The Zhent's eyes expected death and feared it greatly. Such it must be, Algorind thought with sudden pity, if all that awaited a man was the dubious mercy of Cyric or the other dire gods that the Zhentarim favored, or—most terrible of all—the numbing emptiness of no faith at all.

"Only answer my question, and you may go free and unharmed," Algorind vowed.

The man's eyes narrowed suspiciously. "And if I don't talk?"

"Speak freely, or die swiftly," the paladin said. "It is your choice."

"Easy enough, put that way," the soldier muttered. "What do you want to know?"

"You are of Darkhold, and you are far from your fortress. Do you hold another stronghold nearby?"

The man's quick, wicked grin reminded Algorind of a buzzard preparing to feed. "As of last night, that we do."

Algorind's heart seemed to turn to stone. "Thornhold. You have taken it."

"Made a nice piece of work of it, too."

Algorind nodded and knew at once that he would not be able fulfill his charge and carry a message to Hronulf. He himself would gladly fight to the death to protect a stronghold of the order from Zhentish capture. He did not know of a paladin who would not. Even so, he had to ask. "And the paladins who held it . . . are they all dead?"

"To a man. I saw 'em burn."

The black smoke, Algorind realized. His wrath kindled, prompting him to slay this evil man who recounted the destruction of goodly men with such unconcern.

But Algorind had given his word. He could not break it, nor had he learned all that he must. Since he studied the lore of the order with scholarly devotion, he knew that Hronulf of Tyr wore a great artifact, one of the Rings of Samular. It was Algorind's duty to learn what had become of it.

"You answer plainly. For that, I thank you. Tell me one thing more. What became of the paladins' possessions?"

The man lifted one shoulder in a shrug. "The usual. Weapons and valuables went to the commander. His captains sorted through them and passed them out as booty."

"The paladin commander, known as Hronulf of Tyr, wore a gold ring. Do you know who now holds it?"

"That damn ring," echoed the soldier in a resigned voice. "Bane's balls, but I'm tired of hearing about the thing! The commander had us search the whole damn fortress for it more times than I know how to count. As far as we can figure, the old knight gave the ring to a pretty young wench who escaped. No one knows how she escaped or where she went. My patrol was one of several out looking for her. That is the truth, and it's all I know."

Algorind studied him for a long moment, then stepped back. "I believe you," he said. "You may go."

The soldier stared at him for a moment. "Just like that?" he said in disbelief.

"You fulfilled your part. You may go."

The man laughed—a bitter, mocking sound. "It sounds easy, the way you put it. Do you know what Dag Zoreth will do to me when he finds out that I lost my patrol to a single man? When he learns what I've told you? And he *will* learn. He has ways of finding out things that I don't even want to know about. If I go back to the fortress, I'm a dead man."

Algorind was thoroughly confused. "Then why did you speak?"

"You offered me a quick death. I figured that was the best bargain I could make."

This appalled the young paladin. It was a terrible thing that a man must fear his superiors as this one did. He studied the Zhent for a long moment, silently calling on Tyr to help him judge the true measure of this man. What he found surprised him greatly and made the task of disposing of the soldier all the more perplexing.

And what of his own quest? The capture of Thornhold and the death of Hronulf put an end to it. Yet what of the ring and the woman? This matter was grave indeed and required the wisdom of an elder paladin. Perhaps Sir Gareth was still at the Halls of Justice. And if not, what better place for Algorind to start his search for the mysterious "pretty wench" than in that decadent city?

"We are both at something of a loss," Algorind said. "I made a bargain with you, not expecting it could go awry in this manner. As for myself, I think it best to travel south to Waterdeep. You might come along, if you desire. Surely, in so large a place, you could lose yourself and find a new, better life."

The soldier dragged himself up on his elbows, staring incredulously up at the young paladin. "What are you offering? A conspiracy?"

"Companionship on the way south," Algorind corrected, "and my word of honor that I find little true evil in you. I can also offer you, in the name of Tyr, the gift of redemption. Accept, abandon the path you have chosen, and when your time comes you need not die with such horror in your eyes as I saw this day. But be warned," he cautioned the wary man. "Tyr is the god of justice, and it may well be that your life among the Zhentarim has left deeds that require restitution. Tyr's redemption does not come without a price."

"What does?" grumbled the soldier, but he took the hand that Algorind offered him and let the young paladin help him to his feet. In this soldier's eyes, Algorind read the flickering rebirth of the gifts that Tyr could bestow: hope, honor, and the grim yet comforting belief in stern justice.

"I can travel with you as far as Waterdeep," the soldier said.

* * * * *

Bronwyn ran with the dwarf until she was certain her sides would split. When she was sure she couldn't go another step, the dwarf veered off the river path into an utterly black tunnel. She stumbled along behind, aware only that they turned several times. Finally her guide came to a stop.

For many moments she stood, her hands on her knees, and struggled to regain her breath. The dwarf sounded in about the same condition, only louder. Air rasped in and out of the stout fellow with a force and volume that suggested a forge bellows at work.

"How'd you get in that shaft, anyhow?" he demanded when he'd gathered enough breath for speech.

"Believe me, it wasn't my idea." Bronwyn sank down to sit on the cold stone floor of the tunnel. "There was a battle. Zhents got into the fortress—through the midden, by the smell of them. When it was clear that the fortress would be taken, one of the paladins dropped me down that hole."

She did not say who or what the paladin had been too her. Her loss was too new, too raw, to bear the burden of words.

"Hmmph." The dwarf considered this. "Well now, that fits into the picture. Zhents mean trouble, plain and simple. A few dwarves in my clan used to trade with them. Don't do it, I told them. Never pays, I said. Well, it *paid*, all right."

The bitter grief in the dwarf's voice smote Bronwyn's heart. She began to put together the pieces. Most fortresses had escape tunnels, but these were secret and closely guarded. Even the midden, a necessity of any settlement, was always warded from possible intruders. The presence of a dwarf clan would provide a powerful shield for these escape routes. The angry mixture of shock and sorrow in the dwarf's voice suggested why the midden shoots were suddenly accessible.

"The shaft led into your tunnels?" she asked gently.

"That's right. Not many knew of the slide, even among the dwarves. Only the head human was supposed to know of it. Guess you happened to be in the right place at the right time."

The heavy irony in his voice did not escape her, nor did the ragged sound of terrible grief. For several moments Bronwyn and her unseen companion sat in silence. Nothing she could say to him would ease his pain. She knew, for she could think of no words of consolation that would make any difference to her own loss.

A small, strong hand gripped her wrist. "Come on," he said gruffly. "We'd best get out of this place."

They walked in silence for perhaps an hour before Bronwyn began to notice shapes and shadows emerging from the darkness. "There's an opening ahead?"

"That's right. Oh, *damnation!*"

Bronwyn stopped, startled by the dwarf's sharp tone. "What is it?"

"I'm-a gonna have to put a blinder on you. No human knows this opening. Best I keep it that way."

That struck Bronwyn as a sad variation of locking the barn door after the horse was stolen, but she wasn't about to point that out to the grieving dwarf. "I understand. Rip a strip of cloth off the bottom of my cloak if you want."

The dwarf busied himself with the task, then led Bronwyn out of the tunnel and into the open. Since being blindfolded was not much different from walking through the black tunnel, she didn't mind it as much as she thought she would. And even if she couldn't see, the sound and feel of the sea winds lifted her spirits. Until she'd left the tunnels behind, she hadn't realized how oppressive they'd felt.

Finally the dwarf stopped and removed her blindfold. She blinked and shielded her eyes from the sudden stab of light. When her vision cleared, she noted that they were on a wide dirt path—the High Road. She was also able to form a detailed impression of the dwarf.

He was, well, square. Probably just short of four feet tall, he was built like a barrel with thick arms and shoulders of a width that most six-foot men would envy. Curly reddish-brown hair rioted over his shoulders, and a beard in a brighter hue of auburn spilled down over his chest. Unlike most dwarves, he wore no mustache, and that lent a slightly boyish look to his broad face. A horseshoe hung about his neck on a thong, another bit of whimsy, but there was nothing of the child in his eyes, which were the color of a stormy sky and just as bleak.

She extended her hand. "I'm Bronwyn. Thank you for getting me out of the tunnels."

He hesitated, then clasped her wrist in a brief adventurer's salute. "Ebenezer."

His answer was curt, almost challenging. Bronwyn didn't expect anything different. Dwarves were slow to trust and loath to give more of their names than absolutely necessary.

By unspoken consensus, they started south along the road. Bronwyn noted the dejected slope of his shoulders. "You lost people in the tunnels," she said with deep sympathy.

A moment of silence stretched out, growing ever more tense until it exploded into an earthy dwarven curse. "My clan," he admitted. "Most killed. Some gone."

"Some of them escaped," she pointed out. "That's something."

"Bah! You don't know dwarves after all, if you're thinking that way. Running away when there's fighting to be done? They're not gone by choice, I'm telling you that for free."

Bronwyn's eyes narrowed as this sank in. She stopped and seized the dwarf's arm, spinning him around to face her. "They were taken by the Zhents? Why?"

"Why indeed?" he raged helplessly. "Why would a human learn to read the stones or sweat himself dry chipping ore and gems out of solid rock? Why spend twenty years learning the craft of sword smithing, another thirty making practice pieces, then start turning out swords at the cost of a decade apiece? Why go through the trouble to cut and polish gems until they sparkle like the Tears of Selûne on a clear night? Why do any of that when you can steal someone else to do it for you?"

"Slavers," she gritted out. Her own past rose up before her, lending that single word more venom than a nest full of pit vipers could muster.

The dwarf eyed Bronwyn with curiosity. "That'd be my guess. What's it to you?"

She dropped his arm and started down the road at a brisker pace. After a moment, Ebenezer jogged up to her side. "With the spring fairs coming up, a southbound caravan should be along soon," she said briskly. "I've enough coin to buy us a horse. Can you ride?"

"Yes, but—"

"Two horses then. We should be in Waterdeep before nightfall day after tomorrow. If we're lucky, we'll be in Skullport by midnight."

"Skullport!" he scoffed. "More of your tall tales. Tavern legend. No such place."

"There most certainly is, and it's the nearest port for slave transport. If you want to find the surviving members of your clan before they're halfway to Calimport, that's where we'll have to go. Live with it."

He jogged along, considering this. Finally he turned a skeptical gaze upon her. "What's this to you, human?"

"My *name* is Bronwyn," she said grimly. "You might as well get used to using it. Where we're going, singing out 'Hoy, human!' will get you too many responses. Most of them, you won't like."

"Bronwyn, then," he agreed. "And it might be that you could save your coin. I got a horse stashed. Here you have Ebenezer Mac Brockholst 'n' Palmara, of Clan Stoneshaft."

She nodded, understanding the honor he conferred upon her by giving his full name and lineage—and seeing in his eyes the effort it cost to name his parents, whom he had probably just laid to rest. He was agreeing with her plan, trusting her to help him find his lost family. The enormity of that staggered her. She couldn't think of anything to say, but tried anyway.

"Stoneshaft," she repeated. "Your clan were miners, then?"

"No, we got that name because my grandsire managed to

sire himself thirteen kids," he shot back.

Bronwyn raised her eyebrows, acknowledging the bawdy sarcasm. "Fine. Straight to business."

"Speaking of which," the dwarf asked with a sudden return of suspicion, "what did you say you did to earn your keep?"

"I didn't say, but I'm not a slaver, if that's what you're thinking. I find lost antiquities. You'd probably call me a treasure hunter."

He nodded, clearly understanding this bias; after all, collecting treasures was a very common dwarf impulse. "Whereabouts do you keep your hoard?"

"It's more of a shop, really, and I'm seldom there. Most of my days are spent on the road, searching for new pieces. I often work on commission, but everything I find is for sale."

"Practical," approved Ebenezer. "Don't need stuff lying around gathering dust. Too much trouble to be toting it around. Where'd you learn to fight?"

Bronwyn chuckled helplessly, feeling somewhat dizzied by the quick change of topic. "By doing, mostly. I've had no formal training as a fighter, but so far, I've won more times than I've lost."

"Best training there is," he said. He cast her a stern look. "You always fight dirty?"

She shrugged. "When I have to."

He nodded again. "Good. Well then, let's have a look at this Skullport of yours."

Eight

Algorind and his newfound companion headed south on foot toward the great port city. One of the Zhentilar horses had been regrettably lamed during Algorind's attack and had to be put down. The men tried without success to recapture the other horses. It seemed that the steeds lacked the sense of loyalty and duty that was trained into a paladin's mount.

Jenner, the former Zhent, was a surprisingly good companion. He could sing rather well, and he knew some old ballads that spoke ringingly of deeds of heroism and valor—strange songs indeed to come from the throat of a man who had spent his youth riding patrol around Darkhold. This puzzled Algorind greatly.

"How is it that you fell into the service of evil?" Algorind asked him.

The young paladin's words drew a rueful smile from the man. "I didn't see it that way. It was more like survival. I was born in the Greycloak Hills, grew up herding my father's sheep. The land and the sheep would go to my older brother. I always knew that, but then came three bad years running with no crops and few lambs. Didn't have much of a choice but to take whatever work came to hand."

"There are always choices," Algorind said firmly. He laid one hand on the man's shoulder. "You have made a good choice this day, the first of what I trust will be many."

"Trust, do you?" Jenner chuckled without amusement. "Seems to me that you're a trusting sort. That'll bring you to grief, come soon or late."

Algorind could not dispute that. The treachery of the dwarf he'd saved from the zombies still troubled him deeply.

"There is a travelers' rest not far ahead," he commented. "We can fill our waterskins at the well and gather some of the berries that grow in profusion nearby."

Jenner let out a sigh of great longing. "I like spring berries. They're good any way you can get them, but best with honey and new cream, heaped over a pile of sweet biscuits. I mean to have some of that, first thing, when we reach Waterdeep. After a nice roast of venison and a few mugs, that is."

The paladin was mildly offended by this picture of gluttony. "You would do better to seek gainful employment for yourself."

Jenner winked. "And what better place than in a tavern? That's where men come to hire swords and to hire their swords out."

"You would find work as a sell-sword?"

"It's what I know. Don't worry yourself," he said, casting a wry half-smile at Algorind. "I'll do well enough as a caravan guard or some such. Well, there's the rest house."

Algorind nodded, then froze. The sight before him was one of such boldness and villainy that it stole his breath.

The red-bearded dwarf came out from the stone structure, leading Icewind by the reins. With him was a young woman with exceptionally long, thick hair plaited back into a single braid. She was comely enough to suit the Zhent's description of "a pretty wench," and, since women traveling alone were uncommon in these wild lands, she was probably the one that the Zhentarim of Thornhold sought. The dwarf tossed her up into Icewind's saddle as if he had every right to dispose of the horse, and then hauled himself up onto the back of a squat, nasty-looking pony. He glanced back and did an astonished double take when he caught Algorind's dumbfounded gaze.

The dwarf lifted a hand in an insouciant salute, then kicked the pony into a surprisingly quick canter. The woman followed along behind on Algorind's stolen horse.

"The woman you seek," Algorind said grimly, "she is allied with the Zhentarim?"

Jenner shook his head, obviously not following this line of reasoning. "Not that I know of. Why'd you ask?"

"That white horse is mine," Algorind said, pointing. "The dwarf stole him from me in an act of base treachery. If the woman consorts with horse thieves, one must ask if she could be allied with the very scum of evildoers."

The former Zhent let out a snort of laughter. "No offense intended, I suppose."

Algorind looked at him in puzzlement. "No, I had no wish to offend. Why do you ask?"

Jenner chuckled dryly and shook his head. "Never mind. Let's just get us to Waterdeep the fastest way we can—or let me put it better, the fastest way your scruples will allow."

*   *   *   *   *

Late in the afternoon, two days after the fall of Thornhold, Bronwyn led her new companion into the Curious Past. When they entered the shop, the dwarf looked around in begrudging wonderment at the old and rare things that crowded the shelves and tables in glittering display.

"Lot of dusting to do," he concluded gruffly.

A loud huff announced Alice Tinker's presence. The gnome rose to her full height, her brown face peering over the rim of the large brass vase she'd been polishing, her small form quivering with indignation. "Dust, nothing! I challenge you to find a single pot, gem or book in this entire place that isn't polished to a gleam."

Ebenezer folded his arms. "If I were a betting sort of dwarf, I *still* wouldn't take that one. You can stuff that so-called challenge in the who-cares bucket and take it on out to the slop heap."

"Alice, meet Ebenezer Stoneshaft," Bronwyn said dryly. "He'll be with me for a tenday or two."

The gnome's face went wary. "And staying where?"

"Neither of us are staying. A bath and a meal, and we'll be on our way."

Alice huffed. "Well, by the looks of you, child, you could certainly use a good meal." Her eyes slid disdainfully over the dwarf, leaving the last part of her insult unspoken.

Bronwyn noted this exchange with great puzzlement. Alice was the most genial of souls; it was not like the gnome to so mistreat a visitor to Curious Past. She was about to admonish her assistant when she noticed the delighted battle gleam in the dwarf's eye. He had spoken little on the journey south, and she'd given him silence and time to deal with his loss. Judging by the animation on his face, maybe she would have done better to pick a fight or two with him.

"Grow a beard, woman," Ebenezer gruffly advised Alice. This comment baffled Bronwyn, but Alice seemed to understand it perfectly. The gnome's eyes widened, then turned coy, and bright color bloomed on her already rosy cheeks.

Belatedly, Bronwyn got the point. Dwarven women were as bearded as their men. Apparently, Ebenezer was expressing his approval of Alice's gruff reception, even flirting with her a bit. Bronwyn cast her eyes toward the ceiling—which, despite Alice's claims, was liberally festooned with cobwebs. "Did anything interesting happen while I was gone?"

The gnome collected herself. "Your friend Lord Thann has found excuse to stop by, or send someone on his behalf, at least thrice a day. He seems most concerned about you."

"I can just imagine," Bronwyn muttered. "I suppose he has been watching me and reporting back to Khelben all this time, too. No offense meant, Alice," she added hastily when she saw hurt and self-reproach creep into the gnome's eyes.

Watching. Reporting back.

Suddenly something else occurred to Bronwyn, something that widened her eyes with shock and fury. When she had wanted to identify herself to her father, she named her tell-tale birthmark. Surely that identifying mark was one measure used by those who once searched for Hronulf's missing daughter. The Harpers might have heard of the search, and remembered that birthmark. Was it possible that the invitation to join the Harpers, to move to Waterdeep and work under Khelben Arunsun's direction, was not motivated by the skills she could bring to the Harpers, but by who she was?

All these years, she had searched so desperately for her family, and they had known.

If that was so, then the brief days and nights of merriment that she and Danilo had shared several years before suddenly took on new and ominous meaning. And with that realization came a stab of betrayal so painful that it almost sent her to her knees. Danilo had known who she was—or at least suspected. By the time he left Amn, he knew beyond doubt.

"Oh, my god and goddess," she whispered in a appalled voice, stunned by this duplicity in a man she had long called friend. "Sweet sister Sune."

"Some might think it's a bit early in the day to be invoking the goddess of love and beauty," observed a familiar, languid male voice behind her. "Myself, I see no reason to put off what I might want to do again later."

This observation, coming on the heels of her sudden and disturbing insight, raised Bronwyn's temper past boiling. She fisted her hand and spun toward the shop door, swinging out high and hard.

Danilo dodged the blow and caught her wrist. "Really! Is that any way to greet an old friend?" he chided her.

Bronwyn wrenched her arm from his grasp and backed away. "You son of a snake," she said in a low, furious tone.

"Ah."

Just that. He didn't bother to ask her what she meant. Of course not. But if Bronwyn had not known what a chameleon her fellow Harper could be, she would have sworn there was real regret in his eyes.

He took a step toward her, one hand held out in entreaty. "Bronwyn, we need to talk about that."

"The hell we do. Get out of my shop."

Ebenezer came to stand beside her, and the expression on his bearded face suggested an entire battalion taking flank position. He folded his arms and looked Bronwyn's visitor up and down. He snorted when his gaze fell on Danilo's jeweled sword. When his scrutiny was completed, his upper lip curled, leaving no doubt concerning his opinion of the faired-haired dandy. "Haven't killed anyone today," he announced. "Might be I ought to, just to keep in practice."

"Hold that thought," Bronwyn told him, secretly rather touched that the dwarf would come to her defense without question or hesitation. It helped a little, especially when all her perceptions and alliances seemed to be shifting, and her emotions in such chaos that she couldn't think things through with her usual clarity.

But at that moment, another disturbing piece molded itself into the spreading puzzle. It suddenly occurred to Bronwyn to wonder about the reason for the Harpers' recent, intense interest in her. Did Khelben suspect the Zhentarim had designs on her father's keep? If the Harpers had known and had done nothing to stop it, then she was finished with the lot of them!

She whirled back to Danilo, her pain over his earlier transgression forgotten. "How much of this did you know?"

He spread his hands, palms up. "I swear to you, Bronwyn, I had no idea who you were when we met in Amn," he said earnestly, "nor did I know of your lineage until a few days ago. There was no subterfuge or design in our friendship. We were young and congenial. When I vouched for you as Harper many months later, I did name your distinguishing marks. Such things are important for a Harper Master to know, and when Khelben asked the question I thought nothing amiss. I told him, but I made no mention of how this knowledge was acquired."

"Ever the gentleman," she sneered. "But that's a small thing. A few moments ago, I wouldn't have thought so. This new betrayal outshines all that went before."

This clearly took him aback. "What is this about?"

"You deny it still!" Furious now, she snatched up a carved ivory statue and hurled it at him. It missed and crashed into the lintel, breaking into several pieces. "You killed my father! If you hadn't withheld information, he might still be alive."

Bronwyn was raving and knew it, but she was beyond caring. The bitter words tore from her like living things determined to be born, regardless of the pain of their birthing.

Danilo stooped and gathered up the ivory bits; Bronwyn suspected he wished to buy time to gather his composure and shape his next remarks. But when he rose, his face was still bewildered. "Bronwyn, what is going on?"

"Tell me this: did you know that Thornhold would come under attack?"

Danilo looked honestly and thoroughly stunned by this news. He sank down to sit on a carved chest, and he rubbed both hands over his face. "Thornhold was attacked?" he echoed.

"And taken," she said shortly.

From the corner of her eye Bronwyn noticed that Shopscat was showing keen interest in her visitor's ear-cuff and was starting to edge closer for the attack. Out of habit, she started to grab for the raven—then thought better of it and left the bird alone to do as it willed.

"The fortress of Thornhold is now held by the Zhentarim," she said, her voice gaining volume and passion as she spoke. "Isn't that why Khelben Arunsun was so concerned about my dealings with Malchior? He was afraid I might give away family secrets, is that it? Or perhaps you thought I was in collusion with the Zhentarim?"

"Not that. Never that." Danilo rose and took a step toward her. His progress was halted when a very angry dwarf stepped between him and Bronwyn.

"Back away," Ebenezer growled. He reached up and thumped the Harper's chest with his stubby forefinger. "Seems to me the lady of this here shop told you a ways back to git. And you ain't got yet. Now, I see a problem there that we could solve one of two ways."

The Harper took a long breath and exhaled with a sigh. "I

have no quarrel with you, good sir. Bronwyn, even if you are content to lay to rest the old matter, we must discuss this new one. Send word, when you are ready."

Her only response was a stony stare. After a moment Danilo nodded a silent farewell and left, unwittingly evading the quick stabbing attack of Shopscat's beak.

"I could get to like that bird," Ebenezer observed, eyeing the raven with grim approval.

* * * * *

Danilo strode through the streets toward Blackstaff Tower, hands clasped behind him and brow deeply furrowed in thought. He caught a glimpse of himself in the polished glass of a milliner's shop window, and the sight pulled him up short. It took him a moment to realize what bothered him about the reflected image. He had seen that stance before, and the expression was a mirror image of that he'd often beheld on the visage of the archmage he served.

"I have been at this business far too long," Danilo murmured as he took off down the street again, this time at a saunter.

He found the archmage at his table, which did nothing to brighten his mood. Khelben had a perverse fondness for such foods as pottage of lentil, thick oat porridge, and fruit unadorned by pastry or sugar. If that was the secret of the archmage's long life, Danilo fervently hoped to die when his naturally allotted span was through.

As they exchanged greetings, Danilo selected a ring of dried apple from a tray. He sat down across from the archmage, munching the leathery fruit as he pondered how best to pass along the dire message Bronwyn had hurled at him. Danilo had given his word to Alice, albeit tacitly, that he would not report to Khelben word of Bronwyn's trip to Thornhold. Nor would he tell the archmage that Bronwyn was back in the city. Khelben would find that out soon enough. Danilo's days of reporting on his old friends were over.

A simple ruse came to him. Nothing annoyed Khelben

more than reference to Danilo's bardic pursuits. Perhaps that very pique would serve to keep the archmage from examining the tale too closely.

"I heard a most amazing ballad last night at the Howling Moon," Danilo began, naming a new tavern popular with traveling bards of all stripe. "The singer described the fall of Thornhold and claimed that this dire event occurred but two days past. I am inclined to believe him, Uncle. I do not wish to criticize a fellow bard, but the song sounded rather hastily composed."

Khelben stared at him for a long moment. "Wait here," he commanded.

The archmage rose and swept from the room. In Khelben's absence, Danilo nibbled away at the plate of dried fruit and studied the dining hall. There was not overmuch to see. Polished wood covered the walls, and the stone floor had been neatly strewn with fresh rushes mingled with sweet-smelling herbs, as was the custom. The room was dim and cool, lit only by the light that filtered in from the ever-shifting windows. The archmage had remarkably simple habits and insisted that there was no need to waste candles unless they were needed for reading.

Khelben returned in moments, his visage even grimmer than the reflection of his own face that Dan had glimpsed in the shop window.

"It is as you say," the archmage said. "How could such a thing occur without word or warning? How could a siege force of sufficient size march not more than two days' ride north of this city and no one notice anything amiss? What good are we doing here in Waterdeep?"

The last question was a challenge, leveled at the Harpers in general and Danilo in particular, and delivered with the force of a thrown lance.

"It is possible," Dan ventured, "that the Zhentarim have been preparing for this attack for a long time. There would be no time better, given the coming of the spring fairs and the heavy traffic on the High Road. Soldier and horse could easily be disguised as part of a merchant caravan and could pass unnoticed. Small groups could slip away into the hills and mountains and gather at the appointed time."

Khelben looked at him with surprise. "That is well said."

"But said too late. We should have thought of this possibility." Dan sighed and reached for a dried plum. He slipped a jeweled knife from the cuff of his shirt and deftly pitted the fruit. "I have no expertise in siege tactics, but surely some of your Harpers keep watch for such things."

"We have not seen the need," the archmage said shortly. "Thornhold was considered a secure fortress."

"And?" Danilo prompted, seeing a familiar film of secrecy settle over his uncle's face.

Khelben considered, then threw up his hands as if resigned to yield up the truth at once rather than endure the pestering that would surely ensue if he did not. "If truth must be told, the Harpers and the paladins of the Knights of Samular have a wary relationship. The source of this conflict is a tale too old to profit from retelling."

"Really?"

"Really." This time, Khelben's forbidding expression declared his intention to hold firm. "And though your assessment of the possible strategy of the attackers has merit, it is not sufficient to explain the fall of Thornhold. The paladins send out patrols into the hills. If a force large enough to scale the walls was camped about, slowly gathering in number, the paladins surely would have discovered it. No, there is something else here, something hidden." He cast a quick, sharp look at Danilo. "Something that should remain hidden from casual eyes. Where did you say you heard this ballad?"

"The Howling Moon," Danilo repeated, "and a dreadful ditty it was." Or would be, he amended silently, given the time he would have to compose it!

"Good." Khelben nodded with satisfaction and began to spoon up his now-cold soup. "A poor tale has less chance of being repeated."

"It is clear that you have not spent much time in taverns of late," Dan said dryly. "I assure you, Uncle, the Ballad of Thornhold is the sort of song most frequently requested in the taverns, most eagerly sought by young bards and minstrels who make their living traveling about with news and gossip."

"You couldn't squelch this ballad?" Khelben demanded.

More easily than you could imagine, thought Danilo with a stab of guilt. He could simply leave it unwritten and unsung. But in truth, what would that profit? His words to Khelben painted the picture clearly enough; if he himself did not write such a ballad, someone else would, and the tale might grow dangerously larger in the telling.

"How so? Forbid a song? That would only spread it the faster. And you must admit, this has in it all the elements of a fine tale: heroism, tragedy, mystery. It will strike a particular chord with retired men of the sword, in which Waterdeep abounds."

"How so?"

"Well, other than the men who rode patrols, Thornhold was manned by aging paladins, veterans who chose to serve rather than retire. The paladins of Thornhold defied their age and infirmities. They died fighting, as heroes, long after their time. This holds much appeal."

Danilo reached for the ladle of the soup tureen, then thought better of it. "There is more. Although listeners expect tales in which good triumphs over evil, many are surprised and secretly delighted when evil triumphs—as long as the results do not touch them personally."

The archmage wiped his lips with a linen napkin. "That is a harsh thing to say."

Danilo shrugged. "But true, nonetheless. Since there is much mystery about the fall of Thornhold, there will be speculation. All who listen to the ballad become storytellers themselves, as they spin tales about what might have happened."

"But not all men are content with gossip," the archmage said. "How long before small forces gather to throw themselves against Thornhold? The paladins at the Halls of Justice will probably make a quest of it, not to mention the knights of Summit Hall. I don't need to tell you what a waste that would be. Only an enormous, full-scale assault of massive power could bring down those walls."

Danilo examined his fingernails. "Thinking of trying your hand, Uncle?"

The archmage sniffed. "As to that, I have but one word: Ascalhorn."

"Ah. Excellent point."

For a time, the men fell silent, and the air was thick with the memory of dire, unforeseen results of powerful magic wrought. The fall of the fortress that Khelben had named opened the gate to darker, more deadly powers. For years Ascalhorn had been aptly known as Hellgate Keep and represented the failure of extreme magical remedies. Evoking it declared Khelben's firm intention to keep himself free of direct involvement in the matter. Danilo often suspected that Khelben had a deep, personal stake in the matter as well, but he had never found a way to broach the subject.

"So, what do you propose that the Harpers do?" Danilo prodded.

"You are not going to like my suggestion," the archmage warned him, "but listen to my concerns, and weigh them well. Hronulf of Tyr was one of the men slain. Lost with him was an artifact, a ring of considerable and mysterious power. We must get it back."

"There is that 'we' again," the young man said in a voice heavy with foreboding.

Khelben's smile was grim and fleeting. "This task will not fall to you. There is one better suited for it."

"Bronwyn, I suppose."

"Who better? She has demonstrated great skill in searching out artifacts. And what she does not know of her heritage this day, she will soon find out. It is only prudent to bind her to the Harpers' service in this matter."

Danilo was more than a little unhappy about this turn of events. "This task would put her in great danger."

"Is that so different from many other assignments she has willingly taken?"

There was truth in that, yet Danilo still scoured his wits for a compelling argument against this plan. Then it occurred to him that Bronwyn might already possess this ring. If she had managed to see her father, perhaps he had passed it on to her. It was a possibility that bore looking into. If that were the case, Danilo could conceive of nothing important enough to warrant taking from Bronwyn the only family treasure she had ever possessed or was ever likely to possess.

"Bronwyn will do as you direct," Danilo said, letting a bit of anger creep into his voice. "She always has. But why is this ring so important that you consider its worth above hers?"

"I didn't say that," Khelben cautioned him. "Finding the rings and keeping them safely away from those who wish to use their power is the only course that will guarantee Bronwyn's safety. As long as the rings are obtainable, any descendant of Samular is a much-desired commodity."

Danilo reached for the pitcher of ale and poured himself a mug. "Uncle, do not send me out blind. There has been too much of that, and I won't be party to it any longer. Tell me plainly what these rings do."

"Some old tales say—"

"Let us dispense with prevarication," the bard cut in impatiently. "What do they *do?*"

Khelben tugged at the silver hoop in his ear, a sure sign that he was ill at ease. "I do not know," he admitted. "When the three rings are combined, they produce a powerful effect that is, unfortunately, unknown to me. The wizard who created them on behalf of Samular and his knights was not inclined to share his secrets."

Aha, Danilo thought. Some of Khelben's earlier comments took on more meaning, when considered by this light. "An old rivalry, perhaps?"

The archmage merely shrugged. "Find the ring," he repeated.

Danilo leaned back in his chair and took a sip of the ale. The beverage was flat and bitter. He grimaced and set the mug down.

"That might prove difficult," he said. "As I reported earlier this tenday, Bronwyn is away on business. My scouts have not found word of her in Daggersford, so it is possible that she had this story put about as a blind. My guess would be that she had another, *deeper* destination in mind."

He spoke those words with heavy portent, deliberately misleading the archmage. Khelben scowled. "Skullport, again, eh? Well, check it out. Help her complete her business, so we can move on to the matter at hand."

Danilo smiled, relieved to be able to speak whole truth at least once. "On that, Uncle, you may depend."

*   *   *   *   *

Ebenezer waited impatiently as Bronwyn held council with the aging human who kept the inn. The Yawning Portal, it was called. The yawning customer was more like it. He was beginning to nod off over his third mug of ale when the young woman strode over to his table, an expression of grim triumph on her face.

"Durnam will let us in," she said softly. "This is not the only entrance to Skullport, but it's the quickest. It's like being a bucket in a well. He ties a rope around you and lowers you down."

"A well, eh? A dry one, I'm hoping."

"At first." She grinned fleetingly, fiercely. "Skullport is neither dull nor dry, not by any measure."

The dwarf perked up at this news. He'd been doing too much sitting around for his liking and was about ready for a rowdy hour or two. He hopped up from the chair. "Well then, let's get to it."

Ebenezer followed Bronwyn back to the locked room and watched as the old man slid the cover from a gaping hole in the floor. The dwarf insisted on going first, figuring he'd be the better one to look around for danger, seeing as he could see in the dark and she couldn't. She agreed and told him briefly what to look for.

It was a good thing he'd chosen to go first, for the ride down was far longer than Ebenezer had expected. If he had had to sit and twiddle his thumbs while they cranked Bronwyn down, he might have changed his mind and demanded they take another route. It was hard to rethink the matter in the middle of a dark, narrow well shaft.

Finally he caught sight of the opening Bronwyn had told him would be there. He swung back and forth on the rope a bit to get some momentum, then seized the first of several iron handholds set into the stone wall. He hauled himself into the side tunnel, then wriggled out of the leather harness and gave the rope a couple of good tugs.

Instinct prompted him not to holler up a got-here-just-fine. Darkness and silence surrounded him, but there was a watchful quality to the place. Ebenezer wasn't keen to alert who-knows-what of his arrival.

The dwarf waited impatiently, hand never far from the handle of his hammer, until Bronwyn came into view. He grabbed her by the belt and hauled her into the tunnel. She touched down with a whisper of soft-soled leather. She shrugged off the harness and gestured to Ebenezer to follow her—a bold gesture, considering that she herself could not see in the utter blackness of the hole.

Ebenezer fell into step beside her, moving comfortably though the darkness. His eyes, like those of all dwarves, slipped easily past the range of light and color to perceive subtle patterns of heat. Humans had no such abilities, but Bronwyn moved along well enough, finding her way by running the fingertips of one hand along the wall.

They passed two passages before Bronwyn turned off into a side tunnel. This one sloped down swiftly in a tight, curving spiral, widening as it went. Slowly, the heat patterns faded from the dwarf's vision to be replaced by a faint, phosphoric light. Glowing lichen clung to the damp stone walls, and globs of luminous, mobile fungi inched along the walkways.

Ebenezer booted one out of the way. It splatted against the wall in a smear of weirdly glowing green, then oozed down to meld with a passing fungus.

"Looks like a deep dragon sneezed in here," he muttered darkly.

"It gets worse. Take care what you step in."

This proved to be good advice. Some of the leavings were more disgusting than others, and more than once they skirted the rotting carcass of some poor critter who'd been ambushed and half eaten.

They walked for hours without talking, listening intently to the sounds of the tunnel—the hollow, echoing sound of their footsteps, the dripping of water, the squeak of rats and the distant roars of prowling monsters. In time the faint clamor of a settlement edged into the tunnels.

"Almost there," Bronwyn murmured.

Ebenezer nodded and lifted one hand to cover his nose. The unmistakable stench of a seaport filled the air. They turned down another passage and came out into a huge cavern, the floor of which was scattered with low, dark buildings

They made their way through a squalid marketplace crowded with more beings, hailing from more races than Ebenezer had ever seen in one place. It was almost a relief when Bronwyn veered off into a narrow side tunnel.

The tunnel ended abruptly, opening into a small cavern glowing with faint, flickering blue light. At the entrance stood two of the largest illithids Ebenezer had ever seen. They were hideous brutes—man-sized, bipedal creatures whose mis-shapen bodies were not recognizable as either male or female. Large, bald heads of a sickly lavender hue rose above robes the color of dried blood. Their faces were utterly without expression—at least, none that the dwarf could read. Illithid eyes were large, white, and blank, and the lower half of their face comprised four writhing lavender tentacles. The guards clutched spears in their three-fingered purple hands, but their real weapon lay behind those impassive eyes.

"I need to talk to Istire," Bronwyn told the guards, jerking her head toward Ebenezer. "Got a dwarf for sale." In response, the guards stepped aside, and a third illithid emerged from the shadows, beckoning them to follow.

Ebenezer threw his friend a derisive glare, which he kept firmly in place as he followed the woman into the cavern. The way he saw it, a scowl would look well matched with the swagger he threw into his walk. Maybe these purple critters could look into his mind and know what he thought of all this, but he'd be damned as a duergar if he'd *look* scared!

"Not a bad plan, I guess, but you couldn't have warned me about it ahead of time?" complained Ebenezer in a low whisper as he and Bronwyn fell into step behind their guide.

"Hard to do, considering that I'm making this up as we go," she countered.

"Hmmph! Just see that you don't go selling me off to some two-legged squid," the dwarf returned with more bravado than he felt.

When they emerged into another small cavern, their guide disappeared back into the thick shadows and yet another illithid, this one draped in expensive-looking silks and fine gold jewelry, glided forward. Apparently, the message had been relayed through the mysterious mind-speak the creatures employed. Since there was little point in lying to a creature who could pluck thoughts from another being's mind, Bronwyn sensibly got right to the point. "Istire," she said, nodding a greeting. "We're trying to locate a shipment of dwarf slaves. I want the whole lot of them."

That is not the message the guard relayed, responded the illithid Istire, its unearthly "voice" sounding in Ebenezer's mind.

"I want an Arbiter," Bronwyn said calmly, ignoring her own lie. "We are entitled to one, by Skullport's laws of trade."

A touch of emotion—irritation, frustration, and perhaps respect—emanated from the illithid. *This way,* it said grudgingly.

The creature led them deeper into the cavern. As they went, the bluish glow intensified, until the gleam forced Ebenezer to shade his eyes. He just barely made out the source of the light—and promptly wished he hadn't bothered.

A strange, malformed illithid sat on a pedestal on a square dais with steps leading up on all sides. Instead of four short tentacles, this one had nine or ten extremely long ones that branched out from all sides of an enormous, glowing head. These tentacles undulated softly through the air like a cave octopus feeling about for prey.

"An Arbiter," Bronwyn explained softly. "You need to hold the tip of one of those tentacles. As long as you do, we're all equal. The illithid can't influence us, any more than we can control it."

Ebenezer eyed the writhing tentacles with dismay. "When we find the rest of my clan, those dwarves are going to owe me big for this," he muttered.

Istire took up one of the tentacles, nodding at Bronwyn and Ebenezer to do the same.

The experience was every bit as unpleasant as the dwarf feared. Immediately Ebenezer was enveloped by a cloud of strange sensations. He'd never much thought about evil—other than the natural impulse to pull out his axe and get to work whenever a critter bent on such mischief got in his way—and he'd had no idea that evil had a sound and shape and stench all its own. Linking thoughts with an illithid convinced him of that beyond debate. Even worse was the hunger—the dark, grasping, endless hunger that was the illithid's power.

Fortunately, Bronwyn seemed better able to twist her thinking to the illithid way of doing business. After some brisk bartering, Istire answered Bronwyn's questions readily enough. Who had dwarf slaves, where they were being kept, what ship they were going out on? Ebenezer suspected that the discussion cost Bronwyn, though, far more than the ridiculous price she'd agreed to pay. Glad though he was for the information the creature sold them, he would rather crawl into a dragon's gullet than ever again willingly enter an illithid's head.

On his way out, Ebenezer didn't bother trying for bravado. Speed seemed more sensible. He practically dragged Bronwyn out of the blue-glowing cavern and into the relative darkness and purity of the tunnels beyond.

"A pouch of silver and a long rope of black pearls," Ebenezer muttered, marveling at the cost Bronwyn had paid for the information, but not wanting their guide to hear his words. Since it was easier to think ahead, to the settling up of scores and debts, than to ponder the grim reality before them, he added, "The clan will be hard pressed to pay you back the price of that ransom, but we're good for it. Just might take a little time, is all."

She cut him off with a scowl. "We'll talk about that later. Right now, we're nowhere close to discussing reimbursement."

"Yeah," he admitted with a sigh. "What's this place we're bound to, then?"

"The Burning Troll. It's a tavern frequented by pirates and smugglers. It's one step up from a midden, but we should be able to get the information we need."

* * * * *

About an hour later, Ebenezer sat slumped on a high, rickety stool, getting the elbows of his jacket sticky on the unwashed bar in front of him. He sipped gloomily at his ale, too downcast to care overmuch that it had been desecrated by the addition of water.

The ship had already sailed. The ship that carried his kin away to slavery had sailed just that day, and they had missed it. No tunnel could reach where they'd gone. Even the cold comfort of vengeance was denied Ebenezer. The murderous, thieving humans who had done this were beyond the reach of his avenging axe.

Ebenezer let out another curse and signaled for a third mug.

"Game o' dice?" suggested a coarse, grating voice beside him.

Ebenezer swiveled on the stool to find himself nearly nose to snout with the ugliest excuse for an orc he'd ever seen. The critter was not much bigger than a dwarf, though it was as broad and powerful as most of its kind. It struck Ebenezer that some god with time on his hands and a twisted sense of humor had placed the orc lengthwise between his palms and compacted the critter like a snowball. In Ebenezer's opinion, the god in question should have kept squishing until the task was done.

Ebenezer pointed to his chest. "You talking to me?"

"Why not?" The sawed-off orc bared his fangs in a drunken grin and swatted Ebenezer companionably on the shoulder.

A satisfying, cleansing flood of dwarven ire swept through Ebenezer. Earlier, he had pitched a kobold through the window of the tavern—not first bothering to unlatch the shutters—for taunting him about his lack of a mustache. That really hadn't taken the edge off, though. But a friendly orc, now, that was enough to raise a considerable froth.

"Since you asked," the dwarf growled, "I'll *show* you why not."

His hand flashed out and seized the offered dice from the orc's palm. He slapped them down on the table and pulled the hammer from his belt. The orc's roar of protest rattled the mugs on the bar as he understood Ebenezer's intent. He grabbed for his dice—just in time to get one finger smashed under the descending hammer.

Several patrons, most of them just as ugly as the orc, came over to investigate the disturbance, their faces made memorable by scars and fangs and the uniform expression of menace that they currently wore. Ebenezer acknowledged their approach with a nod.

"Lookit," he said grimly, pointing to the shattered dice. A small, iridescent blue beetle, sort of a pretty thing that looked like a sapphire with legs, scuttled frantically away. Smart little critters, they could be trained to throw their weight against the colored side of their tiny prison.

A low, angry murmur rose from the cluster of men, orcs, and worse that surrounded Ebenezer and his orcish challenger. Using loaded dice didn't win many friends, Ebenezer noted with satisfaction, not even in a place like this.

The orc's howl of pain and outrage died suddenly as he realized how the tide of opinion had turned. He backed away a few steps, his piggish eyes wary and his shattered finger clutched close against his chest. Then he turn and ran with the whole pack of his former dice-mates roiling after him. Ebenezer raised his mug in mock salute, then turned back to the bar and his intended goal of waking up to find himself facedown on the bar after a few hours of hard-won oblivion.

An hour or so later, Bronwyn found the dwarf still at the bar. Ebenezer looked so defeated that her own shaky resolve firmed. She had found a solution—one that terrified her, but it was the best she could do. And it was the only chance the dwarf's lost family had.

She strode over to the bar, slapping away a few grasping hands on the way, and seized the dwarf's arm as he lifted his mug. Ale splashed over the bar and dampened the dwarf's beard. He turned a dispirited face to her. "Now why'd you go doing that?"

"I've got us a ship," she said urgently.

His eyes narrowed. "A ship?"

"And a crew. Smugglers waiting for cargo. It's been delayed, and the captain is losing too many men while he waits. He's eager for a job and will work cheap."

"Now hold on there. You're saying we should go out on the sea?" the dwarf asked. "In a ship?"

"That's the usual method," she hissed impatiently. "Now, come on. We haven't much time to get to the docks."

The dwarf still looked uncertain, but he hopped off the bar stool and followed her out of the Burning Troll. They wove their way between rows of leaning wooden buildings, taking a confusing maze of narrow alleys that led to the docks.

The prospect of a sea voyage left Bronwyn so edgy she felt as though several layers of skin had been peeled off, leaving her incredibly vulnerable. She started to chatter softly, to provide a distraction.

"Getting a ship was easier than I'd dared hope. The captain even took credit against plunder or payment. If you're a praying dwarf, you might want to hope that the ship has some plunder worth keeping, or this could break us both."

"Clan's good for it," Ebenezer repeated.

"I'm sure you are. It seems to me, though, there's more to the captain's story than he's letting on," she said absently, suddenly aware of a soft, rhythmic sound behind them. In Skullport, sound seemed to be everywhere, echoing through the vast sea cavern and bouncing off stone walls, resounding through tunnels. But this particular cadence was too regular and too constant to ignore.

"We're being followed," she murmured. She took a small

bronze disk from her bag and cast a quick glance over her shoulder. She caught the reflection of a squat, ugly orc peering around a corner at them.

Ebenezer was not so discrete. He turned around and glared, then sniffed dismissively. That clearly angered the orc. Lowering his head like a charging bull, he came at them. Bronwyn reached for her knife and dropped into a crouch.

But the dwarf pushed her aside and stood waiting in the center of the alley, hammer in hand. "Sit this one out," he said. "Won't take long, him having a smashed hand and all."

Bronwyn looked from the gleam in the dwarf's eye to the hammer in his hand and sighed. "Made friends in the tavern, did you?"

Ebenezer grunted in response and hauled the hammer down and back for the first swing. He caught the orc's chin with a wicked uppercut that halted the creature's charge and jerked his lowered head up and back. Ebenezer punched out with his free hand, slamming into the creature's chest. The orc's eyes bulged, and the gray hide of its face turned a ghastly blue. Slowly, it tilted forward and fell facedown into one of the fetid puddles that dotted the alley.

"Stops the heart, if you get a good clean shot," Ebenezer commented. He tucked his hammer back into his belt and turned to Bronwyn. "You was saying?"

She shut her gaping mouth and turned back down the alley.

"The captain is an ogre," she said, picking up where they left off. "But he was knowledgeable, well dressed, well spoken. Not a desperate second-rate thug by any means."

"Your better class of smugglers," Ebenezer said dryly.

"There's truth to that," she rejoined. "Think about it. There's a city below and a city above. There is traffic between the two, and you can bet that hammer of yours that many of Waterdeep's merchants know someone who knows someone who can pay someone to do a favor. Are you following?"

"Easily enough, but the question is, do *you* know someone who's in a position to do all that other knowing?"

Bronwyn hesitated, not certain but wanting to believe.

"You remember that man who came into the shop? Tall, fair-haired, good-looking?"

"No beard. Too much jewelry," Ebenezer remembered. "You were mad enough at him to chew trade bars and spit nails. What about him?"

"He's a friend, and he's also a member of a rich merchant family. It's possible he made some arrangements, helped pave the way. Here we are," she said as they emerged from the alley onto a broad, rotting boardwalk. "And over there's our ship."

Ebenezer's gaze followed the line indicated by her pointing finger. His dubious expression darkened into a scowl as he took in the maze of docks and the ships bobbing alongside them in an expanse of undulating black water. A flock of sea bats whirled and shrieked over the ship Bronwyn had indicated, which was being rapidly prepared to sail. Burly dockhands hauled barrels of supplies aboard, and a huge ogre captain clung to the rail and bellowed down orders in a voice that held all the music of a bee-stung mule's bellow.

"That friend of yours," Ebenezer said darkly as he eyed the ship with trepidation, "might not have done you as big a favor as you seem to think."

*   *   *   *   *

Dag Zoreth stood on the wall of Thornhold and watched the caravan pass. Three wagons, plus a mercenary guard. Nothing of interest. He would not even suggest that his men attack and demand toll from the traders. He looked past them, seeking for another, smaller caravan, one with a much more precious cargo.

Several days had passed since Dag's victory. With each day he found himself spending more and more time walking the walls, searching the High Road for signs of his daughter's caravan. The escort of Zhentilar soldiers should have retrieved her by now from her place of secret fosterage. She was late, and Dag was growing ever more concerned.

He was therefore greatly relieved to see a group of riders

turn off the road onto the path that led up to the fortress, and gladder still when they lifted the standard of Darkhold by means of introduction. Dag gave a few terse orders to one of the guards to carry word to the castellan and then hurried down to meet his daughter.

To his great consternation, the gate opened to reveal a group of men familiar to him but not under his command. At their head rode Malchior. Dag quickly arranged his features into a expression of honor and welcome and strode forward to help his former mentor and superior down from his horse.

Malchior landed heavily and swept an appraising look over the fortress bailey. "Very impressive, my son. I never thought the day would come when I saw the interior of this particular Caradoon stronghold—except, perhaps, for the dungeons."

Dag smiled faintly to acknowledge the jest. Malchior seemed in a rare mood, so jovial that he looked likely to break into dance at any moment. "You've had a long ride from the villa. Come, I will show you to your room and have the servants bring refreshment."

"Later, later." Malchior flapped his hands, brushing aside this notion as if he were shooing flies. "You've gone through Hronulf's papers?"

"Yes," Dag said coolly. There had been little enough to see. Three or four lore books, recounting stories of past glories attributed to the Knights of Samular, and a few blackened, curling bits of parchment that he had found in the hearth fire next to his father's charred heart.

The older priest rubbed his hands together in his eagerness. "I would be most interested in seeing any papers you have."

Dag shrugged and began to lead the way up to the tower. He had claimed the commander's quarters as his own, of course, and in them he kept the few goods that Hronulf of Tyr had left behind. "There is not much to see," he cautioned.

"What of treasure? Some holds, even those of religious orders, have a considerable hoard. Silver reliquaries holding the finger bone of some hero or saint, ancient weapons, an occasional artifact. Even lesser treasures, such as jewelry."

Malchior's voice dropped on the last observation, becoming a subtle note softer, more casual. Dag's quick ear marked the difference and the probable reason for it. Malchior knew of the ring.

As Dag showed Malchior up to the tower chamber, he pondered what to do about the ring. Say little, he decided, in hope that Malchior would reveal more of the rings' true purpose. So Dag waited until Malchior was seated behind Hronulf's—no, Dag reminded himself, *his*—writing table. He noted the open greed in the older priest's eyes as Dag placed a pile of lore books before him. Perhaps the rings were not the treasure that Malchior held most dear.

"You mentioned jewelry. You were speaking, of course, of the ring of Samular that Hronulf wore," Dag said coolly. "Regrettably, it was not on Hronulf's hand when he died. My sister arrived before me, it would appear, and made off with my inheritance. She will be found."

The old priest looked up, his eyes shrewdly measuring his former student. "And the other rings?"

"I will find them, as well," Dag said confidently. No need to tell Malchior that one was already in his possession. He waited until Malchior opened one of the books and began to leaf through it.

"How long will you be able to stay?" Dag asked.

"Not long," the priest murmured in a distracted tone. "This is most interesting. Most interesting. Three or four days' study should suffice, unless, of course, you can see your way clear to loan me these books."

"By all means," Dag said quickly—too quickly, judging from the shrewdly calculating look that Malchior sent him. The priest always suspected, and rightly so, that every other priest of Cyric knew more on any matter than he was willing to reveal.

At that highly inopportune moment, there came a sharp knock from the open door. Dag glanced over, and his throat clenched with apprehension as he recognized the captain of the escort he had sent for his daughter. The man's too stiff posture and the tight, grim lines of his face announced more clearly than words that the news was not good.

"Excuse me," Dag murmured to a very interested Malchior. "Please help yourself to any of the books and papers, and wine as well, if you will."

He hurried into the hall and shut the door behind him. "Well?" he hissed.

The captain blanched. "Lord Zoreth, there is grave news. When we arrived at the farm, the child was gone. Both the elf and his woman had been slain."

The sound like a roaring sea rose in Dag's ears, threatening to engulf him. He summoned all of his iron control and pushed away any response at all to this, the apparent ruin of his dreams. "And then? What did you do?"

"We followed. One man, on horse, headed swiftly toward the city of Waterdeep. We lost the trail once he took to the roads, but his destination was clear enough." The man stood straighter still. "What would you have us do?"

Dag turned a coldly controlled gaze upon the failed soldier. "I would like you to die, slowly and in terrible pain," he said in an expressionless voice.

Surprise leaped into the man's eyes, and an uncertainty that suggested he was unsure whether or not his commander was jesting with him. Then the first wave of pain ripped through him, tearing this notion from his mind—and tearing his lowermost ribs from his chest.

The soldier looked down in disbelief as the two slim, curved white bones sprang from his chest like a door flung open. His eyes glazed, and his mouth opened to emit a scream of agony and horror. But all that emerged was a choked gurgle as blood rose into his throat and poured down over his ruined chest.

Dag watched impassively as the power of his focused rage tore the soldier apart. When the man lay dead, he calmly walked back into the room and tugged at a bellpull. A servant arrived in moments, his face pale from the shock of what he had discovered in the hall.

"Have this mess cleaned up, and send Captain Yemid to

me," Dag said calmly. The man gulped and turned away. "Oh, and one more thing. Prepare my horse and guards. I will be leaving tomorrow at first light for Waterdeep."

Nine

 By dawn the following day, Dag Zoreth's horse and guard stood ready for the journey south. He was not pleased, therefore, when one of Malchior's servants came down to the gate to bid Dag to await his guest, who wished to accompany him.

An hour and more passed while the older priest lingered at breakfast and carefully supervised the packing of Hronulf's lore books into his bags. That accomplished, the members of the party mounted and began to wind their way down the hillside to the High Road.

The size of the group worried Dag. Although none of the guards wore the symbols of Darkhold, and neither of the priests their vestments, the addition of Malchior and his score of attendants made them more suspicious and more subject to scrutiny. A group of two score armed men arriving at the gates of Waterdeep might attract too much attention and too close an examination into Dag's affairs.

He had worries enough without the close attention of Waterdeep's officials, both overt and secret. The city was a veritable nest of Harper activity, and the secret lords of the city were nearly as intrusive and pervasive as the Harpers.

The inquiries Dag needed to make in the city were extremely sensitive, and he could use none of his usual Zhentilar informers. If Malchior discovered that Dag had a daughter, and that he had kept the girl's existence secret for over eight years, there would certainly be trouble.

And there was always the possibility that Malchior *did* know and that the girl's disappearance had been the work of the Zhentarim. Dag had reason to know that the society he served used such methods.

He cast a sidelong glance at Malchior. The fat priest rode like a sack of grain, but his face showed no sign of the discomfort his body must have been experiencing. He caught Dag's eye.

"You have met Sir Gareth. Are you finding that liaison useful?" Malchior asked pleasantly.

Dag considered his words carefully; after all, he intended to use the paladin to find his missing sister and his stolen child. "He managed to get Bronwyn to Thornhold. He handled the disposition of some newly acquired . . . cargo for me. In short, he seems able enough. I would hesitate to trust him too far, however, as he demonstrates a remarkable capacity for self-deception. I have no doubt he could justify any treachery."

"Well said," Malchior agreed. "That is always the risk of any agent, is it not? A man who is willing to betray his comrades at arms is not likely to show absolute loyalty to the men who bought him."

This presented as good an opening as Dag ever expected. "You presented Sir Gareth as an ambitious man, jealous of Hronulf's fame and lineage. That I can readily accept, but how did the Zhentarim hope to profit from the raid on Hronulf's village, and what do you personally intend to gain by pointing me toward my heritage?"

Malchior cast a glance around to ensure that the guards were beyond earshot. "The answer to your first question is easy enough. Paladins and Zhentarim are natural enemies, much as mountain cats and wolves. Hronulf had more enemies among us than I could count or name."

"You state what is known rather than answer the question," Dag observed, keeping his voice cool only with great effort. "You taught me better than to accept such sophistry. Please, do not insult your own fine instruction."

The priest chuckled at this tactic. "Again, well said!"

"Why were some of Hronulf's children taken?" Dag persisted.

Malchior sighed and flapped away a fly that buzzed about his horse's ears. "That I cannot tell you. It is the nature of the Zhentarim that one hand does not always know what the other is doing. There are many ambitious men among us. Who knows? Perhaps there was intent to seek ransom, or vengeance. Who is to say what is in the heart of any Zhentilar?"

Again, Dag noted grimly, a question evaded. "And how did you come to learn of my family's history and to connect me, a child lost some twelve years by the time I came to your attention, to Hronulf of Tyr?"

"Ah, that. I have made a study of the Caradoon family, you see. Sometime I must show you the old portrait of your ancestor, Renwick Caradoon. You are enough like him to be his son, perhaps even his twin. I saw the resemblance instantly when you were brought to Zhentil Keep for testing as a lad, and I made a point to look into your history. Tracing your path was no easy thing, I assure you. Years passed before I was convinced that you were indeed the child stolen from the Jundar's Vale and lost by the Zhentish soldiers who took you."

Dag listened carefully, but habit prompted him to study the path ahead, the seemingly endless stretch of hard-packed dirt shaded and scented by the stand of giant cedars growing on the eastern side. He absently signaled to his captain and pointed to the trees, thus indicating the need for additional vigilance. The man saluted and sent a pair of men off into the trees to scout ahead for possible ambush.

"You have grown quite practiced in the art of command," Malchior observed. "Perhaps there is something of Hronulf of Tyr in you, after all."

Dag's eyes narrowed. His first impulse was to believe the

remark a deliberate taunt. Then, upon consideration, he realized that Malchior had at last given him the answer to his question—albeit in the roundabout manner that the priest favored. "And that is why you sought me out," Dag summarized bluntly.

"There is power in the bloodline of Samular," the priest agreed, "as I have said before."

"Then why not Hronulf himself?"

Malchior scoffed. "I would have a better chance of turning the tide itself than bending a man such as Hronulf Caradoon to my purpose. No, the only way to deal with a noble paladin is the manner that you chose—and no doubt executed yourself."

Dag stiffened. "I did not mention Hronulf's fate."

"You did not have to. I trained you well, and we both know that only fools leave the destruction of an enemy to even a trusted underling. The important thing now is that Hronulf's power will be yours. When you discover what that is, and how to use it, then I trust that your gain will also be mine."

"You are a trusting man," Dag said with heavy irony. "I suppose that is why you also seek my sister. You are, perhaps, placing bets on more than one horse?"

Malchior laughed heartily, slapping one fleshy thigh with his hand. "Alas, betting upon racing horses is one vice I have not yet had occasion to develop. But you are astute. I would like to have this woman under the influence of the Zhentarim. Yours, mine—it makes no real difference. Are we not like father and son?"

An interesting comparison, Dag thought wryly, considering the history of betrayals that lay between him and his blood father. But Dag carefully considered the older priest's words, reading between and behind them for the true meaning. Perhaps his first conclusion was off the mark. Perhaps Malchior did not need him *or* Bronwyn. Perhaps he needed them both.

The family rings. There were two of them, that he knew of. One was on his daughter's hand, the other most likely in his sister's possession. But the inscription on the ring he found in his ruined village indicated that there were three and that when they came together, "evil would tremble."

The third ring, then. Three rings, in the hands of three of Samular's descendants. That had to be what Malchior wanted.

Dag's jaw clenched, and again he turned his eyes to the road ahead. No, he certainly could not rely on the Zhentarim to help him find what he had lost. Sir Gareth, for all his limitations, was Dag's best recourse. Two days' travel, and then he would confront his paladin "ally" face to face. There was grave danger in this, of course. If the paladins under Sir Gareth's command recognized the ring on the little girl's hand, Dag might be hard pressed to get her back.

"And your sister? Have your men found any sign of her yet?"

Dag lifted a hand to his lips to hide his knowing smile. Yes, Malchior seemed very interested in finding Bronwyn. "As of this morning, no. But, sooner or later, she will return to her place of business in the city, and I shall find her there. There is no real harm in the delay. I shall have my little family reunion in due time."

He turned a bland expression toward his former mentor, carefully studying his reaction to these words.

But the priest's face gave away nothing. "I'm sure you are right. Now, on to more practical matters. We have been on the road for hours. Surely we should break for the midday meal."

Dag glanced toward the east. The sun was barely visible over the tall cedars. Highsun was at least two hours away. He suppressed a sigh and gestured for his quartermaster's attention.

The trip to Waterdeep, it seemed, would take considerably longer than Dag had anticipated.

* * * * *

Ebenezer Stoneshaft had never been so thoroughly and completely miserable in his nearly two centuries of life. He slumped on the deck of the ship, his back against a barrel and his eyes fixed with determination on the sky—rather than on the heaving waves beneath.

Every jolt and roll of the ship sent shivers of atavistic terror through him. How humans and elves put up with sea travel, he would never know. The feeling was too much like that of the first shivers of an earthquake, that unpredictable and devastating force that was every dwarf's deepest fear. Being on a ship was a constant, terror-filled waiting for the damn quake to start.

The rolling motion, and the unrelieved state of expectant dread, kept the dwarf's belly in turmoil. Ever since they'd left that cesspool of a port in this floating excuse for a coffin, Ebenezer hadn't been able to keep much down.

Not that he'd stopped trying. When Bronwyn found him, he was doggedly spooning up salty chowder.

She crouched beside him. "The ship's food is terrible," she commiserated.

"Aye," he agreed sourly, regarding the small bowl is his hands. "And the portions are pretty damn skimpy."

For some reason she found this amusing, but she sobered quickly as she sat down beside him. "We're making good progress. Captain Orwig was able to bribe the Gate Keepers in Skullport and learn where they sent the ship we're seeking."

Ebenezer nodded. He remembered all too well the trip up from the subterranean port through a series of magical locks. "How much longer, do you figure?"

"This caravel is fast and light. The ship we're chasing is single-masted, with a deep hold for cargo. It was fully loaded. According to the captain, if we keep to the course the Keepers gave us, we should outrun it soon. If not today, then surely tomorrow."

"Good," the dwarf said stoutly. He wiped the bowl clean with a bit of hard biscuit, which he popped into his mouth. "Like the old saying goes: Nothing settles the stomach like the scent of an enemy's blood."

"I missed that one," Bronwyn murmured. "Must be

strictly a dwarven proverb."

It seemed to Ebenezer that she sounded a mite peaked. He looked keenly at her. "You're looking green around the gills, yourself. Sea travel don't agree with you, I take it."

"No."

Her grim, curt answer hinted at a tale. A tale, Ebenezer suspected, that might do her some good to tell. "So, this wouldn't be your first voyage, then?"

"Second." She glanced at the dwarf, her expression forbidding. Clearly, she didn't want to take this particular tunnel.

But Ebenezer was not easily put off. He nodded expectantly, inviting the tale. When that yielded no result, he leaned forward slightly and pointedly raised his eyebrows.

With a sigh, Bronwyn capitulated. "I was taken south on a ship after the raid on my village. I was, maybe, three or four at the time."

"Stones," he muttered. The thought of a child, any child, being submitted to the terror of a sea voyage set Ebenezer's blood simmering with rage. Which, in his opinion, was a big improvement over a churning belly. Danged if he shouldn't a-got riled up early on in this voyage, and stayed that way. "Hard thing, especially on a kid that age," he said darkly.

"It was." She fell silent for a moment. "I never actually saw the sea."

Ebenezer's gaze dipped down to the endless silvery waves. He gulped and yanked his attention back up to the billowing clouds that dotted the sky. "No loss there."

"There's bad, and there's worse," Bronwyn pointed out. "At least this trip, I have a choice. On my first voyage I was kept in the hold, along with maybe a dozen or so other prisoners."

Imprisonment. The dwarf didn't quite manage to suppress a shudder. "That's worse," he admitted.

They sat in silence for a few moments. Ebenezer caught Bronwyn looking in the direction of his belt, and tracked her gaze down to his "wine skin." He had replaced it in Skullport. The Burning Troll, whatever its other shortcomings as a tavern might be, kept dwarven spirits in stock. He untied the string that held the skin to his belt and handed it to Bronwyn.

She uncorked it and took a long, fortifying swig. To Ebenezer's surprise, she swallowed the strong spirits—known among dwarves as "molten mithral"—without a cough or a sputter. He didn't know a human who could do that, leastwise, not without practice. Maybe, he mused, she *had* had more than a little experience with dwarves and their ways. Later he'd probably be tempted to ponder on that a mite.

Bronwyn corked the skin and handed it back with a nod of thanks. "For some reason, I was the only prisoner not chained. They treated me well enough, I suppose. I had enough food, a blanket, and a corner of my own to sleep in, and even a couple of toys. The others were destined for slavery—they spoke of it, wept over it. I don't think I was. Not at first."

"What happened?" the dwarf prompted.

"There was a storm," she said shortly. "A terrible storm that tossed the ship around like a leaf. The mast snapped, and some of the planking tore loose. The hold took on water."

She shuddered from the memory. "I climbed as high as I could onto a pile of crates. Everyone else was chained. I could do nothing but watch as they drowned, slowly, screaming and cursing like creatures damned to the Abyss." Her voice dropped to a near whisper, husky with the remembered horror.

"Hard thing on a kid," the dwarf repeated.

"Nothing else in the hold survived except me—and a few rats. They could climb, too, and they found any footing they could. By the time the water rose to my chin, there weren't many places left for them to perch."

Ebenezer suspected what was coming, and muttered a heartfelt oath. He stopped himself, just barely, from reaching for her hand.

"Two of the rats climbed onto my head. They fought each other for the right to be there. Nothing I could do would dislodge them." She smiled faintly. "When my hair is wet, and parted just so, you can still see the scars."

She drew in a long, ragged breath. "The sea calmed suddenly. I learned later that we had been caught in the wake of a waterspout, thrown off course and into the path of some

Nelanther pirates. Without the mast, the ship could neither fight nor flee. Most of the crew were killed. The pirates seized the valuables and took all the survivors to be sold as slaves. It was night then," she added, "and there was no moon. That's why I never once saw the sea."

Ebenezer sat bolt upright. "So you ended up a slave after all?"

"That's right. This time, I *was* chained. The rest of the trip is a blur. I vaguely remember the marketplace, and standing on the block while people gawked and poked. I was sold. There is a dark cloud over the next bit. I think I was resold, or maybe I escaped and was recaptured. I really don't remember."

She sighed, and to Ebenezer's eyes she looked exhausted and drained by the recounting. He was sorry he had asked, but glad to know just the same. A good thing, it was, to know the measure of your friends.

That measure he could summon up in one short statement. "And after all that, you came out on this ship."

Their eyes linked in understanding. After a moment, the dwarf reached for her hand. Her long, fragile human fingers intertwined with his stubby digits. They sat together, gazing up at the cloud castle that floated gently past and at the silver sea beneath. It didn't bother Ebenezer quite so much now to see the heaving sea. His own kin most likely didn't have his kind of choice in the matter. As Bronwyn had said, there was bad, and then there was worse.

*   *   *   *   *

Algorind arrived in Waterdeep footsore and dusty. His boots had been made for riding, and the soles were nearly worn through by his days of walking. His once-white tabard was dingy with the dust of the road. He hated to present himself at the gates of the Halls of Justice in such a state, but his brothers must learn of Thornhold's fate.

He hurried through the streets. As before, he was struck by the noise and the crowds. How did men of Tyr hold fast to their faith, surrounded by such distractions and decadence? It puzzled him why the brothers would see fit to build the Halls of Justice in the heart of this teaming city. Better the remote hills, or the purity of a windswept mountaintop.

The gatekeeper at the Halls of Justice looked him up and down with obvious disapproval.

"It is most urgent that I speak with Sir Gareth," Algorind said. "Please bear word to him that Algorind of Summit Hall begs audience."

"Summit Hall, is it?" the guard said, his face showing a bit more warmth. "You'll be in good and abundant company, then."

Algorind's brow furrowed in puzzlement. "Sir?"

"You don't know? There's a group of young paladins and acolytes from the training school, led by Laharin Goldbeard himself. They are making a paladin's quest of it," the man said. His eyes grew warm and distant with remembered glories. "I would go myself, but for the injuries that keep me tending gate."

"Yours is an honorable task and a service to Tyr," Algorind said, noting the wistful note that crept into the knight's voice. "But sir, of what great task do you speak?"

"You *have* been out of the thick of things. Taking a time of solitude, like old Texter?"

"Not by choice. Sir, the task?"

The knight's face turned grim. "Why, the reclaiming of Thornhold, of course. Riders are taking word throughout the northlands. The Knights of Samular are gathering to march north. Paladins of other orders are joining in, and those who claim no order at all. It has been many years since such an army of righteousness gathered together. May the Zhentarim tremble."

Algorind caught the gatekeeper's arm. "Sir, I have just come from Thornhold. I was but a few hours' foot travel away when the capture was complete. I saw the smoke of destruction rise, and exchanged blows with a Zhentish patrol from the army who took the keep."

The knight's eyes widened. "Why did you not say so at once? You, Camelior! Come here, and take this young knight to the council room with all haste."

Algorind fell into step beside his guide. He was led into the largest of the three buildings and into a vast hall. Six long tables dominated this hall, their edges cunningly shaped so that all fit together to form a single large hexagon. Paladins sat around the outer edge only, so that all could converse. Bright banners hung from the ceiling, proclaiming the standards of the many orders and the solitary knights who served the Halls of Justice.

Algorind's gaze sought out Sir Gareth, and he noted the stunned look on the old knight's face. This made him exceedingly self-conscious. Neatness and cleanliness were rules of the order and for him to appear thus was an affront, but Algorind had little time to consider his hero's response, for Camelior quickly relayed the message that Algorind had given the gatekeeper to the assemblage.

"Another seat, if you please," called Laharin.

Pages—young boys brought to the temple to be tested for suitability to the life of Tyr—leaped to do the Master Paladin's bidding. Algorind found himself escorted and seated with discomfiting ceremony. All eyes were upon him when Laharin urged him to speak.

Again Algorind's eyes sought out Sir Gareth. The old knight solemnly tapped one finger to his lips, reminding Algorind of his pledge of discretion. The conflicting duties made Algorind feel uncomfortably like a tethered hawk bid to fly and hunt.

"I rode north to Thornhold to carry a message of a personal nature to Hronulf," Algorind said carefully. Sir Gareth's faint nod assured him that these words were well chosen. "When I was but a few hours away, I saw black smoke rising into the sky. From the scent, I knew it to be a bier."

Algorind fell silent for a moment in respect to the fallen. All around him knights and priests bowed their heads or formed the hand gestures that affirmed their faith and commended the spirits of their brother knights into the hands of Tyr.

"I heard a patrol and lay ambush." Algorind blushed to admit this, but he was sworn to the truth. "There were four men, mounted and well armed. They were searching for a woman who had been in the fortress at the time of the attack. She escaped, and none knew how, but it seems likely that she took with her a ring that belonged to Hronulf."

Murmurs of consternation rippled through the hall. "And did you seek this woman?" demanded Laharin.

"Sir, I believe I caught sight of her. She was in the company of a dwarf and riding south for Waterdeep. If it is your wish, I will seek her out."

Sir Gareth rose slowly, and his expression was that of a man determined to meet a fate of his own making. "Brothers, I may be able to shed some light on this matter. Some days ago, a young woman came to me earnestly seeking word of Hronulf of Tyr. She gave me the name Bronwyn. A slight woman, with large brown eyes and very determined bones about the cheeks and chin, and a very long braid of brown hair. Is this the woman you saw?"

"By your description of her size and hair, it seems likely," Algorind agreed. "I was too far away to stop her, much less look carefully at her face."

Sir Gareth sighed and sank down to his chair. "I have gravely erred," he admitted. "I spoke of Hronulf to this woman, and perhaps my words sent her to Thornhold."

"Do not reproach yourself, brother," Master Laharin told him. "You had no reason to doubt the motive for the young woman's questions."

"No, none, but I did not pray to Tyr to test her heart and her chosen path. That was a terrible oversight." Sir Gareth's brow furrowed suddenly, and he looked to Algorind. "How is it that you are come so late with this news?"

This was the moment Algorind had been dreading. "My horse was stolen from me by the dwarf who accompanied the woman. I had to walk back to the city."

"In that case, your progress is most noteworthy," Laharin said dryly. "Tell me, did you fare any better in retrieving the child of Samular's blood?"

"Oh, yes, sir." Algorind said earnestly. He looked to Sir Gareth for confirmation.

The old knight swept the room with a steady gaze. "Upon

hearing of the fall of Thornhold, I feared for the child's safety. She was taken to a place of secret fosterage, outside of Waterdeep. It seemed a wise precaution."

"But—"

Sir Gareth shot Algorind a glare that stopped his protest as surely as an arrow to the heart. How was it, Algorind marveled, that the knight could make this claim? He himself had delivered the child to Sir Gareth well before the fall of the stronghold and had been told at that time that the girl was to be taken to secret fosterage. Perhaps she had been moved to a safer place, Algorind concluded, finding consolation in this reasoning.

"How, then, are we to proceed?" asked a knight whose name Algorind did not know, a man of middle years and exceedingly ruddy visage.

"This young paladin has a quest to complete," Laharin suggested, nodding to Algorind. "He is able. The loss of his horse is the first fault I have seen in him in nearly ten years of training and service. Let him find the woman and the ring she carries."

"I agree," Sir Gareth said quickly. "With your permission, brothers, I would like to lend Algorind a horse from my own stables. This matter is too important to await his earning of another steed."

"That might not be needed," put in another knight. "A tall white horse was delivered to our gates just yesterday. Is it possible that this horse thief had a change of heart?"

"I will stop by the stables and see if the horse is mine, sir," Algorind said gratefully, "but I cannot speak for the dwarf."

Greatly relieved to have discharged his duties, and eager to see if the white horse was in fact his lost Icewind, Algorind requested permission to leave so that he might attend his new task.

Laharin's stern face softened as he studied his former student. "No, you are sorely tired and no doubt in need of food and rest. Clean the dust of the road from you, then return and break bread with your brothers. Lord Piergeiron has consented to dine with us. The pages will show you to the barracks, where you may wash and find fresh clothing. Return in all haste."

Algorind did not need prompting. One of the pages led the way to the barracks. He made short work of washing off the road dust and exchanging his worn garments for new. There was nothing to be done about the holes in the sole of his boots, but after the page attacked them with goose grease and rags, they were at least clean and well shone.

He hurried back to the hall, arriving just as the echoing call of horns announced Lord Piergeiron. He found his seat beside Master Laharin and rose with the others to greet the Lord of Waterdeep.

Piergeiron was a most impressive man, tall and well made. His brown hair was thick and only lightly touched with gray, though by all accounts he had lived more than threescore years. He nodded graciously to the assembled paladins, bidding them to take their seats. He carried himself with becoming modesty, Algorind noted, and wore none of the trappings that might be expected of a ruler of such a decadent city. But then the lord was a paladin, and the son of a paladin—the great Athar, the Arm of Tyr, who in his time was as famed as Hronulf and Sir Gareth were in theirs.

Algorind felt himself humbled in the presence of such men, and he was grateful when no call was made on him to recount his recent misadventures. Indeed, there was little serious discussion over the meal. Men shared news they had picked up on the road and reminisced with comrades they had not seen for many years. It was a most congenial meal, ably attended by the pages who served it.

Algorind watched the boys at their work, approving of their skill and diligence. Service was the goal and the delight of a paladin, and all young men who aspired to Tyr's service began their chosen path in similar fashion. Boys were given menial chores and taught to do them cheerfully and well. It had been so with Algorind and with every man he knew. Better training than this he could not conceive. Tales of glory and heroism attracted many young men and a few young women to seek a paladin's path, but it was service, long and hard and inglorious, that tested out those whose dedication was true.

The meal was unusually grand for a paladins' hall, with three removes and wine with each course. Fine, boat-shaped salt cellars were placed every six men, and there was such an abundance of fine plate that only the youngest paladins and knights' squires were given bread trenchers to hold their meat. Algorind was dazzled by the variety. There was roasted venison, eel pie, pigeons stuffed with finches that were in turn stuffed with herbs, a fat rump of pork and another of rothé, fish, and small, savory pasties. There was even a sweet, a flummery rich with cream and dried apples. Algorind ate sparingly, not wishing to fall into gluttony and trying mightily not to harshly judge those who seemed less devoted to the keeping of that rule.

At last the final remove was carried away and sweet wine poured to end the meal.

"Lord Piergeiron, we have a grave matter to bring before you," Sir Gareth began. "We seek your assistance in finding a certain young woman, whom we believe might have stolen an artifact sacred to the Knights of Samular. Her name is Bronwyn. She is comely and brown as a wren, of small stature. We wish to learn more about her and her associates."

The paladin politely wiped his lips on the edge of the table-cloth, as was proper in good company, then turned to his brother knight. "I do not know of this woman, but I will have inquiries made. You have my word as the son of Athar, what I learn, you will know."

*   *   *   *   *

Solitude was a rare pleasure, and Danilo had intended to make the most of it. He had set aside the afternoon for private study and informed Monroe, his able halfling steward, to admit no one. He was more than a little annoyed, therefore, to have his fierce concentration broken by a tapping at his study door.

"Yes? What is it?" he said, not bothering to look up from the arcane runes.

"Lord Arunsun to see you, sir. Shall I show him in?"

This time he did look up from the spellbook, startled by

these most unexpected words. He met the halfling's gaze with a rueful smile. "Only if you can't think of a better plan," he said dryly.

"None comes to mind, sir," Monroe said with an admirable lack of inflection. He bowed and then hastened out to fetch his master's guest.

Danilo sighed. Khelben did not often visit him in his home, most likely because he was discomfited by the extravagance of the house's furnishings, the many musical instruments that lay readily at hand, and the bards and revelers who always seemed to be gathered at table or making merry in the parlor. Today Danilo was alone but for the discrete ministrations of the steward and the half dozen or so servants under his command. Dan had planned to learn a new spell. Hastily he opened a drawer in his table and thrust the book out of sight. Although he still kept to the study of magic that his uncle had started twenty years before, he was careful to downplay his interest in the art. It would not do to raise the archmage's hopes overmuch.

"Uncle!" he said heartily, rising to meet his visitor. He beckoned the archmage in and reached for the decanter of elven feywine that stood on his writing table. "Had you sent word you were coming, I would have had cook stir up something thick and bland in your honor."

"I've eaten." Khelben waved away the offer of wine and took the seat across from his nephew's writing table. He glanced at the new Calishite carpet that covered most of the polished wood floor with a tapestry in rich shades of red and cream, but for once did not comment on this latest extravagance. "You have heard of the recent influx of paladins to the city?"

So that was it, Danilo mused. No doubt Khelben was concerned about the possible connection with Bronwyn and had come to hear a report and deliver advice—advice that Danilo almost certainly would not wish to follow.

"Rumors travel," Danilo agreed lightly. Suddenly he dropped his façade of determined cheerfulness and sank back into his chair. There were times that Danilo sorely regretted his increased role in Harper activities. His existence had been much more congenial when the only life he was required to endanger or to answer for had been his own. Making decisions that could have grave consequences for friends such as Bronwyn, and for the other young Harper agents and messengers under his direction, was a heavy responsibility.

"The presence of so many paladins in the city worries me," he admitted, "and has given me cause to reconsider my belief that there cannot be too much of a good thing."

"For once, we are in accord," Khelben said. He looked as if he wished to say more, yet there was a most unfamiliar hesitancy in his manner that greatly increased Danilo's sense of unease.

Danilo bit back the flippant comment that came to mind. This was a time for straight and honest words.

"A paladin," he said thoughtfully, "may well be the finest, purest example of what a man can be—the epitome of all that is noble. And a paladin mounted for battle on his war charger, filled with holy zeal and absolute courage, might well be the most inspiring sight that many mortals could hope to see. He can, and does, accomplish much good. But a hundred paladins, a thousand? United in purpose, single-minded and driven by their sense of duty? I tell you truly, Uncle, I can think of no better definition of terror."

"These are not words you should repeat to most men," Khelben cautioned him, "and only to you will I say that, once again, we are in complete agreement. For this reason, I have long been wary of the paladin orders. These good men have a disturbing tendency to ride their war horses over whatever perceived obstacle they find in their path."

"You are either with a paladin, or you are against him," Danilo agreed. "There are no half measures, and few shades on their moral pallets other than black and white. I regretfully parted company with my old friend Rhys Brossfeather shortly after he entered Torm's service. My ways are not his, and that was too much of a stumbling stone for him. In fact, in the eyes of many paladins, I would dare say that a Harper is nearly as much an enemy as a priest of Myrkul."

The archmage nodded slowly. "That is well said, and therein lies our problem. It is impossible for Harpers to come out against one of the Holy Orders without incurring not only the wrath of the paladins but the suspicion of many of the common folk. In this matter, I am of divided mind. What would you suggest that we do?"

This question was the first of its kind, and Danilo quickly hid his surprise. "What we do best. Watch, report, and shape events in small ways. In the old days, the Harper who was most effective was usually unseen. I have already taken steps to measure the knights' interest in Bronwyn and their intentions."

"Oh?"

"Clearly, sending men to infiltrate the Halls of Justice would be a waste of time and effort, considering a paladin's ability to weigh and measure the intentions of those about him. So I have people watching over Bronwyn's shop, her usual contacts, even the shops and taverns she frequents. If the paladins seek her out, we will know."

The archmage nodded, satisfied. "Good. Have you made any progress in your studies?"

Danilo blinked. For a moment, he thought that the canny archmage referred to the half-learned spell hidden in his drawer. Then he remembered the other matter of contention that lay between them: Bronwyn, and the secrets of her past.

"Indeed I have," he said. He rose and crossed the room to a wall lined with books. Selecting one bound in fine red leather, he returned to the archmage's side.

"I read all I could find concerning the Knights of Samular. Quite an impressive group, with a long history. There were a few things, though, that did not ring true, not even when I discounted a bit of bardic exaggeration and the usual way legends have of growing in the telling. The capture of Thornhold was one such incident."

Khelben eyed him keenly. "You are not referring to the recent battle, the capture by the Zhents?"

"No, indeed. The original battle, in which the knights wrested the fortress from some petty warlord. Samular himself

was involved, and apparently took personal title of the hold.
Paladins were less conscientious about personal possession in
those days, it would seem. And as Samular was from an
exceedingly wealthy family, I suspect he was so accustomed to
ownership that he considered it his right, not a violation of his
vows."

"Leave such matters for the Heralds," the archmage said
impatiently. "Continue."

"Well, according to the best information I can find, the paladins under Samular's command took the fortress in a single
day, with a force of fewer than fifty men. Brunyundar, the
warlord, had three times that many. Even taking into account
the fervor and skill for which paladins are renowned, that
seems an impossible feat."

Khelben nodded, following Dan's reasoning to the conclusion. "You believe they called upon the power commanded by
the three rings of Samular."

"It is reasonable," Danilo said. "What that power might be,
I do not know, but I think I can tell you how the third ring
came to be lost."

He lay the book open on the table before the archmage.
"This is a new-made copy, not more than five years old, of a
very old lore book. The original was copied several times
before over the years, but the scribes and artists were among
the finest of their times, and I believe the reproduction is
true. Look closely at this etching."

The archmage bent over the desk and studied the page.
Danilo leaned over his shoulder and gazed at the drawing he
had nearly committed to memory. It was an exceptionally
well drawn picture of a battle's aftermath, rendered with an
accuracy that suggested that the artist had not only been present, but had possessed some skill or enchantment that
enabled him to capture the moment with a near-magical pre-
cision. In the background was a stone stronghold, two towers
surrounded by a stout, curving curtain wall. The doors were
open, indicating that the fortress had already been taken. The
stonework was sharp of edge and unworn by time. The terrain
was rough and hilly, and seabirds wheeled overhead. Here

and there about the outer wall lay fallen men, arrows bristling from their chests or throats. These unfortunates wore chain mail of larger, coarser links than had been in use for centuries, and wore crude helmets of a type not seen in many years. In the picture's foreground was a young man, his white cloak and robe deeply stained with his own blood. He lay supported in the arms of the burly knight who crouched beside him, and whose face was marked by deep grief. The two men were recognizable as brothers or at least near kin, though they were in many ways very different. The wounded man was young, slight, and small of stature. His face was narrow, his prematurely white hair dipped in the center of his forehead into a pronounced inverted peak, and his gesturing hands had long, supple fingers. He wore a single ring on the index finger of his left hand.

Danilo marked the sudden flash of recognition, quickly covered, that entered the archmage's eyes. "Do you know him?" the bard asked.

"I did. Or thought I did. That was many years ago," Khelben said shortly. "It is not a tale I wish to relate, so do not bother to ask."

It was rare that the archmage was so blunt. Clearly, this old wound had healed badly.

"Note those hands," he said, pointing to the dying wizard—for wizard he certainly was. That distinctive gesture, frozen in time by an artist who most likely did not understand what he recorded, was part of a long, difficult, and dire spell. A spell born of unquenchable pride and ambition, and a last recourse for a dying wizard who was not content to yield to death.

Khelben's eyes widened as the implication of that gesture struck him. He shot a concerned glance over his shoulder at his nephew. "How could you know what this means? What in nine hells possessed you to learn *that* spell?"

"Curiosity," Danilo assured him. "Not intent. I wished to know how such a thing might be done, but I have no wish to experience it myself."

"Good." Khelben expelled a long, shaky breath. "You are trouble enough as you are now."

"But you see my point."

"Indeed I do," the archmage said grimly, "and I believe I know where the third ring may be found. Unfortunately, Bronwyn is the only person alive who has a chance of retrieving it."

Ten

On the morning of their third day at sea, Bronwyn awoke to the sound of angry voices on the deck above. She groaned and rolled out of her hammock, placing her hands on the small of her back as she straightened up. As she had expected, Ebenezer's hammock was already empty.

Bronwyn could barely stand straight without banging her head on the low ceiling beams. With four paces, she could easily cross the cabin she shared with her dwarven "partner." Even so, they were traveling in comparative luxury. In the identical cabin across the narrow walkway that served as a hall, clearly visible through the two open doors, slept six occupants: four men and two ogresses.

One ogress snarled in her sleep, half-roused by the woman's movements. Bronwyn grimaced and eased toward the cabin door, going one small, stealthy step at a time. The small porthole in the cabin wall showed a sky that was still more sapphire than silver, and her shipmates would not thank her for waking them so early. All six had been late to bed, scorning sleep to sit on the floor of the cabin recounting tales, playing dice, and swigging away at some syrupy, spice-laden drink.

Rough though they were, these crew members shared an odd companionship born of long acquaintance and battles shared. Bronwyn almost envied them. She, a newcomer and their employer, had been excluded from this fellowship, but she had seen enough to know better than arouse their collective ire.

Bronwyn stooped at the door to pick up her boots and carried them with her as she slipped through the open door. She crept down the short hall to the ladder leading above deck and climbed it one-handed. On deck she found pretty much what she had expected to find.

Near the bow, standing nearly toe to toe with arms folded and eyes blazing, were Captain Orwig and Ebenezer Stoneshaft. The top of the dwarf's curly red head barely reached the ogre's belt, forcing him to tip his head way back to glare at his adversary, but Ebenezer's angry expression conceded no disadvantage. The two of them were engaged in yet another round of verbal warfare, lobbing insults at each other with a force and fury that brought to mind flaming pitch balls and a pair of trebuchets. Bronwyn was no delicate spring flower, but she caught her breath in surprise at the sheer creativity of the dwarf's pungent explanation of Captain Orwig's parentage.

The small sound startled the combatants. They glanced over, and identical sheepish expressions flooded their unlike faces. The captain collected himself first, and after acknowledging Bronwyn with a curt bow, he strode aft to sound the morning rise bell.

Bronwyn's gaze tracked him. Near the stern was mounted an old cart's wheel that had been adapted as a steering device suitable to the ogre captain's strength and size. Two paces to starboard was a huge brass triangle hanging from what appeared to be a miniature gibbet, upon which was a hook holding the long brass rod used to sound the alarm. But Orwig ignored the brass clanger. He drew his cutlass, which he thrust into the triangle and spun in several quick, impatient circles.

An urgent clanging shattered the morning quiet and brought sailors roiling up to the deck. They came with their weapons in hand, feet still bared, sleep forgotten in the promise of coming battle. For a few moments, the crew scanned the waters for the threat, and then, when it was clear that there was nothing to be seen, they turned incredulous faces to their captain.

"Practice drill?" one of them ventured.

"*Morning!*" Orwig roared in response. "Layabouts, the lot of you! To your tasks, and quickly." He spun away and scampered up the rigging, nimble as a squirrel despite his vast size.

Bronwyn sighed and sat down on a low barrel to pull on her boots. Captain Orwig seemed an able sailor, but he was still an ogre. The captain had no more love for Ebenezer than the dwarf bore him, and the exchange of insults and challenges was growing steadily hotter. Bronwyn suspected it was a matter of hours before the two of them came to blows.

The crew, too, were getting restive. She'd overheard some grumbling about their canceled shore leave, and she had marked their muttered expectations that this unplanned trip would have to pay well, and pay soon, to be worth the while.

She rose and looked about for Ebenezer. He stood with his ankles crossed and his back leaning against the mainsail mast. His current occupation was staring out to sea and puffing at a small clay pipe.

"That's an interesting notion you shared with Orwig," she said in a casual voice. "That particular use for lizard man eggs had never occurred to me."

The dwarf jumped and then colored. "Wasn't meant for your ears," he mumbled.

Bronwyn took the pipe from his hand and sipped a bit of the fragrant smoke, then handed it back. "Orwig has a good record as a captain, and a good reputation as a smuggler— odd though that may sound. Everyone I talked to said he delivers what he promises, no tricks, no excuses. He'll take us where we need to go, but mark me, Ebenezer, you can only push any ogre so far."

"Itching for a fight, isn't he?" Ebenezer said with immense satisfaction. He dragged at his pipe, then blew out a trio of smoke rings in quick, expert puffs.

As the implication of this sank in, Bronwyn gaped, then shook her head in disbelief. "You're doing this on purpose? To work him up for the fight ahead?"

"There's that," Ebenezer agreed. "And it's a bit of sport, to keep my mind off. . . ." His voice trailed off, and he nodded at the sea.

"It's almost over," Bronwyn said, as much for her own assurance as the dwarf's. "We should catch up with the slave ship today. Tomorrow at the latest."

"Yeah? Big place, that sea. Easy to miss one small boat."

She shook her head. "Orwig bribed one of the Gatekeepers in Skullport to tell us where the slave ship was sent. We know where the *Grunion* emerged and have a good idea where it's bound."

Ebenezer shuddered at the reminder of the journey up through the magical locks linking the subterranean Skullport with the open sea. Dwarves, it seemed, did not take kindly to magical travel. Ebenezer's dense, compact body resisted the process. Unlike any of the other people aboard the ship, he had felt the magical passage as burning physical pain. "Like being ripped through a thick wall all at once, but in lots of little bits," was how he had described it to Bronwyn after he'd recovered from the ordeal.

His hand shook a little as he lifted the pipe for another long drag. "Lotta water out there," the dwarf repeated. He glared at Bronwyn, as if daring her to prove him wrong.

Bronwyn understood completely, and she chose her next words as much for her own reassurance as his. "We were set on the same place on the sea as the *Grunion* emerged. Now, the slavers are going to want to get where they're going as fast as possible. This time of year, the warming air over the land causes a strong coastal wind. They'll take full advantage of it. Much farther out to sea, the wind diminishes; much closer to shore, they'll run the risk of shoals, rocks, and harbor patrols. The corridor is not that wide. As long as Captain Orwig follows the wind, we should pass within sight of them."

The dwarf glanced up at the sails. There were three of

them, mounted on a pair of tall oaken masts. All three were curved tight, so full of wind that not even a ripple disturbed the taut white sheets, but he still looked doubtful. "They got a jump on us."

"True, but the *Narwhal* flies three sails to the *Grunion*'s one. This ship is built for pursuit and battle. The *Grunion* is a tub—an old ship, with a deep keel designed to hold a great deal of cargo, and according to the dock manifesto, it's heavily loaded. It can't possibly outrun us."

He slid a sidelong glance up at her. "For a person that don't like water, you know a lot about this sort of thing."

"I'm a merchant," Bronwyn said shortly. "I have to know how things are moved from place to place."

"There's that," he agreed, but his shrewd, sympathetic gaze suggested that he understood far more than Bronwyn wanted to say. She had spent many years learning all she could about the slave trade, in hope of tracing her own path back to her forgotten home and family. And yet, this was the first time she had taken action on behalf of people who, like herself, had been stolen away from all that they knew. She was relieved that the dwarf did not ask her why this was, or press her to explain why she suddenly felt compelled to help him and his clan. That she could not explain, not even to herself.

They fell silent, both of them gazing out over the sea. It had faded to silver, and on the eastern horizon a deep rose blush shimmered over the water to herald the coming sun.

Far above them, a harsh undulating howl tore out across the water—a sound like that a wolf might make had he the capacity for speech, but in a voice far deeper and more ominous that any beast of forest or tundra could muster.

Bronwyn spun and squinted up at the crow's nest. Captain Orwig shouted the make-ready alarm, pointing toward the east. He vaulted over the side of the crow's nest and scrambled down the ropes, shouting orders as he went.

The crew went into action immediately. Several of them dragged coils of rope to the starboard side, fastening one end of each coil to iron loops set into the deck and tying grappling hooks on the other. Some sailors ran for weapons, and still others tended the sails.

"Mount the bowsprit!" roared Orwig as he leaped down onto the deck. He shouldered his way through the chaos and shoved the first mate away from the wheel. He took his place at the helm and hunkered down, his piglike eyes narrowed on the ship ahead. "Shift the ballast!"

Several crew ran to the enormous pole that stretched down the middle of the deck, from bow nearly to the mainsail. They deftly loosened the knots that kept it from rolling and then crouched, ready to lift. On the count of three they heaved it upward, grunting with exertion, then staggered to the bow. They lowered the weapon into the slot built to hold it—which was reinforced inside and out with iron plate—then tightened the bolts. Meanwhile, other sailors put their shoulders to heavy barrels of ammunition—ballista quarrels, scrap-iron grapeshot, and wicked spiked balls—and slid them down toward the stern to balance the ship.

Bronwyn whistled softly as she took the measure of the ship's weaponry. The bowsprit resembled a giant lance, banded and tipped with iron. With it in place, *Narwhal* really did resemble the deadly, spear-headed fish for which it was named. She understood why Captain Orwig had designed his ship thus and why the crew suffered the inconvenience of stepping over the bowsprit in its usual resting place in the center of the deck. When it was in place, *Narwhal* was clearly a battleship, and as such would be regarded warily in all legitimate ports and even in Skullport.

She shaded her eyes and looked across the brightening sea at the fleeing ship. It looked much as it had been described: old, nondescript, hardly worthy of notice. The sail was much-patched, and the ship gave the impression of being the last possession of some down-on-their-luck fisher family. But the number and weaponry of the small figures clustered on the deck gave lie to that illusion. *Grunion* was well defended, and her mercenary crew appeared more than ready for a fight.

"Prepare to ram!" Orwig bellowed. His massive arms corded as he wrenched the wheel around. The call echoed

throughout the ship. Several sailors hauled at the ropes of the
sails, intent upon seizing every possible breath of wind. The
ship rolled precariously to one side as it hurtled forward.
Bronwyn had thought *Narwhal* was moving fast before, now
it sliced through the sea with a speed that etched a deep path
in the water behind them.

The slave ship tried to evade, but it was far too slow and
clumsy. To Bronwyn's eyes, it looked like a rabbit, frozen by
fear as it awaited a raptor's claws.

"Brace!"

The ogre's shout thundered out over the sounds of the
rushing wind and water. All over the ship, sailors seized
handholds and braced themselves for the coming impact.
Bronwyn threw her arms around the mast and held on tight.
Ebenezer took a grip on the anchor's chain with one hand and
Bronwyn's belt with the other. A fleeting smile touched her
lips at this instinctively protective gesture.

The two ships jolted together like giant knights in an
uneven joust. The first thundering, shivering boom was followed by a sharp, splintering noise. Wood shrieked against
wood as the bowsprit plunged through *Grunion*'s hull.

As soon as the shudders of impact subsided, *Narwhal*'s
crew leaped into action. Eight sailors snatched up large
shields and knelt in a row, providing a shield wall. Behind
them a dozen archers and half as many loaders kept a storm
of arrows arching up toward the slave ship's deck. Bronwyn
hurried over to join them and soon fell into the rhythm of
reloading the small, deadly crossbows.

Left alone, Ebenezer looked about for something to do. At
the railing gathered the largest and strongest crew members.
They were taking up the coiled ropes and hurling grappling
hooks toward the other ship's rail.

The dwarf shrugged, willing to try. He darted over to the
rail. Grabbing one of the lines, he gave it a twirl as he'd seen
the others do and let fly.

The grappling hook whistled through the air—and
plunged into the side of the ship a foot or two below its
intended mark. Though the aim was a mite off, Ebenezer gave

himself full points for force. Wood gave way with a splintering crash, and the hook disappeared into the side of the ship.

This feat earned him a brief, incredulous stare from the sailors. Ebenezer just shrugged and picked up another line. This time his aim was better. The hook sailed *over* the railing and into the chest of a black-bearded mercenary who was busily sawing off one of the other lines. Iron hooks bit deep, curved under and through ribs. The man flew backward, messily and unarguably dead.

Seeing as how the human didn't need his body any more, Ebenezer thought he might as well try to make use of it. With a fierce tug, he pulled the line back. The dead mercenary's head crashed through the hole Ebenezer's last throw had created. The dwarf gave the line an experimental tug.

"That should hold," he said with satisfaction, and turned to the next rope.

But the task was completed; all the hooks had been thrown, and there were so many connecting lines that the slave ship looked like a netted fish.

Some of the more agile sailors ran up the ropes under a cover of arrow fire from their comrades and took the fight to the slave ship. Ebenezer marveled at the cat-footed humans and then leaned cautiously out over the rail to survey the dark expanse of water below.

Bronwyn came to Ebenezer's side. The dwarf noticed that she didn't look any keener about the idea of crossing than he felt. "I don't suppose *you* can swim, either," he ventured.

Her response was a grim smile. "We'll just have to make sure we don't fall in."

She climbed over the rail and took up one of the ropes with both hands. With a deep breath, she dropped to hang over the hungry sea. She began to work her way across, hand over hand, her feet swinging precariously from side to side to aid her momentum.

"Stones," breathed Ebenezer, both as curse and compliment. "That woman's got a barrel full of 'em!"

Determined not to be outdone, he hauled himself up to the rail and tugged at a couple of ropes before he found one he thought might hold his weight. He dropped and began to inch his way across.

Bronwyn made it over in moments. Swinging herself over the side of the slave ship, she darted a quick look back at the still-struggling dwarf. She beckoned impatiently, then pulled her long knife from its sheath and hurled herself into the battle that was raging across the deck.

"Hurry up, she says," Ebenezer muttered as he gingerly eased his way along, never quite letting go of the rope with either hand. "Easy for her to say. Long arms, nothing to haul but a scrawny little—"

A sudden, sharp downward jerk stopped him in mid insult. He sent a glance over his shoulder, and his eyes widened in pure panic. His rope was fraying, threads of twine flying free, just at the point where it rubbed against *Narwhal*'s rail.

The dwarf frantically redoubled his pace, his arms pumping, intent upon getting over while the getting was good. He was perhaps ten feet from the ship when the line behind him gave way.

Howling in terror, Ebenezer swung toward the dark water. He hung onto the rope for dear life, and instinctively brought his boots up before him, legs stiff and braced.

He slammed into the ship, just above the waterline, and with a force that rattled his bones and sent white-hot flashes of pain shimmering through every fiber and sinew. Old wood gave way with a mighty crack, and his feet plunged through the hull. He wrenched them free, and with a few determined kicks he punched a hole big enough to crawl through.

Ebenezer wriggled through, cursing at the thought of the splinters he'd be picking from his legs and backside. The sight inside the hold stopped him in mid curse.

There were his lost clan, looking thinner and more bedraggled than any dwarf should ever have to look. They were chained to wooden bunks so closely packed that they looked like bookshelves, too close for them to so much as sit up. Barrels and crates were spilled about every which way. In the center of the chaos stood a small, brown-haired child, her face utterly white and her big brown eyes rounded with terror.

The ship rolled suddenly as the sea rocked it lose from the caravel's lancelike prow. Water spilled in through the shattered hull. For a moment Ebenezer had the uncanny feeling that he was reliving Bronwyn's personal nightmare.

"This is no damn time to be taking a bath!" exclaimed a querulous and much beloved female voice. "Are you gonna cut us loose or just pass the soap?"

A grin split the dwarf's bearded face. Tarlamera was alive and feisty as ever! He hurried toward her voice, picking up the child as he went. He placed the girl on a crate, well out of reach of the frigid water that sloshed around his ankles. Before he left her, he took a small knife from his belt and pressed in into her hand.

"For rats, with two legs or four, just in case they trouble you," he explained kindly.

The child's fingers closed on the knife, and her eyes were steady as she nodded in understanding.

Ebenezer grinned and chucked her under the chin. Durned if there wasn't yet another female lacking nothing but a beard. The tunnels were full of them these days.

Then he was off, axe in hand, chopping at Tarlamera's prison like a deranged forester. The way he saw it, there was no way he could cut through so many chains—the best and quickest way to turn the dwarves loose was to demolish the bunks.

The moment she was freed, Tarlamera rolled off the shelf, one wrist trailing a length of stout chain and the hunk of splintered wood. She moved stiffly, and with obvious pain, but her face was glad and fierce.

"I never once saw a prettier sight," Ebenezer swore, and meant it down to the depths of his soul. Tarlamera was bedraggled and filthy, and her festive wedding garments stiff with blackened blood, some of it her own. Her red ringlets were lackluster and wildly disheveled, and her beard nearly as stringy as a duergar's, but she was safe and whole.

Tarlamera's grin matched his own, and her eyes were as suspiciously bright as his. She seized her brother by his ears and dragged him forward. She planted a kiss smack on the tip of his nose, then slapped him upside the head. And then she was off, running toward the ladder that led to the deck and clutching the remains of her bunk like a deadly club.

Ebenezer sighed happily, delighted by this unusually sentimental reunion. He didn't have long to ponder it, for his clan was setting up a clamor fit to wake their ancestors. Each dwarf loudly demanded to be next, offered scathing comments on his axe technique, and just generally abused him left, right, and center.

It was good to have them back.

Each dwarf he freed took off up the ladder to join the battle. Not a one stayed to help him free the others. Although Ebenezer grumbled, he understood them well enough. If he'd been packed in here like a heap of coal by a bunch of damn dwarf-stealing humans, he'd be wanting to get his own licks in, too. Even the dwarf children went, as grimly determined for blood as any of their elders, and with no time out for a by-your-leave.

All but Clem, a dwarf lad who was kin to Ebenezer by way of a couple of cousins. The little scamp paused long enough to throw his arms around his rescuer's middle for a quick, fierce hug. When he straightened up, he had a huge grin on his beardless face—and Ebenezer's hammer clenched in his hand. Raising the stolen weapon in salute, he turned and darted for the ladder.

"Git back here, you durned thief!" roared Ebenezer, but though he mustered some impressive volume, his heart wasn't in it. In fact, his grin was so wide it threatened to raise up his ears a mite and leave them there. Better Clem went up armed than not. And if Ebenezer couldn't get in on the fighting, at least his hammer would shatter a skull or two.

"What's the holdup? Dull blade?" taunted a gruff dwarven voice.

Among dwarves, that insult was roughly on a level with a reference to an orcish ancestor. Ebenezer whirled toward the direction of the sound and stabbed his forefinger at the dwarf who'd spoken. "Damn it, Jeston, you could *shave* with this blade!"

"I'd be willing to, if'n you'd turn me lose."

The faintly pleading note in the tough smith's voice smote Ebenezer's heart, and he wavered in his decision to leave this ornery cuss for last. He hefted his axe for the first blow. "Just might be I'll hold you to that," he muttered.

*   *   *   *   *

On the deck above, Bronwyn heard her friend's shout resounding from the hold. Her first response was relief that he had made it across safely. Her second reaction was a quick stab of concern. Judging by the number of grim-faced dwarves staggering about the deck, whacking away at their captors with rough, makeshift clubs, she suspected that Ebenezer had little fighting support below decks.

Bronwyn edged toward the hatch. A mercenary lunged at her, his cutlass whistling down toward her in a quick, deadly sweep. She sidestepped the attack and struck down hard with her knife, pressing the cutlass down to the deck. Then she pivoted toward the joined blades and kicked out high and hard with her left foot. Her boot sank deep, just above the man's weapon belt. The cutlass clattered to the deck, and the man staggered back—into the outstretched hands of a waiting ogress. The sailor grinned horribly, her fangs flashing. She spun the man around a couple of times as if they were children playing at blind man's bluff, and then flung him back toward Bronwyn.

"Catch!" she roared.

Bronwyn brought up her knife. The man fell heavily on it, and his weight slumped against her. For a moment they were eye to eye.

Bronwyn had seen death before, more times than she liked to count, but never at such close range. The life drained away from his face, surely as a receding tide, and his black eyes went empty and flat. Then he jerked back with a suddenness that left Bronwyn staggering for balance.

The ogress held the man by the collar as a boy might hold a puppy by the scruff of the neck. She grunted with approval at the sight of Bronwyn's dripping knife, then flung the dead man aside.

Bronwyn turned back to the hold and was nearly knocked over by the dwarf lad who exploded from the hatch as if he'd been launched by a smoke-powder canon. She noted the hammer he held clenched in his hand and understood the source of Ebenezer's ire. Reassured that her friend was not besieged by foes, she picked her next battle.

Narwhal's first mate, a hugely muscled barbarian woman, was pinned down by two fighters, her back against the mast and her sword flailing. Bronwyn noted the jerky motion of the blade, the huge beads of sweat on the massive woman's brow. Just then one of the attackers ducked, and Bronwyn caught sight of the wound that slashed across the sailor's collarbone. It didn't look fatal of itself, but the woman's tunic was sodden with her own blood, and the cold sickness that followed a battle wound was settling upon her.

Bronwyn waded in, dodging a pair of dwarves who carried a human male between them, one dwarf holding the man's hands and one holding his feet. Their captive writhed and struggled and cursed, but the dwarves moved inexorably toward the rail, intent upon hurling him over.

She seized one of the first mate's attackers by the hair and jerked his head back. Without hesitation, she lifted her knife and drew it hard and fast across the man's throat. His startled oath, though quite quickly and literally cut short, drew his partner's attention. The second man turned toward the sound, only to be hit in the face by the sudden spurting flow of his shipmate's lifeblood.

The man shouted and slashed blindly with his blade. Bronwyn still had her grip on the dead man's hair, and she spun around to duck behind him. The body jolted from the impact. Bronwyn released him and danced back, almost losing her footing on the blood-slick deck.

Again the slaver lashed out. Bronwyn dropped into a crouch, ducking the blow so narrowly that she felt the wind of it. Before he could reverse his swing for another attack, she tensed for the spring and came up, knife leading.

Her blade punched hard into his ribcage. The blow registered in his eyes, but he did not go down, and his grim expression proclaimed his intent to take her with him to the gates of death.

Bronwyn wrenched her knife free and jumped up, bringing her knee up high and hard as she came. She connected in a profoundly debilitating blow. The man's forgotten sword clattered to the deck.

She stepped back, breathing in quick, shallow bursts.

"Behind you, girl!"

The woman's shout snapped Bronwyn back into the battle. She whirled to face the grim-faced dwarf who was preparing to apply the spiked nail in his club to the base of Bronwyn's spine.

Instinct and memory took over. "For Stoneshaft!" she shrieked in the dwarvish tongue, remembering what her long-ago dwarf friend told her about rallying cries.

Her response clearly startled the dwarf. He lowered the club, and the red haze of battle-lust faded from his face. For a moment he peered keenly at Bronwyn. Apparently he recognized her as someone other than one of his captors, for he gave a curt nod and went off in search of another fight.

But the battle was nearly over. The sounds of fighting had dwindled to a few clashes of steel, a few screams of pain—some of which ended with chilling abruptness.

Captain Orwig's bombastic voice could easily be heard over the ebbing tide of battle, ordering his crew to round up the dead of both sides and all the slavers and toss them into the sea as Umberlee's due. This rallied even the dwarves, who cared not a wit for the Sea Goddess. They took to the task with such grim gusto that they didn't even seem to notice that they were taking orders from an ogre.

Bronwyn tucked her knife into its sheath just as the barbarian's eyes rolled back in her head. Bronwyn caught the woman as she fell and lowered her to the deck—not an easy task given the difference in their size, but at least she managed to ease the woman down to a gentler landing than she would otherwise have had.

Bronwyn tore a strip from the hem of the woman's tunic and pressed it to the wound, holding it firm until the bleeding stopped, then shrugged off her cloak and tucked it over the woman's broad shoulders to keep her warm until the cold sickness ebbed. That was all the help Bronwyn could give her, and she hoped it would be enough.

Narwhal's crew had not gone unscathed. Some of the dead tossed overboard wore familiar faces. One of them was the ogress who had played the deadly game of catch with Bronwyn, thus accepting her, if for one brief moment, as a comrade. Bronwyn took a deep breath and headed back to the stern, where stood a small, wooden shack built over the helm.

In this, as she had expected, she found the ship's records. Quickly she thumbed through the pages, looking for something that would provide a clue to the identity of the people who had destroyed the dwarves' home and stolen from them their freedom—and from her, her father.

But the transaction was coded. In time, she could probably figure out what it said. There was, however, a lengthy list of cargo neatly written up in Common, the language of trade. Bronwyn skimmed it and whistled softly. This would be enough and more to satisfy *Narwhal*'s captain's and crew's desire for booty. It might also help her negotiate with Orwig on a delicate matter. He was an ogre. Even in tolerant Waterdeep, he would be closely watched. And he was a smuggler, which meant his affairs would not hold up to close scrutiny. Yet she could not subject Ebenezer and his kin to the punishing journey back through the magical locks into Skullport.

She tucked the log book under her arm and walked out onto the deck. Captain Orwig stalked by and she caught his arm.

"The battle was a great victory. I want to thank you for your help," she began.

His gold-capped tusks flashed in what she hoped was a smile. "You don't have to thank me. You have to *pay* me."

"You'll have your full fee," she assured him, "and as a bonus, I'll yield my right-of-hire ownership of the cargo." She told him what the hold contained: unworked gems, bolts of wool, valuable pelts, weapons, coin, barrels of mead.

The prospect of such treasure touched the ogre's soul. "All?"

"Except for the dwarves. You don't want them, of course."

He snorted as if to indicate that this went without saying.

"I will yield my right to the cargo in exchange for two things," Bronwyn continued, "this book with the ship's logs and records, and your promise that we'll make port in Waterdeep rather than return to Skullport."

The ogre hesitated, but temptation danced in his small red eyes. He scratched his snout and considered. "There'll be a dock fee to pay and a tax on the booty."

"And after paying the tax, you'll still have far more than you expected. I'll pay the fee. Agreed?"

Still he looked doubtful. "One dwarf is trouble enough. Eats enough for two humans. How many did we turn loose? Fifty?"

"Close enough," she responded. "But the stores from the *Grunion* should serve to feed them until we get to Waterdeep."

The ogre scowled, but gave in with an ungracious shrug. "Very well, but keep that red-bearded dung heap away from me, or I won't be responsible for his safe arrival."

"Done," she agreed, though she doubted she had enough influence with Ebenezer to persuade him to leave his favorite new toy alone.

She strode to the hatch and listened. No sounds of battle emerged, but a rhythmic thudding indicated that Ebenezer was still busy with his axe.

Bronwyn clattered down into the hold. She blinked, startled by the destruction. Shards of wood were scattered about, looking like the blasted limbs of trees in the aftermath of a volcanic eruption. Ebenezer was doggedly chopping away at the far end of the wood pile.

"You got them all?" Bronwyn called.

"This one's the last of 'em," the dwarf said. "The others all took to fighting but me, the selfish sods," he grumbled. He nodded toward a small stack of crates. "All but that one, that is."

Bronwyn tracked his gesture. Her gaze fell upon the small girl-child who crouched upon the stack, the dwarf's table knife clutched in her hand.

Terrible memories flooded back into Bronwyn's mind, striking her like a sword to the heart. For a moment her ears rang with the cries of the doomed and drowning slaves, the shrill piping of the rats. She absently raised her hand and rubbed the long-healed place on her head where two of them had clawed her.

But that was long ago, Bronwyn reminded herself firmly. This was now, and another small girl required comfort. She could not slay her own demons, but perhaps she could keep them from laying claim to this tiny victim.

She swallowed hard and fixed what she hoped was a reassuring smile on her face. Slowly, as if she was approaching a spooked horse, she began to move toward the girl.

"I'm Bronwyn," she said softly. "You've already met my friend Ebenezer. We came to set free the dwarves. You are safe with us. We will take you home."

She extended her hand, the offer of her pledge. The girl studied her with large, somber brown eyes, then placed her own small hand in Bronwyn's. The contact seemed to reassure the child, and her fingers slid up to Bronwyn's wrist and tightened into a desperate grip.

"But I don't know where my home is," she said in a high, clear voice that retained just a hint of early childhood lisp.

"I'll help you find it. Don't you worry," Bronwyn assured her in the same soothing voice. "What's your name? How old are you?"

"Cara Doon. I was nine last winter."

The child looked younger than nine, perhaps because she was small and exceedingly thin. When she raised one tiny hand to tuck a stray bit of brown hair behind her ear, Bronwyn saw another explanation for her size and seemingly delayed development. The child was a half-elf. Her ears were slightly pointed, and the fingers that gripped Bronwyn's wrist were long and delicate.

And on one of them, she wore a very familiar ring.

Bronwyn's eyes widened in shock. Her heart thudded painfully, then picked up the beat at a quickened pace. The child's ring was golden, and richly carved with distinctive, mystic designs. Bronwyn had one just like it in her safe back in Curious Past.

"That's a very pretty ring," she said, pointing. "May I see it?"

Cara snatched her hand back and hid it behind her. "My father said no stranger was to look at it, and I was to give it to no one but family. And you can't take it from me, you know. The bad men tried," she said, pointing to the deck. "It won't come off unless I take it off myself."

This was news to Bronwyn. She wondered if the ring her father had given her would display a similar magical loyalty. But that thought came and went, overwhelmed by one of much greater importance. Cara's ring was identical to her own. Hronulf had referred to the ring as a family heirloom, meant to be worn only by the blood descendants of the great paladin Samular Caradoon. Once more Bronwyn's eyes went wide.

"*What* did you say your name was?"

"Cara," the girl said with a hint of impatience. "Cara Doon."

Eleven

Dag Zoreth had been to Waterdeep only once before, and the proximity of so many enemies of the Zhentarim left him uncharacteristically edgy. He waited until the maidservant shut the door behind her, then he slid the stout oaken bolt firmly into place. Since one could never be too careful, he walked around the sumptuous chamber, checking for magical spying devices and chanting softly as he sought out any invasive magic.

There was none to find. The Gentle Mermaid, a festhall and tavern in the heart of the staid North Ward, was renowned for its discretion. Private rooms were precisely that, and in this magic-rich city, that was rare enough. The other rare things that crowded the chamber were merely pleasant extras.

There was a fine writing table and chair of polished Chultan teak, a large bed heaped with silken pillows in bright rare shades of yellow and blue, velvet draperies and fine tapestries to keep out the chill, a washbasin and pitcher of delicate porcelain, a small table upon which was laid out silver goblets and a bottle of wine, as well as a tray of small savory bites and another of sweet pastries. Dag missed none of this, for he had a keen appreciation for luxury. As he sampled a small wedge of herb-scented cheese, he vowed to have such amenities brought to Thornhold, to soften and brighten the stark quarters of the former paladins.

But at the moment, Dag Zoreth had another, more immediate task to tend. He took a small dark globe from its hiding place in the folds of his cloak and settled down into the cushioned chair. Holding the globe before him on his palm, he stared intently into its depths.

At his command, purple flames burst into life within the globe. Dag knew from experience what this would do to the man who received the message. The magical summons would bring cold, searing pain that would last until the man found a private place and took the corresponding globe into his own hand.

It did not surprise Dag that he did not have long to wait. Sir Gareth Cormaeril, for all his courtly airs and sanctimonious pronouncements, had a keen instinct for self-preservation. In mere moments the paladin's lean, dignified face appeared in the globe, looking rather incongruous against the background of sinister purple fire.

"You wished to speak with me, Lord Zoreth? Is there some problem that requires my attention?"

"No, I was merely overwhelmed with desire for the pleasure of your company," Dag said coldly. "What is occurring in Tyr's temple? The place is teaming with paladins!"

"They prepare to march on Thornhold," Sir Gareth responded, forthrightly enough. "Surely you did not think that your victory would long remain unchallenged."

"Let them try. They will not find it as easy to get into the fortress as we did. Unless of course," Dag added, "you gave them the same information you gave me."

The knight's blue eyes widened with a sharp, sudden flash of fear. "I did not, but there might be others among the order to whom Hronulf entrusted this knowledge."

Dag didn't really care—he brought up the matter just to tweak the older man. If the gathering paladin army had this knowledge, it would do them little good. The tunnels beneath the fortress had been so altered that men could wander about for tendays without finding the old passages.

"There is another matter of which we much speak," Dag continued. "I have a daughter. Though her existence has been kept secret for more than nine years, she is now widely sought. What do you know of her?"

"Sir?" inquired the knight, puzzlement on his reflected face. "Why should I know anything?"

It was not a lie—Dag had yet to catch the fallen paladin utter a direct untruth—but it was a blatant evasion. This irritated the priest.

"I run short of time and patience," Dag said through gritted teeth. "Hear me well. The girl was abducted from her foster home by a single man, even though her foster father was an elf of considerable skill at arms. The Zhentarim are not known for such acts of foolish bravery. That leaves . . . who?"

Sir Gareth bowed his head. "I have earned your suspicions, Lord Zoreth. My part in the raid on your childhood village—"

"Is past history," Dag cut in coldly. "I have no intention of making you suffer for past misdeeds, but I assure you, your continued existence depends upon your ability to serve me quickly and well. Is that quite clear?"

"Pellucid, my lord," the knight agreed.

"A straight answer, then. Did you or did you not have a part in abducting my daughter?"

"Alas, the answer to that is not so simple as your question suggests," the knight said, his face deeply troubled. "My *order* was indeed responsible, so some of this lies at my door."

Dag sniffed at the self-serving "confession," but found in these words welcome news. "My men tracked Cara's abductor. He was headed to Waterdeep. I want his name, and soon thereafter, I want his heart on a skewer."

"There are many paladins in Waterdeep," Sir Gareth hedged. "Tell me more of your daughter, so that I might make discrete inquiries. I myself never saw the girl."

That seemed a reasonable request. "She is nine years of age, but small and slight, so that she looks to be no more than six or seven. Her hair is brown, as are her eyes. There is a touch of elf blood in her. Her ears are slightly pointed, her eyes are large and tilt up at the corners, and her fingers are very tiny and thin." As soon as the last words were out, Dag rued them. He did not want to draw any attention to the girl's hands—and the extremely valuable ring she wore.

"And my sister," Dag added hastily. "What word on her?"

"I sent her to Thornhold, as you directed. Did she never arrive?"

Dag decided that was a question best left unanswered. "I want the woman and the child found and turned over to me. Find a way to circumvent the other knights. Is that quite clear?"

The knight lifted two fingers to his brow in an archaic salute. "I am pledged to honor the children of Samular's bloodline. All will be done as you say."

Dag shook his head in disgust and released the enchantment. Sir Gareth's face faded abruptly from the globe—but not before Dag caught a satisfying glimpse of the anguish inflicted by the spell's release.

He despised the old knight. He hated all paladins, and particularly those who, like his own father, took vows as Knights of Samular, but this man simply galled him. Sir Gareth Cormaeril had once been a mighty knight, his father's friend and comrade. He had saved Hronulf's life once and had received the wound that shrunk his sword arm and ended his career in battle. But there was a weakness in the man, a weakness of will and heart that Dag particularly despised. He himself had triumphed over physical weakness—why should another man see in it an excuse to give up all he once was?

That was precisely what Sir Gareth had done. He had fallen prey to Malchior's cunning snares, abusing his new role as exchequer of the order when his younger brother, a rogue and a gambler, ran afoul of Zhentarim-owned pleasure houses. Malchior had assumed the young lord's debts, and Gareth had quietly "borrowed" money to repay the Zhentish priest rather than risk personal or family scandal. That was the beginning. From there, it had become increasingly easy to purchase the man's soul, a few words at a time.

It amazed Dag that Sir Gareth did not yet seem to realize
this.

What Dag was, he had chosen to be. He had great power,
granted him by a mad god and wielded in ways that a man
like Sir Gareth could never conceive. And he intended to get
more of the same, by much the same methods—or worse, if
such path came to him. What he did, he chose. What he was,
he acknowledged. There was a basic honesty in this that Sir
Gareth could not begin to comprehend or duplicate.

As Dag tucked the globe away, an ironic smile touched his
lips as he noted that, in this matter at least, he possessed
more virtue than a man lauded as one of Tyr's great knights.

*   *   *   *   *

To Bronwyn, the three days of the return voyage went all
too quickly. She spent many hours with little Cara, answering her seemingly endless supply of questions. The little girl
had a deep curiosity about the world, and her yearning to see
far places was written on her small face as she listened to
Bronwyn's tales.

True, Cara had other things to occupy her time. She played
with the five dwarf children, holding her own surprisingly
well in tussles and arguments with the much stronger and
stockier dwarves. Ebenezer also took a special interest in the
girl, and he spent hours telling her stories of his adventures,
answering her questions. He even carved a toy for her, a
small wooden doll with slightly pointed ears. The limbs were
jointed and connected with strings so that the doll could be
moved about. Bronwyn, who caught him at work stitching
together bits of sailcloth for clothes, commented on the delicate work—and immediately wished she hadn't. The dwarf
gave her a bit of advice on the merits of minding her own
affairs, in the form of a tongue-lashing that almost, but not
quite, covered his embarrassment at being caught red-
handed and soft-hearted.

To her surprise, Bronwyn found that she enjoyed being
with Cara. She'd never had any experience with children, not

even when she herself had been a child, but she enjoyed the girl's curiosity, approved of her stubbornness, and admired her resilience. By the time the outer islands that protected Waterdeep's harbor came into sight, Bronwyn decided that if she were ever to have a daughter, she would be more than happy if the girl took after Cara.

But Cara had a family—a father, who was almost certainly kin to Bronwyn. The need to find him, for both of them, was growing in Bronwyn like a fever.

Cara, unfortunately, was little help. She remembered her father only as "Doon," and the description she gave of him was what might be expected of any eight-year-old half-elf. He was a grownup. He had dark hair. He was big.

It was not much to go on.

She did have a great deal to say about the man who had stolen her away from the only home she had ever known. He had a sword, which he had used to kill both of her foster parents. He was a tall man, with light blond hair cut short. He rode a white horse and wore a white tunic with a blue design on it. At Bronwyn's bidding, Cara tried to sketch it, but the childish scrawl was far from enlightening. They rode for a long time and stopped at a beautiful house. After that, Cara remembered nothing. She had fallen asleep and awakened in the hold of the ship with an aching head and a fiercely empty stomach. Bronwyn, who listened to this with silent rage, realized that the child had been drugged. She vowed to find who had done this and make certain that they would send no more children to the life that she herself had endured.

Finally *Narwhal* sailed in through the southernmost entrance to the harbor, past the lighthouse known as East Torch Tower: a tall, slender cone of white granite that flamed like its namesake. Bronwyn would have preferred to sail to the northern entrance, for the harbor fees were somewhat less and she would be much closer to her shop, but Captain Orwig absolutely refused to come within a longbow's shot of a place called Smugglers' Bane Tower.

A pair of small skiffs met them at the chained entrance, and a woman clad in the gold and black uniform of the Watch asked to come aboard. At this, the ogre captain bared his fangs in a sneer and started to go for his cutlass. Before he could speak, Bronwyn caught his arm and nodded to the water beyond the skiffs. Orwig tracked her gaze and defeat registered in his small, red eyes. Several heads broke the surface of the water here and there, and shadowy, vaguely human forms swirled around the ship. Mermen, ready to aid the officials if need be. Orwig valued his ship too highly to risk having it scuttled from below.

"Permission to come aboard," he snarled. He shot Bronwyn a glare that left the matter in her hands, then stalked off.

Bronwyn produced the logs stating their cargo, and, on Orwig's behalf, paid out the cargo tax in some of the coins taken from the slave ship. She wrote a note for the docking fee, promising to deliver payment to the Harbormaster within three days. The chain was lowered, and *Narwhal* allowed to sail into the harbor. For Captain Orwig's sake—the ogre was clearly uncomfortable with this port—Bronwyn requested that the ship be allowed to dock at the nearest available slip.

Within an hour, the passengers had disembarked onto a small, barnacle-encrusted pier just off Cedar Street. *Narwhal* took off with such haste that the last dwarf to disembark was still on the gangplank. He fell into the harbor with an enormous splash and sank like an axe. Four mermen managed to drag him the surface, though all of them were visibly worse for wear before the task was done. A grinning dockhand threw down a rope. Glad for something they could do, a dozen of so of the Stoneshaft clan seized the rope and hauled it up with a gusto that brought the unfortunate dwarf vaulting out of the water and skidding along the dock on his belly.

Once that bit of excitement was over, the dwarves gathered into a cluster on the dock, their eyes wide as they gazed around the bustling scene and the narrow, crowded streets beyond. For once, all fifty-some-odd dwarves were struck silent, their contentious voices stilled by their awe of the city.

"Gotta excuse them," Ebenezer murmured to Bronwyn. "I'm the only one been out of the clanhold much. The rest of them, well, you might say they're ducks in a desert."

"The sooner we get them settled, the better," Bronwyn agreed. She hailed a tall, bald man who wore the insignia of the wagoner's guild on his jacket. After a brisk, brief haggle, she hired three wagons to haul the dwarves through town to her shop.

"We could-a walked," Ebenezer complained once they were settled inside a closed wooden wagon that smelled strongly of fish and old cheese.

"Fifty dwarves marching through the Dock Ward?" she scoffed. "It would look too much like an invasion. That much attention, we don't need."

The dwarf considered this, then nodded grudgingly. "What's your plan, then?"

"For now, we'll go to my shop. I'll send out some messengers, call in a few favors. We'll get everyone settled."

Ebenezer looked over to the fistfight that had erupted between two of the dwarf lads. "Not an easy thing," he observed.

The wagon driver, as directed, let the dwarves off in the alley behind Curious Past. Despite Bronwyn's pleas for discretion, they roiled down the narrow path, clearly feeling more at home in the close, tunnel-like corridor than they had for many days.

They descended on the Curious Past like a plague of blackbirds. Alice's response astonished Bronwyn. The gnome produced a sword from under the counter, as well as a smoke-power pistol. These she brandished at the first pair of dwarves in the door.

"You'll not get past me," she said with such conviction that Bronwyn believed her. "Take your looting elsewhere."

"Alice, it's me!" Bronwyn shouted over the heads of the dwarves. "It's all right. They are with me."

The gnome's eyes bulged. "*All* of them?"

Bronwyn raised her hands in a helpless shrug, knowing she was asking a great deal of the gnome. Alice's tiny shoulders lifted and fell in a sigh, but she stepped aside.

In roiled the dwarves, their eyes rounded with awe at the sights around them. "Quite a trove," Tarlamera said with grudging admiration. She picked up a bangle bracelet studded with large gems. Instead of slipping it onto her wrist, she fisted it in her hand so that the raised stones augmented her knuckles. She lifted her fist and admired the effect. "Nice. Yours, gnome?"

"I should say not! That piece was commissioned by Lady Galinda Raventree."

Tarlarmera's eyes glinted. "Might could be she'd like to go a round or two, you think? Sitting on that ship has left us all a mite restless and ready for fun."

The image of the iron-willed society queen facing off in battle against the dwarf woman brought a wry smile to Bronwyn's face. That fight, she'd happily pay to observe. "Alice, why don't you go to the market and get something for our guests? Some bread and meat, a keg of ale. Have it delivered."

"Well, I'm certainly not going to *carry* it back," the gnome grumbled. She seized her shawl off its hook and took off—gratefully, it seemed to Bronwyn.

One of the dwarf lads started to climb a shelf after an axe that had caught his eye. A sleek, black form glided from the rafters and landed on his shoulder.

"Think about it," Shopscat advised.

With a yelp, the young dwarf let go and tumbled to the floor. The raven winged off and settled down on a tall urn.

"It talks!" exclaimed a dwarf woman with delight, her stubby finger pointing at the raven. Her eyes took on a battle gleam, and she came over to Shopscat and leaned in close, nose to beak. "Been a while since I had me a roast bird," she said, a challenge in her voice.

The raven stared her down. "Think about it."

The dwarves laughed uproariously. "Might be you could keep that up for a while, Morgalla, if you asked the right questions," Ebenezer said.

She shrugged and grinned, then wandered off to finger a long string of pink pearls displayed on a wooden bust.

They spent a pleasant hour poking through the shop and exchanging insults with the raven. Just as some were starting to get restless, Alice returned with a half dozen strong porters and the requested refreshments.

The instant the first keg hit the floor, the dwarves converged from all three floors of the shop. They snatched up whatever came to hand—silver mugs, gem-encrusted goblets—and clustered about. The gnome cringed as she took in this casual use of the treasures she guarded.

"We can hire someone in to help clean up," Bronwyn told her.

"If you have the coin left to do the hiring," Alice shot back. She nodded toward their visitors, who were making short work of the piles of food. Two of the dwarves were already tapping the third keg.

It seemed that Ebenezer was thinking along similar lines. "Don't you doubt, I'm gonna pay you back every copper," he vowed softly. "Tell me what I can do to help get them earning their keep."

Bronwyn glanced at Cara, who was petting Shopscat and chattering happily. Her heart melted at the sight of the little girl and the obviously charmed raven.

"There are dwarves in the city, but the sort of labor your clan can do is always in demand. I know people who can line up what we need."

"You got a lot of friends, if they can set up this bunch," Ebenezer commented.

"In a manner of speaking." This brought up a matter that Bronwyn had been puzzling over for several days. She had realized aboard ship that she would have to rely upon the resources of the Harpers to get the dwarves settled. Disclosing membership in this secret organization was forbidden, except in extreme situations or to trusted friends. Though she had known Ebenezer for a relatively short time, she counted him as among the best she'd found. She decided to confide in the dwarf.

Taking him by the arm, she led him to a relatively quiet corner. "What do you know of the Harpers?"

Ebenezer scowled and spat—hitting the bronze spittoon by the door with dead-on accuracy and ringing force. "Nothing good. As I hear it, they're not big on minding their own affairs."

"That's true enough," she said hesitantly. "But they *are* good at gathering information and passing it along. If I contact the right Harpers here in the city, by highsun tomorrow I should have every member of your clan set up in business. Sword smiths, gem workers, bakers. Whatever skills they have, I can match."

"How do you know who to—" The dwarf broke off, his eyes suspicious. "You're one of them."

Bronwyn sighed. "Guilty. Is that such a bad thing?"

"Maybe," he grumbled. He slanted a look up at her. "What you did for my clan—was that Harper business?"

"No," she said stoutly, even though she suspected that claiming otherwise might sway the dwarf's opinion on the matter. "That was personal."

"Good." He nodded in satisfaction. "Well, then, you tell me where to go, and I'll be getting the process started."

Bronwyn hurried up the stairs to her chamber—evicting the pair of dwarf children who were jumping on her bed—and sat down at her writing table. Under the false bottom of her drawer were sheets of parchment bearing the sigil of Khelben Arunsun. This rune, his personal symbol, gave force to whatever was written on the parchment. The Harpers under his direction were to use them only in dire circumstances. Bronwyn had but two. She dipped a quill in her inkwell and began to write a letter to Brian Swordmaster.

Even as she wrote, Bronwyn's mind skipped ahead to the consequences of this measure. Khelben would know when one of his special edicts was used, and by whom. Brian Swordmaster, though a common tradesman and a quiet, modest man, was a great friend of the archmage. The story would get to her Harper master all too soon.

And then, she wondered, what would she be required to do?

This thought didn't set well with her. All her life, she had been told what to do. As a slave, she had been given little choice about anything. As an antiquities dealer, she had taken commissions and fulfilled them. Her methods were her own, and she prided herself in being resourceful, but the task itself was given her. The same could be said for her involvement with the Harpers. The first act that she could call truly her own was her decision to rescue the Stoneshaft clan from slavery. She regarded that with pride and was not reconciled to tamely accepting that all her decisions would henceforth be made for her by others.

And yet, had that ever been truly the case? Even as a slave, she had directed her path. She worked hard at the gem trade, and before she was a woman grown, she was crafting better counterfeit pieces than any of her master's servants—or her master himself, for that matter. He'd taken an interest in her, and taught her about the rare pieces that they copied in the shop and sold as originals. Bronwyn had developed a genuine love of the old, beautiful things that came into her hands. Unlike her, they had a history, a past. These stories had more importance to her than the pieces themselves. And so she wheedled her master into letting her learn about the background of the pieces—so that they could make better, less detectable reproductions, she'd argued. This idea had pleased him, and Bronwyn had begun the path she now trod. When the master died, his son sold off the shop, including the slaves. She had bought her freedom by apprenticing herself out to a treasure hunter who'd done business with her master. Soon she went her own way. And, she realized with deep surprise, she had been doing so ever since.

Bronwyn sat for a long moment as she absorbed this. Then she nodded slowly and rolled the parchment into a scroll. She went down the back stairs and through the alley. There was always a messenger or two available for hire at the cobbler's shop two doors down.

The messenger was a youth she knew well. She gave him the scroll with instructions and an extra silver coin, then returned to her shop with a light step.

Whatever came of this venture, she would handle it as she always had: her own way.

* * * * *

It took Ebenezer the better part of two hours to round up his kin and get them headed out of the shop. "Like herding cats, it is," he grumbled as he shoved the last of them out of the door. The look of pure, desperate gratitude that Alice sent him brought a wry grin to his face. The Stoneshafts were a handful, and no mistake. He only hoped that Bronwyn's mysterious "friends" had pickaxes big enough to chop through this particular problem.

Once the dwarves were out on the street, the problems compounded. Bronwyn's shop was on the Street of Silks, a nose-in-the-air piece of town where folks thought their shoes too good to sully with walking. Fancy carriages rattled past, drawn by teams of horses.

"Lookit the size of them mules," marveled Benton, a cousin who'd never been out of the tunnels before his capture.

"How'd they get four of 'em to go in the same direction?" demanded Tarlamera, whose only experience with mules involved small, dusty pack animals nearly as stubborn as herself. The clan had kept a few for hauling back the gems and ore from the outermost mines.

That image suggested a solution to Ebenezer. "Miners, ho!" he hollered. "Tunnel size, seven. Fall in by clan rank."

His clan scuttled into place with an alacrity born of long practice. A size seven tunnel meant that three dwarves could march abreast, and clan rank was easy enough: oldest first. Every dwarf knew where he ranked in comparison with any other dwarf, so they found their places readily enough. The only break with tradition was when Ebenezer took his place at the head. Not a dwarf argued with him for that honor, though, seeing as he was the only one who'd ever been to the city before.

He marched them down the Street of Silks, past shops brimming with the fashionable doodads that humans seemed so all-fired fond of. These the dwarves passed without missing a step, but as they neared the Jester's Court, the scents drifting from the Mighty Manticore inspired wistful sighs from some of his kin. Ebenezer had some knowledge of the tavern owner, a half-dwarf but a good sort for all that. Coopercan, his name was, in honor of a backside as big as a barrel. When Coop settled down to keeping tavern, he'd kept some of his dwarven ways. There was no mistaking the smell of rothé roasting on a spit, stuffed with mushrooms and the tasty black rice that grew wild in the marshy hollows hidden among dwarven mountains. Coopercan always seemed to have a rothé roast going, and there were few scents that could get a dwarf to drooling better than that.

"Hoy, brother!" shouted a gruff female voice. "I'm-a coming up."

Ebenezer lifted his hand to his lips to hide his smirk. He'd been too long among humans, if he found humor in the usual dwarven method of "asking permission."

Tarlamera huffed up to his side. For several moments they marched in silence as he waited for her to speak her mind. "We gotta go back to the clanhold," she decreed.

He'd been afraid of that. Knew it was coming. Even so, he tried to scoff away the notion. "And how might you be planning to do that? There's not enough of us left to take back the tunnels, much less hold them secure. The men that stole you away in the first place would be back, and the second harvest would be all the easier."

The dwarf woman scowled and folded her arms. "What are we to do, then?"

"There's dwarves in the city," he told her. "Bronwyn has friends what can find us work. We'll fit in, make our way. Make a life."

Tarlamera glowered. "Seems to me like you're putting too much weight in that human's say-so. Mountain dwarves in a city? What kind of life is that?"

"Better'n the one 'that human' stole you from, I'll tell you that for free," he shot back.

She shrugged. "There's that. But all I got to say is— *Almighty Clangeddin by the short hairs!*"

Ebenezer pulled up short, startled by his sister's oath and the force with which it was delivered. "How's that again?"

She seized his arm and pointed. The road had widened up into a broad, cobblestone courtyard. At the far end was the

enormous, elaborate palace built for the first lord of the city,
and behind that swept the majestic summit of Mount Waterdeep. But somewhat closer was the sight peculiar enough to
stop Tarlamera in mid-complaint, a tall, slender tower before
which stood a skeleton, arms raised high and feet not quite
touching the ground.

"Don't be going too close to that tower," Ebenezer said
casually. "Alghairon's Tower, it's called. Been empty for a
long time. Seems it used to belong to some big-axe wizard,
long since gone to his ancestors. It's a monument now. The
folks hereabouts let it alone mostly, except for the fellow you
see there."

"Good warding sign," one of the dwarves behind them
offered. That sent a weak chuckle rippling through the group.

The company got some strange looks as they marched in
formation through the courtyard. Ebenezer didn't suppose
they looked like much of a threat, as scrawny as they were,
and not more than three weapons among the lot of them, but
still he raised his hand in a conciliatory salute whenever a
curious member of the guard looked their way.

They veered east onto Waterdeep Way, toward the massive castle that was the heart and strength of the city.
Ebenezer had always admired that castle. "Lookit that," he
said grandly, pointing up at the far towers. "Four hundred
feet high, that is."

Tarlamera sniffed. Dwarves, as a rule, weren't terribly
impressed with *up*. They were more interested in *through*.

"Got walls some sixty feet thick," he added.

"That's a wall," she admitted, impressed at last.

Ebenezer pointed ahead. "See that sign what's a-hanging
from that lantern pole? Marks the Way of the Dragon. Big
street. Goes down to the Trade Ward and the man we gotta
see."

"I seen a man already," the dwarf maid grumbled. "Seen
hundreds of 'em so far today."

"This one's a smith. They say his pieces are as good as any
human can make. Better than some dwarves."

She scoffed. "I'm not buying that at the asking price. How

can you get a good forge going without the tunnels to pull a powerful updraft?"

Ebenezer pointed up toward the blue dome of the sky. "Got lotsa wind."

"Yeah." She scowled and plucked at her ruined clothes. "And I'm feeling every breath of it in these rags. Back at the clanhold, I got me a new linen kirtle and a leather apron."

A bleak, wistful note crept into her voice. Though her eyes kept steadily fixed ahead, Ebenezer could read the pain in them. The kirtle and apron were part of every dwarf maid's wedding chest. By all that was right, she should be home scrapping happily with her new-made husband. But Frodwinner was dead, as were their four brothers and their sister, their mother, their da. They hadn't spoken of their slain kin, not once since the day Ebenezer had chopped her loose from the slave ship.

"Frodwinner fought well," Tarlamera said. A struggling smile rippled across her face, as if she were trying to accept that this was enough. "I saw that much before they dropped me. How many did he take?"

"Fifteen," Ebenezer said promptly, upping the number without a qualm.

"Good," she said. "That's good."

They walked in silence for a while. "I made them a cairn," he said softly. "Just one, for all of them."

"That's the way things are done in time of battle," she agreed. "You accounted for all?"

"Not all," he said grimly. "Didn't see old Hoshal, but I'm pretty sure they got to him ahead of time. Found one of his chisels in an osquip trove."

"They got him," Tarlamera agreed. "Hoshal's particular about his tools. Da always said Hoshal could put a hand to any one of his tools quicker than he could grab his own—"

She broke off, her jaw dropping in astonishment. Ebenezer tracked her gaze into a side alley, and his own eyes widened in astonishment. "Now, that's something you don't see every day," he admitted.

An enormous, disembodied hand, each finger longer than a

dwarf was tall, floated aimlessly down the alley. In the center of the palm was a huge mouth that worked its way through some silly tavern tune. Ebenezer shook his head in utter bemusement.

"What does it want?" one of the dwarves behind him hissed.

"A better song?" snapped Ebenezer. "Do I know everything there is to know about this city? Step lively, now!"

They stepped, with a liveliness that had the lot of them huffing like a gnome-built tea kettle.

"Gotta get back to the clanhold," Tarlamera moaned.

Ebenezer shook his head and pointed to the road ahead. The streets were getting narrower, and the tall, timber-framed buildings crowded so close that dwellers in the top floors could lean out and kiss their neighbors, providing they were on good enough terms. They were coming up on the Street of Smiths, and black smoke from a dozen forges rose into the sky.

Many of the houses—the foundations at least and sometimes up to the second floor—were masoned over with stone as a deterrent to fire. If a body squinted just so, he could pretend they were cavern walls.

"Kinda cozy, isn't it?" he said hopefully.

Tarlamera snorted again.

As they rounded the corner to Brian's Street, a huge, utterly bald man came striding to meet them. He came to Ebenezer and stuck out his hand. "You'd be the Stoneshaft clan," he said. "Brian here. Been expecting you."

Ebenezer gave the ham-sized hand a good squeeze, which was returned with a force that made his eyes cross. "He's a smith, all right," he told Tarlamera.

His sister was doing her own evaluation. Her eyes scanned the man from his bald head to his massive, gray-streaked black beard, measuring the width of his shoulders and arms heavily corded with muscle and blackened with soot. "He's a likely-looking lad," she admitted, and then sighed. "All right, boy, let's see this forge of yours."

* * * * *

During the voyage back to Waterdeep, Bronwyn had managed to decipher some of the code in the slave ship's log. Enough, at least, to assure her that *Grunion* was owned by the Zhentarim. No large surprise, that, considering the destruction of Thornhold and the capture of the dwarves by Zhentish soldiers.

But what of Cara? What was there about the ring she wore that attracted the ire of the Zhentarim, that they would steal children away from their homes? Cara's father, whoever and wherever he was, might also be in danger.

That thought spurred Bronwyn as she made her way into Dock Ward. This unknown man was her kin. Perhaps he had answers for her that Hronulf had not lived to give. That possibility made the chance she was about to take worthwhile.

She hurried to the Sleeping Snake, a rough and noisy tavern where thieves of many races gathered to trade stories, blows, and stolen goods. The Zhentarim contact she had used a few times before frequented the tavern.

Raucous laughter burst out into the street when Bronwyn shouldered open the door and pushed her way into the crowded room. The smell of stale ale and staler bodies assaulted her. Most of the dockhands who came to drink here didn't bother to bathe after a hard day's work. She spotted the informer—a dockhand and occasional assassin—slumped over a table near the hearth.

He glanced up when she kicked at his chair. "Well," he asked drunkenly, "what are you looking for this time?"

She bent down low so that she could speak the words in a normal voice rather than shouting. "A man who recently lost a child."

He leaned back and eyed her with speculation. "Don't have much use for brats, myself."

"No one's asking you to have anything to do with this one. Have you heard anything?"

"Can't say I have. Who's this man that got shed of his brat?"

"His name is Doon. He's a dark man, probably not exceptionally tall."

There was a flicker in the man's eyes, but he shook his head. "Sorry. Can't help you," he said as he reached for his mug.

Bronwyn caught his wrist. "Can't, or won't?"

He shook her off and turned aside in obvious dismissal. "One way or another, it's much the same to you."

A trickle of fear ran down Bronwyn's spine. Always before, this man had tried to sell her something, spinning out any scrap of information into something she might wish to buy. His outright refusal and the gleam of avarice in his eyes alerted her to danger.

Bronwyn nodded and worked her way back to the bar. The fighting had spread into the main floor, and it would be a while before she could get to the door. She ordered an ale and took a stool to wait out the storm.

A hand seized her arm. Bronwyn spun, gripping the hilt of her knife. She measured the man with a glance and decided that this would be an easy battle. Though still south of midlife, he was the thinnest, frailest person she had ever encountered. The spark of life had apparently drained from his body to center its last flame in his small black eyes.

"Move your hand, or I'll slice it off," she said in an even voice.

The man halted her with an impatient gesture, an upraised palm. Her eyes bulged. Tattooed, or perhaps branded, into his palm was the emblem of the evil god Bane—a small, black hand.

Instinctively she eased away, raised both of her hands in conciliation. Though the god himself was considered dead and gone, and no longer a power to be feared, Bronwyn had no desire to tangle with someone who purported to be an acolyte of such evil.

"I heard you. You want a man who is seeking a child. Where is this man?" he insisted in a voice that recalled a viper's hiss.

Bronwyn licked her lips nervously. "That's what I'm trying

to find out. If you know anything of him, I'd be willing to trade for the information."

A terrible chuckle wheezed from the former priest's lips. "If the item you have to barter is his yellow hide, then you have a deal, wench. I want him. I want him dead," he specified, as if there could be any doubt concerning his intentions.

Bronwyn quickly weighed the risk against the possible gain. If this priest had knowledge of Cara's father, she really had no choice but to endure conversation with a Banite and accept the danger inherent in such company. She reached for her mug and signaled the barkeep to bring another drink for her "friend."

"I don't know where he is, but I'd be happy to turn him over to you once I locate him. Because of the child," she said quickly, when he turned a suspicious stare upon her.

"Ah." He smirked, then tossed back the contents of the mug the barkeep set before him. "Your tale rings true. He always was one to walk away from what he started."

A horrible suspicion took root in Bronwyn's eyes. "He was once a follower of Bane?" she asked, striving mightily to keep her voice neutral.

"That he was. Defected, the damn traitor," he sneered, raising and clenching his fists.

Bronwyn let out her breath in a long sigh. The possibility that Cara's father might be a follower of an evil god was chilling, but, perhaps, in seeing the error of his ways he had made enemies. It was better so than that he should earn the fate of the man beside her, with his skeletal face and wild eyes. Bereft of spells, cut off from the source of evil power, the former priest of Bane was little more than an insane shell.

"When I find Doon, I will send word here," she said, her mind racing as she planned how she could kept this promise without endangering Cara's father. "I will write the name of the place where he might be found on a sketch of a black dragon and post it on the cloakroom door. Watch for it."

"*Doon?* What are you talking about, wench? The man's name is Dag Zoreth."

She quickly covered her surprise. "Of course," she said

with feigned bitterness. "He would not want to be known by
the name he gave to a woman he'd betrayed and abandoned.
He was always cautious. Most likely, he is also frank and
earnest—*Frank* in Luskan, and *Ernest* in Neverwinter!"

To her surprise, the hoary old jest earned a wheezing
chuckle from the Banite. She supposed that, in the company
he was accustomed to keeping, humor was not a common
commodity.

Bronwyn rose and tossed several silver coins onto the
counter and nodded her intent to the barkeep. "Drink what
you will, with my thanks, until the coins run out."

She left quickly, while the former priest was still contem-
plating this unexpected bounty, and all the way to the door
she felt the eyes of her Zhentilar informer following her.

* * * * *

Algorind rode swiftly through the crowded street on his
tall white horse. He still did not understand how Icewind had
returned to the Halls of Justice. The horse had been well
treated and seemed none the worse for having been stolen by
a treacherous dwarf.

He scanned the wooden signs that hung from the many
shops, looking for the Curious Past. What he found was a bit
of a surprise. Unlike most of the signs, it did not rely on an
image of shoe or cloak or mug to convey what goods could be
had within. The name was carved with runes in Common, as
well as in several other languages. A learned woman. That
did not fit the picture he carried of Bronwyn, who would steal
from Hronulf and consort with a dwarven horse thief.

He pushed open the door. A bell tinkled merrily, and a
white-haired gnome woman appeared from behind a counter.
"How can I help you?" she said cheerily.

Algorind heard a door bang in the back room. "I am looking
for Bronwyn."

"Then I'm afraid I can't help you," the gnome said with evi-
dent regret. "She is out of town on business."

The young paladin nodded. "You expect her?"

"That I do. No more than two, three days. Would you like to stop back or leave a name?"

"I will return," he said simply. "Thank you, good gnome, for your time and help."

He left the shop, walking briskly toward the narrow alley he'd seen by the cobbler's shop a few doors down. That banging door interested him.

A small figure darted toward him in hot pursuit of a young alley cat, her hands outstretched for the grab. She hauled up short when she caught sight of him, and her large brown eyes rounded in terror. She shrieked and whirled away, dashing back down the alley.

It was the child! The same girl he had taken from the farm and turned over to Sir Gareth's keeping. What she was doing in this city, and on her own, Algorind could not begin to fathom. He took off after her, ducking low to avoid a string of long wool stockings hung out to dry in the alley.

The girl could run like a rabbit. She darted down the alley and out into a small, open area. A wooden sign proclaimed the site to be Howling Cat Court. A few women strolled about, their faces garishly painted and their bodices laced indecently low. They mocked Algorind as he dashed past in pursuit of the child, bidding him leave off with his playmates and learn some adult games. His face heated when he realized what they meant.

His quarry swerved and dodged, evading his grasp nimbly. She turned and darted toward another alley. Algorind began to follow suit when a heavy *thunk* resounded painfully through his skull and stopped him where he stood. He turned, dazed, and looked incredulously at one of the over-ripe women. There was a small oak cudgel in her hand. She gave him a hard smile and kissed her fingertips to him in a mocking salute, then melted away into the shadows of an alley.

Algorind shook off the numbing pain and took off after the girl. He was almost to the alley when a loud, trembling horn call resounded through the court.

"You, there! Stop where you are."

The young paladin knew authority when he heard it. He

stopped and slowly turned around. Four men and two women, all wearing leather armor dyed green and black and reinforced with gold-colored chain mail, strode toward him, small clubs in their hands. A band of mercenaries, no doubt. He decided to try to fight his way clear.

His resolve must have shown in his eyes. "Yield to the city watch," the speaker said. "You will not be harmed unless you resist."

This put Algorind in a quandary. The rule of his order stated that he was to obey all lawful authorities unless they constrained him to do evil. These city guards were standing between him and his duty, but that was not necessarily evil.

"Good sirs, ladies," he said earnestly. "You do not understand."

"We *understand* that you were chasing a little girl. She yours?"

"No, but—"

"You responsible for tending her?"

In a manner of speaking, that was true, but not plain enough truth to give Algorind comfort in speaking it. "I wished to return her to her rightful place," he said, which was more precise.

"Uh-huh," the watch captain said, skepticism deeply etched on his bearded face. "What was her name?"

Algorind was utterly at a loss. "I do not know," he had to admit.

The captain sniffed. "Thought as much. Take him in. We'll let the magisters deal with this one."

This was utterly beyond Algorind's comprehension. "I cannot go with you."

"You don't have much of a choice. You can come easy, or we'll take you in trussed and hooded. You choose."

"I will come with you," Algorind said, bowing his head in defeat. "Will you grant me one kindness, though? Carry word to the Halls of Justice, and tell them of my fate?"

"There are messengers in the castle. They'll get around to your cell sooner or later, and you can send word to whomever you like. Now, move."

* * * * *

Bronwyn hurried back to her shop, cutting through the back ways. As she came through Howling Cat Court, it seemed to her that one of the low-rent courtesans who strutted along the far walk sent her a knowing smile. The woman looked vaguely familiar and harmless enough, so Bronwyn lifted a hand in friendly response as she strode past.

She found Alice in a fit, wringing her tiny hands and pacing the floors with enough fervor to raise a cloud of dust. Bronwyn's first thought was for Cara. She pounced on the gnome, seizing her shoulders and turning her so that they faced each other. "Where is she?"

"Gone!" mourned Alice, confirming Bronwyn's worse suspicions.

Bronwyn ran a hand over her forehead and back, smoothing her hair in a gesture of pure frustration. "Did you see anything?"

"A young man came looking for you. A paladin, I think. He wore a blue and white tabard and carried a broadsword. He was young—no more than twenty—but taller than most men. Pale yellow hair, curly. He left his horse at the door."

Bronwyn had a very bad feeling about this. "A big horse? White?"

"I believe so. I didn't get more than a glance. Why?"

"Long story," Bronwyn mumbled. Ebenezer had told her of his rescue by a man who could turn undead to dust. That would make the man a priest—or a paladin. The man who came looking for her, who might have taken Cara, was near Thornhold. What he knew, what he wanted, she could guess all too well.

At that moment the shop bell tinkled, startling them both. Woman and gnome jumped and whirled to face the door. In it stood Danilo Thann, a broad smile in his face and a small, half-elf girl in his arms.

"Cara!" Bronwyn cried. She rushed forward to reclaim the girl, gave her a quick hug, then she set her down and turned her attention to the man. "Danilo, what happened? Where did you find her?"

"Actually, I did not. Cara was brought to me by some Harpers who happened upon her."

Bronwyn's face clouded. "Still watching me?"

"Strictly speaking, no. We've been keeping an eye out for the paladins, and one of them happened by your shop."

"I should thank you, then," she said softly, looking at the child. Cara was happily chatting with Alice, telling her all about the ginger cat that she'd almost caught, and wouldn't it make a fine pet?

Bronwyn sighed. "I promised I would find her father, but I don't know if I can keep her safe until then."

She spoke softly, but the girl looked up. "I will be safe, Bronwyn. Look at this. Come to me, Shopscat!"

Before the raven could respond to the summons, the child disappeared. Bronwyn blinked rapidly, as if she could conjure the girl by clearing her vision. There was nothing, save for a childish giggle outside the front door. Before Bronwyn could move, Cara was back, just as abruptly as she left.

"Look!" she said proudly, showing Bronwyn the three bright gems in her hand. "A ruby, a blue topaz, and a . . . citrine?" she asked, looking up at Danilo for corroboration.

He nodded, his eyes bright with the child's reflected pleasure. "That's right. You remember well."

"Gemjump," Bronwyn murmured, remembering tales she'd heard of stones that enabled the holder to magically transport to the location of any of the gems. They were rare, and exceedingly expensive. Three of them was a princely gift.

"With these, Cara can get herself out of the occasional tight spot," Danilo said lightly. "Put them back in their bag, Cara, the way I showed you."

The child beamed and did as she was told. Danilo drew Bronwyn aside. "You've got a remarkable new friend," he said softly. "I think you will have your hands full, though."

Bronwyn nodded. "Cara is no trouble, but I think she's *in* trouble. I just don't know how much, or what kind."

"Let me help you," Danilo said earnestly. "Tell me what I can do."

She smiled at him, her anger nearly forgotten. "You

already have. The gemstones give her a bit of control over her fate. She needs that. And a little control," she added somberly, "is usually the best any of us can expect."

Twelve

Dag Zoreth had seen his former teacher Malchior give way to anger on only one occasion. Before his ire had cooled, a half battalion of inept soldiers lay on the ground, some fried black by Cyric-granted lighting, a few still jerking spasmodically. As Dag looked at the older priest's angry countenance, he silently rehearsed his own prayer to Cyric. If one of them had to end this conference writhing and twitching on the carpet, Dag would prefer it not be he.

He rose from the chair in deference to the higher ranking priest. "This is a surprise," Dag said mildly. "I did not expect to find you in Waterdeep."

"No doubt!" the priest retorted. "What is this I hear about you?"

Dag strolled over to the table and helped himself to a piece of the spiced shrimp that the maid had brought along with the midday meal. A fine place, this inn. This meal was enough for two, and to spare. He took the entire tray and handed it to Malchior. The older priest hardly seemed to notice. He popped one shrimp into his mouth, chewed briefly, and kept talking.

"You have not yet found your sister, but one of our informers has," Malchior said, punctuating this statement by snatching another shrimp. "She was asking about a child. Said it was yours."

Dag shrugged. "She would not be the first woman to make such a false claim of me. Since I did not know I had a sister, you cannot hold me to account for violation of consanguinity laws."

The priest stuffed his mouth again and chewed angrily. "You are sidestepping the question."

"It has become a habit," Dag said lightly. "You have taught me well."

The priest's eyes narrowed, and he studied the younger man as if he was suddenly considering whether his lessons might have been learned too well. Then the look of speculation was gone, and with it Malchior's ire.

"These are excellent," he said easily, nodding at the nearly empty tray. "Perhaps we could start on that savory pie while we speak of other matters? You have heard of the gathering of the paladins. I have some advice on the administration and safeguarding of your new command. That is, if you are willing to listen."

Malchior's jovial expression was back in place, but Dag was not fooled for a moment. This man was a dangerous enemy, and he wanted Cara. If Dag had to, he would kill him. Until then, he would learn from him.

"My dear Malchior," Dag said with a smile, "I am interested in every word you have to say." And even more interested, Dag thought, in what you choose to keep shrouded in silence.

The glint in the priest's eyes suggested that he sensed Dag's unspoken addition and marked it well. Smiling at each other like a pair of circling sharks, they sat down to play out the game.

* * * * *

"I tell you, Bronwyn, your friend will be a resident at the castle for the rest of the day," Danilo swore. "Several of the messengers who attend the prisoners are Harpers. They will take care to leave young Algorind's request until last."

Bronwyn nodded and shot a glance toward Cara. The child was kneeling on the floor of the shop, playing some elaborate game of make believe with some chess pieces, and singing softly to herself. "That's something," Bronwyn admitted. She bit her lip, considering.

"What?"

"This might sound frivolous," she warned him.

That amused her friend. "Remember to whom you're speaking."

She chuckled and got to the point. "Cara has spent her life on a small, remote farm. Other than her trip to Waterdeep as a prisoner and a brief voyage on a slave ship, she hasn't had a chance to see the world. What better place to begin than Waterdeep?"

He nodded. "Your reasoning is sound. And you should be safe enough. With your permission, I'll make certain that you are discretely followed and amply protected."

The years of unseen Harper eyes still rankled. "And if I did not give my permission?"

"Then I would respect your wishes," he said. "Regretfully, but I would respect them."

He spoke firmly, with not a hint of his usual lazy drawl. Bronwyn believed him. She smiled and turned to Cara. "Cara, what is your favorite color?"

The little girl looked up, startled by this question. "I don't think I have one."

"Well, if you could pick out any dress you liked, what color would it be?"

Feminine longing lit her eyes. "My foster mother wore purple but said I was not to," she said. "She would not say why."

Bronwyn had a suspicion concerning this, but she did not want to put words to it, not even in the silence of her own mind. "How about blue? Or yellow?"

Cara nodded, clearly willing to play the game. "Pink, like a sunset cloud."

That struck a memory. Ellimir Oakstaff, a seamstress

whose shop was also on the Street of Silks, had a bolt of soft pink silk, a rare color that would be quickly seized by ladies looking for spring gowns. "Come on," she said, extending a hand. "I know a lady who can make you a dress the color of clouds and just as soft. Let's go and let her take your measure."

Cara was on her feet in an instant. "Truly?"

"Truly," Bronwyn answered. "And then we'll go for tea and see all there is to see in the City of Splendors."

Cara looked suddenly suspicious. "This is not just a game?"

Bronwyn laughed, but her eyes stung. At Cara's age, she had had none of these experiences, either. She thought she knew what this would mean to the girl.

Bidding farewell to the Harper bard, Bronwyn kept her promise and bought Cara the pink gown and two more along with it. They had tea and sugared wine at Gounar's Tavern, a glittering eatery in the heart of the Sea Ward. The taproom was brightly lit by dozens of magical globes, and mirrored glass tossed back the light to every corner, there to be captured by the cunningly faceted crystals and imitation gems that studded everything from plate to chairs.

As Bronwyn expected, Cara was enchanted by the display. Too excited to eat, she clutched her goblet of sugared wine and water—much more sugar than wine, and more water than either—and looked around with boundless curiosity. Her silence lasted until they left the tavern, then she exploded into questions, wanting to know about everything they passed.

Bronwyn shook her head as she followed Cara down the street, amazed at her own feelings. Every moment she spent with the child only made the prospect of giving her up more difficult. But this gift, this single day of adventure and light-hearted pleasure, this she could give.

Wanting to show Cara as much as possible, she hailed a carriage and bid the driver to show them the sights. They rode down along the sea wall, marveling at the vast and ornamental mansions, and the ninety-foot statue of a warrior that looked out impassively to sea. They drove past Alghairon's Tower, and Cara shivered at the story of the long-ago wizard and the skele-

ton of the man who had tried to steal this power. She oohed over
Piergeiron's Palace, craned her neck to watch the griffin patrols
pass. At the Plinth—the obelisk that served as a house of
prayer for people of all faiths—she looked faintly puzzled.

"My foster parents prayed—so did my father—but they
would not teach me or name a god I should pray to."

Bronwyn's suspicions regarding this mysterious faith
deepened, as did her puzzlement as to why this Dag Zoreth
seemed so determined to keep his daughter ignorant of his
faith. "You'll find the god or goddess who speaks to your
heart," she said softly.

"Who speaks to yours?"

Bronwyn considered this. She was not a religious person,
but it occurred to her that there was only one answer.
"Tymora," she said. "The lady of luck. She bids you take a
chance and make your own way."

Cara pursed her lips. "That sounds good, but not quite
right for me."

"And that's fine," Bronwyn said, feeling slightly out of her
element with this conversation. She had never given religion
much consideration, but the longing in the child's eyes for a
god or goddess of her own convinced Bronwyn that it might be
a matter worth pondering.

"Now let's go to the South Ward," she suggested. "The sun
will be setting soon, and I believe there's a full moon tonight."

At such times, the Moon Sphere hung above a large courtyard. People could enter the huge, magic-rich globe and float
or soar as they wished. Bronwyn could think of no wonder
more likely to capture the child's fancy, or no better ending to
the day.

*   *   *   *   *

The dungeon of Waterdeep Castle was not the dank and
fearful place that Algorind had expected. Granted, his prison
was well underground—the watch had brought him down two
flights of stairs—but the stone walls were smooth and dry,
and torches sputtered in wall brackets placed every few

paces. The cells were small, but clean and provided with the basic comforts: a straw mattress on a plank frame, a chamber pot, a washbasin, and a pitcher of water. He had been offered food the night before, and again this morning. In all, he could not complain, and he trusted in Tyr's justice to see that his confinement would not be long.

Keeping his mind fixed on this thought, Algorind raised his voice in the traditional morning hymn. It was not, he supposed, the sort of thing one usually heard emanating from these particular halls of justice.

The sound of footsteps echoed down the halls, growing louder. Algorind's face brightened when he caught sight of Sir Gareth, but he finished the last two lines of the hymn before speaking. "Thank you for coming, sir."

"You sound surprised to see me," the knight said curtly. "You are wiser than you appear if you suspect that I considered leaving you here. How did this thing come about?"

Algorind glanced at the prison guard. The older knight followed his thinking and affirmed it with a curt nod. Once the young paladin had been released, they walked in silence from the prison and did not speak until they were riding side by side back to the Halls of Justice.

"I saw the child," Algorind finally said. "The child of Samular's bloodline."

The knight's face turned so white that Algorind feared he would fall from his horse. "Here? In Waterdeep?"

"Yes, sir. I pursued her, thinking to bring her back to the temple. She eluded me, and the watch detained me."

Sir Gareth sat in silence for several moments as he mulled this over. Finally he turned a stern face to Algorind. "Your failure to apprehend a small child is serious. It speaks of lack of skill or lack of will. Perhaps you allowed the girl to escape."

Algorind was deeply shocked. "Sir!"

"Incompetence is a grave offense. You are certainly guilty of that," the knight said coldly. "By all reports, you are well trained and able. Any future failure will be regarded as deliberate and as treason against the order. Do you understand?"

"No, sir," Algorind said with complete honesty. In truth, the knight's words baffled him.

"What part was unclear?"

"Well," he began, "I am not certain how the girl came to be in the city at all."

"You would do better to concern yourself with finding her," the knight said in a severe tone. "And when you do, bring her to me at once. Not at the temple, though," he added in a milder voice. "The other brothers need not hear of this single lapse. We will keep the matter between us. Obey me in this."

"Yes, sir," Algorind responded, but never had he found obedience so heavy a burden. If he had done wrong, then he should have the censure of his brothers. To seek to avoid it was impious. He had no wish to shrug off his burdens or cover his lacks, but he was sworn to obedience, and he must do as Sir Gareth bid him. Once his duty was clear and his choices simple. That was no longer the case.

Deeply troubled, the young man settled back into his saddle and pondered the fog-shrouded path ahead.

*   *   *   *   *

Once Malchior had polished off the last bite of raspberry tarts and drained the decanter of wine, he went on his way. Left alone in his rented room, Dag Zoreth prepared to summon the image of his paladin spy. Sir Gareth had once reported to Malchior. Perhaps he still did.

It took much longer for Gareth to respond this time. Despite his impatience with the delay, Dag was not entirely displeased. A prolonged summons could be immensely painful, and he was not averse to giving the fallen paladin some of the pain he had earned.

The face that finally appeared in the globe was pale as parchment and tightly drawn. "So good of you to come," Dag said with heavy sarcasm. "I had an interesting visit from our mutual friend Malchior. Perhaps you have also spoken with him of late?"

"I have not, Lord Zoreth," the knight said flatly.

Dag believed him. By now, he understood that Gareth cloaked his lies in elaborate self-deceiving half truths. Any statement put that baldly was likely simple truth.

"What word on my sister and my daughter?"

"I have just met with a young paladin, the man who stole the girl from the farmer folk. His name is Algorind. The child got away from him. He was pursuing her through the city and was so mindful of the task before him that he did not notice he had drawn the attention of the city watch." He paused. "You know how single-minded the followers of Tyr can be."

"Indeed," Dag agreed dryly.

"The young paladin is very earnest. He reminds me of your father, when he was of like age," Sir Gareth mused.

Dag wondered, briefly, if the knight was deliberately trying to stir up his hatred of this Algorind. "And where is the girl now?"

"I do not know. She was seen near the Street of Silks, coming from the shop known as the Curious Past. This shop is owned by your sister. The paths of our quarry converge, which makes matters somewhat neater. I have sent this Algorind to redeem himself, with the instruction that he is to come only to me. When the child and the woman are in my hands, they are as good as yours. This I will do, without fail."

"See that you do," Dag said absently, then dismissed the enchantment.

The Street of Silks was not very far from the festhall where he rented a discrete room. Perhaps it was time to meet this long-lost sister of his.

Dag hesitated for a moment, wondering whether he should discard his black and purple clothing for less distinctive garb. He decided against it. He had worn no other color nearly ten years. His lord Cyric might take umbrage with any change now.

The priest left the festhall and walked to the shop. He did not go directly, but took his time, moving from one shop to the next as if he had no thought but to consider the wares offered. He tried on a pair of boots in one small shop and in another spoke briefly with a comely half-elf girl who was busily stitching a small, pink gown.

He was impressed with the Curious Past. A fine building, two stories tall and stoutly constructed of timber frame filled with wattle-and-daub. The plaster was in good repair and freshly whitewashed. Small panes of good, nearly translucent glass graced the large window, and a tempting display of her unique merchandise—but not too tempting—was arranged on a table before the window. There were interesting touches everywhere. The banding on the wide-planked door was cunningly worked in a spiral, the symbol of time passing, but on several panes of glass was etched the pattern of an hourglass, tilted so that the flow of sand was arrested.

He lifted the door latch and walked in. A gnome woman came to greet him and to shoo away the raven that studied him with an intensity that bordered on recognition. Dag was not the least discomfited by this. He felt a certain affinity for the raven and the wolf, for these carrion-feeders benefited from strife. Indeed, some of the ancients believed that the ravens carried the souls of the dead into the afterlife. Dag's god had once been the lord of the dead, and Dag had sent many souls to Cyric's kingdom. In all, he had much in common with the shrew-eyed bird.

"How can I help you, sir?" the gnome asked, sliding an expert eye over him. Obviously marking his lack of interest in personal ornamentation, she ran through a likely litany; a set of goblets, a small statue, this carved chest, a scrying bowl?

"Nothing, please. I would like to speak with Bronwyn. I might have a commission for her."

The gnome's eyes cooled just a little. "She isn't available, I'm afraid. Would you like to leave a name and word of where she can contact you?"

"I will return. Perhaps tomorrow?"

"After highsun," the gnome said quickly. "That is the best time."

He thanked her and left, not believing a word of it. Remembering the friendly half-elf seamstress—and reconsidering the possible importance of that small pink gown—he retraced his steps to the dress shop and struck up a conversation.

The woman was quickly charmed and soon was chatting easily. "Yes, spring is late to come this year. The markets are just starting to open, and folk from here and beyond coming into the city. . . ."

"Quite an influx of paladins, I notice," he said casually. "I rode past the Halls of Justice this morning. Such a racket they made, with their endless bashing away at each other."

She made a face. "Let them keep at it, and leave the rest of us alone. One was around the other day." She glanced down at the pink silk, which she had fisted in both hands. She smoothed out the wrinkles and seemed to reconsider saying more.

But Dag had already learned quite a bit. He leaned closer to the woman. "Perhaps you can help me. If I were to need a special gift for a lady, something different and rare, where should I go?"

"Oh, to Bronwyn's shop, of course. The Curious Past." Her face fell slightly. "You have a lady who requires a special gift?"

"My mother," he lied smoothly. The woman brightened again. So predictable, he noted with a touch of scorn. No wonder he found so little time to waste on women.

But this one had been useful. The half-elf knew his sister well. She was working on the little gown with quick, neat stitches, not even putting aside her work for their flirtation. She expected to deliver the dress soon. It would seem that the child would soon return, and Bronwyn as well.

Dag spoke with the half-elf for a few more minutes, making an appointment to meet later in a certain discretely lit tavern—an appointment he had no intention of keeping.

It was a small cruelty, but satisfying. And more important, it served a purpose. If the half-elf wench thought herself jilted, she was less likely to speak of her embarrassment and the man who had caused it.

Dag promptly forgot the half-elf as soon as he left her shop. He had more important things to tend. Somewhere in this city was a paladin who called himself Algorind. Before the day was through, Dag intended to roast the paladin's heart over purple fire.

*   *   *   *   *

Bronwyn returned to her shop with her linen shopping sack laden with treats. She'd left Cara sleeping and intended to have a special breakfast of pastries, fruit, and lemon tea ready for her, but the look on Alice's face stole such pleasant thoughts from her mind.

"A man came by just a bit ago," the gnome said tersely. "He was about your height and small enough to balance you in a scale. He had black hair, dipping here," she said, tapping at the center of her forehead.

The contents of Bronwyn's sack spilled unheeded to the floor. That was the one detail Cara had been able to give them about her father. "Just like Cara said," she muttered.

"Just like."

"Did you tell him Cara was here?"

Alice looked insulted. "What do you take me for—a kobold? He didn't ask, nor would I have told him. It was you he wanted. A commission, he said."

Bronwyn stooped to gather up the fallen groceries. She picked up a lemon and dropped it into the sack. "One more thing. Did he wear purple?"

"Purple and black," Alice confirmed. "Why?"

Bronwyn just shook her head, for her throat was too tight for her to form an answer.

"Child, it's time," the gnome said. "If that was the girl's father, you'll have to turn her over. Cara would be the first to insist."

"I know," Bronwyn said, but she meant nothing of the sort. Never before had she felt less sure of anything. Before she could decide what to do with the little girl, she needed to find some answers. It was time to face down Khelben Arunsun, and test her ability to hold to her own path against the Master Harper's powerful will and subtle manipulations.

Thirteen

As it turned out, Bronwyn did not have to seek out Khelben Arunsun. He came to her.

The street outside of her shop was always alive with a pleasant clamor during the day and well into the evening. So the sudden lull in this bustle held a portent that few warning horns could match.

Bronwyn peered out the window and understood at once. Lord Arunsun and his lady, the mage Laeral Silverhand, strolled arm in arm down the street, stopping at shops to admire this or that trinket. This was far from a common sight, but Bronwyn suspected that this visit was for her benefit and that the other stops were visited so that she would not seemed to be singled out.

At that moment one of Ellimir's helpers came running out, a bolt of cloth-of-silver in her arms. She held up a length of it to show that it was of near color to Lady Laeral's hair. The two women haggled pleasantly for a few moments. Bronwyn watched, troubled by something but not quite able to pinpoint her concern. Then the young seamstress turned, and Bronwyn noted the heavy kohl that lined her eyes, the smudge of henna still on her cheeks.

So that was why the three-copper courtesan in the alley had looked so familiar, Bronwyn thought grimly. She was willing to bet good gold coin that this shop assistant was one of Danilo's Harpers.

That flustered and angered her. She drew back from the window and busied herself with some rare volumes as she collected her thoughts.

The bell over the door rang too soon for her comfort. The archmage and his lady were met at the door by Alice Tinker. Bronwyn had to admire the gnome's performance. Alice's response was perfect. She seemed overawed by the presence of two of the city's most powerful magi, and so eager to please that she resembled a puppy who regretted she had but one tail to wag. Anyone who witnessed the gnome's performance would have a difficult time believing that she had been a Harper informer for many years. Since Alice's admission, she had spoken freely to Bronwyn of her past. It was difficult to equate the motherly gnome with the fierce fighter she once had been, but Bronwyn could see how that very dichotomy would make Alice a more effective Harper agent.

Khelben looked somewhat bemused by the presence of a child in the shop. Bronwyn noted how his eyes followed Cara, but his countenance was too difficult for Bronwyn to read. She studied Cara herself and tried to imagine what the archmage saw. Cara was a small girl, exceedingly thin, and brown as a wren. Half-elf, that was obvious, but except for her delicate frame and the slight point to her ears, she looked more human than elf. Did the archmage also note that the girl followed Bronwyn like a second shadow? That, like her apparent mentor, the child had an eye for rare and pretty objects? Following Alice's lead, Cara brought choice baubles to show Laeral. Soon she was giggling and chattering, utterly charming the lady mage.

Khelben was not long content to stand to one side and watch the womenfolk exclaim over trinkets. Bronwyn caught his eye as she bent to hold a hand mirror so that Laeral could admire the effect of a necklace of rosy pearls. She put the mirror into Alice's hand and straightened. "Can I show you anything, my lord?"

"Old tomes, perhaps? I see none about, but perhaps you have some that are not on display?"

Bronwyn took the hint and led him into the back room. He waited until she had lit a small oil lamp and shut the door. "You no doubt have many questions about your past," he said without preamble. "I believe I have the answers you seek. Or at least, I can tell you where they might be found."

Bronwyn listened as he gave her directions to the monastery of Tyr and a description of what she would find there. "That's two days' ride," she calculated, her face troubled. "I hope Alice won't mind looking out for Cara."

A hint of suspicion edged into the archmage's eyes. "This child. What is she to you?"

"She's a stray, like me," Bronwyn said lightly.

"Do you plan to adopt her?"

She sighed, her face wistful. "I wouldn't mind—she's a dear little thing—but she has a father."

Khelben considered this. Bronwyn wondered if he was comparing Cara's face to hers and seeing the resemblance. "She is kin to me," Bronwyn admitted. "She says her father's name is Doon. I have heard him called by another name."

"Dag Zoreth," Khelben said flatly.

Bronwyn blinked, startled but not really surprised to hear that Khelben knew of this. "Yes. Who is he?" she said urgently.

The archmage picked up a tome bound in green leather and put it back on the shelf, unopened. Fidgeting, perhaps? marveled Bronwyn, who had never thought to ascribe such simple mortal failings to the archmage.

"Dag Zoreth is a strifeleader . . . a priest of Cyric. Until lately, he served Darkhold as a war cleric," Khelben said bluntly. "He is also your brother."

Bronwyn sat down hard. "My brother," she echoed.

"Yes. You knew him as Brandon. He took the name Dag Zoreth shortly after he was abducted."

"Brandon," she murmured. "Bran." An image came to her:

a small, pale face, narrow and intense, capped by hair the color of a raven's wing. He was a presence both fiercely beloved and vaguely feared. Bran and Bron, they'd called each other. Yes. It came to her again—not quite a memory, but at least the shadow of one.

She had a brother.

The thought struck her again, this time hard enough to hurt.

"It appears that your family has access to considerable power," Khelben continued. "Dag Zoreth wants that power. So do the paladins. This might be considered heresy in some circles, but I would no sooner see one side get their hands on it than the other."

"And Cara and I are in the middle," Bronwyn murmured.

"You are in a most delicate position," he agreed, "a fulcrum between the Zhentarim and the Order of the Knights of Samular."

She gave him a rueful smile. "Not exactly what I signed up for when I pledged to protect the Balance."

"Nevertheless, it is the task that has come to you," Khelben said with a wry smile. "You are well suited for it. As a finder of lost antiquities, you must find three rings that once belonged to Samular and his brother and bring them back to safe keeping."

Bronwyn rose, her eyes intent upon Khelben's face. "Why?"

To her surprise, he didn't seem to find her question impertinent. "The rings are but part of the puzzle. There is a larger artifact, a power of some sort that the three rings together can trigger. This you must recover."

She thought it over and decided to speak the truth. "I already have two of the rings. One was given me by my father, the other Cara wears."

The archmage nodded as if he had expected to hear this. "I suppose I cannot persuade you to yield the rings into my keeping. Would you at least consider leaving the child behind? There are few places more secure that Blackstaff Tower. Laeral seems quite taken with her, and I am sure she would not mind tending her until your return."

Bronwyn's eyes narrowed with suspicion. "This seems too neatly planned. You knew of her, too."

"Not until this moment," Khelben said plainly. "I had no knowledge of the child's heritage, and I would not have known her for who she is had I not seen the two of you together. Only then did I look for the ring and note it on her hand. But consider this: if one man can discern this resemblance and see the ring she wears for what it is, so can another."

Bronwyn's shoulders rose and fell in a sigh as she accepted the truth in the archmage's words. Poor Cara had been tossed around like a cork on the waves, and Bronwyn wasn't looking forward to telling the child that she would be left in the care of a stranger.

"I'll bring her around first thing in the morning," she said. "She'll need some time to get used to the idea."

The magi left the shop soon after, leaving Alice happily counting and recounting a pile of coins, and Cara sighing and starry-eyed over the gems she had helped to sell and the pretty lady who would wear them. Bronwyn noted this and was grateful. It would make things a little easier.

She crouched down so that her face was level with Cara's. "You liked Lady Laeral, didn't you?"

The girl beamed, and her head bobbed happily. "She's nice. She bought me this. It is mine to keep, she said." She showed Bronwyn a small brooch, shaped like the shadow of a leaping hart. It was a simple, pretty thing. It was also silver, and elf-crafted, and over two hundred years old. There were other pieces in the shop of greater value, but not many.

Bronwyn gently took the brooch from the child and fastened it to the shoulder of her new gown. "That was kind of her. I like Laeral, too. She's a good friend."

"She has magic," Cara said matter-of-factly. "Lots of it."

That surprised Bronwyn. "You can tell?"

Cara drew herself up. "Of course. Can't you?"

Well, this was an interesting twist, Bronwyn mused. She was no expert on the subject of magic, but she knew that the ability to recognize magical talent in another almost certainly meant that Cara was gifted. "Would you like to learn magic?"

She nodded avidly. "Today?" she said, hope ringing in her voice.

Bronwyn chuckled. "It takes a bit longer than that, but you could get a start. How about this," she said, twisting around so that she could sit on the floor and pull Cara into her lap. "Tomorrow morning, I will take you to the wizard's tower where Lady Laeral lives. She will play with you and take care of you and show you some magic. Would you like that?"

Cara considered. "Will you be coming, too?"

"Yes, but I can't stay," she said ruefully. "I have to go away for a while."

"Why?"

"We're not going to find your father if we don't look, right?"

The girl brightened. "I'll come with you."

"You can't. I'll be riding for several days. It will be dull and tiring, and it may be dangerous. You've had quite enough of that sort of thing to last you a long while. You'll be safe with Laeral."

The girl folded her arms. Her lip thrust out and her face turned, as portent as a thundercloud. "I'm *tired* of being kept safe and quiet and out of the way! I'm tired of staying in one place! I want to go with you. I want to see the places you and Ebenezer told me about."

Bronwyn sighed and stroked the girl's nut-brown hair. "Believe me, I know how you feel. If I stay too long in one place, I start feeling itchy, like ants are crawling all over me."

Cara giggled, then shivered. "I can feel them, too," she confided.

Bronwyn smiled faintly, both touched and grieved that this foundling of hers was such a kindred spirit. But perhaps, because of all they shared, she could make Cara understand.

"You know that the ship you were on was a slave ship, right?"

"Yes, but I was not to be a slave. The men said I was a sort of princess, and that I was being taken to a palace." Cara frowned. "They didn't listen to me, though, when I told them to take me back. You'd think a princess could decide where she wanted to go, wouldn't you?"

"I suspect that princesses have fewer choices than the common, everyday sort of girl," Bronwyn told her. "But sometimes things go wrong. I was on a ship like that, once, when I was much smaller than you. Pirates came and stole me, much as Ebenezer and I stole you and the dwarves, but they didn't set us free. I was sold to be a slave. The first person who bought me was very . . . unkind. I got away but was captured and sold again. This time, a gem merchant bought me. I had clever hands, and I could draw and use tiny tools very well by the time I was your age. I worked very hard. There was no time for play, no children to play with, and never quite enough to eat. All that I had of my own was a sleeping mat in a corner of the kitchen."

"They were mean," Cara decreed.

"They did not set out to be," she said, "but they didn't give me much thought one way or another. That was almost worse."

The child considered this, and nodded. "I'm glad you stole me back."

Bronwyn hugged her. "I am, too. I would do anything to keep you from that life—even leave you in Blackstaff Tower for a few days, if that is what I must do."

"All right," the child conceded. Her face turned stern, and she shook her finger. "But if you stay too long, Ebenezer and I will come looking for you and steal you back!"

* * * * *

Later that morning, Bronwyn rode down to the South Ward to say good-bye to Ebenezer. The courtyard surrounding Brian Swordmaster's forge was alive with glowing fires, the ringing of hammer against anvil, and the voices of contentious dwarves.

As she tied her horse to the gate, Ebenezer caught sight of her. He immediately dropped his hammer and bounded over to her. "Where's the lass?" he asked. "You found her da yet?"

She told him what she had learned so far and of the attempt by Ebenezer's paladin friend to snatch her. His face clouded with concern as he listened.

"Smells funny to me," he said. "Paladins are supposed to be a rare breed, aren't they? They've been popping up far too frequent for my liking."

"The paladins are the lesser of my two problems," she assured him.

"Seems to me we don't know that just yet. You can't prove by me that paladins are all that different from any other breed of human. As I always say, think the worst, just in case," he offered. "And I don't like you walking into their den with nothing more than a how-d'you-do as shield and armor."

"I don't have time to argue, Ebenezer. I'll see you when I get back."

"And lots of times in between," he said. "I'm going with you."

"I'll be riding."

His eyes lit up. "You know I can ride. You still got that pony?"

"No," she said regretfully. "I left him at the public stable, with instructions that he be sold."

"Well now, that's too bad. I liked that horse better'n most men I've met. Got more sense. But I've got a few coins now, and the clan owes me. Might could buy my own pony."

"You don't want to be spending your earnings," she cautioned.

"Oh, don't I? One way or another, I'd-a go with you, if it means riding piggyback on a winged elf. You stood with me; I'm prepared to do the same."

At that moment a female dwarf hollered his name. He cast a look over his shoulder then leaned in to whisper, "And they've put me to work at a forge. Nothing wrong with that, but my feet start to itching if I keep 'em in one place too long. You'd be doing me a kindness," he wheedled.

Bronwyn capitulated with a grin. "Well, let's be off. We're going to need to get you a horse."

* * * * *

Algorind took his leave of Sir Gareth and returned to Curious Past, the scene of his previous failure. He puzzled over what he was to do when he found Bronwyn and the child. In this city, a man was not left alone to tend his duty. As he rode along, he noted many small watch patrols, busily tending the affairs of the city and minding the business of better men.

To compound this matter was the difficulty in tracking anyone through a city. He had learned to follow the sign of man, horse, or monster through the hills and moors, but a woman's passage through Waterdeep? A child's? How was such a thing measured?

He was still pondering this when he saw a small, furtive figure dash down a dark passage between two tall buildings. He caught a glimpse of a long, brown braid flashing around the corner.

Algorind swung down from his horse and quickly tied the reins around a lamp post. He no longer felt secure that his mount would be there when he returned, but he could not afford to worry about that now. He hurried down the narrow way in pursuit.

The woman ducked down two more alleys and then disappeared into the back door of a large frame building. Algorind could hear the clatter of looms as he approached, and above the noise, the sound of frantic footsteps dashing down wooden steps.

He followed her into the building and down the stairs. The smell of moisture, dirt, and root vegetables grew stronger, and a bit of light came in from a small, iron-grated portal placed high on the cellar wall.

When Algorind reached the dirt floor, he pulled his sword and squinted into the gloom. His eyes could not yet discern anyone else in the cellar, but he was certain he had heard her come this way.

A sharp, short, grating sound broke the stillness, and a torch flared high. Algorind found himself facing four men, all armed with swords and wearing enormous, evil-looking grins.

The biggest smile was on the man he had followed—a scrawny runt of a man with a face much pocked by some forgotten sickness, and a long, braided tail of brown horsehair in his hands. This he brandished mockingly at Algorind, fluttering his eyelashes in a parody of feminine wiles.

His comrades laughed uproariously at this and then began to close in. From above them, the steady clack and clatter of the looms never once faltered.

Too late, Algorind realized the trap into which he had been lured. These men knew the ways of a city and had prepared a place where they might fight undisturbed. Well, by the grace of Tyr, he would give them the fight they sought.

He held his sword out slightly to the side, his every muscle alert and ready. The first man dashed at him, sword held high and two of his fellows hard on his heels. Algorind lunged forward with a quick, precise motion and ran him though the heart. He ducked under the next attack and stabbed upward at the third man, felling him, too, in a single blow. A skitter of feet behind him dragged to a quick stop on the dirt floor. Algorind rose and spun toward the man who had run past him. It was the man who had tricked him, and he came in with a vicious, upward-sweeping backhand. Algorind caught the sword in a ringing parry. He pressed in close and with his left hand punched out over the joined blades. The man staggered back and again Algorind lunged. His sword sank between the man's ribs and darted back out.

The paladin turned swiftly back to his fourth and final foe. This one was the wiliest of the group, and the worst—content to watch his comrades die as he took the measure of his opponent.

The man was nearly as tall as Algorind, and though not as broad, he had a lean, sinewy look and a way of holding the sword that bespoke long acquaintance with a blade. He lifted the sword to his forehead in a salute that seemed only partially mocking.

They began to circle each other, then exchanged the first ringing blow. His foe was quick, Algorind noted, and fought with a clean economy of motion. The man had been trained, and trained well.

The paladin feinted high. His blow was met and then matched by a quick, spinning cut downward. Algorind parried and answered with a lunge. In all, three fast strokes of steel on steel, coming quickly one after another and each delivered with strength.

Speed, then. The paladin began a stunning routine, raining a quick series of blows upon the man. His opponent stopped each, and got his own in beside. For several moments the two swords rang in rapid, steady dialogue.

The fighters fell apart by unspoken agreement, answering the unique rhythm of their deadly dance. Again they circled, tested, parried.

This time the assassin came in, his blade working Algorind's low and his hand hovering over the knife strapped to his belt. The paladin understood. The man intended to come in over the swords with a knife, much as he himself had served the trickster with a barehanded punch.

But Algorind was ready for him. The young paladin's masters had trained him in many styles of fighting. This one marked the man as from the Dales, a rough but generally peaceable area far to the east and inhabited for the most part by goodly farmers, rangers, and foresters. What had happened to his man, Algorind wondered, to bring him so far from where he once stood?

Some of the pity he felt must have crept into his eyes for the former dalesman to see. A convulsive twitch darted up from his clenched jaw to his anger-filled eyes, and the man drew the knife. But emotion overpowered strategy and he drew too soon and swung too high.

Algorind easily caught the knife on the hilt of his own and sent the man's wild blow out wide. He reversed the direction of the swing and brought the hilt of his knife in hard against the man's nose. Bone shattered, and bright blood spilled down over his worn leather jerkin.

The man came on again, swinging wildly now, all discipline gone. Algorind easily stopped and sidestepped the blows. With a sense of something like regret, he swiftly ended the battle with a stroke across the man's oft-exposed throat.

He stood for a moment over the body of the man, to murmur a prayer for a soul gone astray, a worthy opponent fallen to his own weakness.

Algorind cleaned his sword on a handful of straw that covered a bin of last summer's carrots and slid the weapon back into his sheath. His knife he kept in hand, and he took the torch from the wall holder into which it had been thrust. He had been caught unaware by treachery once this day, and that was all he intended to yield.

At the top of the stairs, he snubbed out the torch, tossed it into the alley, and retraced his steps to the street. To his great relief, his horse was where he left it. He untied Icewind's reins and pondered what next to do.

It seemed likely to him that the woman Bronwyn and her dwarf comrade were somehow behind this. He would immediately report this information to Sir Gareth and leave the matter in his hands.

The knight was in his office, going over a ledger and wearing an expression of martyred resolve. He looked up when Algorind announced himself, and his gray brows rose in question.

Algorind told him what had occurred. The knight considered this for several moments, then reached for parchment and quill. "Go to the barracks and clean yourself up. We will bring this matter to the First Lord himself."

In moments they left the Halls of Justice, bound for the First Lord's palace. It was an easy matter for Sir Gareth to gain an audience with Lord Piergeiron. When he and Algorind rode to the gates of the lavish palace, they were met by uniformed guards and taken at once into the First Lord's presence.

Once again, Algorind found himself discomfited by the unseemly splendor around him. The palace was an elaborate structure built entirely of rare white marble, crowned with a score or more of turreted towers and much elaborately carved stonework. The inside was even more lavish. A fountain played in the center of the great hall, and marble statues of heroes, gods, and goddesses encircled the room. Tapestries of incredibly fine detail and brilliant color hung in lavish profusion. The courtiers were richly dressed in silks and jewels—even the servants wore finery appropriate to a young knight's investiture.

They were led up a broad, sweeping stairway, down a succession of halls to the tower that Piergeiron claimed as his own. Here, at least, Algorind found himself in familiar surroundings. The First Lord's study was simple, almost austere. The walls were bare but for a single tapestry. The only luxury was a profusion of books, and the only comfort a small fire on the grate.

Piergeiron rose to greet them both, with bluff good nature and a comrade's firm handclasp. "Welcome, brothers! You have been much in my thoughts. How goes the preparation for battle?"

"Well, my lord," Sir Gareth said. He nodded his thanks when Piergeiron indicated a seat, and waited until all were seated before speaking again.

"Paladins from all over the northland are gathering for the assault on Thornhold. In another tenday, perhaps two, our numbers will be sufficient for the march north."

"That is good news," the paladin lord agreed. "The sooner the fortress is back in the hands of your good order, the safer will be the High Road for all who travel it."

Sir Gareth inclined his head to acknowledge this praise. "There is other news, my lord, that is not so pleasant to hear. This woman we spoke of. She had been up to mischief since last we met."

Briefly, the knight told the story of Algorind's arrest and the ruse played on him by assassins who lured him into ambush. He also mentioned, much to Algorind's chagrin, the theft of the young paladin's horse by a dwarf known as Bronwyn's companion. He told of her visit to Thornhold at the time of the assault, and her suspicious escape—doubly suspicious in light of the fact that the Zhentarim commander who took the stronghold was Bronwyn's brother. Sir Gareth ended his litany by repeating that Bronwyn stole a valuable artifact belonging to the order.

Piergeiron absorbed this in troubled silence. "I have had information gathered on her, but none so dire as this. The young woman has an excellent reputation in her chosen business, and she appears to live a quiet life."

"Yet she has interesting associates. A brother among the Zhentarim, a dwarf horse thief, a rogue gnome. Did you know that Alice Tinker, the shopkeeper employed by Bronwyn, was once known as Gilanda Quickblade? She was a thief and 'adventurer,' later recruited to the Harpers."

"I did not know this," Piergeiron admitted.

"There is more," Gareth continued. "A frequent visitor to her shop is a young nobleman, one Danilo Thann. Is he not the Harper involved with the new barding college?"

The First Lord nodded grimly.

"I must wonder what he wants with this Bronwyn. She is no bard. Either she is a lightskirt or a Harper." Sir Gareth's tone suggested that there was little difference between these two evils.

"I have met young Lord Thann on several occasions. He is exceedingly fond of gems and other fine things. Perhaps he merely purchases items from Bronwyn's shop."

Sir Gareth lifted his eyebrows. "Do you believe that?"

"No," the First Lord sighed. "I will look into this matter and send word to you as soon as I can. Will that content you?"

"It does indeed. The word of Athar's son is a bond that no steel can break," Sir Gareth said heartily. He rose to leave, but hesitated. "There is one thing more. I have no wish to forestall any efforts your officials of law and order might wish to take, but may we also search for this woman ourselves and bring her to Tyr's Hall of Justice to answer for herself? Will you trust me in this matter?"

It seemed to Algorind that Lord Piergeiron looked relieved to hear a question that could be answered simply. He rose and extended his hand in a pact. "Who could deny a brother paladin? And who could better dispense justice than Tyr?" he said heartily.

The two men, paladin and knight, clasped wrists in an adventurer's salute. "Who indeed," echoed Sir Gareth.

* * * * *

Bronwyn packed up Cara's few belongings and prepared to deliver her to Blackstaff Tower. Cara appeared to take it in stride. It made Bronwyn proud to note how adaptable and resilient the child was.

What made this more remarkable was that the child had no true anchor other than her own inner strength. Cara would be fine, Bronwyn assured herself as she packed for the trip ahead, and that indeed seemed to be the case until they got to the base of the smooth, black wall that surrounded the archmage's tower.

Bronwyn dismounted and went over to Ebenezer's pony to lift Cara down. To her surprise, the child threw herself on the pack horse. She scrambled up onto the bundles and glared down at Bronwyn with a defiant, tear-streaked face. "I want to come with you!"

Bronwyn sighed. "We've been over this, Cara. You can't. It will be very dangerous."

"Take me with you," Cara insisted.

"I'll take you into the tower," Bronwyn bargained. "And I'll stay for some of Lady Laeral's tea and biscuits. How's that?"

The girl folded her arms and sniffed. "Not good enough."

Ebenezer elbowed Bronwyn. "Make a decent merchant, she would," he said in a low, amused voice.

"You're no help," she muttered. She cast a look of appeal toward the smooth black stone on the tower, wondering if someone within could see her plight.

Her silent plea was quickly answered. Laeral emerged, walking through apparently solid stone and looking like a living waterfall. She was a tall woman, taller than most men, and slender as a birch tree. Silver hair, thick and abundant, had been left unbound to cascade in waves over her bared shoulders and fall past her knees. The mage's silvery gown, cut low and cunningly fitted to both cling and swirl, was appropriate for an evening of dancing and revelry. Earrings like a shower of falling stars glittered at Laeral's ears, and her necklace was an intricate web of silver filigree and still more crystal. The outfit was extravagant, absurd—and perfect.

Cara's jaw dropped, and her eyes rounded in wonder. "You look like magic," the child pronounced. "And lots of it."

The mage's eyes lit with warmth and humor. "And so shall you, Cara. We will have some breakfast, and then we will begin. Would you like that?"

The child was utterly and obviously enchanted. Even so, her eyes slid to Bronwyn's face, and she bit her lip in indecision. "Yes . . . " she said hesitantly.

"And I got a new flitterkitten," Laeral continued, "just this very morning. She is a very pretty little white kitten with snowy white wings, but she is just learning to fly and she truly needs someone to take care of her."

This was just the extra bit of inducement that Cara needed. She promptly put out her arms for help. Bronwyn lifted her down from the pack horse, giving Laeral a grateful look over Cara's brown head.

"We will do just fine here, you and I," Laeral said as she took the girl's hand. Noticing how Cara gaped at her glittering rings, she selected a ring that flashed with fire and ice and slid it onto the child's small hand. Instantly the ring sized itself to fit the tiny finger.

Bronwyn nodded in approval, understanding how this would appear to Cara. The child had a ring from her father and knew it to be important; she would view another such gift as a very significant thing. Laeral was apparently as wise and insightful as she was beautiful.

Wrapped in a nearly tangible delight of magic and each other, the two turned and disappeared into the seemingly solid black wall. Neither of them looked back.

Bronwyn sighed again and wiped the back of her hand across her eyes. She swung herself up onto her horse and started out for the Northgate.

They rode in silence for several minutes. Ebenezer glanced over at her. "You look like you got something on your mind."

She managed a faint smile. "I was just now wishing," she said softly, "that I had thought to give Cara a ring."

*   *   *   *   *

Beneath the streets of Waterdeep lay a maze of tunnels, and beneath that another and then yet another, layer upon layer of secrets carved deep into mountain stone. Two men strode through one such tunnel, a simple passage that ran between Blackstaff Tower and Piergeiron's Palace, a tunnel accessible only to the men who ruled in those places. It was by its very nature a lonely place. The only sounds were the drips of water falling from the rounded ceiling, the clicking of their boots upon the stone floor, and the occasional squeaking of rats—creatures that went wherever they pleased, in casual defiance of lordly might.

They walked in silence, their thoughts on the meeting ahead. Khelben Arunsun's stern face was more solemn than usual, creased with something approaching dread. His nephew thought he understood, at least in part. Such power as the archmage wielded put him on a summit few could hope to climb. But for his lady, Khelben was very much alone, and he carried burdens more diverse and wearisome than most mortals could bear to contemplate. Khelben had lived long and outlived many; lovers, friends, comrades, even his own children. That Danilo could not begin to comprehend—how could any man bear the burden of life, when his own children had long ago turned to dust? He suspected that the archmage was soon to suffer yet another loss, the loss of one of the best and oldest friends remaining to him.

The passage ended at a tightly spiraling stairway. Danilo stepped aside so that Khelben could ascend the stairs first. At the top of the spiral, the archmage tapped at a stout wooden door, a door that, on the other side, was simply not there at all. At Piergeiron's summons, he opened the door and the two men stepped *through* a tapestry, into an oak-paneled sitting room.

Piergeiron greeted them warmly, his famed charm very much in evidence. He poured wine from a jeweled decanter, had a servant bring a tray of fruit and cheeses. He inquired after the archmage's household and the bard's work, chatted about songs he had heard and people they all knew. Danilo had been well versed in the art of meaningless words, and for some time they chatted pleasantly about small and inconsequential matters.

Through it all, Khelben watched his old friend with an expression that suggested he was seeing him anew, by a different light. Danilo observed this with growing unease. He had seen Piergeiron and Khelben together several times, and though their friendship was as unbalanced as that which sometimes occurred between a barn cat and a draft horse, it was of long standing. There was usually an easy comfort between them that today was utterly missing. Nothing the First Lord did or said could be faulted in the slightest, but Danilo sensed the change in the man, as surely as a forest elf could scent the coming of snow in the autumn wind.

He wondered how many more moments would pass before Khelben broke the awkward pattern. The archmage was not by nature a patient man, nor inclined to calmly endure such treatment at the hand of an old friend. Better a sharp insult, a sudden blow, than this polite and mannered scrambling for distance.

"A young woman reputed to be a Harper agent has run afoul of a paladin brotherhood," the archmage said bluntly. "I assumed you summoned me here to discuss the matter. If so, speak plainly, and I will do the same."

"Very well, then." Piergeiron set his wine goblet down. Far from insulted, he looked relieved to be back on familiar ground. With admirable directness, the First Lord set his concerns out, based on Sir Gareth's report.

"Let me put your mind at rest," the archmage said at once. "Bronwyn is indeed a Harper agent. She does have an artifact of Tyr in her possession, that much is true, but she is on her way, even as we speak, to Summit Hall, a monastery of Tyr."

Piergeiron's expression eased. Danilo cast a furtive look at the archmage, wondering if he felt even a twinge of guilt for misleading his old friend. Khelben had not actually stated that Bronwyn was returning the ring, but clearly Piergeiron thought that this was the case. It did not seem that Khelben intended to disabuse him of that notion.

"I am relieved to hear this, my friend, but I must admit to

some lingering doubt about Bronwyn's intentions. According to Sir Gareth, she has been asking around for a priest of Cyric. Her brother, no less."

Khelben did not so much as blink. "She has reason to seek him out. The Harpers and the Zhentarim have long been foes."

Another truth that cloaked a lie, Danilo mused. Was this, then, what Harpers must become? As time went on would he, like Khelben, so manipulate his oldest friends and twist the truth to serve the Balance? Later, he would have to give this matter serious consideration, but this was not the time. He schooled his face to reveal nothing of his troubled thoughts.

Khelben leaned forward. "To speak truly, Piergeiron, I would be wary of Sir Gareth's motives in this matter."

The First Lord looked offended. "He is a paladin of Tyr!"

"He is of the Order of the Knights of Samular," Khelben specified. "I do not argue that the paladins are anything but good and holy men, but I am wary of the orders. One man's righteous conviction is a fine thing, but imagine the evil that could be done by so many, of such power, in the single-minded pursuit of a goal they believe to be good. I would hate to see Bronwyn swept up in such a rushing tide."

Piergeiron shook his head in astonishment. "I do not believe what I am hearing."

"At least consider my words. I have long looked askance at the military orders, especially the followers of Samular. Recently, I have come to suspect that there might be good and sufficient reason for this."

The First Lord rose, his face stern and his eyes shuttered. "When, and *if,* you find evidence to support this unease, please tell me at once. You will forgive me if I do not wish to speak of this again until that time."

Khelben rose in response to the dismissal. If he felt the chill of his friend's tone, it did not show in his eyes. "Believe me, my friend, when I tell you that I hope I am wrong on this matter."

They moved swiftly through the polite gestures and words of leave-taking, and the Harpers left the palace. As they made their way back through the tunnel, Khelben's silence was heavy, troubled. It occurred to Danilo for the first time that the archmage might finally have entered a battle that he could not hope to win. How could any man go against paladins without appearing to side with evil? And what man alive—especially a man who had lived Khelben's long years and wielded his vast power—did not have in his past some secrets that would support this supposed charge of wrongdoing? Danilo did not know of any particulars, but Khelben's reaction when they discussed the history of the Knights of Samular led him to believe that at least a few of the archmage's secrets might be bound up with this order.

"What you said to Piergeiron . . ." Danilo ventured. "You spoke of this thing ending badly, but hoped that your predictions would prove wrong. Do you believe that a likely possibility?"

The archmage sniffed. "Do you want an honest answer?"

A wry smile lifted the corner of Danilo's lips. "I suppose not."

"I've noticed," Khelben said in a voice heavy with weariness, "that people seldom do."

Fourteen

The ride to Summit Hall passed more swiftly than Bronwyn had anticipated. Ebenezer's blue pony, for all his disagreeable nature, had a tireless stride and a stubborn streak as wide as the dwarf's backside. Blue Devil, as Ebenezer aptly named the beast, would not concede the pace to Bronwyn's swifter mare, and he trotted along as if challenging the horse to match him.

Shopscat came along with them, sometimes perched on the pack horse, sometimes taking wing and flying in wide circles overhead. "Why the raven?" Ebenezer wanted to know. "You're looking to scare off shoplifters out here?"

He gestured to the wide expanse of wilderness about them. This was their second day of hard travel. They had forded the Dessarin River early that morning and were now following the Dessarin Road north. The day before, the path had followed several small villages and outlying farms, and riders and caravans waved a friendly salute as they passed. Today they had seen only two other bands of travelers, and both of those early that morning. But for the path itself, this place had little sign of habitation. The trees over much of the road were dense and tall enough to meet overhead. The summer shade would be pleasant, but Bronwyn was just as glad that the trees were still lightly clad with buds and leaflets of golden green. When fully leafed, the trees would provide ample cover for bandits and predators.

"Why the raven?" she echoed. "Sometimes he carries messages back to Alice. Why the pack horse?"

Ebenezer shrugged. "Habit. Never know when you'll find something worth hauling to market."

She chuckled. "Now you're sounding like a treasure hunter."

"Been known to do it. There's worse ways of earning your keep. Harpering being one of them, I'm guessing."

She slid a speculative look at the dwarf. His studiously casual tone proclaimed a certain interest. Dwarves, as a rule, liked to keep to themselves and avoided meddling like they avoided water, but Ebenezer was a curious sort with interests that ranged far beyond those of his kin.

"It's not really the way I earn my keep, although I suppose some people do. Being a Harper is one way to be a part of something, rather than one person alone."

"Sort of like a clan," he reasoned.

"I don't know much about the ties of family, but I suppose you could say that. Look up ahead," she interrupted, pointing.

For about an hour now, the trees had been thinning out and getting smaller. To the north of them, the scene opened up, changing from forest to wild, rolling hills. In the distance, the path twisted up the side of a particularly steep knoll.

"Caves hereabouts," the dwarf proclaimed, eyeing the rocky hills to the north. "Prime goblinkin country. Orcs, mostly likely. Best to look for a defensible camp before nightfall."

They rode until twilight and set up camp on a hill not far from Summit Hall. Ebenezer found a small cave, one with a small opening so hidden that Bronwyn couldn't see it until he pulled aside the brush to show her.

"Wait a mite," he said, and then disappeared into the opening. He emerged in moments, briskly dusting off his hands. "Good cave. No orc sign, and the ceiling's too low for orcs to stand and fight. Even has a small escape tunnel. Tight fit for me, but I'll keep the stew down to two helpings tonight."

The hopeful tone in his voice brought a grin to Bronwyn's face. "Isn't it your turn to cook?"

"How about I catch the rabbits?"

"Fair enough." Bronwyn turned toward the packhorse to unload their gear. There, perched on the packs and grinning like a cream-sated tabby, was Cara.

Bronwyn fell back and yelped in surprise. "How did you get here?" she demanded.

But she knew even as she spoke. Suddenly Cara's behavior at the wall of Blackstaff Tower made perfect sense. Her reluctance to part was a ploy—a way for her to plant her gem stone in the horse's packs. Bronwyn wasn't sure whether to be amused, touched, or exasperated. She pressed her fingers to her temples as if by so doing she could still her pounding pulse.

"Well, now. This is a fine how'd-you-do," Ebenezer said, folding his arms and pretending to scowl. "Can't hardly march into that nest of paladins with the kid, seeing as how the ones in Waterdeep are so all-fired-up to keep her."

"True." Bronwyn went over to Cara and lifted her down. "You should go right back."

"Let me stay tonight," the child wheedled. "I've never slept under the stars."

Bronwyn had, so many times that she no longer gave it much thought, but it was a lovely notion when said with such wistful longing. She looked to Ebenezer. "Will you stay with her while I go in and talk to the knights?"

"And miss jaw-boning with that crowd? Glad to do it. Let's you and me set up some traps and snares around camp," he said to Cara.

Cara, it seemed, was an old hand at snares. It had been one of her tasks to tend the small rabbit traps her foster parents kept around the garden. Once she learned to adjust for size, she was tying and weighting snares as nimbly as the dwarf. "Might be you know how to cook, too?" he wanted to know.

"No, but I can make a fire. Watch." The child turned her brown eyes onto the pile of kindling Bronwyn had gathered in a stone circle. Wisps of smoke began to rise from the sticks, and then the first bright tongues of flame.

"There!" she said triumphantly, turning to an open-mouthed Bronwyn for praise. "Laeral showed me that. It's called a cantrip."

"That's very good," Bronwyn managed. She was no expert in magic, but it seemed remarkable to her that anyone, particularly a child, could learn a spell so quickly. For the first time, she wondered about Cara's mother. What elf woman had borne her and bequeathed her daughter such incredible talent? And where was she now?

Since Cara had never mentioned her mother, Bronwyn thought better than to ask. She threw some dried meat and roots into the travel pot, and by the time the first stars winked into being, the three of them were spooning up stew and listening to the piping calls of spring peepers from a nearby marsh.

*   *   *   *   *

The complex was impressive—more like an enclosed town than a simple holdfast—surrounded by a thick wall perhaps twenty feet high, fashioned of the sand-colored stone that abounded in the hills. Watchtowers rose from the corners, and a large keep stood at the summit of the hill. To the north, outside of the complex itself, was an old, weathered tower.

Bronwyn rode to the gate and was cordially, if distantly, received by the followers of Tyr. An elderly knight showed her to a guest chamber in one of the smaller buildings that clustered around a large, open arena of hard-packed dirt. The room was sparsely furnished, and she wondered if she would rate better quarters if the paladins knew of her heritage. But at the moment, the wisest course seemed to be to keep her identity private. She'd left her ring hidden back at the camp rather than risk alerting the paladins and losing the ring in the process.

"Good thinking," Ebenezer had approved. "Not a good thing, to be putting too much trust in humans."

It had been on the tip of Bronwyn's tongue to ask the dwarf what exactly he thought *she* was. But in recent weeks, she herself had not had many experiences with humankind that she could claim as proof against his cynical assessment.

A bell rang from one of the keep towers. Bronwyn heard a flurry of activity and glanced out her window. Several dozen young men were gathering in the large, open field that formed the heart of the monastery. They stripped to the waist and formed pairs, then fell to practicing with swords, staves, and a wide variety of smaller weapons. All of them fought well—impressively so. There was not a single man whom Bronwyn felt she could take in a fair fight. On the other hand, she got the impression that any one of them might be susceptible to some creatively dirty tactics.

Presently, one of the young paladins directed her to Master Laharin Goldbeard. She made her way up to his austere study and politely hailed him.

The man looked up, and his eyes widened. "Gwenidale," he breathed.

It was not a common name, and Bronwyn had heard it only once in twenty years—when Hronulf spoke of her mother.

Bronwyn had not intended to reveal her identity, but she quickly adapted her course. "Not Gwenidale, but her daughter," she said. "My name is Bronwyn."

The knight recovered his composure and came toward her, both hands outstretched. He took her hands and spread them wide, as a family friend might do to a child whose growth he wished to fondly measure. "It is you, beyond doubt. Little Bronwyn! When last I saw you, you were no more than three. By the Hammer of Tyr, child, you have become the very image of your mother."

She found herself liking Laharin and thought she would have even if he had not spoken of her mother. The man seemed to possess more warmth and kindness than any of the other paladins she had met—her father included.

"Come, sit down," he urged. "You must tell me everything.

How is it that you are come home to us at last?"

"You know about the raid on my village. I was lost—sold into slavery. For years I tried to find out about my family, but I was too young to remember. Recently I finally learned my father's name."

Deep sadness flooded the knight's face. "Too late," he mourned. "Your father was a great man. A good friend."

"I met him," Bronwyn admitted. "I went to Thornhold to see him."

Sudden light dawned on the knight's face. "You met with Sir Gareth in Waterdeep, did you not? I did not until this moment make the connection. Child, the brotherhood is gravely concerned about you. It was thought that you were in collusion with those who seized the fortress, that you took with you an artifact sacred to our order. How is it that you escaped the destruction?"

"There was an escape shoot. My father insisted that I take it."

"Ah. That explains all. Hronulf would know of such. The fortress has been in your family for many years."

This created an opening Bronwyn hadn't considered using until this moment. "It was Hronulf's wish that I come to you, Master Laharin. He said I should avail myself of your good council regarding the future of my family. . . ." She let her voice trail off uncertainly and dropped her eyes as if she were overcome with maidenly modesty.

"Ah." Laharin clearly understood Hronulf's thinking. "Yes, you must find a suitable match. There are several young men here who might suit. I will think on the matter."

"In the meanwhile, can you teach me of my heritage? I am not accustomed to being the daughter of a paladin. If I am to be a mother of paladins, I should know more about the order."

"I will show you Summit Hall, and gladly!"

Laharin rose and tucked her hand into his arm. Together they strolled through the fortress. He showed her the training field, the barracks where the young men slept, stables filled with beautiful horses, armories well stocked with nearly every weapon Bronwyn could name. There was a library with some old books and maps. "You may read anything here, at your leisure," Laharin assured her. "All the stories and lore must be passed to your sons. Do you remember hearing the tales?"

"Vaguely," she admitted. "Just the shape and rhythm of them." Her eyes followed a thin boy who bustled down the hall toward them. She judged him to be a page by the cut of his tunic, and the pile of linen in his arms. He was thin and boasted a mop of bright auburn hair and a liberal sprinkling of freckles on his face and bare arms. He looked all of eight years old.

Laharin followed her gaze, noting the puzzlement in her eyes. "The lads who wish to enter Tyr's service come to us before they have reached ten winters, and stay usually ten years."

"So young. . . ."

He gave her a look that was both stern and sympathetic. "It is the way of men to dedicate their lives to the service of Tyr. Women, I suspect, have a harder task. They must dedicate their sons."

Bronwyn murmured something suitably docile and followed the knight down a long, narrow flight of stone steps into what appeared to be a dungeon. There were a few cells, none of which were occupied, and at the end of the hall another flight leading further down. Laharin took a torch from a wall bracket and bid her follow.

"This tunnel leads to the kitchen cellars," he explained.

She pointed to a low, curved wooden door. The latch was chained and locked, rusted almost to dust. "What is that?"

"Nothing of great consequence. It is a tunnel leading to the old tower outside the walls. No one has used it for centuries."

This struck Bronwyn as very strange thinking indeed. "You are not afraid that someone will gain access to the monastery through the tower?"

"No," he said shortly. He squared his shoulders and smoothed the frown from his face with visible effort. "The tower is clearly visible from the guard tower. No one has gone in or out for centuries."

"Then why—"

"It is part of our heritage," he broke in. "Few know this story, but you should hear it. The tower once belonged to the brother of Samular, a wizard of great power known as Renwick 'Snowcloak' Caradoon. It was Samular's wish that a training monastery be built around that tower, and that it remain undisturbed for all time in honor of his brother, who died in battle as bravely as any knight."

At least, that was Samular's story, Bronwyn thought as she recalled what Khelben had told her about this place, and what she should look for. "That is an inspiring story. Samular knew the value of family," she said, arranging her face in a wide-eyed, guileless expression.

Laharin gave her an odd look, as if he was suddenly considering how much Bronwyn truly knew about her family's value. The moment passed swiftly, chased by a glimmer of self-reproach. He was not a man, Bronwyn noted with a touch of guilt, who was often or easily suspicious. She truly hated abusing his good will. On the other hand, she was not ready to turn herself and the power of her family heritage—whatever that might be—over to the order.

She spent a pleasant day with the knight, but begged off dinner by claiming travel weariness. She waited until the paladins and priests were at their evening devotions. Then she sneaked through the courtyard and back into the keep. Khelben had bid her look for a tower outside the main fortress. That old tunnel was her best way in. She took a torch from the upper level, as Laharin had done, and made her way to the low wooden portal.

Breaking the rusted lock was easy. Three sharp taps with the hilt of her knife, and the old chain fell away. Bronwyn crept through, one hand sweeping the air before her to tear away the tangle of spider webs that curtained the place like mist. The floor was alive, too; beetles and worse crunched underfoot as she made her way through.

The tunnel seemed to rise as she walked. To her surprise, the passage ended with a solid stone wall. Refusing to give in to discouragement, she lay one hand on the stone. A tingling sensation ran up her arm, and a sweet, wordless summons beckoned her in.

Bronwyn snatched her hand back, startled. Beset by a sudden sense of urgency, she again flattened her palm on the stone of the keep and again felt the compelling invitation. She followed her impulse before she could understand it and stepped through the stone wall into the keep. The passage through the solid stone sent an odd, tingling sensation through her entire body and left her feeling strangely chilled.

She wrapped her arms around her shoulders and took a look around. The interior was larger than it looked from the outside, dimly lit by candles thrust into wall sconces. The flickering light revealed stone walls festooned by cobweb drapery and a ceiling that vaulted up farther than her eye could follow.

"Welcome, daughter of Samular," intoned a faint, rusty voice.

Bronwyn whirled, startled by the unearthly sound, and found herself looking straight into glowing red eyes, set into a skeletal face.

She swallowed a scream and fell back. At second glance, she understood what manner of being she faced. Ancient, rusty robes hung in tatters about the lank form. Where flesh once had been, there was only bone wrapped in papery gray. Lank strings of white hair straggled out from beneath the cowl of a once-white cape. Yet there was life, of a sort, in those glowing red eyes. This was a lich, an undead wizard, and one of the most feared and powerful beings known.

The creature advanced. "Daughter of Samular," it repeated. "You have little need to fear me. I have waited long for this day and for one such as you. The Fenrisbane—its time has come? You have come for it, and for the third ring?"

Because it seemed the thing to do, and because she was not certain her voice would serve her, Bronwyn nodded.

The lich darted forward with a skittering rattle. It seized Bronwyn's arms with bony fingers, and tears of dust and mold leaked from its glowing eyes. "At last you have come! The wonders we will know, and the glory! Wait here."

Bronwyn was released so abruptly that she almost fell. She rubbed her arms where the lich's touch had chilled her. She watched, bemused, as the creature hobbled up the stairs that wound around the inside wall of the tower. Several minutes dragged by, and she was considering attempting a retreat when the lich reappeared, a small box in its skeletal hand. "The third ring," it said reverently, and handed her the box.

Bronwyn opened it and slipped the ring onto her left hand as her father had done. As with the other, this one magically sized itself to her finger.

"What of the Fenrisbane?" she asked, remembering the name the lich had spoken, and assuming that this was the much-sought artifact.

"It is not here, of course. I had the siege engine hidden away for safe keeping years ago, much as one would hide a tree in a forest," the lich said slyly. "It is in the attic of a toy and curiosity shop, in a remote town not too far from the monastery."

Siege engine. In a toy shop. Bronwyn was beginning to understand what part the rings might have in this. "Why did you do this?" she asked. "I would think the Fenrisbane would be safer here."

A bony finger waggled in admonition. "There is danger in having the rings and the tower in the same place. The four artifacts should be reunited only when there is a force gathered sufficient to use and to protect the artifacts." The lich paused, tilted his head, and leaned forward in a menacing gesture. "You don't have the other rings with you, do you?"

"I know where they are, but I do not have them with me," she assured the lich. "One is in the hands of another child of Samular's blood, a child who is protected by powerful magic. If threatened, she can magically flee within strong walls." Some instinct prompted her not to mention Blackstaff Tower.

"Good. That is good. Your forebears have prepared you to wield the Fenrisbane in Samular's name?"

There was a cunning note in the dry tone that Bronwyn mistrusted. The lich obviously sensed her heritage—perhaps this was a test of her knowledge and worthiness. She answered as truthfully as she could. "My father gave me the ring just before he died in an attack on his fortress. He would want me to use the Fenrisbane to right this wrong."

The lich nodded avidly, shedding flakes of ancient skin in the process. "Good, good. You have two children of the bloodline, two who are agreed in how to use the rings. That is a needed thing—one person alone cannot fully awaken the Fenrisbane's magic. Go now, and do."

Bronwyn was only too glad to obey, but at the wall, she turned back. "The toy shop."

"Gladestone," the lich said impatiently. "An old town of elves with long lives and longer memories. Seek out Tintario or his heirs. There is a dweomer on these elves and their shop. They will never sell the Fenrisbane or close the shop. If the need to protect it arises, they will do so or die. See that you do likewise."

She had one more question, one that she feared to ask. "Who are you? Or, if you prefer, who *were* you?"

The lich hesitated. Bronwyn got the impression that it was more saddened than aggrieved by this impertinence. "I no longer recall the name I once wore. What I was is lost. What I am now is the Guardian of the Order." A dry, heavy sound wheezed from the lich, one that might have been a sigh had it come from a living throat. "This puts me in a paradoxical position. Paladins cannot abide undead and would destroy me on sight. For good or ill, few of the paladins and priests in yonder fortress knows who or what inhabits this ancient tower. They simply consider it a holy place and are restrained by their order's edict from disturbing it."

The lich shook itself, staving off despair as it must have done many times in its long years of undeath. "But now you have come. I entrust the third ring and the Fenrisbane into your care. This I do because you are of the bloodline of Samular, and because I cannot give these things to the paladins for whom they were intended." The creature darted forward with startling speed and loomed threateningly over Bronwyn.

One bony hand parted the robe. A small black bat flew out from the empty ribcage. The lich paid it no heed, but slipped a tiny scrying globe from an inside pocket of the robe and showed it to her. "I will know what you do," he said. "Fail, and I will seek you out."

*　　*　　*　　*　　*

Cara and Ebenezer spent a pleasant day on the hillside. He taught her to spit for distance and how to hold a knife for whittling. She took to both with gusto and soon had a pile of wood shavings around her feet. Wood chips and toothpicks, the dwarf observed, pretty much average for a first-time whittler.

The girl pestered him for stories, as she had on the ship. Ebenezer had used up most of his best tales, but he didn't mind telling the second-rate ones. They didn't tell bad, once he added a bit of gloss and color. While he talked, he whittled away at a toy for her. An orc, she wanted, just like the ones in his stories.

Orcs were much on Ebenezer's mind. He knew the signs better than he liked. The scuffling big-footed prints, scat that showed small game eaten raw and whole, and the fetid, musty smell that emanated from some of the hidden caves. There would be trouble, of that he was certain. Orcs always meant trouble.

But trouble, when it came, took a very different form. Cara's soft, sharp intake of breath startled him. She seized his wrist and pointed. "There! See that white horse coming along with the gray dappled? That's the man who stole me from my farm and chased me in the city."

Ebenezer strained and squinted, but his eyes weren't made for distance in the same way the sharp-sighted child's were. He couldn't make out the man, but oh, he knew that horse!

"More paladins," he muttered. "And heading to the keep."

He didn't like this, not one little bit. His every instinct told him this put Bronwyn in a bad way. But how could he warn her?

Cara whistled sharply. A few feet away, Shopscat was tearing at the bones left from their breakfast of roast rabbit. The raven looked up at the sound and flew to the child's shoulder. "We could send Shopscat to warn her," she suggested.

Ebenezer pursed his lips and considered. "He'd know how?"

"He can fly. He can find her and bring her a message," she said confidently. She suddenly bit her lip in consternation. "I don't write very well yet. Can you write the note?"

He could, but not in Common. The sign on Bronwyn's shop bore Dethek runes along with Common lettering and curling, sissy Elvish script. Ebenezer hoped she hadn't needed to hire a dwarf scribe to write the Dethek for her. He took the stump end of charcoal pencil Cara handed him and scribbled a few runes on a scrap of parchment. "Guess it's time to see if that dwarf what she boasted of taught her anything useful," he muttered as he wrote the message.

*   *   *   *   *

The sunset colors were fading as Sir Gareth and Algorind rode swiftly toward Summit Hall. They hailed the watch towers as they came so that they need not slow to wait for the gates. They swept in through the wooden doors and bore down upon the startled group emerging from chapel.

"Where is the wench?" demanded Sir Gareth as he slid down from his horse.

Master Laharin strode forward, his yellow brows drawn down in a scowl. "Courtesy is a rule of this Order, brother. The only woman in this fortress is an honored guest."

The rebuke was a harsh one to a man of his station, but Gareth didn't seem to take notice.

"She is a traitor and a thief. Lord Piergeiron of Waterdeep told us she was bound here. Find her!"

Such was the knight's urgency that most of the paladins obeyed at once. Algorind dismounted to join in. Before he took a dozen steps, Yves, a young man perhaps a year behind

Algorind in training, came running back to the courtyard. "The chain on the tower tunnel has been disturbed!"

Algorind had never seen such unbridled rage on a paladin's face as Sir Gareth wore. The knight quickly mastered himself and turned to a suddenly pale Laharin. "You see? This woman has made fools of you."

It seemed to Algorind that the knight took an unseemly relish in delivering this news.

"This woman was at Thornhold when it fell," continued Gareth. "Did it not occur to you to ask how a single woman walked out unscathed?"

"She is Hronulf's daughter," Laharin stated simply. "She told me that she met with Hronulf and that he showed her a secret tunnel whereby she might escape."

"Did she also say that Hronulf had given her his ring? Did she mention that the lost child of Samular is in her keeping, held in the fastness of Blackstaff Tower?"

Laharin paled as the enormity of the situation hit him. "She did not."

"And she has been to the old tower," Sir Gareth concluded grimly.

Although Algorind did not know what that signified, Laharin clearly did. The master paladin was fairly wringing his hands. "It seems likely. By the Hammer of Tyr! The three rings will again unite."

Sir Gareth turned to Algorind. "Find her. Take another man with you. Do what you must, but retrieve the rings of Samular."

The utter coldness of the knight's voice chilled Algorind, but he could not fault Sir Gareth's reasoning or question the duty ahead. He whistled for his horse and beckoned for Corwin, a comrade of about his own age, to follow.

The two young paladins struck out for the tower. Algorind assumed that if Bronwyn had left by some hidden door, she could not be far. They would pick up the trail.

Twilight was deepening swiftly toward night when Algorind saw the first tracks—prints made by small, worn boots. There was a single set, and they ran behind a rocky hillock.

He swung down from his horse and knelt for a better look. The woman was small, and these prints looked a little big to be hers, but not so big that a match was impossible. For safe measure, he drew his sword and motioned for Corwin to do the same. Together, they rushed the hillock.

No woman awaited them there, but a small band of orcs did—scrawny, hideous creatures, with their piggish red eyes and jutting canine fangs. This band was armed with nothing but evil grins and bone knives. Most were naked, or nearly so, and only one greenish-hued female had a pair of boots. She must have left the deceitful tracks. This, then, was an ambush.

These creatures were smaller than any Algorind had seen, and younger. The female wore nothing but her ragged boots and a small leather loincloth, and her small young breasts rode high against her clearly delineated ribs. Likely she was not yet of breeding age, and some of the males looked younger still. But they were orcs. The paladins charged as one.

The ambushers lacked the courage for honest battle. When it was clear that the fight would not be easy, most of them shrieked and tried to flee. Algorind cut down one orc who charged him with a knife, then gutted a second with his returning stroke. He lunged forward and high, cutting deeply between the ribs of the coward trying to scramble up and over the rocks.

The survivors scattered and fled. The boot-shod orc had the wit to try to steal a horse. She hauled herself onto Corwin's black steed and frantically kicked the horse into a run, but she did not reckon with a paladin-trained mount. As the horse cantered past, Corwin gave a sharp whistle. Instantly the black horse reared, pawing the air. The orc rolled backward and fell heavily onto the rocky ground. Corwin was there in a moment, his sword at her throat. The little orc wench managed to spit at him before she died.

Algorind leaped onto Icewind's back and called for Corwin to follow. Working together, they managed to slay all but two, and even those did not escape unscathed. The two surviving orcs were wounded and promptly left their companions to slink away and lose themselves among the rocks and shadows.

"That is the way with wild animals," Corwin observed when at last they gave up their search. "Even a wounded dog will seek out a small, quiet space to lick his wounds."

Algorind nodded. "Let us find a place to make camp. In the morning, we will surely find the trail. If Tyr is willing, we will find Bronwyn before the sun sets again."

* * * * *

Bronwyn stepped through the tower wall and collapsed onto the ground. Never had she felt so chilled, so drained of life, so utterly despairing. Dimly she noted that the terrain looked different and that the walls of Summit Hall were not where she expected them to be. Later, she would think about that. She pillowed her cheek on the rocky ground and let the darkness claim her.

When Bronwyn awoke, twilight had nearly passed, and the sky's silver was tarnished with the coming of darkness. A sudden flutter seized and focused her groggy thoughts. Shopscat landed beside her, batting his wings and cawing furiously.

Bronwyn groaned and turned her head so that she was face down. The raven's raucous voice made her temples throb. "Think about it," she pleaded with him.

The familiar thunder of Ebenezer's iron-shod boots came rumbling toward her. The dwarf picked up her head by her braid and scrutinized her face.

"Thought you forgot how to read, woman. Where in the Nine Hells were you—an ice cave? You're blue as a Moon elf!"

Bronwyn rolled up into a sitting position, hugging her knees and shivering uncontrollably. "A lich. Gods, I'm cold. I didn't realize how cold until I got away."

"Fear's a good thing," the dwarf commented. "Keeps you going. And speaking of going, we'd best keep on. Can you stand?"

She let him haul her up and after a few trembling steps,

her legs held her well enough. She listened as Ebenezer told
her about the paladins' arrival, and how Cara's idea enabled
them to find her. In turn, she told him what the lich had
revealed.

"We're going to Gladestone," she told him, "a village perhaps two hours' ride north of here. It's a small community of
elves and half—"

"Stones!" the dwarf spat. "An elf village. Never thought the
day would come when I'd be heading to one on purpose. And
what's this thing that we're looking for?"

"A toy siege engine. I'll explain later." She cast a glance
over her shoulder. "We'd better move. If that paladin was following me before, odds are he's still at it."

They rode by the light of the rising moon, keeping a cautious look out for paladins and orcs. Before long Cara started
nodding off, and Bronwyn was riding with one arm wrapped
around the girl to hold her in place. By the time they got to
Gladestone, Cara was not the only one sleeping. Most of the
houses and shops were dark.

The village was small, a cluster of homes and shops
arranged along two narrow streets and some connecting
alleys. It was a homey enough scene, and a place that Bronwyn had enjoyed the time or two she had passed through.
Most of the houses were low and small, cozily thatched with
straw. A stork dozed in a nest built on an unused chimney.
The large, outdoor clay oven that baked all the village bread
still gave off a pleasant heat and a warm, yeasty aroma. The
toy shop was closed, the doors and shutters barred, and the
whole guarded by a large and rather hungry-looking dog.

"Might be this should wait until morning," Ebenezer suggested as he eyed the softly growling guardian.

Fifteen

Bronwyn awoke in the grip of a nightmare, thrashing at her covers and struggling to get away from the demons that howled and roared through her dream.

"Hush, now!" admonished a stern dwarf voice. Strong hands seized her arms and shook her awake. "You're to stay here and watch over the girl."

As she emerged from sleep, Bronwyn realized that the nightmare had roots in reality as well as memory. Beyond the window was a hellish cacophony of shrieks, thundering hooves, and the clash of steel on steel. Above it all roared and hissed the hungry voice of fire. Bright tongues of it leaped up to lick at the night sky.

Bronwyn kicked off her covers and tugged on her boots. Her mind shoved old fears into the background and nimbly assessed the situation. Their rented room was large, a single open chamber that took up the entire second floor of the cottage. There was but one door, and the windows had shutters. She could keep invaders out for quite some time, and if need be, Cara could always use her gems to escape.

She shot a glance over at the little girl. Cara's face was set, but calm. She walked over to the window and stared at the orc who had pinned two half-elven villagers against the clay oven. Suddenly a fire leaped up from the ground, licking up high between the creature's splayed legs. The orc yodeled in pain and surprise and stumbled back.

"I can help," Cara said adamantly, turning to face Bronwyn. Her brown-eyed gaze dared Bronwyn to try to send her away.

"You'll go if necessary," Bronwyn felt compelled to say.

"And not until."

She nodded in agreement, and they settled down to wait.

* * * * *

In the streets below, Ebenezer had to chuckle when the bit of wizard fire roasted the orc. He wondered, briefly, if Cara could do that again.

Not that they needed any more fire. Four cottages at the east side of the village were ablaze, utterly beyond saving. The orcs didn't seem interested in putting the torch to anything else, though. They were here to loot, and fairly desperate about it.

It seemed to Ebenezer, though, that there was a bit of vendetta thrown in. There was a craziness to the attack, a wild, bloodlusting lack of know-how and think-it-through that made the critters harder to fight. Like bee-stung mules, they were. No way to tell which way they'd be going or why.

One of the orcs caught sight of him and came at a run, a farmer's pitchfork held like a lance under one arm. For just a moment, Ebenezer puzzled over how to best meet this attack. Then he remembered where he stood—directly in front of one of the thick plaster walls of the rooming house.

The dwarf took out his hammer to make the fool orc think he planned to stand and fight, and let him come on. At the last moment, he dropped and rolled to the side. The orc kept coming, and the pitchfork's tongs dug deep into the wall.

Ebenezer was up before the orc's startled grunt died away. He swung his hammer hard, crunching into the base of the orc's spine. Down went the orc, sped on his way by another crushing hammer blow to the back of his head.

The dwarf looked around for something else to do. Not far away, an elf woman with a tumble of pale yellow curls and a nightdress of a matching hue stared with dismay at the broken sword in her hand. Two dead orcs lay nearby, but it seemed like she wasn't quite through.

That, Ebenezer could respect. If he'd had a chance to defend his clan and home, he wouldn't care to stop until the job was done.

"Hoy, Goldie!" bellowed the dwarf. He pulled his axe from his belt and brandished it. "Need a blade?"

Doubt flickered across the elf's face, then disappeared in resolve. She darted over to the dwarf and took the axe. "Like chopping kindling?" she asked as she hefted the blade.

"Pretty much." He nodded with satisfaction as she took after an orc who was creeping off with an armload of loot. She held the borrowed axe poised high overhead and brought it forward with a respectable downward chop. "Lacks for nothing but a beard," he mumbled as his blade cleaved thick orcish skull.

He saw an uneven fight over by the well. A hulking orc had pinned down a scrawny elf lad, who had no weapon at all that Ebenezer could see. He barreled over to see what might be done and pulled up to a stop just as the orc slammed down hard with a short sword. The elf dodged, but not by much. Wood chips flew as the blade slammed against the well's cover.

A second boom followed quickly as Ebenezer brought the hammer down on the orc's hand. The elf lad, no fool, snatched up the dropped sword and did what he had to do.

The dwarf noted the lad's stricken eyes and remembered back a century and more to when he stood in the same boots. "Hang onto that sword," he advised kindly. "It don't never get much easier, but it generally won't be any worse."

And then he was off, looking for someone else in need of a chance to fight.

*   *   *   *   *

Algorind was awakened from a deep sleep by the sounds of battle and the flicker of fire against the sky. He shook Corwin awake and they quickly mounted and set off at a gallop to give aid.

They had not far to go. Even though the paladins from Summit Hall did not patrol this area, Algorind knew of the village from a map in the monastery library. The villagers were mostly elves and half-elves, but peaceable folk.

The reason for the disturbance became clear as they drew closer. Mingled with the crackle and hiss of the fire and the screams of the wounded was the guttural, roaring battle cries of an orc band. Algorind's jaw firmed with resolve.

But Corwin hung back, naked horror on his face. "This is our doing! The orcs tracked us. We led them here."

"This is a village, and they are orc raiders," Algorind argued. "Come!"

But Corwin caught his arm. "Don't you see? We killed their children when we truly did not have to. This is vengeance, but these people were in our path and are paying the price."

"If that is so, justice belongs to Tyr," said Algorind. "Stay or come, as you will. This is no time for words."

He reined Icewind toward the village and leaned low over the horse's neck as they sped toward battle. Behind him he heard the sound of the black horse's hoof beats and was glad that Corwin had found his way back to duty.

Some of the orcs were escaping. The paladins beat them back, cutting them down when they could or pressing them back toward the blades of the grimly determined villagers.

The work was Tyr's, and Algorind served with all his strength and conviction. Yet even as he fought, his eyes scanned the hellish melee for some glimpse of a small, brown-haired woman and the child she had unrightfully claimed.

* * * * *

Upstairs in the cottage, Bronwyn waited by the door, a wooden chair held high overhead. She counted the steps as heavy feet thundered up the stairs.

"Do you have your gem ready?" she asked Cara.

The girl nodded, but her words were swallowed in the shattering crash. The door buckled and splintered, but held. It gave way entirely with the second assault, and a large, gray-skinned orc came stumbling into the room.

Bronwyn smashed down with the chair, hitting the orc before he could regain his balance. He went down hard, but he quickly brought up his arms and pressed his palms against the floor as he prepared to push himself back up. Bronwyn reacted, attacking with the weapon at hand—a leg of the chair that had splintered at one end into a jagged point. She drove the stake home like a crazed vampire hunter and stomped on it for good measure.

Another orc thundered into the room. Bronwyn pulled her knife and deflected a sword slash. For several moments they exchanged ringing blows, moving about the room in a shifting pattern of advance and retreat. She was beginning to think she might be able to take the match when the sound of more footsteps in the hall below dashed her chances.

She heard the scrape of a small wooden chest across the floor, and instantly knew what Cara had in mind. The blanket chest would hit the orc at just the right spot, if only she could maneuver him into position.

Bronwyn went into furious attack, slashing and jabbing at the orc and forcing him into a defensive stance. Slowly she beat him back across the room. He stumbled over the chest and went down heavily. Bronwyn leaped, knife leading, and threw her weight against his suddenly unprotected chest.

She rolled aside, wrenching her knife free. Two orcs roiled into the room. Bronwyn flipped her knife and caught it by the tip. In the same motion, she hurled it at the first orc. But the knife was slippery with blood, and her aim faltered. She went for the throat. The knife went considerably lower.

The orc roared and stumbled, doubling over as if he'd been gut-punched by a giant. Bronwyn snatched up the dead orc's sword and leaped up, swinging out wildly. The blade sliced across the chest of the orc just entering the room and he slumped over his doubled-up comrade. They both fell.

Bronwyn finished first one, then the other with quick, decisive strokes.

She straightened up, breathing hard, and looked to the far side of the room for Cara. The child had flattened herself against the wall. Her face was white and her eyes huge. It made Bronwyn heartsick that the child had seen all that.

"You should have gone," she panted.

"I moved the chest," Cara reminded her in a small, pale voice.

Bronwyn smiled faintly. "You did well, but you aren't safe here."

The child's eyes darkened, and suddenly they looked far too old for her tiny face. "I really don't think," she said softly, "that I'm safe anywhere."

*   *   *   *   *

Back in Thornhold, Dag Zoreth paused before the altar and studied the purple flame that leaped and danced in an ever-changing sunburst, and the enormous black skull that leered out from the fire. It was a symbol of his god, proof of Cyric's favor. Such a thing would bring him great honor, and inspire men to consider him with fear. It was more than he had hoped for.

But it was not enough.

Dag carefully knelt before the altar, lowering a round, low bowl to the floor. The bowl was brass and so finely crafted that not a single ripple or flaw marred its surface. A perfect receptacle for power, it would seize mystical force and throw it back, much as mountains playfully turned a shout into an echo. Filled with water, the bowl became a scrying pool of enormous power.

Filled with blood, it begged the level of dark power that only an evil god might grant.

Dag braced his hands on either side of the bowl and stared intently into the dark pool. He began to chant, an arrogant prayer that importuned a god for power, and scorned the price that would surely come due. He would pay it in time, and consider it worthwhile—as long as he found Cara.

He formed an image of the girl in his mind and reached out to her through the dark thread of the chant.

The words of the prayer enveloped him, gathering in power. Magic rose like incense toward the purple flame, carrying with it a heady scent of night-blooming flower, musk, and brimstone.

That scent prodded at his memory. Through the ritual-induced haze, Dag felt the first sharp tugs of alarm. His chanting faltered, then broke off altogether as blood began to rise from the bowl.

The blood rose swirling into the air, taking on the shape of a slender, furious elven woman. The image of Ashemmi floated before him, clad in a gown a shade deeper than her usual crimson.

It occurred to Dag suddenly that he was still on his knees. Quickly he rose to his feet and stared down the apparition. "You take a fearful chance, interrupting a ritual to Cyric," he warned her.

"I felt the magic and followed it!" the image of Ashemmi snapped. "Do not think for a moment that I cannot find you, and that I will not!"

A shimmer of dread rippled through Dag as he wondered if the elf had also found Cara. But no, she would have said so if she had. There was no tie binding her and her child, and her seeking magic did not know the paths that belonged to Cara alone. But Dag she knew to the depths of his black heart, as he knew her.

"What do you want, Ashemmi?" He tried to imbue his words with a weary patience.

"The child!"

Not *my* child, Dag noticed, or even *our* child. A tool, a weapon. That was all. Cara deserved better.

"She is safe," Dag said, and believed it to be so. His best intelligence indicated that the child was being kept in Blackstaff Tower, and he was inclined to believe that she was still there. Still, he wanted to see for himself. No mere scrying device could pierce that fastness—which was why he had decided to seek a god's power.

"Safe?" shrieked the apparition. "I have learned that she was apprehended from a southbound slave ship! Do not talk to me of safety."

This startled Dag. Instantly, he knew who the culprit must be. It would appear, he mused, that he owed his sister a debt of gratitude. It was she who had thwarted this plan and brought Cara back to Waterdeep.

"I had nothing to do with that," Dag assured Ashemmi's magical image. "I have no intention of bringing harm to my own child."

She sniffed. "It does not matter what your intentions are. After a certain level, there is no real difference between evil and ineptitude. I want her, Dag. Find her and bring her to me."

"You relinquished your rights to the child," he protested.

"I reclaim them. When you find her, she *will* be brought to Darkhold. You can bring her, or she will be taken from you. But mark me: the child will be mine!"

The apparition disappeared as suddenly as a lightning bolt. Blood splashed back into the bowl, splattering the floor and the priest.

Dag lifted his eyes to the symbol of Cyric. It seemed to him that the skull had a watchful mien, rather like a wild cat considering the moment to pounce, but the godly manifestation gave no sign of Cyric's displeasure. Strife, intrigue, illusion— all these things were present in the tableau he and Ashemmi had just presented. Cyric must have found it quite diverting.

But Dag was taking no chances. He left the chapel at once and sent his most expendable servants to clean up after the failed ritual.

* * * * *

When the sounds of battle had died away, Bronwyn unbolted the shutter and looked out over the village. A small cry escaped her at the terrible destruction. Four houses had been reduced to smoldering circles of foundation stone. From this height, they looked like large and very sad campfires.

Doors and windows and shutters had been broken, and goods from households and stores lay crushed and scattered in the street. Much worse were the terrible injuries dealt those slumped onto the street, and worse still those who no longer moved.

"Cara . . ." began Bronwyn.

"I want to find Ebenezer," the child insisted, sensing what was coming. "I want to see that he is all right."

She couldn't deny the child this, nor could she leave her here alone. "Come, then," she said, and led the way down into the street.

Bronwyn almost stumbled over the paladin. He had taken terrible head wounds, and her gaze didn't linger on his face, but there was no mistaking that blue and white tabard. A wave of relief swept over her, only slightly darkened by guilt. It did not seem right, to be glad that a "good man"—for he would certainly be regarded as such—had been brutally slain.

They found Ebenezer at the toy store, kicking through the rubble and swearing with impressive creativity. He broke off in mid curse when he saw Cara at Bronwyn's side. "You kept her here?" he demanded incredulously.

"She wouldn't go," Bronwyn responded.

The dwarf shook his head. "Lacks for nothing but a beard, that one. Well, I've got some bad news. You've got ten guesses, and there's your first clue."

He pointed to the back door. The body of an elderly elf stood sentry at the door, pinned to the wooden beam by what might have been his own sword. Inside the store lay two more elf corpses and the remains of five orcs. The elves had fought with a fervor all out of proportion to the apparent value of their wares.

Bronwyn stepped over a gray-skinned female orc and began to survey the devastation. The shelves had been tossed down, and toys littered the floor. Dolls and wooden carts and carved farm animals had been tossed contemptuously aside. Bronwyn noted that there were no small bows and arrows, no wooden swords, no slingshots or miniature catapults. In short, all the toys that trained youngsters for the art of war had been taken.

It was an odd sort of plundering, and from Bronwyn's point of view, the worse possible situation. She sifted and kicked through the rubble, but she had no more luck than Ebenezer.

"I'm-a gonna take a look around outside," the dwarf said. "There's stuff dropped all over. Those orcs were in a hurry. Might be I can find it here. Or—" he broke off suddenly and shrugged.

Bronwyn caught the dissonant note, but was too distracted to dwell on it. "Fine," she muttered. She kept looking, turning over every bit of wood, every scrap of cloth and paper, until she finally had to admit the truth.

The Fenrisbane was gone.

Defeated, she sank down onto an overturned shelf.

"But you're *dead*!" Cara protested.

Bronwyn jerked around to face the open door. There stood another paladin, a tall, fair-haired young man who matched the description she'd heard from Cara, Alice, and Danilo. This was the paladin who had stolen Cara from her foster family, who had followed Bronwyn to Waterdeep, then to Summit Hall. He simply did not quit. Like a troll, he just picked up the pieces and kept coming. Exasperation swept through Bronwyn.

"What the hell are you?" she demanded.

"I am Algorind of Tyr, and it is my duty to take this child back to the Order of the Knights of Samular for proper foster-age."

"You did that once," Bronwyn snapped. "It didn't turn out so well. I found her on a ship, bound for the slave markets of the south. You will take this child only when I'm too dead to stop you."

The young man looked saddened, but determined. "Lies will not help you. It is not my wish to harm you, but I will take the child. It would be better if you returned with me to the order to answer for your crimes of theft and treason. Perhaps doing so will bring you peace."

"I don't lie." Fury swept through Bronwyn, and she went for her knife. "But I'd be happy to do what you say, just as soon as you turn that sword of yours point up and sit down on it hard."

Algorind colored, but did not flinch. "It is plain that you are no fit guardian for a child." he said. "Stand aside, or face Tyr's justice."

"No!'

Cara's small, piping voice startled them both. She walked forward, placing her small body between the armed paladin and Bronwyn. "Don't hurt Bronwyn. I'll come with you."

"Cara, don't!" Bronwyn appealed. "Just leave. *Now!*"

The girl shook her head stubbornly. "I won't leave you here with him." She walked toward Algorind, holding out her tiny hand.

The paladin watched as the child approached. She was pale, but trusting. She came close and placed her hand in his. "I will go with you and not give you any trouble, but first you must answer a question. Will you give me your word on this, and keep it?"

The paladin gave her a puzzled look. "I am pledged to always keep my word."

"Well, that's fine, then. Here's the question: what is my raven's name?"

Algorind was not greatly gifted with imagination, but he dredged his memory for names that he had heard given to such birds. "I do not know. Midnight? Blackwing? Po?"

"No, no," Cara said impatiently. She withdrew her hand from his, then held it in a fist over Algorind's palm. "What do you call a cat who lives in a shop?"

"A shop's cat, I suppose."

As soon as he spoke the words, she opened her hand. A large, red gem tumbled into his palm. Instantly he felt himself being sucked away, as if by a strong wind.

Algorind tried to fight it, using every vestige of his iron will and his disciplined strength. To no avail. The ransacked shop began to blur and fade, and a sound like an angry sea began to crescendo in his ears. Above the tumult, Algorind heard the merry music of the child's laughter. His fading vision fell upon the treacherous woman. She was on her knees beside the child, her arms around the girl and her face both glad and proud.

And then it all disappeared, and Algorind's world became a terrible, terrifying white whirl. He was taken away, torn away from his duty by some treacherous magic.

* * * * *

The tunnel that lay between Danilo's posh townhouse and Blackstaff Tower was a great convenience. In Danilo's opinion, it was becoming too damned convenient. He strode down the tunnel to answer his third summons in a tenday.

The tunnel ended in a magical gate. Danilo murmured the phrase that enabled him to pass, then walked through the apparently solid stone wall and into Khelben's study.

The archmage was painting again, which was certainly a sign of duress. Danilo glanced at the canvas. It was a seascape, with livid streaks of lightning darting down from a heap of billowing purple clouds. Despite the pending sky, the sea was an inexplicably calm shade of green.

"An interesting work, Uncle. Might I name it? 'Umberlee having a nightmare' is one that comes to mind."

Khelben stabbed a paint brush in his direction, splattering him with dabs of purple paint. The fury on the archmage's face convinced Danilo that it might be unwise to protest the matter.

"What possessed you to do such a stupid, orc-brained thing?"

Danilo lifted one shoulder. "You will have to be more specific. I do a great many stupid, orc-brained things."

The archmage dug in the pocket of his artist's smock and took out a bright blue stone. "What is this?"

Bluffing was hopeless, but Danilo gave it a try. "A topaz?"

The archmage snorted angrily. "Gemstones. You gave the child enspelled gemstones and taught her to use them. You have done some foolish things in your life—"

"But this is not one of them," Danilo cut in. "Cara is just a child. She's smarter than most, but few people of any age have the sort of enemies she's collected. A paladin saw her outside Bronwyn's shop and gave chase. My agents saw to it that the watch was called and the would-be abductor of children summarily dealt with."

"Yes, I know," groused Khelben. "And thank you very much for your quick thinking. As a result, I still have Piergeiron's boot print on the back of my breeches."

"The paladin had it coming," Danilo said without a touch of his customary humor. "No one has the right to take a child from her family."

"Her *family* is Dag Zoreth, a priest of Cyric."

"Bronwyn is Cara's family, too," Danilo argued. "She is Dag Zoreth's sister."

"Yes, I believe that came up in conversation with Piergeiron, too. Or don't you recall?"

Danilo folded his arms. "With a little help, Bronwyn can take care of Cara. If you have no regard for the concept of family, consider this: Wouldn't it be better to have whatever power this family wields in the hands of the Harpers, rather than at the disposal of the Holy Order of the Knights of Samular?"

The archmage considered this. "You make a good argument, but understand that whatever we do could place a wedge between the Harpers and the paladins. That is a dangerous situation. We cannot afford to anger the Knights of Samular any more than we have."

A sudden breeze arose in the room, an intangible wind that spoke of gathering magic. Before either mage could respond with a defensive spell, a flash lit the room. A man stumbled out of the invisible white whirl, almost into Khelben's arms.

Both men drew back, staring at each other with startled faces. Danilo regarded the newcomer. He was a young man, tall and broad, with curly fair hair cropped unfashionably short. The description was unmistakable, even without the telltale colors of the Knights of Samular. This was the paladin who had been chasing Cara, and this was how the clever little wench had served him back.

Danilo burst out laughing, laughter that rolled from him in waves, that had him clutching his belly and bending over as he gasped for air.

The paladin barely glanced at him, but advanced on Khelben. "What manner of fell sorcery is this?" he demanded in an aggrieved voice.

"None of my doing," Khelben replied sternly.

"Oh, go ahead and take credit for it," Danilo gasped out through his laughter. "It would better serve his dignity to be bested by the archmage of Waterdeep than a half-elf child not yet ten."

The paladin reached for his sword, and that sobered Danilo somewhat. He wiped his streaming eyes and subsided to a chuckle, all the while forming the one-handed gestures needed for a cantrip designed to heat metal. The grip of the paladin's sword began to blush with heat. With a startled gasp, the young man released his sword, staring down at his hip with an expression that suggested he thought the sword guilty of deliberate treachery.

That set Danilo off again.

"From whence have you come?" Khelben demanded, raising his voice to be heard over his nephew's laughter. "I will send you back."

Danilo broke off in mid howl. "Uncle, that would not be—"

"I will send him back a reasonable distance from the place he left," the archmage specified, and turned back to his "visitor."

"Gladestone," the paladin admitted.

"That's near Summit Hall. I will send you to the monastery, which is about a half day's ride. *If* that is acceptable to *you*," Khelben added, sending a dark look in Danilo's direction.

Danilo lifted both hands in a gesture of surrender. "Leave the stone behind, though," he told Algorind.

The young man looked down at his hand, remembering what he held. He dropped the stone on the floor as if it were a loathsome insect. "I want nothing to do with such things. But you, sir, your assistance I will accept," he told Khelben stiffly. "For the sake of my duty."

The archmage began the casting, a complex weaving dance of the hands accompanied by a brief but powerful chant. With this, he wove a silver path through the magic that encircled and sustained the world—which was no small thing, even if magical trinkets such as the gemstones made it appear so to the untrained. Danilo knew the effort of magical travel, and he certainly knew the cost of the trio of stones needed for the gemjump spells.

At the time, he'd had the feeling that little Cara Doon was worth it and more.

As he watched the paladin slowly dissolve, only to be whisked away as a smattering of silvery motes of light, he considered what Cara had done and knew that his decision to give her this magic had proven to be the right one.

Sixteen

 By the time the sun rose above the trees, the villagers had buried their dead. A few of the survivors sorted through what was left of their stores, hoping to find enough to feed their exhausted and dispirited kin. They gathered together what food remained and tossed it into a large kettle, so that all might share.

Ebenezer wandered into the village about the time the soup was ready. Bronwyn caught sight of him and hurried over, her footsteps sped by mingled relief and anger. He'd been missing since last night, leaving her nearly sick with worry. As soon as she was within arm's reach, she smacked him upside the head, as she had seen his sister do. Hard.

"Good one," he admitted, rubbing at the side of his head. "Been off orc hunting. Hand me that bowl there."

She passed it over and ladled some soup into it, then took a bit for herself. Bronwyn took a few spoonfuls before setting the bowl aside. Cara was sleeping, exhausted by the terrible night. She would be hungry when she awoke, and there would be no more soup. "How did it go?"

"Got me a few," the dwarf said with relish. "Didn't have as much fight in them as I'd-a liked, though. Scrawny things."

"There's a reason for that," said a soft, angry voice beside them. They looked up into the thin, careworn face of a half-elf woman.

Since the villager clearly wanted to talk, Bronwyn patted the ground beside her in invitation. The woman sank down and after a moment's hesitation took the package of trail rations Bronwyn quietly handed her. She slipped it into her apron. "For my children," she said grimly. "They will have little enough until the new crops come."

"This is not the first time the orcs attacked," Bronwyn surmised.

"No, nor will it be the last. They are desperate creatures, and they are fighting for their survival. As I understand it, the paladin order destroyed an orc settlement in the hills to the south. The orcs cannot hunt the hills without running afoul of paladin patrols. The paladins hunt the orcs with great fervor, for this provides practice—*practice!*—for young knights who wish to learn to fight and kill."

Bitterness seared through her every word. "Strange talk, coming from an elf who just lost kin and home to orcs," Ebenezer observed.

"I have no love for orcs," the woman stated, "but I know what is happening, and I do not place all the blame on the monsters who attacked. What choice do the displaced orcs have when their hunting grounds are taken from them? They must raid towns and farms in order to survive, and so they do."

"Gotta keep the orcs down," Ebenezer put in, his face showing puzzlement over this dilemma. "If you just leave 'em be, they breed like rats."

The half-elf sighed. "I suppose. But now we are the ones who must move. Those of us who are left." She rose, briefly touching Bronwyn's shoulder. "Thank you for your kindness, and for hearing me. Talk doesn't change anything, but all the same, I needed to have my say."

Ebenezer watched her go, looking clearly uncomfortable with any conversation that put orc-hunting in a bad light. He shrugged and turned to Bronwyn. "You ever find that toy thingabob you need?"

"No." Bronwyn raked a hand through the stray wisps of her hair, wishing as she did that she could smooth over this problem as easily as she tamed her fly-away locks. She untied her braid and loosened it, meaning to gather up the loose bits in a fresh plait.

"Here, lemme," the dwarf said, pushing her hands away. "You got a moon-eyed look, like right about now you couldn't walk and spit at the same time. Braided me many a horse's tail, so don't you be worrying."

Bronwyn obediently turned her back to the dwarf. True to his word, he started to deftly braid her hair for her. "The 'toy' is gone," she said wearily. "The orcs cleaned out the village of almost every useful thing, and a few extras. It looks to me as if they stole all the war toys and left the rest."

"When times are hard, young ones hurt plenty. Hard to see it," Ebenezer mused, "but I'm guessing even an orc gets a bit of a grin out of handing their whelp something that'll help the little one forget an empty belly or a hurting heart." He cleared his throat. "Not that I'm in favor of orcs, mind you."

"So noted," Bronwyn said. "What next?"

"Well, we go get the toy back. A heat-blind dwarf could follow the trail. The orcs are holed up in some caves not too far off the mountains."

"There are only two of us," she pointed out. "We certainly can't ask the paladins of Summit Hall for help."

"I'm with you there," Ebenezer agreed. "Lemme study on it a mite."

They fell silent until the dwarf finished his soup. "Seems to me this is a pretty nice place. People hate to leave their home. Might be, they don't have to. Gotta get rid of that orc tribe for once and final, though."

A passing elf woman pulled up short when she heard this. She dropped to a crouch beside them and shoved a lock of thick blond hair from her face. "Tell us how."

The dwarf studied her. "You've just done fighting. You ready for more?"

"Tell us how," she repeated.

*   *   *   *   *

The villagers set to work at Ebenezer's instructions. Skills used as peaceful farmers came into play as they grimly sought to reclaim their homes. Some of them hung snares along the trails, while others dug a deep pit in the center of the village. An early morning hunt had yielded a boar, and this roasted on a spit out in the open air so that the inviting fragrance wafted out into the hills—a statement to any orc scouts that the villagers still might have a few things worth stealing. A handful of villagers stayed behind to prepare for a renewed raid. Cara did not. She had reluctantly agreed to return to Blackstaff Tower and await Bronwyn there. As much as Bronwyn hated to see her go, she could not risk leaving the child behind with so few defenders.

When the village was in readiness, a dozen elves and half-elves who wanted to fight crept along with Ebenezer and Bronwyn through the hills south of the village.

Finally Ebenezer called a halt. "It's close to twilight," he said in a soft voice that was just above a whisper. "The raiders will be stirring around now, wanting to get an early start of it. The rest will still be sleeping. You know orc lairs."

The elves nodded. Bronwyn remembered what she had been told. Most lairs were a series of caves. The warriors slept toward the front, and next would be supplies of food and weapons. Finally, in the deepest and most secure position, would be the young.

Ebenezer pushed aside some boulders and shouldered through the opening of a narrow cave. The elves squeezed in after the dwarf, one by one. Bronwyn crawled through the utter darkness on her hands and knees. The tunnel widened as they went—at least that's what she surmised, for she no longer felt the walls pressing in on either side. Bronwyn heard up ahead a dull thud followed by an orcish grunt. Ebenezer had found and taken out the tunnel guard. As she edged past the body, she was almost glad for her limited vision. She had seen too much death already.

The path slanting up now, winding up to the top of the

cavern. They emerged onto a ledge that overlooked the cave devoted to food and weapon storage. Crouching down, they peered over the rock ledge into the den.

As they had anticipated, the warriors were preparing for yet another raid. They were ugly creatures, taller than most men and covered by a thick hide colored the range of swamp-like hues from green to brown to gray. Some were donning leather armor, and all took up weapons scavenged from their victims—an odd and daunting assortment of swords, axes, pitchforks, and fishing spears. They also slung sacks over their shoulders. More looting was clearly on the agenda.

The orcs left in waves, a few at a time. Ebenezer's troops waited until there were but ten of the creatures left. Each of the elves picked his or her target, communicating intent through emphatic hand gestures. Ebenezer pantomimed the count of three, and the elves launched themselves into the air.

Bronwyn winced as they slammed into the orcs, catching them off guard and sending the much taller creatures crashing to the stone. Most hit their targets, knives or daggers leading; those who didn't bounded up, weapon in hand, and dispatched their chosen foe with a few deft strokes.

A clamor arose from the inner chamber, and another wave of orcs came running out. Some were bandaged and lame, some were females or toothless elders, but all had blades and the will to use them.

Bronwyn turned and began to slither down the cavern wall to join in the fight. A thrown rock hit her hand, hard enough to startle her into losing her grip. She tumbled down and landed squarely in Ebenezer's arms.

He hefted her, as if surprised at how light she was, and then set her on her feet. "The village folk can mop up here. We're going to the back," he said.

She nodded and followed him, hugging the walls of the cavern and holding her knife out ready.

The back was nearly deserted. Two orc females stood guard, and three hideous, yellow-skinned children, naked and blatantly male, huddled against the far wall. Ebenezer stooped and seized a handful of small rocks. With deadly

accuracy, he hurled first one, then the other, and struck the
adult orcs squarely between the eyes. The creatures' red eyes
crossed, and they went down.

The youngster set up a fearful wailing. Ebenezer's face
went grim, and he turned to Bronwyn. "Get what you need."

She glanced around the dimly lit cave. It was more orderly
than she would have expected, with sleeping skins piled
neatly to one side, and a cracked barrel that served as a
receptacle for bones and other leavings. Small shelves had
been carved into the stone wall. These held the orcs' treasures. Bronwyn noted many of the stolen toys. Her gaze swept
the cave, looking for the one she wanted: a small, detailed
model of a siege tower. It was in the center of the shelf, right
over the cowering orc young.

"There," she said, pointing.

She started forward, but Ebenezer caught her arm. "You
go back with the others. Wait by the mouth of the main cave.
You don't need to be seeing what I'm about to do," he said
grimly.

Bronwyn's heart ached for the necessity facing her friend.
She suspected that the pragmatic dwarf could not allow three
such potentially deadly enemies to grow into a threat, but
Ebenezer's deep love for kids—be they dwarf or human or
even orc—made the hard task even more terrible. She swallowed hard. "You go. I'll do it."

"I said *git*!" Ebenezer roared. He seized the siege tower
from the shelf and hurled it into her hands.

Clutching the artifact, she darted from the cave. As she ran,
she heard the dwarf tell the orc young to "Stop your damn
sniveling." Harsh words, but with a note in them that prompted
Bronwyn to linger at the entrance to the children's cave.

She peeked around the side as the dwarf took from his pack
an intricately carved toy soldier—an orc, if the faint light did
not deceive her eyes, and handed it to one of the orc lads. "Take
this, in exchange for the tower, and you other two each pick a
favorite. Then get some clothes on you, and a knife and a packet
of food. There's a back way out. You three are going to take it."

They just stared at him. He swore and said a few words in

a halting, guttural speech. This time they understood and scurried to do his bidding. "Follow this path out, but don't wander too far. Your two hearth dames here will wake up and come looking for you. Tell them you're to travel north, and join a new clan. Go!"

One of them babbled a few words, and Ebenezer, or so Bronwyn surmised, repeated his instructions. The scramble of small feet announced that the orcs were only too happy to comply. Bronwyn hurried out to the first cavern. If Ebenezer knew that she had heard all, he would never again be able to look her in the eye.

"Dwarves," she muttered, then grinned as she realized how much she'd come to sound like her friend.

The battle was long over. Six of the elf fighters stayed at the cave to dispatch any orcs who might circle back, and the rest began the walk back to Gladestone.

As they neared the village, they noted that the snares had done their jobs well. Orcs dangled upside down from young trees like hideous, wingless bats. Elven arrows bristled from their chests. Only a few ringing clashes, a few grunts, and screams of pain, emanated from the village. When they arrived in Gladestone, it was all but over. A trio of villagers stood at the edge of the triggered pit trap, raining arrows at the trapped orcs.

After what she had witnessed in the cave, Bronwyn expected Ebenezer to protest this unchivalrous treatment of an enemy, but the dwarf just nodded with grim approval and joined the villagers in dragging the rest of the slain orcs to the pit.

An elf male rolled a barrel of lamp oil over and let it fall into the opening. Another elf dropped a torch. Flames leaped high into the night while Bronwyn and Ebenezer bore silent witness, and the villagers took stock of the price they had paid for this victory.

After the fire had died away, they all pitched in filling the hole. By the time the sun rose, the task was done. A plume of thick, black smoke rising from the south indicated that the rear guard had likewise cleansed the orc den.

The village of Gladestone was secure at last.

Bronwyn, however, felt anything but safe. They were too close to Summit Hall. She said her farewells to the villagers, and she and Ebenezer rode out into the fields.

"That's that," he commented. "Did what you came to do."

She wasn't so sure. Yes, she did have the Fenrisbane, but she felt a bit like a farm dog who habitually chased—and finally caught—a horse-drawn cart and thought, what now?

"Best be getting back to the city," the dwarf commented, breaking her troubled reverie. "Way I figure it, that Brian Swordmaster fellow has only two more days to talk my kin into staying around for good. I'd just as soon add my voice to the matter."

"True. And I've got to make arrangements for Cara and decide what to do with these trinkets."

The dwarf scratched his chin. "After all the trouble we went through to get that toy, I'd like to take a look at it. You feeling up to a little magic?"

Bronwyn thought this over. She had only two of the three rings and only one of the two people whose agreement was needed to activate the siege tower's power, but even a partial result, if that were possible, would be enlightening. She certainly owed the dwarf that much.

She took the tower and gestured for him to follow her. They walked out onto the rye field, beyond the sight of the villagers. She set the small tower down on a furrow and took the two rings from the thong around her neck. "I don't know if this will work, but here it goes," she said.

Bronwyn slipped first one, then the other ring into the slots on the tower. For a moment nothing happened. Then the tower began to grow, a quick, smooth spreading motion that looked as if a massive tidal wave was rising from the young rye.

Ebenezer hauled her up by her collar, and they both kicked into a run. After a hundred paces or so, they turned to look.

"Stones," whispered the dwarf.

The tower rose into the sky, tall as the forest trees. The front fell in a straight line, the back was sloped down. Strips of wood offered footing to soldiers who needed to climb up to the massive attack deck. A huge counterweight stood ready to drop, thus flinging the contents of an enormous trebuchet. The ballista was an monstrous machine. Next to it, stacks of bolts stood ready. The whole structure was built of thick, solid oak planks, with a sheen on it that suggested some sort of protective coating far superior to the wet animal hides that draped most siege towers. Bands of iron and thousands upon thousands of spikes held the massive construction together. But for all its size, it was little more substantial than a strong wind. Bronwyn could see through it, to the trees beyond. The rising sun caught and shimmered on its faintly luminous outline.

The Fenrisbane was a marvelous, indestructible, death-dealing . . . ghost.

It was also larger than Bronwyn had anticipated, and thus clearly visible from the village. She turned around to see if they had witnesses. Indeed, most of the villagers came at a run, swiftly at first, then dropping off at a safe distance to take stock of this marvel.

Ebenezer whistled softly. "Nice piece of work," he admitted, eyeing the Fenrisbane with naked awe. "Not much starch to it, though."

That was true, and it left Bronwyn with a bit of a dilemma. How to get the rings from the attack deck? But either the incomplete magic wavered, or the magical tower responded to her thoughts, because the monstrous attack machine swiftly shrank back down to a toy, and Bronwyn pulled out the rings and slipped them onto her fingers.

The dwarf glanced over his shoulder at the gaping villagers. He did a quick double take and swore. "Lookit there," he said grimly, pointing to the hills south of the village. A white horse was clearly visible and approaching fast. With the rider were four others. "Now that they've seen this thing, they've got one more reason to run you down. We'd best be riding, and fast."

* * * * *

The incident in Thornhold's chapel weighed heavily on
Dag Zoreth, as did the disturbing information that Ashemmi
had passed on. He went to his chamber and took his scrying
globe out once again. Ashemmi's "visit" had left him seething
with helpless fury. He used this, letting it fuel his prayers. As
a result, so intense was the purple flame that leaped into the
heart of the scrying globe that he could feel the pain he was
inflicting himself.

Sir Gareth came into view almost at once. "Where are
you?" the priest snapped.

"Summit Hall," the knight said, his voice somewhat
slurred by intense pain.

Dag pulled back the power just enough to allow the man to
function. "I had a most enlightening conversation with one of
my . . . comrades from Darkhold. She informed me that my
daughter was shipped south on a Zhentish slave ship—the
same ship that was to dispose of those wretched dwarves.
The same shipment that you so ably helped to arrange. I am
most eager to hear your explanation."

Hope drained from the fallen paladin's eyes. "She was
taken by the paladins, that much is true. I intercepted her
and tried to have her taken away to safe fosterage."

"On a slave ship?"

"The Knights of Samular have few outposts in the south,"
Gareth argued. "She would have been safe enough, tended in
the villa of an old associate who has reason to be grateful and
discrete. There she could have stayed until it was safe to
return her to you."

The truth hidden behind these self-serving words began to
come clear to Dag. Perhaps Sir Gareth had had a role in the
original abduction of Cara. Perhaps not. But certainly, he
used the situation to position himself well. Cara wore a ring
of Samular and thus had the potential to wield power. Of
course Gareth would want to have her in his secret control.
And if he was forced to do so, he could "discover" the child's
hiding place and make himself a hero to whomever he relinquished the child. It was not a foolish plan, but it had gone
awry.

"I want her back," the priest demanded. "Now."

"That could prove difficult, Lord Zoreth," the knight said. "She is in Blackstaff Tower, under the protection and tutelage of the lady mage Laeral Silverhand."

Dag hissed out a foul curse. The beautiful mage was as unconventional as she was powerful. If she took it upon herself to keep Cara, a small flight of dragons would be hard pressed to sway her from this course. But the archmage, the ruler of Blackstaff Tower, was another matter. Khelben Arunsun was not only a mage, but a ruler, deeply involved in the politics of the city and the surrounding area. If the matter were posed to him as a political expediency, he might be willing to see reason.

"Use your name and contacts. Get the child to Thornhold at once," Dag commanded. "And my sister as well, or you will find the same end as Hronulf."

"That is unlikely," the old paladin said. "Unfortunately, I am no longer fit to face armed men in a siege."

The priest laughed softly. "Hronulf did not die from his battle wounds. I tore out his heart with my own hands. You might want to bear this in mind, as you tend this task."

Seventeen

For two days Bronwyn and Ebenezer rode as hard as they dared push their horses. The paladins were never far behind them, though Bronwyn used every trick and shortcut she had learned in her years on the road.

Finally, the walls of the city lay before them. The late afternoon sun glinted off the spires of the Trolltower and bathed the huge arch of the Northgate in a welcoming glow. Bronwyn drew in a long breath and released it on a sigh. Some of the tension slid from her neck and shoulders, and she reached out to pat her horse's lathered neck.

"Stones!" exclaimed Ebenezer with more vehemence than usual. "Lookit there!"

Bronwyn followed the line of his pointing finger. Far to the north was a small, dark cluster, moving toward the High Road with a stolid determination that suggested a migration of ants.

She rapidly skimmed through a mental roll of days. So much had happened since Captain Orwig had left them on the docks of Waterdeep that it was hard to realize that ten days had passed.

"Ten days," she said aloud. "Tarlamera agreed to stay in the city for ten days."

"A dwarf of her word, is my sister," he said grimly. He cast a helpless look at Bronwyn. "Well, I'm off."

A deep sense of loss smote Bronwyn's heart. She reached down and clasped his shoulder. "I've got to see how Cara is doing in Blackstaff Tower. Or whether she's still there, for that matter." She smiled faintly. "That child's feet are almost as itchy as yours and mine. I'll come just as soon as I can."

"Don't," he said. "Chances are there won't be much to find."

This confirmed Bronwyn's unspoken fears. Ebenezer believed that he was going north to die with his clan. "Don't go," she said softly.

"Gotta go. I wasn't there last time. Couldn't live with myself if it happened again."

They sat for a moment, staring out after the determined dwarves. Bronwyn accepted what must be. She forced a smile, reached down, and cuffed the dwarf's curly head in farewell.

Ebenezer caught her hand in his and brought it to his lips. Then he abruptly released her and kicked his tired blue pony into a reluctant trot. His grumbling comment floated back to Bronwyn on the brisk sea breeze.

"Been spending too much time with humans, is what."

Bronwyn blinked back tears and turned her horse through the Northgate. Since secrecy was unlikely, she settled for haste. She left her horses at the nearest public stable and hired a closed carriage. At her instruction, the halfling driver set his horses at a brisk pace down the High Road, and when Bronwyn arrived at Blackstaff Tower she gave him the silver he'd requested for his hire and half as much again. She jumped from the carriage and hit the cobblestones running.

Her heart quickened with worry when Danilo emerged from the black wall to meet her, his expression as dark as the marble edifice behind him. "You do not want to go in there," he said grimly. He caught her arm and began drawing her along with him at a brisk pace.

She fell into step with him. "What's going on?"

"Lady Laeral is packing for an unexpected trip. It seems

she returned to the tower after a night's revel up in the Sea
Ward to find that our mutual bane, the great archmage himself, had relieved her of her promising new apprentice."

Dread stopped Bronwyn cold. "Cara! What did he do with
her?"

"Keep walking," he said shortly. "I doubt you have much
time. The archmage did precisely what he thought he must. It
seems that our good friends at the Halls of Justice got wind of
Cara's new apprenticeship. They convinced the First Lord
that this child was and should be a ward of the Knights of
Samular, that her destiny was with the chosen brothers of
her illustrious ancestor, and many other songs of a similar
tune."

"And Khelben just turned her over?" Fury and incredulity
battled for supremacy in Bronwyn's voice.

"He believed he had little choice in the matter. Three
young paladins came for her, bearing an edict from Piergeiron
himself. Khelben is many things, not the least of them a
canny politician. He understands the rift growing between
the various paladin orders and the Harpers. If he openly
defied Piergeiron's direct edict, he would give the impression
that Waterdeep's Master Harper considers himself above the
law. This, he contends, would endanger the work of the
Harpers and the agents themselves."

"And you agree."

"Did I say that?" he retorted. "The archmage and I
exchanged many words on this matter. Suffice it to say that
we used up most of the truly vile ones, but my anger was a
pale thing compared to Laeral's wrath. I fear that the lady
mage's visit to her sister's farm will last much longer than
previous jaunts.

"But Khelben must handle his own problems," Danilo concluded. "Let us discuss yours. What did you find?"

She sent him a long, considering look. "Why should I trust
you?"

"Whatever you think, I have never betrayed your trust.
Nor will I." He stopped and pushed his fine green tabard off
his left shoulder, revealing a tiny, weathered silver harp

nestled in a crescent moon. He took off the pin, the symbol of his Harper allegiance, and handed it to her.

"This was given me by a man I deeply admire, whose regard I hope always to retain. Hold it for me until this matter is done. If you find me in any way false, return the pin to Bran Skorlsun and declare me foresworn before that noble ranger and his half-elf daughter. I will not gainsay you."

The man could make no other oath that Bronwyn would trust more completely. The odd pairing between this light-hearted nobleman and his quiet, serious half-elf companion was one that Bronwyn never fully understood, but she knew that nothing meant more to her friend than the regard of the woman to whom he'd given his heart. She took the pin and dropped it into her bag. "It will be in my safe. When this matter is over, Alice will return it to you if I cannot."

"You will," he said, in a tone closer to his usual light manner. "Now, tell me what you found."

Bronwyn told him the story of the lich's tower, and the power of the Fenrisbane artifact. "I sent it ahead to my safe," she said, "and it will stay there until I decide what to do with it."

"The paladins would dearly love such a device."

"Wouldn't they, though?" she said bitterly. "And now that they've had a look at it, there will be no denying them."

"They saw it? How?"

She sighed wearily. "After we retrieved it from the orc lair, Ebenezer wanted to take a look at it. I had but two of the rings, and only one descendant of Samular, but I took a shot. The tower was not what it could be, but it was enough."

The Harper swore fervently. "Are you sure they saw this?"

"It would be hard to miss something that big rising out of a rye field."

"Then we must hurry," he said. "We must find a way to get Cara away from the paladins before they catch up with you and demand the artifact."

They slipped through the city, taking a route that led through the back doors of shops, through several private homes and adjoining tunnels, and even, on one occasion, a short dash across a rooftop. There were many such routes in the city, known only to the Harpers and open only to them. Despite her fury with Khelben, Bronwyn found some comfort in the web of support her Harper alliance offered—not the least of which was the determined friend at her side.

Alice met them at the back door and pushed them back into the alley. "Go right back the way you came. There's a paladin here looking for you."

A sense of ill news oft-repeated swept over Bronwyn, and she sighed tiredly. "Tall man? Blond hair?"

"Might have been. There's no telling, as it's long since gone white. He gives his name as Sir Gareth Cormaeril."

Bronwyn glanced at Danilo. "I should see him. He was a friend of my father's. Perhaps he will tell me what's going on."

The Harper shoved one hand through his hair and shook his head uncertainly. "I would be wary."

"I will be. Listen in, if you want," she said, knowing very well that he would do so anyway.

She hurried through the back room into the shop. The knight rose to greet her, his handsome and well-worn face tight with worry. "Thank Tyr, child! I hoped that I might have word with you before the watch found you."

That stopped Bronwyn in her tracks. "The watch?"

"Yes. Lord Piergeiron had decreed that you should be arrested on sight. You are not safe in this city."

She sat down, hard, on a small bench. "Why?"

The old knight gazed intently at her for a long moment. "It is as I suspected. You are innocent of the charges against you."

"Tell me."

He sighed. "The three young paladins sent to escort the child from Blackstaff Tower to the Halls of Justice were found dead. The girl is gone. Most of my brothers suspect that you and your brother, a priest of Cyric allied with the Zhentarim, are behind this abduction." He hesitated. "There is more."

"Of course there is," she muttered. Feeling utterly dazed, she dropped her head into her hands.

"Your brother, Dag Zoreth, commands the forces at Thornhold. I have learned on good authority that he killed Hronulf with his own hands. I would not tell a woman, especially one of your delicate years, the nature of the injuries dealt the young paladins who guarded Dag Zoreth's child, but they bear that villain's stamp. Unless I am far wrong, the child is with him . . . in Thornhold."

"Oh, Cara," Bronwyn breathed.

"The child is in grave danger, and not only from the corrupting influence of her father's faith. The paladins are gathering to mount an assault on Thornhold. It appears that this attack will take place sooner than my brother paladins anticipated. There are not enough men to mount a conventional siege, but the brothers have faith that they can prevail regardless. Not more than an hour ago, a young man of our order, a promising youth known as Algorind, rode in from Summit Hall with four of his brothers. Do you know this man?"

"We've met," she said shortly, not bothering to look up. "He and his friends followed me back to the city."

"They are seeking you even now—you, and the artifact you carry with you."

This time she did glance at the knight. "The rings," she hedged.

"And the siege tower," he added. "Few among the Knights of Samular know that story, but I heard it from Hronulf, and recognized the Fenrisbane from Algorind's story. Unfortunately, so did Laharin Goldbeard. You see, once, long ago, the great Samular himself captured Thornhold with the help of this artifact. My brother paladin desires to use it again, for the same purpose, and for the greater glory of Tyr."

Bronwyn rose and started to pace. "Why are you telling me this?"

The knight came to her and took her shoulders. "You are the daughter of my dearest friend. I see in you Hronulf's spirit. A terrible injustice has been done to you. As a servant of Tyr, it is my duty to try to see it put to rights."

She stared up into his face. "What do you mean?"

"Your destiny was stolen from you when you were too young to understand it. Now that you are a woman grown, men seek to do this again. This is not well done, even though it is done in all good conscience, and for a great cause."

"So what are you saying?"

"The power is yours, Child of Samular. You must decide for yourself how you will use it." He glanced over his shoulder toward the door. "Now go, and quickly! They will find you if you linger."

"He's right." Danilo emerged from the back, holding out his hand for her. "Though I must say, sir, your words surprise me. Bronwyn, I'll get you out of the city. Once you're safe, you can decide what to do."

Alice came up and pressed a leather bag into her hands. "I heard everything. Here are the things from the safe. You might well be needing them."

Bronwyn nodded her thanks and turned to the Harper. She clasped his offered hand. "I'm ready."

As Danilo began the words of a spell, Bronwyn felt a whirling force gather about her. She felt as if she was about to be sucked into a tunnel, torn away from her own body. Never had she traveled magic's silver paths—never had she had occasion to do so, she told herself. But in truth, the notion terrified her more than the prospect of sea travel.

But she had conquered that old fear. Suddenly Bronwyn knew that she need never again yield to lingering demons from her past—or to a belief that meaning and order for her life could only be found in the secrets of the past.

As the roar and whirl of magic carried her away, Bronwyn lifted her chin and stared straight ahead into the white void. The answers she now sought lay not in the hidden past, but the untried future.

Eighteen

Bronwyn emerged from the magical journey at the Thann family estates not far
north of Waterdeep. The sun had vanished by the time they arrived, so she
accepted Danilo's urging and stayed the
night. As exhausted as she was, as comfortable as the featherbed in the villa's
guest chamber might be, her dreams
were haunted by all that had happened in the last several
days and by the uncertainty and danger that lay before.

She rose before the sun and found that Danilo had been
busy while she slept. Servants brought new traveling clothes
and gear to her room, along with a tray of food. She quickly
ate and dressed, and then followed the servants' directions to
the stable. Danilo was there, directing the selection and
preparation of a suitable horse and the packing of travel supplies.

His face turned somber when he saw her. "I suppose you're
determined to go."

"You have to ask?" She jingled the full coin purse at her
belt. "Thank you for this, and for everything else. I will repay
you for all when I return with Cara."

He hesitated. Though it was clear that he wished to do so,

he did not try to dissuade her from riding north. "My family has mercenaries. I could send men with you."

She shook her head. "I will not be alone."

Danilo considered this, and smiled faintly. "It is fitting," he said simply. "Tymora smile upon you."

She rode swiftly northward throughout the day, avoiding the High Road and taking a network of smaller paths that Ebenezer had shown her on the first part of their journey together. Surely her friend would return to his clanhold the same way he left. She only hoped she would be able to catch them before nightfall.

Twilight came, and still no sign of the dwarves. Bronwyn would have missed them had not Ebenezer's gruff voice called out to her. She pulled up her horse and stared intently into the rocky terrain. A curly, auburn head popped up from behind a rock, and then other shapes—many of which Bronwyn had taken to be boulders—stirred into life.

Bronwyn shook her head in astonishment. She had heard that dwarves, though not innately magical, had an uncanny ability to blend in with the stone. She would not have believed the truth of it had she not witnessed it.

The Stoneshaft clan materialized from the rugged landscape and gathered around her horse. "We ain't going back," Tarlamera informed her in a tone that suggested this was not the first time the argument had been aired.

Bronwyn noted that the dwarves looked much better than they had just a tenday past. They had eaten well, and the grime of battle and sea voyage was a memory. They were all neatly clad in new garments the color of earth and stone, and shod with stout boots. Weapons hung at their belts, and their beards had been neatly braided—a style many dwarves adopted before battle.

Tarlamera took note of the careful scrutiny. "I'm-a telling you what I told that smith lad Brian. The clan is good for every coin he advanced us. So don't be looking at us like you're trying to figure out who got took."

"Probably he figures it was worth every coin and more, just to be rid of you," Ebenezer said in disgust. He looked up at

Bronwyn. "They're determined to fight. Can't talk sense into them no how."

"I think they should fight," Bronwyn said firmly. "How else are they going to get the clanhold back?"

Tarlamera hooted with delight and cuffed her brother. "I think I'm starting to like this human of yours!"

* * * * *

The battle planning with the dwarves had gone about as Bronwyn had expected it to go. The dwarves mulled it over late into the night, argued over every detail of the plans, and settled a couple of decisions through the application of force— though Ebenezer, with a show of impressive diplomacy, persuaded the combatants to decide the matter through arm wrestling.

But settled it was, and when morning came, Bronwyn rode swiftly northward to do her part. For the first time in days— for the first time, truly, in her entire life—she felt as if her destiny was entirely hers to command. What lay ahead would not be easy, but it was worth doing. She felt, if not quite confident, at least buoyantly hopeful.

The terrain became increasingly rocky as she went north into the foothills surrounding Thornhold. She urged her fine, borrowed steed—a glossy bay mare with a long, tireless stride—to the top of the hill and pulled up to allow the horse a brief rest, and herself opportunity to survey the path ahead for dangers.

Her gaze swept over the desolate area. There was nothing to see beyond the rolling foothills, scrubby pines, and jagged piles of rock. The sun was warm, and several hawks wheeled and soared on the spring breeze. One of them dropped to the ground, claws outstretched. Bronwyn heard the small, sharp squeak of its prey and instinctively looked away.

Her gaze skimmed over a small, white form on the path behind her, then jolted back. It was a horse, and upon it was a very familiar figure.

Bronwyn dug both hands into her hair and clenched her

jaws to keep from screaming with frustration. Not Algorind, not again, and surely not now! The paladin could ruin everything.

She kicked the mare into a run and took off for the north. Leaning low over the horse's glossy neck, she raced down the hill and around the path that led to the High Road. There she might have some small hope of outpacing the paladin's steed. The paths that wound through the hills were uneven and treacherous, and every frantic pace was a gamble that the horse would not stumble on the scattered stone.

The mare shied suddenly and violently to the right. Bronwyn clenched the horse's sides with her knees and clung to the chestnut mane in a desperate attempt to hold her seat, but she could not. She fell painfully, rolling several times across the rocky ground. As she hauled herself up, her eyes fell on the source of the horse's fright. Several snakes, newly awakened from their winter's slumber, were sunning themselves on the flat rocks ahead. Had the horse not stopped she might have run right through them—with deadly consequences.

Bronwyn regarded her torn sleeve and the deep, painful abrasion that ran from wrist to elbow. "I owe you thanks," she said softly as she walked toward the skittish mare, "but you'll excuse me if I wait a while before expressing them."

Behind her she heard the thundering approach of the paladin's great white horse. She was almost to her horse, was just reaching for the reins, when the mare turned and bolted. Bronwyn dropped and rolled as the paladin thundered by.

He dismounted in a quick, fluid leap and strode toward her, his hand on the hilt of his sword. "I have no desire to fight a woman. If you will yield peacefully, I will bring you safely back to stand judgment."

Bronwyn pulled her knife and fell into a crouch. As she did, a plan began to formulate in her mind. "Why would you content yourself with performing only half your duty?"

"Half my duty?" The paladin drew his sword and circled in. "What trickery is this?"

"None. You want the child. That, you have made plain. I'm

on my way to Thornhold to fetch her back."

"No longer," Algorind said. He lunged in, with a quick hard stroke designed to knock the knife from her hand.

The force of the blow flung Bronwyn's arm out wide, but she kept her grip. "We could both get what we want, if we work together. I could get Cara. After that, we will take her to Waterdeep. Together."

Algorind was clearly skeptical. "Why would you do this?"

"Would you want to see a child turned over to the Zhents? And what of the coming battle? She has seen enough fighting, thanks mostly to you and yours."

"It is a paladin's duty to fight for good," he said.

"And I'm offering you a chance to do just that," she said impatiently. "Do you think it will be easy to get Cara out of Thornhold? You'll get your chance to fight."

She circled closer and noted that Algorind did not retreat. He seemed to be giving her words careful consideration.

"How would you get the child?"

"I am Dag Zoreth's sister. He has been looking for me, just as you and your fellow paladins have been. Apparently, I have some value because of who my ancestors were." She gave an impatient shrug, to indicate she had little knowledge of or interest in this notion.

"So you would surrender to him."

"In a manner of speaking. They will let me into the fortress, and I doubt they would worry overmuch about my companion."

The paladin's face clouded. "Speaking of such, where is that horse-stealing dwarf?"

She shrugged off the question. "They would view you as a far more likely companion. In fact," she added wickedly, "Master Laharin was giving thought to what young paladin might be chosen to help me continue Samular's line. Perform well in today's task, and perhaps I'll recommend you for the job."

The young man looked flustered, as Bronwyn hoped he might. "You believe the Zhentarim would allow a paladin into their stronghold?"

"Why not? You're good with that sword, but you're still one man. The question is, are you good enough to help me fight our way out of the fortress once we have Cara?"

Algorind gave her question sober consideration. "I will speak truly. It seems to me that your plan holds grave risks and small chance for success. Nevertheless, I will do as you suggest."

She glared at him and brandished her knife. "If you're looking to die nobly, do it on your own time."

"That was not my meaning," he said earnestly. "Your bold plan holds danger, but I can think of none better. It is true that I am sworn to follow my duty, even if it leads to death."

Bronwyn remembered Hronulf's last battle at Thornhold. The same serene courage shone in this young paladin's eyes. Suddenly she found herself hard pressed to hate this man.

"But I am not convinced that death will result from this venture," continued Algorind. "Defeat is never certain while life remains. It may be that Tyr will bless this quest and grant success." A sudden, bleak look entered his eyes. "And if success is not to be, still I am content."

His expression alerted Bronwyn. She remembered the fear she had experienced as a child, and again during her brief reunion with her father, that she would never quite manage to meet the mark set for her. That old ghost haunted Algorind's eyes. For a moment, a very brief moment, she felt sympathy for the young paladin and the harsh life he had chosen.

"Got yourself into a bit of trouble, did you?"

"As to that, you know my failings better than any. I allowed a dwarf to trick me and steal my horse, a child to evade my pursuit—"

"And let's not forget the incident with the gemjump," Bronwyn interrupted, "though I'm sure you'd like to do so."

A pained expression crossed the young man's face. "I admit my failings and gladly pay the price."

The calm, steady acceptance in his voice told all. Bronwyn straightened and tucked away her knife. If Algorind failed to rescue Cara, he would probably face disgrace, and possibly even banishment. Had she needed assurance that he possessed enough reason to face the task ahead, this would have outstripped her expectations.

Bronwyn looked around for her horse. The mare had calmed and was cropping at some grass. She turned back to Algorind.

"All right, then. Let's go. But remember, when we get to the fortress, let me do the talking."

* * * * *

Algorind had little desire for speech. He rode alongside Bronwyn, his thoughts churning with confusion. Had he done wrong, throwing his lot in with this woman? She had already proven treacherous, and her choice of companions did not commend her judgment. Yet she had agreed to travel with him, to work together.

He had to be clear on one thing. "Understand this," he said. "I intend to fulfill the paladin's quest given me. Once the child has been rescued, I am honor-bound to take her back to the paladins at Waterdeep."

"I never doubted it," Bronwyn replied, looking straight ahead.

They rode in unbroken silence until the walls of Thornhold loomed before them. Algorind had never seen the fortress, and he marveled at the strength of the ancient walls. He scanned the citadel, searching for something that might aid their escape.

"See that wooden door, about halfway up the walls?" he said, nodding toward the stronghold. "That is a sally port. When we are within the walls, look for a way up to it. There should be a ramp, or stairs."

"Both," Bronwyn said. "I remember that. When I was in the fortress, Hronulf showed me around."

"That is good. Once you have the child, we will fight our way up to the port."

She shaded her eyes against the setting sun and squinted. "It's a good twenty feet down."

"Nonetheless, it is our best hope of escape. My horse will

come to my call. When we reach the fortress, we will leave our horses outside the gates. If we tie your mare's reins to mine, Icewind will bring her along."

Bronwyn nodded as she took this in. "It might work."

One thing more concerned him. "How will you find the child in the fortress?"

"My brother has not seen me since I was four years old," she said. "He is likely to ask Cara if I am who I claim to be. Knowing Cara, she will not be content to go tamely back to her room afterward."

*   *   *   *   *

In his brief tenure as master of Thornhold, Dag Zoreth had transformed the commander's chambers. The rooms that had once been Hronulf's, and that had reflected the knight's austere life, were now luxurious and comfortable. A bright hearth fire was always burning to stave off the chill that lingered within the thick stone walls, even though it was mid Mirtul and quite warm for that month. Fine furniture had been shipped from Waterdeep, lamps of colored glass from Neverwinter, fine furs from Luskan. His chamber did not quite possess the elegance of the Osterim villa near Waterdeep, but in time it would. Already it surpassed any Zhentarim outpost. But today, this small success gave him no pleasure.

"My Lord Zoreth."

Dag looked up from the papers on his table, almost grateful for the interruption. Already Ashemmi was making good her threat. Swift riders had brought word from Darkhold. Sememmon, the mage who ruled the fortress—and who was in turn ruled by his dark affection for the elven sorceress—wanted Dag to return to Darkhold, bringing the child with him. Thornhold would be turned over to another commander. For hours now, Dag had been wracking his thoughts for some way to keep control over his command and his daughter. Another conquest, perhaps. That might sway the matter. If he proved he could thus enhance the power of the Zhentarim, not even Ashemmi's charms could dissuade Sememmon from approving, even applauding, Dag's ambitions.

"Well?" he asked the messenger.

"The sentry on the north tower reports two riders approaching. A man and a woman."

Dag stood up abruptly. "Is this my sister?"

"It might be. The men who saw her enter the fortress before our attack think it is possible, but they saw her only from a distance."

There was one way to be certain. Dag strode to the door that led into the adjoining room. Cara sat on her bed, looking oddly dispirited. The playthings he had supplied her with lay neatly on the chest, in which, he supposed, were all her new clothes and baubles. She preferred to wear the clothes she came with—a gown of pink silk. Some day very soon he would have to find a way to persuade her to part with it long enough to allow the laundry a chance at it. In the girl's hands was a small, wooden doll, roughly carved and so squat and square that it resembled a dwarf far more than it did a human.

"Cara, we have visitors," he said. "As lady of the castle, you need to greet them."

That pleased her. She rose at once and followed him up a flight of stairs to the walkway that followed the entire wall. The height did not seem to bother her in the slightest—she was an intrepid child, that Dag had noted—but nonetheless, he claimed her hand and held it tightly as they made their way around to the front gate.

A delighted cry burst from the child. "It's Bronwyn! She has come to visit?"

"To stay, if you like," he said, and meant it. If he could find a way to keep them both, to use the power only they could wield, he would surely do it. "And the man with her?"

Cara's brown eyes narrowed, and her lip jutted out. "That is the man who stole me. He killed my foster parents and took me away. He chased me in Waterdeep."

So Sir Gareth was telling the truth after all, Dag mused. Dark pleasure rose in him like a tide at the thought of having this man, this paladin, delivered so conveniently into his hands. The single-minded fool probably expected to fight his way clear or die gloriously.

"He will not hurt you here," Dag assured her, "but we cannot be certain he will not hurt Bronwyn, unless we let them in. Do not be afraid."

Cara shot him an incredulous look. "I am not afraid. I am angry."

He smiled with approval and started forward. They walked until they had reached the small parapet overlooking the gate.

His first glimpse of his sister affected him in ways he had not expected. She was beautiful, and though he had not seen her for twenty years and more, so very familiar. Memory stirred, one of those memories that would forever be branded in his mind with utter, terrible clarity. He saw again his mother's white face, set in grim determination as she leaped to the defense of her children. That expression was reborn in his sister Bronwyn's eyes.

He could use that, Dag thought, striving mightily for detachment. If she was so attached to Cara, she might be willing to do nearly anything for the girl. Their mother had died protecting her brood. Let us see, he mused, if Gwenidale's daughter had inherited her mother's heart as well as her face.

Dag stepped forward, so that he was in full view of the riders who waited outside the gate. "State your name, and your purpose," he called down.

Pain, sharp and stabbing and insistent, thrummed along Algorind's temples. He shaded his eyes and tilted back his head to look up at the wall. There was no doubt in his mind who the speaker was. Evil emanated from the man in waves. Algorind silently prayed for strength and for the shield needed to hold back evil's power long enough to defeat it.

The woman beside him suffered no apparent ill effects. In fact, she looked disturbingly at home, and a small smile curved her lips.

"Ask Cara who I am," she tossed back.

There was a moment's silence. "Very good, sister. You say

much in a few words, but you have answered only one of my questions. What do you seek here?"

Bronwyn slid a quick glance at Algorind and nodded. That was the signal they had agreed upon. They dismounted and walked together toward the walls. Praise be to Tyr, his mental shields held, and the pain caused by proximity with evil did not intensify.

"I am a merchant," Bronwyn called up. "I have learned that there is nothing that cannot be bought, if the price is high enough."

Algorind marveled at her calm. She stood easily, her head cocked and her hands resting lightly on her hips. One would think that bartering for a child's life meant nothing to her.

"Your terms?" the priest called down. There was a hint of amusement in his voice that Algorind found more chilling than shrieking rage.

"Simple enough. I want Cara. In exchange, I will give you all three rings of Samular and the powerful artifact they command. What you chose to do with them is no concern to me."

This betrayal smote Algorind with an icy fist. "Do not!" he protested, utterly aghast at this revelation of her true, base nature.

Bronwyn turned and gave him a small, cool smile.

He reached for his sword, but it was too late. The massive door swung open, and a score of Zhentish soldiers surrounded them. They swarmed him, pushing him roughly through the gates and toward whatever fate this treacherous woman had in mind for him.

Nineteen

 Dag hurried down the gatehouse stairs as Bronwyn and the captive paladin entered the courtyard. He smiled and strode forward to reclaim his heritage at last.

"Hello, Bron," he said, voicing the almost-forgotten nickname with a faint smile.

"Bran." She stood staring at him, her eyes huge and her face a canvas awash with more emotions than he could name. "I suddenly remember . . . so much."

As did he. Bron and Bran, they had called each other. Nearest in age, if not in disposition, they were intense friends and foes during childhood. Images, fleeting and bittersweet, assailed him.

She took a step forward and held out a hand in an unthinking gesture. He took it in both of his own. "You've made an offer, but I would like you to reconsider it. You could stay here, if you wished, with Cara and me."

Her large brown eyes focused on him and went utterly cold. She snatched back her hand. "Under the same roof as my father's murderer? Not a chance. Give me Cara, and I'll go."

He refused to let her response sting. "Not quite yet. There is the matter of the rings and the artifact," he reminded her then tsked lightly. "Same old Bron. Hoarding all the toys." Dag understood the undeniable charm of memory, and he wielded like a sword his knowledge that he once had been the person that Bronwyn loved above all others.

She shook her head, refusing to succumb. "I want to see Cara," Bronwyn said adamantly.

He lifted one brow. "Do you not hear her? She is in the gatehouse, under the care of hardened soldiers who, at this moment, are no doubt wishing they were patrolling the Mere of Dead Men, instead."

She cocked her head and smiled fiercely when the sounds of Cara's angry struggle reached her.

Dag turned to the guard at his elbow. "Have the men send her down."

The message was relayed, and Cara flew out of the gatehouse door like a small brown bird. She threw herself into Bronwyn's arms with a glad cry. "My father said you've come to visit! He said maybe you will stay."

Bronwyn looked at Dag over Cara's head, holding his eyes as she spoke. "Plans have changed, Cara. You are going with me. Give your father the ring."

Without hesitation, the little girl peeled off the artifact and handed it to Dag. That concerned him, and stung more than a little. Hadn't he impressed upon her the importance of the ring and the power that came with her heritage? Did she value it—and him—so lightly?

Dag thrust aside these thoughts and turned back to Bronwyn. "The artifact," he said, and his voice sounded colder to his ears than he had intended to make it.

Bronwyn set Cara down and shouldered off her pack. From it she took a small object, carefully wrapped in a travel blanket. Dag watched avidly as she peeled off the covering, holding his breath and hardly daring to imagine what the item might be.

She handed him a small, wooden object. Puzzled, he took it from her. It was a miniature siege tower. A cunning piece of work, certainly, but a toy for all that.

He raised furious eyes to her face. "What is this?"

"Precisely what it appears to be," she said curtly. "Look at the platform. There are three small grooves. When the rings are placed into them by a descendant of Samular, the tower will grow to enormous size."

Dag looked at the tower with new interest. This was what he needed, exactly what he needed! With it, he could make short work of an escalade and gain another stronghold for the Zhentarim. That is, if it worked as Bronwyn claimed.

He handed her back the tower. "Show me."

She looked hesitant. "You'd do better to wait until morning and take the tower out into the open. I've seen it grow. This courtyard might not accommodate it."

That, Dag doubted. Judging from the depth and breadth of the toy's base, in relation to its height, it could most likely fit into the bailey without difficulty. "How tall does it grow?"

"As tall as it needs to be," she said reluctantly. "The artifact seems to sense the need and intent of the person who wields it. I believe it will adjust to the wall it is meant to conquer."

"Well, then, we have no problem, do we? Nor would we, unless Thornhold's wall were a hundred feet tall."

She struggled to hide her consternation, but Dag took careful note of it. "As you wish," she said, and handed him two rings identical to the one in his hand.

Too easily, Dag thought. He shook his head. "You do it."

Bronwyn took a long breath and closed her hand in a fist around all three rings. "Stand out of the way, Cara," she warned the girl. "I want you to go over to the far wall, by the tower. Just to be safe."

To Dag's surprise, the child offered no resistance. But though she watched from a distance, there was little of her usual curiosity in her brown eyes. In fact, her expression was unusually shuttered.

"Do not do this thing!" burst out the paladin. He struggled mightily against the men who held him. "Better to die than to give such power into the hands of evil."

Dag Zoreth lifted one brow and shot a sidelong glance at Bronwyn. "Earnest sort, isn't he?"

"You have no idea," she gritted out from between clenched teeth.

She threw an angry look at the man and set the tiny siege tower on the ground. She put the three rings into place, one at a time, and then she leaped to her feet and ran toward Cara.

Instinctively Dag followed suit. Behind him, he heard the scrape of a heavy object being dragged quickly against packed dirt and the creaking groans of expanding wood. He darted a look over his shoulder and then redoubled his pace. The size of the tower, and the speed with which it grew, were astonishing. Exhilarating!

In moments, the tower had reached its full height. It stood in their midst, like a shining beacon showing Dag the way to the future he craved.

Not a man moved, not a person spoke. All gazed in awe at the huge siege tower in their midst.

Suddenly the silence was shattered by the sound of splintering wood. A door on the side of the enclosed tower flew open, sending shards of wood spinning as the bolt which had held it shut gave way.

A fierce, red-bearded dwarf erupted from the tower in full charge. Ringlets of bright red sprang from her head in wild profusion and streaked behind her as she ran, giving her the appearance of a vengeful medusa. Though stunned into immobility, Dag remembered that dwarf. His raid had disrupted her wedding feast and had left her new-made husband lying dead from many wounds. As he eyed the female's furious approach, it came to Dag that he might well have done that slaughtered dwarf a favor.

Then the shock lifted, and fierce anger took its place. Sensation flooded into his dazed mind. The thunder of perhaps fifty pairs of dwarven boots, the roars and cries of the vengeful attackers, the sound of axe against sword, the smell of blood and of bodies already voiding themselves in death, and the bright, coppery taste of fear.

Dag whirled and seized a sword from the scabbard of the

soldier nearest him. He ignored the battle raging around him as his eyes sought out the gift his sister had so thoughtfully delivered.

The paladin was not difficult to find. His bright hair caught the faint light of the dying day, and his young, strong baritone was raised in a hymn to Tyr. Dag's jaw tightened. He knew that hymn and could sing along with Algorind of Tyr if he chose to do so.

What he chose to do was to cut that song from the man's throat.

*   *   *   *   *

Never had Algorind seen such a transformation come over a mortal face. As the priest of Cyric gazed upon him, life and warmth and humanity itself drained away.

Dag Zoreth raised a sword and touched it slowly to his forehead in salute, his eyes holding Algorind's. As he lifted it, the silver blade darkened, and began to glow. Purple fire danced along the edges, throwing eerie shadows across the sharp lines and hollows of the Cyricist's face.

"You signed on to fight evil, boy," Dag Zoreth said, in a voice that was less like that of a single mortal man than a chorus of angry beings speaking in concert. The voice rang out easily over the chaos of battle and reached out for Algorind like a grasping, unseen hand. "You are about to realize your fondest ambition."

The force of so much evil, so much hatred, drained the blood from the paladin's face, but he lifted his sword, mirrored Dag Zoreth's salute, and ran to meet the priest's charge.

Black and violet fire flashed forward. Algorind parried, sending sparks flying. He advanced, his eyes steady on that inhumanly evil face, his sword dipping and slashing, working the priest's blade and keeping him on the defensive. He had little choice. The unholy fire gave incredible speed and strength to the Cyricist's sword, more than compensating for the difference in their stature and training. Algorind had found more skilled opponents, but never had he faced one as dangerous.

This victory, if such he was granted, would be not his, but Tyr's.

* * * * *

Bronwyn covered Cara's eyes from the glare of the purple fire and the terrible fury of the duel raging just a few feet away, and—most horrifying of all—the evil incarnated on Dag Zoreth's face. She scooped Cara into her arms and started to rise. "We've got to get away," she whispered.

The child wrenched out of her grasp. "I won't leave him," she insisted. "I can't! It's my right to see what happens."

Bronwyn remembered her own despair at the siege of Thornhold and knew she could not deny the child this. Nor could they leave if they wanted to. They were backed against the inner wall, and the duel had shifted to block their escape.

A clear, baritone voice began to ring above the sounds of battle, softly at first and then gaining in strength and power. Though Bronwyn could not see the paladin's face, she was certain that it wore its usual expression of absolute faith, and she had reason to know that Algorind was not one to be lightly dismissed. Algorind sang as he fought, calling out to Tyr in ringing faith that evil would not long prevail.

Slowly, imperceptibly at first, the light that limned Dag Zoreth's sword began to dim. The Fire of Cyric faltered before the power of Tyr. The purple light began to flicker and then to vanish. In moments, the priest held nothing but a blade.

With three deft movements Algorind disarmed Dag Zoreth. Another stroke sent the priest plummeting to the ground. Cara screamed as her father fell, blood darkening the already-black vestments of his god.

"He's killing him! Don't let him kill my father!"

Bronwyn reacted to the pain in the girl's voice. The Harper leaped forward and hurled herself at the paladin's back. She fisted one hand in his curly blond hair. In one swift movement she pulled her knife, reached around, and placed it at his throat.

For a moment, Bronwyn was sorely tempted to pull the

knife back hard and fast. She could finally end this, and she could do it now, but there was enough of her father in her to reject such a dishonorable act. She had caught the paladin in an unguarded moment, when all his being was thrown into the hymn, all his soul devoted to vanquishing evil. Despite everything Algorind had done, she did not want to kill him. But neither would she let him kill Cara's father before the child's very eyes.

"Bran," she said, calling her brother by his old name. "How badly are you hurt? Can you stand? Can you hear me?"

The priest stirred, grimaced, and pressed his hand to his side. He whispered the words of a healing prayer, and some of the color crept back into his pale face. Using his sword as a cane, he struggled to his feet. His gaze settled on Bronwyn and her captive, and a smile of chilling evil curved his lips.

"Well done, Bron," he said. "You hold him, and I'll finish this."

"No."

Dag looked puzzled, and more than a little angry. "No?"

"If I let go, he will kill you. If you try to kill him, I will let go. You have to leave. Now."

Comprehension swept over Dag's face. "So that is your game. You made one mistake—one that could be fatal," he said in a coldly controlled voice. "Why would you let me go, why would you bother to save my life at all, when you know you may well have cause to regret it someday?"

"I'll take my chances." She lifted the knife at Algorind's throat just a little, just enough to suggest the threat. "Just go."

"Very well." His eyes quickly swept the fortress as he took a last look at what he had lost, and then they settled on the little girl. "Come, Cara."

Bronwyn squeezed her eyes tight for a moment, trying to damp down the sudden, searing pain. This is what Cara wanted, she told herself. She belonged with her family, her father.

"No," the child said, clearly and firmly.

Dag Zoreth looked astonished. "What do you mean?"

"I want to stay with Bronwyn," Cara stated.

"But I want you with me!"

The child's smile was sad and old far beyond her years. "Yes, father. So you have often said."

The silence stretched between them, and in it Bronwyn could hear broken promises, just as surely as her ears rang with the sounds of battle.

Dag looked stricken, but he managed a small, rueful smile. "This is a strange end, indeed," he said in a strangled voice. "After all this, I find that I am more like Hronulf than I would have thought possible."

"Never," said Algorind, risking the safety of his voice to speak what he saw as truth.

The priest sent him a look of purest hatred. "You know nothing. Your kind is known to me—your mind is empty of everything but Tyr. It should be an easy matter, therefore, for you to remember this: I will find you and kill you, in the most painful manner I can devise."

Dag Zoreth took a long breath and chanted the words to a spell. He held one hand poised in an unfinished gesture and looked to his daughter. "Good-bye, Cara," Dag said softly. "We will meet again soon."

His gaze sought Bronwyn, and this time his eyes were hard. "As will we."

And then he was gone, leaving behind a small wisp of purple smoke.

Bronwyn caught Cara's eye, jerked her head toward the still-fighting dwarves, and mouthed the word, *run!*

Then she took her knife away from Algorind's throat and danced back a step. Still holding her grip on his hair, she kicked with all her strength at the back of his knee. His leg buckled. At the same moment, she yanked back hard. The paladin fell backward and landed in a painfully twisted heap. Bronwyn resisted the urge to kick him while he was down, and took off running madly after Cara.

A small knot of dwarves had run out of opponents and seemed to be quarreling among themselves. Cara ran straight at them.

"Good girl," Bronwyn panted as she pounded along behind.

The dwarves looked up as Cara approached and parted to let first her and then Bronwyn past. Bronwyn glanced back to see that they had closed ranks, forming a wall of dwarven resolve against the paladin.

For once again, Algorind was fervently pursuing his quest. Bronwyn groaned. "Stop him," she shouted back.

She snatched up Cara and all but threw the girl over her shoulder. There was an open door before them. The chapel. Bronwyn remembered the steps that ran up the back of the chapel into the towers. She dashed into the low building.

The sight before her stopped her in mid stride. Hanging over the altar was an enormous black skull, behind which burned a lurid purple sun. Malevolence emanated from the manifestation, washing over her with a wave of hatred and evil that was fully as debilitating as the lich's touch.

Algorind clattered in after her, barely noticing the dwarf who clung doggedly to one of his legs. He stopped, as Bronwyn had done, and raised his eyes to the unholy fire. But there was no fear on his face, and his eyes held calm certainty. For a moment, Bronwyn envied him the simple beauty of his faith.

Again he began to sing, the same chant that had banished the purple fire from Dag Zoreth's sword. Such was the power of his prayer that the dwarf—who had given up his hold and was now attempting repeatedly to bash at the paladin with a battle hammer—could not even get close. After several moments of this, the dwarf shrugged and took off in search of something he could actually hit.

The manifestation of Cyric was more difficult to banish than the sword's enchantment, and it resisted Algorind's prayers with a hideous crackling and hissing. The sunburst's rays fairly danced with rage.

Bronwyn did not stay to see the outcome. She put Cara down and took her hand. They edged around the chapel, hugging the walls and keeping as much distance as possible between themselves and the angry, evil fire in the midst of the room. Once, a spray of purple sparks showered them. The skirt of Cara's dress began to smolder. Bronwyn dropped to her knees and beat out the tiny flames with her hands. To her relief, the child was not burned—only a few empty, brown-ringed holes marred the pink silk.

To her astonishment, this loss brought a tremble to the girl's lip. *This*, after all Cara had endured. "I will get you another," Bronwyn told her as she pulled her into a run.

The fire was dying now, and Algorind would not be far behind them. They dashed up the winding stone steps, and out onto the walkway that ringed the interior of the wall. Their way was clear, for all the Zhentarim had flooded down into the bailey to meet the dwarf invaders.

They ran toward the front gate tower, hoping to get to the horses. The dwarves had shut the door and barred it. There were but two horses outside the gate. If they could get to the horses, they could outrun the paladin.

But swift footsteps closed in and a heavy hand dropped on Bronwyn's shoulder. She hurled her elbow back in a sharp jab and whirled after it. Stiffening her fingers, she went for his eyes.

The paladin was quick, and he dodged her jabbing attack. Her hand stabbed into his temple, and she changed tactics—spreading her fingers into raking claws and slashing down over his face.

Algorind had not expected his, and for one instant he fell back on his heels. Bronwyn looked around frantically for an escape.

The only way was down. The roofs of the small interior buildings were neatly thatched, and they slanted sharply down. It was the best she could do.

"Jump," she told Cara, then hurled herself onto the roof, never once doubting that the girl would follow.

They slid on their backsides down the low-hanging eaves and leaped out into the bailey. Bronwyn ran for the gatehouse stairs, pulling Cara after her. She shot a look over her shoulder and stopped dead.

A young dwarf had stepped into Algorind's path, his axe raised and his beardless face set in determination. The paladin never slowed. He cut the lad down with a swift, terrible blow and kept coming.

Bronwyn squeezed her eyes shut to force back the wave of pain and indecision. She could not leave the dwarves here to deal with this man. He was too skilled, too determined. The dwarves were just as stubborn, and they wouldn't give up until Algorind lay dead.

Inspiration struck. She reversed direction, zigzagging across the bailey toward the siege tower. On the way, she cuffed Ebenezer's head. He glanced at her, which earned him a thudding blow from the staff of the man he was fighting.

"Bar the door behind!" she shouted, and then she dragged Cara through the open door of the Fenrisbane.

Bronwyn looked around the siege tower. The inside was vast and equipped with many weapons: piles of spears, swords, barrels full of quarrels. None of these, not in her hands at least, would be sufficient to stop the determined paladin from fulfilling his quest.

She looked up. The interior was a maze of scaffolding, leading up to a second floor and beyond. She hoisted Cara up onto a crate. "Can you climb?"

"Like a squirrel," the girl said somberly. She kilted up her ruined skirt and then proceeded to prove her claim.

Bronwyn came after her, hauling herself up from one timber to another. She knew with absolute certainty the moment when they were no longer alone in the tower.

"Faster," she urged Cara. "He's still coming."

The girl scampered up with an agility that Bronwyn duplicated only through sheer force of will. Algorind came after them, slowly gaining.

But they were almost to the top. Almost clear. Bronwyn put her shoulder to the hatch and pushed.

Nothing.

She tried again, hurling herself at the door and almost losing her balance. "It's barred," she said in despair.

Cara, however, was not listening. The little girl stared intently at the wooden door, on the side opposite the hinges. The wood began to smolder and then burst into flame.

"Try again," she advised, her voice pale from the effort of holding the casting.

But Bronwyn could not get close enough without setting herself afire. She backed off a foot or two and got a firm grip on one of the crossbeams. She let her feet drop and rocked back and forth as she hung over the rapidly advancing paladin. Mustering all her strength, she swung up both feet high over her head and kicked at the burning door.

The hatch flew open. Instantly, Cara released the enchantment and the flames disappeared. Bronwyn worked her way back, hand over hand, and pushed the girl up to the platform, then rolled out herself.

She slammed the ruined door down and looked for something to bar it. Cara snatched up a ballista bolt, staggering under its weight. Together, they worked it through the iron latch handles.

The door bounced and heaved as the paladin tried to fight his way through. Bronwyn doubted that the charred boards would hold for long. She snatched the three rings from their slots and thrust them onto her hands.

"Come on!" she said, and took off down the ramp at a run.

The tower shrank swiftly, sending the ground hurtling up to meet them. The crossbars that gave footing on the ramp were compressed, moving together. Bronwyn misjudged the distance and caught her toe in one of the bars.

She fell forward and went into an uncontrollable roll. The fall was mercifully brief; the landing, less merciful. Bronwyn slammed into the ground, rolled, and came to a stop with a clank of metal. When her vision cleared, she found herself looking into the fixed, staring eyes of a slain Zhentilar soldier. The plate armor that covered his chest had been deeply dented by a dwarven axe.

Bronwyn shuddered and shrank back. Strong hands seized her and dragged her to her feet, held her until her world stopped whirling.

Her eyes settled upon Ebenezer's broadly grinning face. "That was good thinking on your part," he said, nodding to the tiny siege tower standing in the courtyard. "Though I don't envy that human much, getting shrunk like that. Makes magical travel feel like a foot massage, I'm telling you that for free."

She reached out to give the dwarf an affectionate cuff, then changed her mind and simply fell into his arms. His grip tightened around her, squeezed with gentle strength, and then he let her go.

Ebenezer cleared his throat and stepped back, turning his attention pointedly to matters elsewhere in the fortress. Cara came to stand at his side, the Fenrisbane in her hands. She had torn a strip from her ruined gown, and securely tied it around the tower to hold the hatch in place.

The dwarf nodded to the tower. "What you fixing to do with him, now that you got him all boxed and gift-wrapped?"

Bronwyn hadn't thought that far, but the answer came to her. "I'm going to turn the tower over to Khelben Arunsun. Secretly. It will be secure in Blackstaff Tower, especially if no one knows it's there."

"Think you can trust him?"

"On this matter, yes," she said shortly. "Whatever else Khelben Arunsun might be, he is no warmonger looking for conquest. And he doesn't look kindly on those who fit that description. He'll keep the tower secure."

"Well, that's fine, then." The dwarf looked wistfully at the siege tower. "Before you do that, lemme give the thing a good long, hard shake, or at least drop it from a high place."

Bronwyn grimaced, finding herself in sympathy with the dwarf's sentiment. "Algorind is defeated. I can't kill him now."

Ebenezer sighed. "I suppose not. Let the wizard deal with him."

"Khelben is the least of Algorind's concerns," Bronwyn said with sudden certainty. She remembered the look in the paladin's eyes when he spoke of the price of failure. As to that, she could do nothing. He had chosen this life, and he would be paid in the wages of his own choice.

Tarlamera sauntered up, looking almost happy for the first time since Bronwyn had met her. "Nice place. You thinking to be giving this back to the paladins?"

The answer that came into Bronwyn's mind surprised her, but she realized that it was the right one. "No. I'm going to hold the fortress. Thornhold does not belong to the order. It legally belongs to my family. To Cara and me."

"Important thing, a good clanhold," Tarlamera admitted. "How you thinking to hold it, though?"

She turned to the red-bearded woman. "I was hoping you might be interested. The tunnels will have to be cleared and protected. You folk could use the fortress as a base until you have secured the tunnels. And even then, you could hold both. This is a good trade site," she added. "I'm sure that dwarves from Mirabar and farther north would be glad of a place to come and trade, outside of the city."

"Been to the city," the dwarf woman agreed. "No reason to go back."

"I'm sure others feel as you do. Think of how a good fortress, a thriving trade, could help you rebuild your clan."

"Dwarves don't hold fortresses," Tarlamera scoffed, but she looked more than a little intrigued. She scowled and strode off. "I'll think on it," she tossed back over her shoulder.

"She'll do it," Ebenezer translated. "And she thanks you for the offer."

Bronwyn laughed, delighted by the gruff affection in her friend's voice. He had his family back. Now that she had a family of her own—she and Cara were family; there was no longer a question in her mind—she knew its value.

"Ah," she said teasingly. "So that's what she said. I wouldn't have guessed, but family matters can be . . . complicated."

"True enough," he agreed. He craned his head and looked up at the darkening sky. A few stars were coming out, and the only sound beyond the walls was the distant murmur of the sea. "Getting late. Might be we should find ourselves some beds, if we're going to get on the road come morning."

She stared at him, puzzled. "You're not staying?"

"Never do. Not for long, anyway. Having secured the clanhold—and taken the measure of my kin—I'd just as soon head out. If it's all the same to you, thought I'd make my home with you for a while, seeing as how you live on the road and furnish your digs with enough trouble to keep things interesting. Might get myself one of them Harper pins, too, now that I got into the habit of meddling."

A smile spread slowly across Bronwyn's face. "Speaking of trouble, I still have this ring, you know."

"That ought to do it," the dwarf agreed.

Epilogue

Khelben Arunsun seldom dreaded anything, but he would gladly have given up a century of his life to avoid the summons to Piergeiron's palace. He felt somewhat reassured by the presence of his nephew. The boy seemed to understand much more than he was told. Khelben hoped, and almost dared to pray, that the young man he loved as dearly as any son would not learn to know him much better than he now did.

With difficulty he focused upon the conversation taking place in Piergeiron's study.

"The Knights of Samular held Thornhold for nearly five hundred years," the First Lord said earnestly. "They are needed in that place."

"I appreciate your feelings on this matter," Danilo responded with far more diplomacy than Khelben would have mustered, "but we must confront the facts. The fortress is in the name of the Caradoon family. Bronwyn has elected to hold it as a legacy for her niece."

"Two young females cannot hold a keep," Piergeiron pointed out.

"But the dwarves can. Some might even argue that the Stoneshaft clan has a better claim. They have lived beneath those mountains for more centuries than the knights have lived above."

Piergeiron sighed. "You have been passionate in your defense of this woman. Yes, she recovered the rings of Samular, but consider this: only one ring of three is in the proper hands!"

"Scattering the rings among diverse powers might prove to be a wise precaution, if unintentionally so," Khelben put in. "The possibility of anyone combining the rings' power into a single, devastating force is greatly diminished."

"I cannot agree. These are artifacts sacred to Tyr. Yet I am told that the child maintains ties with her father, who is of the Zhentarim, and a priest of Cyric!"

"Yes, that is so. Bronwyn returned one of the rings to the paladins of the order, leaving one ring in the hands of the Harpers. There is balance in that, Piergeiron. Let it end."

The First Lord shook his head regretfully. "How can I? And truly, Khelben, how can you consider the Harpers a sound fulcrum for balance, when there is such turmoil within Harper ranks? Sooner or later, there will be such division that some Harpers will be tempted to seek agreement and support wherever they may find it. Then there is the matter of Cara Doon. The girl should have been turned over to the order for proper training and guidance."

"With all due respect, Cara *was* turned over to the order," Danilo pointed out. "And she ended up with the Zhentarim in Thornhold."

Piergeiron had the grace to look embarrassed. He picked up a scroll from the table and handed it to Khelben. "This letter may shed light on that unfortunate event."

The archmage unrolled the scroll and scanned the ornate, old-fashioned script. It was a letter from Sir Gareth Cormaeril. After the usual salutations and courtly thanks for hospitality received, the old knight went on to report Algorind's perfidy. It seemed that he had committed a number of crimes, among them cooperating with both the Zhentarim and the Harpers, and selling into their hands a child of Samular's blood. He ultimately deserted the order to which he had pledged service, but not before he had consorted with Bronwyn and fought with her first at Gladestone and then at Thornhold.

"I cannot speak to all of the crimes this young man is accused of committing, but at least one of his sins is painted here in far more dire colors than it deserves," said Khelben.

"Sir Gareth is a prudent man and careful with his speech," Piergeiron said adamantly.

"Is that so? Judging from the 'prudent remarks' inscribed here, your friend seems to think that Harpers and Zhents are fit to stew in the same pot," Khelben observed dryly.

"Forgive me, but I am inclined to agree with him."

A long silence followed the paladin's words. Seeing the futility of discussion on this matter, Khelben nodded to his nephew. Danilo placed a small box on the table next to a tray of cheeses and fruit, and carefully removed the lid.

"Here is proof that Algorind did not desert his order. As to his other supposed crimes, let him stand trial for them—when he is tall enough to do so."

Danilo carefully removed from the box a small figure, a man no bigger than his hand, and placed him on the table. The little man stood straight, but his face held more dejection than Khelben would have thought could possibly be squeezed into so tiny a space.

The First Lord bent close, squinting, then sat up abruptly with a sharp intake of breath. "That is Algorind! Whatever happened to him?"

"I am tempted to say that he was cut down to size, but that would be unkind," Danilo said dryly. "This occurred during the battle of Thornhold. He turned on Bronwyn and tried to snatch Cara from her for what was at least a third time. Yet Bronwyn spared him and entrusted him to Khelben. A noble gesture from a paladin's true daughter."

Piergeiron did not comment on this assessment. He turned to the archmage. "Can you not return this man to his normal stature?"

"It is not my magic that did this," Khelben pointed out, not without a certain satisfaction. "This is ancient magic, sacred to the Knights of Samular. Would it be right to gainsay it?"

"He is rapidly returning to size," Danilo said helpfully. "In a few moon cycles, he should be back to normal. But this, I fear, will remain as you see it."

He took from the collar of his shirt what appeared to be a gleaming silver pin. It was in truth a paladin's sword, Algorind's sword, in perfect miniature. Danilo skewered a small square of cheese with it, and left it standing thus upright on the tray. A fresh wave of desolation swept over the tiny paladin's face at this indignity.

"He should be turned over to his brothers," Piergeiron mused, "but in such a state?"

"It would be better so," Danilo urged. "With respect, sir, I have little interest in growing a paladin, and no skill for such tasks."

The First Lord sighed. "So be it, then."

"About Bronwyn," Danilo began.

Piergeiron cut him off with an upraised hand. "I will agree to let the matter of Thornhold stand. But you should know, Khelben, that the Holy Order of the Knights of Samular—and many of their brother paladins—feel they have reason to distrust the Harpers."

Another silence followed Piergeiron's pronouncement. In it, Khelben heard the inevitable turning of another page in the lore book of the Harpers. A very long book, it was, and its pages traced many long years, so many endings and partings and false, fresh starts. But for all that, wasn't the story ever the same? The irony of this brought a small, hard smile to his lips

"I do not mean that as a personal insult," Piergeiron said earnestly, misunderstanding the archmage's grimly resigned smile. "We have been friends for many years. No one, I least of all, could doubt your devotion to this our city or discount the good that you have done. Much of that good you have accomplished through the Harpers whose activities you have directed. I do not claim otherwise."

"But?"

Piergeiron kept his gaze steady on the archmage's face. "I still trust you, Khelben, but I fear that goodly men can no longer put their trust in your Harpers."

R.A. Salvatore

The *New York Times* best-selling author of the Dark Elf saga returns to the FORGOTTEN REALMS® with an all new novel of high adventure and intrigue!

the
SILENT
BLADE

Wulfgar's world is crumbling around him while the assassin Entreri and the drow mercenary Jarlaxle are gaining power in Calimport. But Entreri isn't interested in power—all he wants is a final showdown with the dark elf known as Drizzt. . . . An all new hardcover, available October 1998.

FANTASY ADVENTURE

The Fall of Myth Drannor
Steven E. Schend
The elves of Cormanthyr thought they had a prophecy
that would never come to pass: When a red dragon of
good alignment flies over the city, the enemies of Myth
Drannor shall be free. In this support module for the
Cormanthyr supplement, the prophecy is fulfilled and
war brings to an end the great elf empire and the Arcane
Age. Heroes can't stop the Fall, but they can save a few
good souls, and they may be able to fill some important
holes in the history of the Realms.
(9558, ISBN 0-7869-1235-9)

Villains' Lorebook
Dale Donovan
You've read about them in FORGOTTEN REALMS® novels,
now meet them in the FORGOTTEN REALMS roleplaying
game setting. This 160-page supplement brings to life
the infamous scoundrels who plague the Realms, with
full gaming stats and background information so they
can be introduced into any roleplaying campaign.
(9552, ISBN 0-7869-1236-7)

Empires of the Shining Sea
Steven E. Schend and Dale Donovan
This campaign expansion box opens the way to Cal-
imshan and the Land of the Lions. Once ruled by genies,
this land is rich in potent magic and political intrigue,
and its capital city, Calimport, is the largest and roughest
city in all of Faerûn!
(9561, ISBN 0-7869-1237-5)